THE FLAME OF PROMETHEUS

Book One of
The Prometheus Project

TARYN L. DAVIDSON

PHANTOM HOUSE PRESS

To my husband, Drew.
You are my hero, my confidant, and my soul.
Thank you for fanning my flame.

For more information, address: admin@phantomhousepress.com

First edition January 2024

Cover by MiblArt

Hardcover ISBN 979-8-9885110-7-6
Paperback ISBN 979-8-9885110-6-9
Ebook AISN B0CKPSPPYW

THE
FLAME OF
PROMETHEUS

CHAPTER 1

I lifted my eyes to the dark sky where the stars winked above, silent observers of our misdeeds. Though I trusted they approved of our retribution.

A small reverberation rattled the forest floor. It crawled up the oak tree to the branch I was perched on and echoed faintly in my bones. The tremors sharpened my mind like the steady swipe of a whetstone along a sword.

Twenty seconds.

I glanced to my left. My eyes met those of glittering grey that peaked through an obsidian knit mask.

Balor Owens, my commanding officer, nodded.

The subtle motion should have brought me comfort—it should have eased my increasingly tensing muscles—but this was *my* mission.

Balor would soon be stepping down from his role of Commanding Officer, and this mission would determine if I would take over his position. But the entire Coalition Resistance Force wouldn't be on board unless my team gave their approval. And if they thought Balor was still leading this mission, or, worse yet, if the mission failed—

I glanced away quickly, not wanting my team to sense my

weakness. Though I felt all their eyes on me, each set as heavy as a boulder strapped to my back. My chest tightened.

Focus, Red. You have been on this hit a hundred times. It's the same train supply hit you and your team executes at least once a season.

I closed my eyes and drank in the night. Crisp autumn air stung my nostrils and filled my lungs, the cool tendrils slicing me to the core and revitalizing my soul.

Because today—today, this hit was mine.

I opened my eyes and glanced to my right. I found Ulysses' and Clay's eyes set on me, peering into the darkness, awaiting my signal.

But not yet.

My gaze lingered on Ulysses, his impish smirk taunting. Though we both fought for the Resistance, our common goals made us enemies. We both desired Balor's position, and while competition is healthy, ours was anything but.

I forced my attention from him and pulled out the zip-line rod from my jacket pocket. I hooked it onto the line just above my head, stretched beyond the tree line where my team was perched, and into the woods just beyond the train tracks.

To the East, behind Ulysses and Clay, a round, blue light grew brighter, and the rattling in my bones grew stronger.

My gloved fingers tensed and stretched over the rubber padding of the rod, and the train's front light flickered as it passed an old Pre-Coalition railway sign, the yellow and black painted metal now worn away by rust.

It's time.

I pursed my lips and mimicked the two-toned song of a black-capped chickadee.

My team moved.

Donned in black and swinging from the trees, the four of us descended like forest wraiths into the clearing just as the cargo train approached. One by one, we let go of our rods and tumbled onto the tops of train cars, the *thunks* of my team members hitting the train drowned out by the wind. I was light on my feet as I fell onto the train, my impact little more than a few clinks of metal as I tucked my chin and rolled. My right knee grazed a pin, the joint thumping in pain as I unfolded to a crouch. Luckily for me, pain subsides easily. It was already fading into a dull throb when I glanced to my left. Balor was on his feet two cars down, bolting to his assigned carriage as I paused to count. I was on car seven. I needed to be on nine.

The wind whistled sharply in my ear, whipping at the loose tendrils of my crimson hair as I rose to my feet, turned right, and ran. Ahead of me, Ulysses was bounding over cars to find his target—car thirteen.

I kept pace, light on the balls of my feet as the train rattled beneath me. I skipped over the threshold to car eight, my feet finding purchase as I kept running toward my destination. I pumped my legs a few more paces before I pounced again. My stomach felt like it slammed against my throat as I tumbled onto car nine. On top of my destination, I pumped my legs a few more times before I slid onto my knees, my whole body gliding down the train. My hands caught the ceiling latch, and I grunted as the opposing forces of my body and the train played tug of war against my torso. I pulled myself forward and slammed my knees into the top of the train as I cranked on the metal wheel. My arms buckled against the strain, but my gloves held strong, the rubber gripping to the worn metal until it finally gave way. The screeching of hinges was drowned out by the howling of wind and the jostling of the train. As I crawled down the hatch, my legs dangled in the abyss of the train carriage, and I felt like I was wading in shark-infested waters, not knowing what was beneath me until my left foot found a solid corner of some object, then a smooth surface.

I let go.

I crouched on a large wooden box, the faint scent of damp iron and moth balls lingering in the cool air. Moonlight trickled through the hatch, dimly illuminating the labels on several of the boxes.

Blankets…

Sweaters…

"Ah, there you are," I whispered into the darkness as I found a box labeled 'socks'.

I swung my pack around and pulled out a small pry bar. I aimed the bar for the top seam of the box and jam—

"Intruder Alert. Intruder Alert." Sirens boomed around me as red lights flooded the car, casting eerie shadows around the small space.

Fuck.

My head reeled. This could not be happening.

Holy Skies, damned fuck.

My muscles throbbed as adrenaline poured into my veins, flooding every tissue throughout my body, my heart pumping harder and faster with each ring of the alarm.

Focus, Red. You only have fifteen more seconds to get the hell out of here.

I shoved down the panic and forced every ounce of strength into my core, shoulders, and arms as I jammed the pry bar into the crate. With a loud snapping of wood and creaking of nails, the board came loose, pulling open as easily as roasted boar.

I shoved armful after armful of socks into my pack. There was no time to grab the other supplies I came for. Once my pack was filled, I threw it over my shoulder and bolted for the door. I kicked the large metal slab, and the door flew open, but instead of the dark night, I was greeted by a bright, scarlet light pouring from the open door to car ten. With one arm, I shielded my eyes from the unexpected glow, but over the crux of my elbow, there was a dark figure who stood on the threshold.

My heart stopped.

His shoulders were broad and threatening as rifles peered around his back like metal wings—the devil himself standing before the mouth of hell.

Slowly, carefully, I reached for the Glock strapped against my upper thigh as the soldier stepped forward. But as the moonlight touched his face, my fingers loosened around my weapon.

Stepping out of car ten was my fellow agent, Ulysses Smith. Behind him, scattered pieces of security bots littered the floor, sparking and twitching like de-limbed bugs.

My teeth ground together as I once again noted the weaponry protruding from his back— guns and ammunition that were not present at the start of our mission.

Ulysses, dark eyes blazing, raised his arm, a handgun aiming right at my nose.

My heart dropped into my stomach, not out of fear but anticipation.

"Duck."

I obeyed more on instinct than by his command. A crack reverberated in the air between us, and I felt heat shatter in the air behind me, metal falling to the floor like tiny, blazing meteorites.

I glanced under my arm as a security bot hit the floor, its red light flickering out. Smoke tinged my nostrils, and I returned my attention to my fellow agent. A crooked smile marred his lips.

Red-hot rage burned in my chest. My hands flexed into fists at my sides, and I rose onto the balls of my feet. I wanted to strangle him. I wanted to claw his eyes out. And just as I nearly released my ire upon him, I caught the steady beat of wings from a security chopper thrumming in the distance.

I glanced behind Ulysses, peering into the night. The frigid wind stung my eyes, and my vision blurred with tears, but I could still make out the aircraft's searchlight glowing faintly, scanning the bluffs about two miles off.

Shit.

I reached for my COM strapped to the lapel of my jacket. And, like a gift from the Skies above, just as I was about to request aid, our salvation revved to life. Shooting from the woods, a black Humvee sped toward the train. The vehicle slowed as a figure about six cars down jumped into the trunk and barreled toward us.

Ulysses flagged down the Humvee, then gestured with a gloved hand to the open vehicle as it kept pace next to us. "Ladies first."

I did not hesitate as I jumped onto the moving car, grabbed the top rail, and swung into the trunk. I landed on the far side, right next to Clay, who had already made his escape.

Ulysses landed with a heavy *thud* into the trunk and tapped the top of the vehicle three times, signaling the driver to speed up and aid the last agent.

When we caught up to Balor on car three, he was fending off two security bots as he clung to the side of the train, gun in one hand trained on the bots, while the other grasped a ladder rung. Behind us, the beating of the chopper grew louder. I peered in the humvee's side mirror to find the chopper's light had descended onto the train.

Ulysses must have seen the chopper as well and realized the seconds we had left were quickly dwindling. "We have to leave him!" he shouted over the roar of the train and wind. Ulysses' hand hovered over the top of our vehicle, ready to give the signal for the driver to head toward Base.

But that was not his signal to give.

As I stood up, I slid one foot under Ulysses' and pulled. His knee fell into the trunk, and his head cracked against the top of the car. Blood rushed down his face, but I didn't care.

"Stand down," I ordered, not deigning to look at him as I pulled my Glock from my holster. I planted my feet on the floor of the trunk, my muscles fighting to keep steady under the moving vehicle, and took aim at the security bots that surrounded my commander.

"Jump!" I yelled over the deafening roar of the chopper. "I got you covered!"

As Balor pocketed his handgun, I shot the first and closest

bot down, the machine falling under the train rail and shooting sparks behind us. Balor did not glance at the other bot as he propelled himself off the train. But my aim was too slow. From the bot's center eye, a small red beam shot straight for Balor's leg. The scent of burned flesh singed my nose, and Balor's cry grated down my spine as the crack of my gun rattled the air. The second bot fell from the air as Balor's hands hit the rail of the Humvee, his body dangling over the edge. His right leg smoked, and embers clung to the fabric around the gaping wound.

"Clay! Ulysses!" I yelled, but they were already there, heaving their commander into the trunk. The driver didn't need a signal, not as the scope light from the chopper drew closer, nearly catching our tracks.

I holstered my gun and crouched low, eyeing up the left side mirror. My eyes met the driver's. I gave Niahm Owens a single nod. A flicker of relief swept across his freckled face before he pushed the pedal to the floor, jerked the wheel left, and we disappeared into the night.

CHAPTER 2

Crimson bloomed across my white-wrapped knuckles.

One.

Wet, dark stains spotted the old punching bag swinging before me.

One-two

But I felt nothing.

One-two.

Not my own blood spraying my face.

One-two-three.

Not the ripping of skin from my knuckles.

One.

Nothing.

One-two-three.

All I could feel was the burning hatred for Ulysses as he stood in the threshold of the wrong train car, a feral smirk stretching across his face.

One-two.

All I could see were those damned rifles like iron wings as they loomed over Ulysses' shoulders.

One-two.

And all I could think about were the vials of medicine left

untouched on car thirteen—the medicine that was supposed to be safely stored in our Medical Wing. It was probably being unloaded in some Skies-forsaken Coalition City at that very moment.

One-two-three.

"Calm down, Princess." Ulysses' taunt bounced off the walls of my mind as I replayed our argument in my head.

One-two-three.

But I couldn't—wouldn't—calm down. I was Rowyn Eloise Darrow.

I was Red.

One.

The metal chain bracing the bag to the ceiling rattled with the force of my blow. My chest swelled with satisfaction as clunking heavy boots echoed off empty walls.

I knew those footsteps.

My mind was yanked back to the dim, dank gym smelling of stale sweat and worn iron.

"What do you want, Hoenir?" I panted, my eyes still focused on the blood-stained sack as I continued punching. Hoenir Vasquez walked up beside me, his eyes like dark lasers burning into my cheek.

"Are you going to tell me what happened?" he said, voice cold as the concrete floor beneath my bare feet.

"I'm a little busy," I breathed.

"Agent."

One-two-three-four.

I swung my body in for a hook, bracing my core, but Hoenir grabbed my right wrist, swung me around to face him, and pinned me with his eyes. I didn't dare look away.

"As Director of the Coalition Resistance Forces," Hoenir growled, "I order you to report the details of yesterday's hit."

I ripped my wrist from his grasp and hit the bag one last time, putting all the strength I had left into one final blow. The chain that secured the punching bag snapped, and the sack flew across the room before it landed with a heavy *thud*. I turned back to Hoenir. The Director flinched when the punching bag hit the floor, though his usual stone-cold stare was again etched across his face, hazel eyes unyielding.

I stepped closer, nearly nose-to-nose with my director. Sweat trickled down my temple as my gaze bore into his. "We managed to snag food, socks, and random weapons. Unfortunately, the medicine we needed was…compromised." A knot formed in my throat as I thought of my baby sister all those winters ago—burning with fever, quiet as she clung to her fragile strands of life.

Hoenir crossed his arms. "Compromised? From my understanding, your team made no effort to grab the medicine. Instead, you brought back weapons despite direct orders not to hijack the weaponry car."

"My team? Ulysses is the one who disobeyed direct orders."

"Maybe the orders weren't clear enough."

"With all due respect, sir," I spat, my voice a low, feral growl, "they were crystal. Ulysses hopped on car ten instead of his designated car, thirteen. Car ten was bugged, just as we suspected. Since the alarm was tripped, we had twenty seconds to grab what we could and run."

"According to Agent Smith, he did jump on car thirteen. Was it possible our Intel was incorrect?"

The dim fluorescent lights flickered, casting eerie shadows across Hoenir's angular face.

"He can *claim* all he wants, but I saw him jump off car ten with three packs full of rifles, semi-automatics, Military-grade explosives, and ammunition." I began to unwrap the boxing bandages. My knuckles stung as the flesh ripped away from itself, and bright, fresh blood pooled to the surface. "People will get sick and die this winter because of his deliberate disobedience. The whole Resistance will suffer because of his insubordination."

I saw the wheels turning behind his eyes, but Hoenir remained silent for a moment. "I will talk to him."

The Director turned, hands folded behind his back, and walked out of the gym.

That's what Hoenir always said, but it never changed anything. Not when it came to Ulysses.

Hoenir founded this pathetic excuse for a Resistance about twenty years ago. He fled the city of Imperium in the American Coalition with five of his closest friends and family. They are all dead now, either casualties of disease or helping other people escape the Coalition. I think that's the reason he always plays it safe.

As Director, Hoenir has to approve all missions, and so far, all my requests to enter the Coalition and help more people escape or deal some real damage have been denied. Hoenir only approved supply train hits for things like clothes, medicine, toiletries, etcetera.

As far as Ulysses goes, Hoenir was always too soft on him. He says I am too brash. But I'm not the one who disobeyed orders to snag guns and bombs.

I finished peeling off the boxing wraps, flexing my hands to get a feel for how much pain would develop in a few hours. The answer was a lot. Purple and blue bruises already marred my hands in the gaps between the torn flesh, but wounds never lasted long for me, and the pain faded even faster. For most people—for normal people—the wounds that marred my battered hands would be in bad shape for weeks. For me, they would only last a few days. Tomorrow, the stinging and burning would subside into small aches, with only yellow and green bruises left to prove any damage was done. Within three days, my hands would look like the self-brutality session of mine never happened.

I stood up and stuffed my ruined boxing bandages in the trashcan next to the metal bench. My heart sank at the thought of asking Balor for a new pair. Our stock was limited, and it was selfish of me to ruin yet another set. Balor was never mad, only disappointed by how I brutalized myself.

Maybe I need better coping mechanisms.

I shoved the thought aside and trudged to the showers. I wanted to keep my head held high, but all I felt was shame and guilt for our failed mission.

My failed mission.

The Base was eerily quiet, and the air stale as I padded barefoot down the blanched corridors of the old abandoned Military Base that was now home to the Coalition Resistance Forces.

Some might think it ironic, but the Military Base never belonged to the Coalition. It was here long before us. This Base has stood the test of time—a remnant of a *better* time, of a better America, when it was free. And that is what we stand for, what we fight for... If we ever decide to actually fight.

As I turned the corner, I slammed into a solid force, and my neck snapped back from the impact.

"Look where you're going, Princess." Ulysses peered over me. Though he wasn't much taller than I, he was as broad as an ox. I stifled a groan as his dark eyes met mine, and his lips contorted into a sneer.

"Nice hands." Ulysses grabbed my wrist, eyeing up my bruised and bleeding knuckles. The small hairs on my arm bristled at his touch. "Looks like I'll have *your* promotion in no time. The last thing Hoenir needs is a masochistic agent like you." Ulysses spat in my face, and fury exploded within me. In two swift moves, I had him pinned up against the white concrete wall, my right hand bracing my left forearm as I pressed it into his trachea.

Ulysses *tisked*, his eyes glittering with malice from behind his dark, disheveled hair. "What would Hoenir think of you fighting a fellow agent?"

I glanced down at my arm, my fawn skin stark against his

bronze tone. *How was he able to speak? One quick maneuver and Ulysses' hyoid bone would snap beneath my forearm.*

"Darrow! Smith! Get a hold of yerselves!"

I held firm as my mentor, Dr. Metis Barnes, hobbled down the hallway, the *clack* of his metal cane echoing off the bare walls.

"Now, Darrow."

I released Ulysses, and while he should have crumpled to the floor gasping for air, he stood up straight and smoothed out his black shirt, his movements relaxed and feline.

My heart thumped wildly, each beat shattering a small piece of pride.

I turned to Metis. His scarred face was set in fury.

"Red, Lab!" He commanded, his voice gruff. I hesitated as Metis pointed down the hall toward his Laboratory. "Now!"

Ulysses, arms crossed, gave me a bemused smile.

I made to walk down the hall when Ulysses' low voice stopped me. "Good thing Metis is always around to fight your battles."

I balled my fists, ready to strike.

"Now! We got work to do," Metis growled.

Releasing a deep breath, I set off down the hall.

———

Dr. Metis Barnes was not an organized person by any means, but my feet were frozen to the floor as I beheld the chaos that had engulfed his laboratory. Books and folders were strewn across Metis' desk and the floor around it. Pens and crumpled papers littered my desk adjacent to his, and my chair was turned over. Even the students' desks were tipped and strewn across the lab.

"What are ya gawkin' 'bout?" Metis grumbled as he hobbled through the doorway, shoving me aside with his mechanical arm. Metis' left side was almost completely cybertronic—from his left bionic eye all the way down to his left big toe was plated in a lightweight titanium alloy. Beneath the metal exoskeleton was a complex nerve integration wiring system of his own design. It was state-of-the-art when he was first fitted with the technology over twenty years ago, but the Coalition Resistance Force's equipment was lacking, so improvements and upgrades for Metis' system over the years had been minimal. Several years back, Metis created a cane for himself to support his bionic leg, but I have long suspected the cane does far more than just grant stabilization.

"Metis, what the hell happened in here?"

"Entropy," the old scientist grumbled.

I laughed. "Entropy? That's the best you got?"

Metis hobbled toward his desk and started to stack papers together loosely. "That n' I lost somethin'."

"Yeah, your mind from the looks of it." I wove through the disheveled room toward my desk and righted my chair.

Metis snorted. "Says the one with bloodied knuckles from her own fuckin' temper tantrum."

"They will be healed by morning." Indeed. The familiar tingling sensation had spread across my knuckles, an indication my healing process had already begun.

"Doesn't make ya any less stupid. And maybe if you weren't makin' an ass of yerself in the gym and in the hall, ya could've been helpin' me." Metis' gaze remained averted from my own, his bionic eye's light lens shuttering gently as he shuffled through notebooks and folders.

I gathered jumbled papers and angrily tapped them against my desk to straighten them. "I had it sorted. I can take care of myself, and I can handle Ulysses."

"Ya don't know what ya can handle." His voice was gruff. "Ya don't know what ya' can get yerself into, Red. Do ya wanna get kicked outta the Resistance? Out there, on yer own, without yer sister, might I add?"

In all honesty, I wouldn't mind being on my own, but my

heart tightened at the thought of not having Reign with me. My sister was the only family I had left.

"Hoenir wouldn't kick me out, not if I could sell him out to the Coalition."

Metis snorted. "He knows ya wouldn't do that, not if he kept Reign to ensure yer silence. I think ya may even like me a bit."

I rolled my eyes.

"Red." His sharp tone grabbed my attention. "You're here to do one thing: serve the Resistance. There are bigger problems out there than Ulysses."

"Ulysses is disobedient, cocky, arrogant, rude—"

Metis slammed his fist on his wooden desk, shaking various vials and glass test tubes. "I don't care if he's the damned devil himself! He is distractin' ya from yer tasks. Don't cha' think he would like to see ya kicked out? You're givin' him exactly what he wants. You've gotta stop playin' his childish games, Red. We are at war!"

I avoided his heavy gaze. "It's not exactly war," I mumbled, uncrumpling a piece of paper on my desk.

If this was a war, we would actually *need* the weapons Ulysses snagged. If this was war, we would be on a battlefield or actually be saving people.

"Not exactly war?" Metis growled. "The Coalition is killin' their own one-by-one with disease. They watch every move of those with dissentin' opinions. They bend the minds of their citizens to get the results they want! We are fightin' because the people in the Coalition can't! They are slaves who think themselves free!"

Metis lowered his head, and his greasy gray hair swung in front of his eyes as he shook it. "Red." Metis sighed as he crossed his right human arm over his left mechanical one on a pile of unorganized papers. "You've gotta remember that yer dad took your family 'n fled for a reason. He died out there in The Wastes because he thought it was better than ya growin' up there, in the Coalition."

I did remember. The first time Dad left me to watch Reign by myself while he and Aura, my stepmother, went to hunt, I was on my little cot, holding my baby sister, who was almost two. My father crouched down, held my small hands in his wrinkled ones, and as I stared into his beautiful sky-blue eyes, he assured me I was going to be okay. My father promised he would return with Aura by sun-down. I nodded to him, and he wiped away a warm tear.

"But Wynnie," he said, eyes full of urgency as a strong hand cupped my face. "If Mom and I don't make it back, you will be fine here. You are smart. I know you can take care of yourself and your sister. So stay here. Promise me that you will never go back to the Coalition, promise me that you will never seek out or join the Resistance, and above all, promise me you will always protect Reign."

"I promise," I whispered as he wiped another tear from my cheek with a thick thumb. "But Dad... What is the Resistance?"

"Something dangerous, Wynnie. Something very dangerous."

I shook myself from my memories, my mind returning to where I sat on the corner of my desk in Metis' lab. "I know, but I still don't understand why my father didn't just bring us here in the first place," I thought aloud. "Why wouldn't he have brought us to the Resistance? Why did he say it was dangerous if he didn't like the Coalition, either?"

"The important thing is that you're here now. Best not to dwell on the past."

I focused on the geneticist, on the deep scar gouged from his right temple all the way behind the metal plate on his left jawbone. The air between us stiffened as Metis averted my gaze, and something felt wrong.

"Metis—"

"Red." His eyes were still on the papers he tried and failed to organize. "Yer here now. There's no changin' the past, so ya best forget about it."

I ground my teeth, not ready to move on, but after all these years, I knew when Metis was done with a conversation.

"So," I drawled, breaking the silence. "What were you looking for?"

"Nothin' that concerns ya." Metis stood from his chair, picked up a few books, and hobbled over to the small bookshelf. He started stowing them away neatly as I shifted through papers on my own desk.

I ground my teeth, sick of the secrets—sick of the bullshit.

"But I am sure you are still going to tell me," I said, trying to sound sweet.

Metis cracked his neck and exhaled slowly. "Just 'n old research journal from 'n old project."

"I can keep looking if you would li—"

"No," Metis snapped. "It'll show up. I'm sure I shoved it 'n a weird drawer or left it 'n my dormitory."

I blinked once, then swallowed. "Was it your research?"

"Not exactly." His voice softened.

"What was it on?"

"Nothin' that concerns ya'." Metis hobbled back to his desk. "Now, let's get to work. Since that bastard of an agent didn't grab the medicine, we need to work full force on creatin' our own. Go grab the Petri dish outta the incubator. Let's see how well our new antibiotic worked while you were away."

Metis and I had been working on our own oral antibiotics for months. So far, none have been successful. Before I left for the supply hit, this new experiment looked promising, but antibiotics can work one day, then not the next.

I hesitated, still waiting for Metis to elaborate.

"Now!"

I huffed a sigh and hopped off my perch. As I walked toward the incubator, my eyes wandered around the room, looking for anything unusual. Anything out of place. I wanted to find the journal before Metis did. I needed to know what exactly he was keeping from me and why.

CHAPTER 3

Another failed experiment.

And I was the one who had to tell Aine.

Before I left for the hit, Aine, the CRF Medic, told me our stocks were low.

She was expecting the best from the hit. But our mission was fucked, and now we have another failed experiment under our belts.

My eyes burned from the bright lights and the pungent astringent as I crossed the threshold into the Medical Ward. The room was blanched white, far different than the rest of the dark, musty compound. It was bright and clean and always shocked my senses. While I hated the smell of it, I always welcomed the warmth of the light.

Dr. Aine Owens sat on a stool, her blonde curls pinned messily into a bun. She was hunched over a wincing child as she carefully pulled a thin thread through the child's brow. I recognized the scruffy-haired boy right away.

"Oh, Darragh. What did you do to yourself this time?"

I had to stifle a laugh when I noticed the large, red gouge across Darragh's brow.

Aine nimbly fingered a needle as she threaded the suture string through her son's forehead.

"This genius," Aine said, jabbing the needle through skin again, "decided to take a bunk mattress for a ride down the steps from the Rec Room to the sleeping quarters." Aine pulled on the suture thread bringing the two layers of skin together and tightening the flesh into a thin line. The boy flinched. "He flew off his mattress at the bottom and smacked his head into the wall."

Skies, I love this kid. Darragh was always searching for new adventures, usually alone and always in some sort of trouble. I admired the kid—he was easily the bravest member of the CRF.

I peeked over Aine's shoulder. "Did you go really fast?"

Aine shot me a warning glare.

"Super fast!" Darragh blurted, blue eyes twinkling with mischief.

"So, how can I help you, Red?" Aine asked, returning her attention to Darragh's forehead.

"I just wanted to check our medical supply levels since… well…"

"Yeah," Aine sighed. "I heard about the hit."

I tucked a loose strand of hair behind my ear.

"Whoa, Red! What happened to your hands?" Darragh jerked forward, pulling the string woven through his forehead a little too tight. He shot back in pain, moaning.

"Oh." I shrugged as I bent down closer to Darragh and ruffled his sandy hair, careful not to disturb Aine's work or the boy's wound. "I just got in a fight. Same old, same old."

Aine scowled as she eyed my battered hands, her blue eyes like icicles pinning me through the heart. The needle fell from her steady hands, the thread dangling between Darragh's eyes as it swung back and forth like a pendulum.

She gently held my hands in hers. I tried not to wince as she turned one over and then the other, stretching my fingers slowly to assess the damage.

"Really? On the hit? Who'd you beat up? I bet they look a lot worse!"

Aine rolled her eyes. "Do not encourage him with made-up stories, Red." She turned to her son. "She's teasing. Red got a little carried away with the punching bag. Again."

Darragh crossed his arms. "I like Red's story better."

"Me too, buddy." I winked at the kid.

Aine carefully placed my hands back at my side and sighed. "Well, you know the drill. Ice. Pain meds if you need them.

"I won't."

"I know."

Aine understood better than anyone that I seemed to heal faster than everyone else. A 'genetic anomaly,' she called me once when I fell on a large, sharp rock and sliced open my abdomen. The gaping wound completely healed in just four days. Reign didn't heal from infirmities as fast as I did. If she did, we wouldn't have been at the CRF in the first place.

"Take a look around." Aine gestured toward the medicine cabinets. "I'll finish up with Darragh, and then we can talk."

I nodded, then began to rummage through drawers and cabinets. Some medications I knew, some I didn't. Some we used often, some we didn't. I tried to keep a mental list of medications and ointments we were low on, but the list grew too long. Most items were down to their last bottle or tube.

"Alright," Aine said to her son. "Don't pick. Don't scratch… Eh!" A light slap clapped. "And do not touch!"

I glanced over as Darragh jumped from the stool and darted toward the door.

"And no more mattress surfing!" Aine yelled at the boy as he zoomed past me.

He ignored his mother. "Bye, Red! See you later!"

I chuckled. "Bye, Darragh."

Aine washed her hands, dried them on her smock, and leaned against a steel counter. "As you can tell, we really needed those medical supplies." Aine's usually bright face dim.

With my thumb and forefinger, I rubbed at my golden eyes before pinching the bridge of my nose. "I know."

"We don't have enough meds to make it through winter. Have you and Metis—"

I shook my head, my heart aching. "Another failed experiment today. We are at least another month from maybe a successful trial, but then more testing, and we won't know all the side effects."

Aine nodded slowly. "Can we plan another hit soon?"

"You know Hoenir doesn't like to do them more than a few times a year. It's difficult to get good intel from our internal operatives, and the more often we hit up the trains, well..."

"Our chances of the Coalition tracking us down increases. I know. Balor never lets me forget," Aine said, finishing my thought.

Balor, Aine's husband, was my commanding officer and coordinator of our agent team. Balor, Aine, and their oldest son, Niahm fled the Coalition a few years before Reign and I got here. Balor was in the Coalition Military, and Aine was a nurse. When Aine became pregnant with twins, they knew the Coalition would confiscate one if not both babies, as they did with all multiple pregnancies under the guise of 'population control'. Metis believed, however, that twins, triplets, and the like were confiscated for genetic experimentation.

Balor used his Military clearance to gain access to information the Coalition had on the Resistance, including possible Resistance operatives on the inside. He risked his life and the lives of his family when he visited a Resistance operative in Imperium's lowest ring. The CRF smuggled Balor and his family out of the Coalition City and into The Wastes with only vague directions on how to get there. They arrived one month before the babies were born, but only one baby survived delivery, Lyella.

Balor's Military experience proved invaluable to the CRF, and it did not take very long for Hoenir to make him head of the agent team. With his service in the Coalition's Military, he was the most qualified, and he knew how the enemy's mind worked.

"Sometimes I think it's my fault," Aine continued, "that I give away medication too easily instead of waiting for things to work themselves out."

I stepped closer and put a reassuring hand on her shoulder. "Aine, you are doing the best you can."

Aine's head fell into her hands, loose strands of her hair falling around her hands like golden waterfalls. "It's not enough," she whispered, a slight hitch in her voice.

I took her hands in mine, and when her head slowly lifted, I saw her like I had that first day at the CRF Base. She was everything bright, warm, and beautiful. She reminded me of my mom—well, my stepmom. I resented her at first, as Aine took care of Reign and me like we were her own blood. I didn't want her to replace my dead parents. But as I grew older, I understood she wasn't trying to. She was a kind and gentle soul who simply wanted to keep us safe and healthy.

"It is enough. We will make it through."

Aine's crystal blue eyes welled with tears. I gave her a weak smile. "Metis and I will have a breakthrough soon. I'm sure of it. And we will make sure the kitchen is stocked up with canned fruits and vegetables so we can keep our immune systems boosted through the winter." I embraced Aine. "We will weather this storm."

I let her go. She wiped a tear from her eye and kissed me on the cheek.

"Get some sleep. You need it," Aine said, voice as soft as falling snow.

I squeezed her hand. "Yes, ma'am," I said before I turned to leave. But sleep would wait again. I needed to pack for my journey.

———

I was jarred awake, and my head nailed the bunk above me. I clutched my forehead, which was slick with sweat, and my pulse pounded against my eardrums in an erratic rhythm. Down at my feet, Sirius, the wolf-dog hybrid I found in the woods a couple of months back, cocked his head. The black beast blended into the shadows of our dark room, but his green eyes glowed in the dim light tunneling under the door from the hallway. I reached for him. When I found Sirius, his thick dark fur was matted around a camouflage Coalition Military harness. I was able to coax him back to Base with a few strips of jerky and a ball I stole from the rec room. He finally warmed up to me after I fed him a good meal of leftovers from the mess hall and cut him out of the harness. Stitched in gold against the green and tan fabric were three stars and *Sirius*. Hoenir was furious that I brought a canine into Base—especially a Military dog—and he almost shot Sirius on the spot. Luckily, I was able to reason with him. Sirius clearly had been lost for a while, and if he was chipped or tracked, some soldier would have found him by now. So, I exchanged a new hunting partner for a year of bathroom duty.

Worth it.

After a few good pets, Sirius opened his maw in a large yawn, ready to go back to sleep.

I glanced at my watch. The red light blinked zero-six-hundred.

Time to go.

I gently tapped the hybrid's back, urging him out of bed, and I crept after him, careful not to disturb Reign, my little sister, who slept in the bunk above me. She didn't stir. My pupils dilated, eyes straining to see in the dark as I tiptoed to our shared dresser. The top wooden drawer creaked as I pulled it open to grab my thermal pants and a sweatshirt. I threw them on over my clothes, snuck over to the door, and grabbed my jacket, boots, gloves, rifle, and pack before placing a note for Reign on the dresser and slipping out of our room.

Hoenir hated when I ventured out alone, especially without

telling him. I didn't know if it was a control issue or if he was truly afraid I would leave one day and never come back. But what was he going to do? Kick me out? Kill me?

I snorted at the thought.

Kicking me out would be a security threat for our little Resistance, and the whole lot of them would rebel against the Director if he ever laid a hand on me. I never understood why everyone cared so much about me, but I knew each and every one of the Resistance members would take a bullet for me. If push came to shove, I would do the same for every one of them as well. Except Ulysses. But my gut told me the feeling was mutual.

Sirius followed behind me as I snuck out of the CRF Base. The sun was just beginning to rise over the snow-dusted bluffs, casting orange and purple hues on the white-blanketed forest. I inhaled, filling my lungs with the late-autumn air laced with aromas of rich soil and colored leaves. My spine instantly relaxed.

A crisp wind whipped at the loose tendrils of my hair, nature's silent plea to venture onward. I started my trek east, away from the Great River. It had been a few months since I had been to the Shed— since I had been home.

Home.

A sigh of relief escaped my lips, and the muscles in my shoulders and chest uncoiled slightly at the thought. My father brought Aura, my stepmom, and me to the Shed after we fled the Coalition. He must have been planning to leave the corrupt society for weeks, maybe even months, because when we arrived, the creaky old cottage—our new home—was already stocked with food, medicine, books, and toiletries.

We only lived there together for a short while.

Shortly after we left the Coalition, my little sister, Reign, was born. And a couple of years after that, our parents died. They never returned from a hunting trip, killed and carried off by an

Anoka Bear—a giant mutated grizzly often found lurking in The Wastes.

After a week of my parents missing, I strapped Reign onto my back and went searching for them. About five miles east of the Shed, I discovered a body. Well, what was left of one. Claw marks jaggedly sliced through flesh and muscle, making it almost impossible to identify the person. My feet were frozen. My mind didn't want to accept what was laid out before me. I forced my legs to move, but as I inched closer, it took all my strength not to fall to my knees. It was my stepmother. Her coyote-fur-lined boots that she had sown in that winter were splattered with blood, and a single pearl earring still hung from her mutilated face.

It was Aura, my stepmother, who lay lifeless in a pool of blood, strips of fabric from her shirt flowing in the spring wind, and her golden-brown hair stained crimson.

My father was nowhere to be seen, but I saw the long, jagged lines along the forest floor, like boots dragged through the mud. I didn't dare follow the trail. Reign was barely two, and if what I thought was correct…if a mutant bear had killed our mother and dragged my father off to Skies knew where…then my parents were gone, and I was all she had.

The following winter, Reign got sick. Very sick. Fever ravaged her tiny body, and while my father had stored medications in the Shed and left a chart indicating proper dosages of each medication based on a person's age and weight, I was too afraid of getting it wrong, of killing my baby sister. I had no choice. Despite my promises to my father, I bundled us up, packed a bag, and started trudging through the snow toward the nearest city in the Coalition. Reign was swaddled in my arms, small and weak from days of sickness. Strapped around my feet were my father's too-big snowshoes, and a large pack was fastened around my shoulders. A couple of days into our journey, a blizzard struck, turning us around, and the next thing I knew, I was in the Medical Ward of the Coalition Resistance Forces with Aine watching over me. We couldn't leave—Hoenir wouldn't let us. The way the Director put it, I had to join the Resistance or die. Granted, he said it with more finesse, but that was what my eight-year-old mind comprehended.

Crack.

I whirled, snapping my rifle up and taking aim toward the sound before I switched the safety off. Sirius stilled beside me, head down and ears perked in concentration as I aimed down my scope to find… nothing. Sirius' snout twitched in the air, taking short breaths through his nose, and then his tail started wagging as he stared eagerly at a large maple.

"Umm… Please put that down!" a familiar voice chimed from behind the tree.

"For the love, Reign!" I clicked my safety on and lowered my weapon. Sirius darted toward my sister as she stepped out from behind the tree, her brown hair glinting golden in the early morning light. Reign knelt to pet the oversized canine, and he greeted her with a swipe of his huge, wet tongue across her freckled nose. "What the hell are you doing out here?"

"I think it's pretty obvious." Reign stood up and placed her hands on her slim hips. "I'm following you."

"Well, stop. Go back to Base," I commanded and turned east again, not allowing any further discussion. A few moments later, loud, clumsy footsteps beat hard against the ground, snapping twigs and rustling the driest leaves.

As a child, Reign was never graceful, but as a pubescent teen, I swear to the Skies above her trudging could wake a wolf den twenty miles away.

"You really want me to walk the five miles back to Base all by myself?" Reign yelled after me.

"Five miles? It's only been ten minutes. You can make it back to Base just fine. And I'm hunting," I lied coolly, turning back to my sister. "You don't even like hunting."

Reign cocked her head. "Then why did you leave all your snares in our room?"

My temple throbbed. *It's too early for this.*

"Besides, you just got back from a hit, and I wanna spend time with you!"

"Fine," I said through clenched teeth. "But no whining, no complaining, keep quiet, and keep up." I started hiking again.

"I guess Hoenir has taught you to be a real fun sucker."

I fought the urge to whirl on her and shoot her a glare of impending doom if she kept up the sarcasm, but I remained silent. And to my surprise, she did, too.

CHAPTER 4

We hiked the rest of the way in silence—the only sounds were our labored breathing and the soft crunch of leaves beneath our feet. Even Sirius trotted quietly beside us.

"Where are we?" Reign asked as we approached the Shed, the small decrepit building peeking through large oak trees.

"You'll see."

As we trudged closer, the full guilt of never bringing my younger sister here dropped into my stomach like a brick. I kept an eye on Reign, examining her face for any signs of recognition.

None.

My sister looked as though she was seeing the structure for the first time. When I beheld the Shed, I still saw the wildflowers Aura had planted and tended to along the front of our home and beside the small pathway of stones that led to the door, but maybe all she saw was a small, run-down wooden shack covered in vines and moss.

We padded along the stepping stones leading up to the door. They were covered in detritus and debris, an echo of the beckoning they used to sing.

"What is this place? Did you find it? Is this where you and Niahm always go?"

Her words stung like salt in a wound.

Niahm was Balor and Aine's oldest son. A year younger than me, Niahm was the only one in the Resistance close to my age besides Ulysses. He was my first friend in the Resistance and, in some ways, my only friend. Since Niahm was the only guy my age who wasn't a repulsive asshole, we had been an item…several times—falling in love, then out, then we would plunge back in. Currently, we were out, but deep in my soul, I knew we were inevitable. I mean, who else would I build a life within the Resistance? Who else was I supposed to have children with? It sure as hell wouldn't be Ulysses.

I liked Niahm, I really did. He was cute with his hazel eyes, freckles, and glasses. He was very smart—he actually charged the CRF's security tech lab. But there was just something missing. Maybe it was purely the fact that our relationship felt so inevitable that it made him no longer desirable.

Nevertheless, Reign was right. When Niahm and I were an item, we would come here for some privacy.

"You really don't recognize it?"

"No… Should I?"

"Here, maybe this will help." I pulled out my key to open the rusty lock. I honestly didn't know why I even used the lock. Living outside the Coalition Cities was illegal, so no one was going to come this far into The Wastes and come across the Shed.

According to the American Coalition, The Wastes were uninhabitable—a radioactive wasteland resulting from a 1500-ton nuclear bomb that was detonated above what was once the 48 continental United States of America. That was two hundred years ago. The radioactive isotopes had long since decayed. The CRF was proof of that, but keeping large populations in smaller areas increased the probability of herd mentality—it made people easier to control. A contained farm compared to small flocks scattered throughout a mountain.

I opened the door, the hinges creaking, and stepped aside to let Reign enter first. Sirius squeezed his way through and over the threshold as my sister stepped into the abandoned shelter I still called home. Mice skittered across the floor, disappearing into the crevices of the walls, tiny tracks and wisps in the dust coating the wooden floorboards, the only proof of their existence.

My eyes wandered around the Shed. Well, it wasn't exactly a Shed, but that's what Dad called it. When my father first came across the abandoned structure, that's all it was: one lonely Shed standing deep in the woods. Luckily, it was fitted with old tools —they were dull, and some were covered in rust, but our father used them to make our home. Over the course of the few years we lived here, Dad chopped down timber and used the tools the Shed had given us to add a living space and two bedrooms onto the original structure, which was now the kitchen. There was no bathroom, only a small outhouse behind the cottage. It was brutal during the winter and smelled to high heaven in the summer, but there wasn't exactly running water out in The Wastes.

Aside from the dust, it looked as though time hadn't touched the Shed. Books were still piled next to the make-shift couch of wood and pillows where my father used to read. A rocking chair stood by the hearth where Aura would coax Reign to sleep as a baby. My father's leather jacket still hung on the coat rack next to the doorway. I inhaled, the scent of oak filling my senses.

The smell of home.

I glanced at Reign, hoping to see excitement, but instead, she was pensive, her brows drawn together.

"Welcome home, Reign," I whispered. Sirius roamed from room to room, sniffing every nook and cranny of the Shed, gaining his bearings, but Reign's eyes were now fixed on me.

"What are you talking about? Are you preparing this for us?

To leave the CRF? Hoenir will never let that happen," she countered in disbelief.

"No, Reign. This *was* our home. With Mom and Dad. Your *first* home."

Reign glanced back to the small cottage. "*This* was our home." Reign took a step toward the kitchen table my father had built for us, her hands dangling uncomfortably at her sides, almost like she wanted to touch something but was afraid. "*This* was where we lived?"

I nodded.

"I didn't even think you knew where it was. I thought it was lost to us. To *both* of us."

My heart stumbled in my chest.

Carefully, Reign reached for the table, running her fingers along the wooden surface. "But you knew this whole time."

"Reign…"

She studied the dust now on her fingertips. "Why? Why did you keep it from me?" she whispered, a sob stuck in her throat.

"Reign." I was at a loss for words. "I just—"

"You're just selfish!" she spat, whirling on me. "You wanted this all to yourself! Just like everything else! You are so selfish you couldn't even be bothered to share *our home* with me!" Reign glanced around urgently, hopelessness cast over her face like the shadow of a storm cloud. She ran out the door back into the woods.

Her words cut into me like a long, serrated knife, plucking onto my heartstrings until they snapped. *She's right.*

"Reign!" I cried, following her out the door. But she just ran. She ran until she stumbled over a tree root and fell to her knees. When I caught up to her, tears streamed down her pale, freckled face. I reached for her, but she shoved me away.

"Get away from me!" Reign growled, a venom to her voice I had never heard before.

"Reign, please. You were so young, I didn't think you would have any recollection of this place. I didn't think you would care." I tried to reason with her, and my mind shuffled to think of more excuses, but everything she said was true. I wanted this place to myself—all the memories it held and all the love that was carved into every piece of wood and secured with every iron nail. I wanted it all for myself. On Base, Reign and I shared everything—a room, a dresser, meals. Sometimes, she even stole my underwear! I just wanted this one place to myself, to call my own. But the problem was that the Shed never was my own. I had shared it once, and it was wrong of me to keep it all for myself now.

I knelt beside my sister. "I am so sorry," I whispered, tucking a chestnut strand behind her ear. "You are one hundred percent correct. I was selfish." She glared at me. "I *am* selfish." I corrected, and she huffed a breath of approval. "But let me share it with you now."

"Why? You weren't even going to take me here in the first place," she mumbled into the ground.

"Because you deserve it. You have every right to this place that I do."

"What about Niahm?" she taunted.

I narrowed my brows in confusion. "What do you mean?"

"Doesn't he have more right than I do? He has probably been here more than once."

I blushed at her implication. "You have way more right to this place than Niahm does. This place was never his." I took her hand. "Now come on. If you are going to pout, you can at least do it on a bed."

———

Reign wandered around the Shed and rummaged through crates and drawers. She put a hand on the small stack of books in the corner—the full extent of the library—and sat down to read the spines. Most of them were academic books on molecular biology, artificial genetics, and organic chemistry, but there were a few novels and children's stories scattered throughout.

"Have you read all these books?" Reign called from the small living area.

I nodded. I was in the kitchen cooking a couple of squirrels I managed to snare and canned vegetables I found stashed in the crooked cupboard. Sirius panted excitedly as he circled around me, waiting for scraps to fall on the floor.

"Even these science books?"

"Yup." There wasn't much else to do for leisure in The Wastes—even at Base—so I read everything I could get my hands on. "Okay. Come on, time for dinner."

I wiped my hands on my jeans and gestured Reign over to the table. She popped up from the floor and took a seat on a small stool my father had also crafted. It felt surreal—like we were still waiting patiently for Aura and my father to come home. Sirius gave up any ideas of table scraps and laid curled up by our feet. Reign and I talked, giggled, and shared dreams with each other like we didn't have a care in the world. Then Reign brought up the subject of me and Niahm…again.

"I don't know." I shrugged. "We will probably be together eventually."

"Wow, how romantic." Reign rolled her eyes.

"Well, there aren't exactly a lot of options for me back at Base."

"So, you don't really love him?"

I stared down at my plate of food. It felt weird talking to Reign about my love life, but it was nice to share it with someone. "Not in the way I think I should."

"Not like Balor and Aine love each other?"

I chewed on my lip.

Whenever I thought of real love, I always thought of my father and Aura. I thought of how they would dance in the moonlight after they thought I was asleep. I thought of how Aura would lay her head on my father's lap as they read books and how my father stared at his wife when she was gardening, like she was the only thing that mattered in the world.

I never knew my birth mother. According to my father, she died shortly after I was born due to complications after childbirth. I knew it wasn't my fault, and I knew my father loved me, but the guilt was enough to dissuade any further questions. I couldn't even remember the name my father had given me when I asked—I blocked any and all information about my mother from my consciousness and focused on the life I had with my father. It was just him and me against the world, and the only thing I had to share him with was his job.

Then, he met Aura.

I hated her.

I could not stand sharing my father's attention.

It was my childhood best friend, Callum, who helped me realize how good Aura was for my father and how beneficial she was in our lives. Callum noted how the lingering shadows beneath my father's eyes had dissipated, and my father, in his deep baritone, was singing around our house and garden in Militum. My friend helped me realize my father had changed— and I liked it. Not to mention, Aura always treated me like I was her daughter, and it was nice to be loved that way. It was different than how Dad loved me, but it was refreshing. I could still feel her gentle kisses and soft fingertips as she swept loose strands of hair behind my ears. When we lived in Militum, she would take me shopping and to get our nails painted. Then, when we lived in The Wastes, Aura would comb my hair every evening and teach me small crafts.

I couldn't recall much of my childhood in the Coalition—just a few bleary memories of my father's biology lab, a boy I liked with sparkling green eyes, and my father when he first started dating Aura. But Reign couldn't even remember our parent's love for each other. Maybe she couldn't even remember their love for her.

A lump stuck in my throat.

I was thankful to have known that love, and I secretly hoped that one day I could love someone the way Balor and Aine loved each other—the way my parents loved each other—just so I wouldn't be alone for the rest of my life.

I smiled sweetly at Reign. "Right, not like Balor and Aine. What about you?" I asked, switching the subject from myself back to her. "Anyone you like?"

Reign sighed. "No. The only boy my age is Jonah Grayson, and Lyella really likes him. She already called dibs."

I stifled a laugh over the thought of calling dibs on a boy. "Well, what about boys that aren't your age? Like Harrison Aberfeldy or Tyrion Donalds?"

"Harrison is sixteen and way out of my league! He could never like me."

"Oh, you don't know that. But Tyrion seems nice."

Reign rolled her eyes. "You could land a hovercraft on his nose."

I nearly choked on my squirrel.

"Well, it's true!"

"What about Darragh? Then, if I marry Niahm and you marry Darragh, we could be sisters *and* sisters-in-law."

We just stared at each other for a moment, smiles tugging gently on our lips before we burst out laughing. Darragh was four years younger and still just a child. However, when Reign would be twenty-four, Darragh would be twenty. Eventually, four years might not seem like much of a difference. Still, the thought brought tears to our eyes as we laughed about little Darragh children running around.

"Did you have any crushes in Militum before you came here?" Reign asked after we calmed down.

Militum was the Military headquarters of the Coalition, situated right on the coast of the Severing Sea. My father wasn't a soldier, but he worked in the Military Base on some classified government project. It couldn't have been too classified, though, since he brought me to work with him nearly every day.

I nodded. "Yeah." I swallowed a chunk of squirrel. "His name was Callum."

I thought about my old friend often enough. Far too often for just a childhood crush. He would just pop into my head, and I couldn't help but wonder how he was faring—if he became a doctor like his mom, or a senator like his dad, or if he was just as lost and alone as I was.

"I threw a rock at him once." The memory flickered across my mind like a shooting star.

Reign gaped at me. "That doesn't exactly sound like you liked him."

I shrugged. "When you are young and in love, you do silly things."

"What was he like?"

"Sandy hair, green eyes. Smart. Sweet." I shrugged again. "He was really my only friend, so that's probably why I liked him."

"Why didn't you have any friends?"

"Dad had me tutored, so I didn't go to the school like the rest of the kids in Militum. But Callum's mom and our dad worked together, so we would have play dates."

Reign finished her last bite of food. "Did he like you?"

I shrugged. "I think so. But we were so young, it's hard to say."

"Did you kiss?"

I laughed. "Once or twice."

"So, Niahm wasn't your first kiss?"

"I was five or six, and he was two years older than I was—kisses don't count when you are that young."

"It does, too! Does Niahm know? Will he be upset? Are you going to tell him?"

I grabbed Reign's empty plate. "Okay, that's enough." I got up from my stool and walked over to the sink.

"I'm going to do the dishes. Can you let Sirius outside and then light the lanterns?" I handed Reign a box of matches.

Reign stood up and opened the door for the black dog to dart off into the cool autumn evening, then she set about our small home, lighting the lanterns one by one as I washed the few dishes we used with well water and soap Aura had made years ago. Once I started to dry and stow the dishes, the house was glowing, and it felt like it was just yesterday when I sat on my father's lap as he read to me, Aura nursing a tiny baby Reign in the oak rocking chair next to the fire.

"Are you okay?" Reign asked, returning the matches to me.

"Yes," I lied, my eyes stinging as I walked over to the fireplace. "I'm fine." All this time, I thought I would lose this place if I brought Reign here—if she knew about the Shed. But I finally realized that without her, this place was never really home.

I grabbed some firewood from the pile next to the hearth, stacked the logs in the fireplace, and struck a match. With a little stoking, a small flame soon roared to life.

Reign was still watching me when I turned to face her. The flames danced in her sky-blue eyes.

Our father's eyes.

"Follow me." I led my sister into the room we shared when we were little. Reign's oak crib was still there, but it was stripped of all the blankets. I had wrapped my baby sister with all the soft fabric I could find before we fled all those years ago. My worn cot was in the opposite corner with a small wooden box as a nightstand. I patted the bed, signaling for my sister to come sit next to me, then pulled out the faded yellow book from my nightstand. I opened it up to the front cover page, where my full name was still inscribed in my father's script.

Rowyn Eloise Darrow.

My father must have thought himself clever when he named me—using my initials to spell out the color of my hair. However, Reign was also bestowed the same initials for Reign Elizabeth Darrow—though her hair was a deep chestnut brown. Perhaps he just liked the color red.

Reign gently took the book from my hands and read the title. "Winnie the Pooh?"

I nodded. "You don't remember it?"

She shook her head.

"Dad read it to us all the time. It's also why Dad called me 'Wynnie,' because of Winnie the Pooh Bear."

"Why is it in here and not with the rest of the books?"

"Because it's my favorite."

"And what's that book?"

I turned to where my sister had pointed. Tucked deep in the box, almost invisible against the dark wood, was a leather-bound journal. I grabbed for the book. My fingertips met a smooth, cool surface, though I expected the leather to be covered in a thick layer of dust and grime. A gold symbol that looked like two hands holding a single flame was emblazoned on the cover with the title and my father's name.

"The Prometheus Project. Janus Corneilei Darrow."

CHAPTER 5

I could not breathe.

I knew every book, essay, manual, and loose piece of paper in the Shed. I even read Aura's diary once, a narrative that has scarred me for all of eternity. But this—this was new. The thought chilled me to the marrow. Someone else had been in the Shed, and that someone obviously knew my father and that this Shed had once belonged to him.

My sanctuary was breached, and my little sister was stuck in the crossfire.

Though my heart was pounding in my chest, I kept my face placid. But Reign caught everything, like how my hands were shaking as I stowed the journal back in the box. Maybe if it looked like I never touched it, then no one would come for us.

"What is it?" Reign asked, worry dripping from her words.

"It's nothing important. Just some of Dad's scribblings." I ran a hand through my hair. We needed to get out of here. I glanced around the small, dimly lit room, the lanterns' fire light flickering off the walls like dancing sprites I used to read stories about. The sun had already set, and even one of these lanterns could not chase away the dark creatures that roam these woods at night.

I smiled gently at my little sister. "Let's go snuggle in Mom and Dad's old cot, and I'll read you a story. It's big enough for the both of us."

And I know where Dad kept his Glock.

———

"What were they like?" Reign asked. We just finished reading a chapter from *Winnie the Pooh Bear,* Reign snuggling in the crook of my arm and chest as we lay on our parents' old cot. But even she couldn't warm me from the chilling thoughts of someone sneaking into our home, leaving a journal on my nightstand, and probably touching my bed. Shivers like spiders crawled down my spine.

I clapped the yellow book shut and set it on the makeshift nightstand beside me. "Wonderful," I told her, pulling her in tightly.

"Well, I need more than that. You hardly talk about them."

I took a deep breath, willing my tears to remain at bay. "Dad was incredibly smart. When I was little, it always seemed like he was receiving an award for some new scientific research or breakthrough."

"What did he research?"

"I'm not really sure, but it was in biology. Genetics, I think."

Reign lifted her head slightly to look at me. "Like Metis?"

"Yeah. Like Metis."

"What did he look like? Was he handsome?"

I laughed. "In a rugged sort of way. Dad let his hair and beard grow out while we lived here. His blue eyes reminded me of storm clouds. He was strong. Very strong."

"And Mom? Was she pretty?"

"Beautiful," I said. "And you are the spitting image of her. Warm, hazel eyes and wavy, chestnut hair. She was gentle and petite. She always wore the pearl earrings Dad bought for her when they first started dating, and her smile was as wide and bright as yours." I brushed back some of Reign's silken hair and kissed her brow.

"What about me is like Dad?"

"Your curiosity. And your eyes." I tapped a finger on her freckled button nose. "Though, just the color—the shape is more like moms. And maybe your chin. I think you have Dad's chin."

A long moment of silence passed between us, and I thought my little sister had fallen asleep, but then she whispered, "Did they love me?"

"Of course." I squeezed Reign again. "They were infatuated with you, really. Every milestone you met as an infant was celebrated like you were the brightest star in the sky." I kissed the crown of her head. "Okay, it's time for bed."

I untangled myself from Reign. I tucked her in tightly on the other side of the bed and turned back over. My lips pursed, ready to blow out the antique lantern flickering on the nightstand next to me, but my eyes wandered to the doorway—to where the journal lay next to my cot.

Alone.

In the dark.

It called to me.

I waited until I was sure Reign was sound asleep before I gently crawled out of bed, grabbed the lantern, and crept from my parent's old room—a loose floorboard creaking slightly—and padded to my room.

I set the lantern on the nightstand, and the gold lettering of the journal glinted, the emblazoned flame flickering to life in the candlelight. I sat on my cot and peeled apart the old pages. It opened to the middle, where a piece of faded ivory cloth with faded pink roses and green leaves was tucked between two pages. I picked it up and fingered the cloth. It was incredibly soft —it reminded me of the textile blankets my family had in Militum—a far cry from the animal pelts and few knitted blankets we had in the Shed. Two of the edges were jagged like it was torn from a larger blanket, and the other two obviously made a corner, a thin, intricately woven lace stitched into the seams. It smelled like old parchment. I tucked it back into the page and continued to flip through the journal. Most of the pages were worn and frayed. Some were even ripped from the binding completely.

According to the dates listed in the top right corners of the legible pages, my father had used this journal for a little over ten years. It was filled with equations, measurements, and data, often referring to either another journal or recorded work of some sort. Nothing I recognized to be in the Shed, but it was definitely my father's handwriting—I had seen enough of his scrawl in the margins of books to know.

The more I analyzed the journal, the more I realized that his work dealt largely with experimental genetic research. Some pages were even just lines and lines of genetic code. Others were laced with various proteins and nucleotides he was trying to separate.

I came across one page that revealed the findings of a short DNA sequence. At the end, he had written:

Verified sequence 14B5284 through 14B5863 with Dr. Freyja Osouf as an ancient viral sequence that had been embedded into the Human Genome about 1.3 million years ago. Not vital for gene expression.

Osouf.

I recognized the name. It was the mother of my childhood friend, Callum Osouf.

As I flipped through the pages, Dr. Osouf came up quite frequently. I knew they were colleagues, but it seemed they were partners tasked with the same project. I skimmed over data, equations, and calculations, trying to find any clue on exactly what they were researching—a name, anything.

June 6th, 2298.

I consulted with the head of the Epimetheus Project today, Dr. Metis Barnes. It seems that gene sequence 08D6798 through

18D8054 is found in other homo species and is necessary for gene expression. More data is needed on exact function.

Dr. Metis Barnes.

Metis knew my father. *Worked* with my father.

I felt the betrayal wrap around my lungs like a python.

Why didn't he tell me?

"Fucking Metis," I mumbled to myself as I stood up from my cot.

I grabbed my bag from the corner of the room, stifling the urge to stomp around angrily, not wanting to wake Reign, but I was so incredibly furious!

We had no time to waste tomorrow morning. First, an intruder, and now this. As soon as the sun rose, we were leaving, and I was going to get some damned answers.

Quietly, I slid the kitchen table off the faded rug and lifted the thread-bare fabric to reveal a hidden door. I unlatched the panel and pushed down on the ladder that led into our vault. Lantern in tow, I descended fifteen feet underground to the bottom. The cool, damp air crawled along my skin and smelled like stale dirt and rock.

Aura stored most of her canned foods and dried herbs at the far end of the vault. There was also a tiny room that was her root cellar. My father had kept some things down here, too, including the medicine he stocked before leaving Militum. The vault had a few crooked shelves ladened with ointments, pills, and vials that were good for anything from simple cuts and scrapes to bacterial infections—things that should have come in handy to save Reign all those years ago.

Despite the small medicine manual my father had scribed, it was no use to me when Reign got sick. I stood in front of these shelves for hours examining all the bottles and tubes, searching for something that would help my little sister—something that could relieve her cough or stop her fever. But as I read all the long, complicated names, each drawn-out syllable seemed like a foreign language. I was afraid that for my sister—as a toddler—any amount of treatment would poison her.

I decided I would much rather venture out in the middle of winter to find someone—anyone—risking both our lives in the frigid journey than to either accidentally kill my sister or watch her suffer a slow, agonizing death.

Standing here again, years later, I knew I'd made the right choice, but I was still pissed that I was forced to break one promise to my father to keep the other two. But life…it's always about choices.

Shelf by shelf, I pushed all the medicine stored in the vault into my pack. Vials, bottles, tubes, bandages—it all went. I didn't know what we would need for the winter, but I couldn't risk lacking anything, and Skies knew the medicine wasn't doing any good sitting here.

I trudged up the ladder, shut the vault door, and placed the rug and kitchen table back over the entrance. I continued to stock my pack with various items from the Shed, including my father's journal.

I set my pack on the kitchen table and returned to my parents' old bed. Just as I settled under the blankets, I heard what sounded like long, thick claws scratching in short, quick movements across the Shed door.

I bolted upright, then bent over the bed, popped the loose floorboard, and pulled out the handgun stashed there. As I stalked toward the front door, I switched off the safety and cocked the handle. The scratching persisted, the sound grinding on my skull and teeth. I aimed the gun at the door with my right hand and unlocked the door with my left. Slowly, I cracked the door open, and a dark shadow darted through the space, forcing the door wide open. With a start, I jumped back, gun trained on the creature.

"Holy, fucking damn, Sirius!" I yelled in a whisper.

The hybrid wagged his tail as he sat before me. I tripped my safety back on and lowered the gun. "You are a Skies-damned idiot."

I trudged back to my parents' old bedroom, careful not to wake Reign. Sirius trotted after me, his paws pattering softly on the wood floors. I stowed the gun back under the floorboard and crawled into bed. Sirius hopped up as well and snuggled at Reign's feet. I stared at my little sister. Though she was fifteen, when she was sleeping, all I could see was the little toddler I was so afraid to hurt—the only family I had left.

"It's nice to have you here," I whispered, kissing my little sister gently on the cheek. Reign didn't respond, but I swear a slight smile tugged at her pink lips.

———

Fucking Metis.

Those two words were the beat of every footstep as Reign, Sirius, and I hiked back to Base the next morning, and when we reached Base just before noon, I was ready for answers. But as Reign and I entered the compound, sirens were blaring, bouncing off the walls of the dimly lit corridors, and people rushed through the halls, their eyes frantic.

"Level Two Security Breach. All Committee Members report to Director Vasquez immediately."

This wasn't a drill. The siren continued to sound throughout the whole Base as I tugged my sister through the chaos, making my way to Hoenir's office until I finally found him in the stairwell to the second floor.

I approached the director. "What the fuck is going on, Hoenir?"

Hoenir's back stiffened. "Where the hell have you been, Agent?"

I opened my mouth, but the Director cut me off.

"Committee meeting. My office. Now." He turned on a heel, fingers angrily tapping on his COM-device.

I whirled to my sister. Her face was painted in worry, and I cupped her cheek. "Take Sirius and go find Lyella, Darragh, and Aine. Stay wherever they are. I will come for you after the meeting."

She nodded once. I pushed her and Sirius in the direction of the dormitories as I followed after Hoenir.

The Advisory Committee consisted of Hoenir, Metis, Balor, and myself. Metis was our skilled scientist, and Balor's priority role was RAC. Though, technically, Balor was also head of security, it was a responsibility he pretty much handed over to his eldest son since Niahm was more skilled with technology. Hoenir was our CRF Director, and I was the newest member of the Committee, though the only reason I was a part of the Committee was due to my constant pestering. I had called Hoenir sexist because the Committee consisted of only men, and once Balor started training me to take his place as RAC, my position in the Committee was secured. Of course, Metis pulled for me as well.

However, as I entered the office today, two more members joined us: Niahm and—

"Well, hello, Princess! Where have you been?"

I stiffened at the sound of that dreadfully cheery voice—a voice that ground like nails on concrete against my spine. "What the hell are you doing here?" I asked Ulysses, not deigning to look at him.

"Oh, I was invited."

I gave Hoenir an exasperated look, but the Director merely shrugged. "You have got to be kidding me, Hoenir! What the hell is going on that Ulysses has to join in on our committee meeting?"

"Agent, sit down!" Hoenir commanded.

I rolled my eyes and plopped into my chair.

Hoenir sat on the corner of his desk. "Sorry for the delay of the meeting, gentlemen, but if one of our top agents wasn't MIA, we could have addressed this problem much sooner."

"What problem?" I interjected.

Hoenir's glare was icy. "Where the fuck were you, Agent?"

I sucked on a tooth. "Hunting trip."

"With little Red?" Ulysses scoffed, arms folded over his chest as he casually leaned back in his metal folding chair. I ground my teeth. I hated it when people called my sister 'little Red'—it was like her fate of being devoured by a wolf was sealed.

Hoenir held a hand up to his dog, eyes still pinned on me. "Unauthorized?"

I kicked my pack under my chair. "Yes, sir."

Metis tapped his cane angrily on the ground. Niahm flinched next to the bearish man. "Reprimand Agent Red later, Director. What in blazes is goin' on?"

Hoenir pinched the bridge of his nose. "Apparently, our firewall was breached, and our server has been hacked by the American Coalition."

"What?" I glanced at Niahm. "How?"

Hoenir gestured for Niahm to continue.

Niahm pushed his too-large glasses up the bridge of his nose. "We are not exactly sure. All I know is that at zero-five-hundred this morning, our main computer in the lab had a window pop up initiating 'Routine Data Transfer' from our server to server CL535743. I was able to trace the server back to the Coalition's capitol of Imperium, but not a specific location within the city."

"What did it mean by 'routine,' boy?" Metis asked.

Niahm adjusted his glasses again. "I am not sure. But it would suggest that it has happened before."

Balor sat across from me, one leg propped on a chair. Through his slacks, I could see the bandage bulging from where Aine had cleaned him up. Luckily, the security bot's laser left a clean wound, but it would be weeks until his right leg was healed. My Commanding Officer rubbed at his salt-and-peppered beard. "Were you able to find the initiation sequence and look back on the log to see if it had occurred previously?"

Niahm shook his head. "The sequence was encrypted. It would take weeks, maybe even months, to figure it out."

"What do they know? What did they take?"

"They didn't take anything, but they copied everything. Hit plans, resource spreadsheets, security cam footage, even the kids' school assignments."

"Well, why didn't you stop it?" Metis asked pointedly.

We all looked to Niahm. He grew small under our stares. "Well, I did not find out until zero-eight-hundred when my shift began, and the process was already complete."

"Who the fuck was supposed to be on shift?" Metis' cane again stomped on the tile floor.

Niahm glanced at Ulysses. "Agent Smith was scheduled for the overnight shift."

"What?" I snapped my attention to Ulysses.

Ulysses held his hands up. "I had just returned from a four-day-long mission. I told you I needed the shift covered to rest."

Niahm's cheeks reddened. "And I denied your request. Dan and Quince just pulled two double shifts each while we were on the hit. There was no one else."

"Except you."

I stood from my chair. "Oh, hell no. The mission took *four* days because we had to shake the Coalition off our tails. And why was that? Oh yeah, because of you! Niahm doesn't owe you anything after the shit you pulled."

"Sit down, Agent," Hoenir commanded.

"He disobeyed direct orders and then didn't report for a scheduled shift. That's damn well near treason, Director."

"And, why is Ulysses here, Director?" Balor questioned, clearly annoyed but always the diplomat.

"It is important for Agent Smith to learn how to clean up messes, especially if he is in line to take over your position one day, Balor."

"Excuse me?" I coughed, choking on my saliva. I glanced over to my RAC but Balor's eyes were as wide as mine.

"Yes." Hoenir stared me down. "I think Ulysses would be a better fit for the position, Agent Darrow."

"Better fit, my ass!" Metis shouted.

I also started to object, but Hoenir hushed me with a hand. "I think this conversation is best suited for a different time, Agent. Right now, we need to focus on our next steps. The most logical option, and the option I have initiated the protocol for, would be to dismantle this Base and move."

"That would take too much time," I argued. "Not just packing, burning, and scouting for a new Base but actually traveling to a new location. We would be out in the elements for too long, and it's nearly winter."

"I agree," Metis stated. "We could lose people. The young 'n' the elderly would be at great risk. Not to mention, we would be sittin' ducks. Even if we did get to a safe location without the loss of lives, movin' as many people as we have would leave a trail. We would lead 'em straight to our new Base."

"We could travel in smaller teams," Ulysses suggested. "Each team could take a different route to our rendezvous."

"I doubt we have enough experienced people to lead the number of teams we would need. Our groups would have to be extremely small for the Coalition to have trouble tracking us," I rebutted.

"What are your thoughts, Balor?" Hoenir asked the RAC.

Balor considered me. "I think Agent Darrow knows what to do. *She* should oversee damage control."

I stared blankly at Balor in disbelief and gratitude.

"I second!" Metis shouted, pounding his cane on the floor again.

"A child in charge of a cleanup this big?" Hoenir's eyes widened.

"That *child*," Metis pointed to me with his cane, "is your

most skilled asset, Director. You're doin' yourself a disservice by not utilizing her.

Hoenir rolled his eyes. "Any ideas then, Agent?"

Everyone's attention turned toward me. Waiting. Expecting.

I couldn't help but smile. "One… But it will be unlike any mission we have ever done before."

Hoenir leaned back in his chair, rubbing his temples with his fingers. Metis, for once in his life, had a huge grin spread across his face, and his bionic eye seemed to glow brighter. For a moment, I had forgotten about his betrayal.

"What do you have in mind, Agent?" Hoenir mumbled, already irritated by the absurd plan I was about to propose. Or maybe it was my prolonged dramatics.

"We break into the Coalition and take back what is ours."

CHAPTER 6

We outlined the mission parameters and assigned our best agents to the team. The final details were to be sorted with Hoenir and his operatives within the Coalition city of Imperium.

"Agent Red, a word." Hoenir stopped me after the Committee had been dismissed.

Metis turned in the doorway. "Surely, ya need to talk to yer operatives before ya ream her out, Director. Or maybe ya need a serious conversation with Agent Smith since this colossal fuckup is all his doin'." With his cane, Metis pointed to Ulysses, who was still lounging in his chair, clearly in no hurry to leave his new and comfortable committee seat.

Hoenir's dark eyes narrowed into slits. "You would do well to remember your place, Dr. Barnes."

Metis hobbled deliberately toward the CRF Director. "And you would do well to remember yers, Vasquez. We are not much more than a tick on the back of the Coalition. If we're gonna be effective at poisonin' their bloodstream, then ya need to get yer damned head out of yer ass and focus on the real internal problems here, and it's not that girl."

Ulysses stifled a sneer as he leaned back in his chair and crossed his legs on top of the conference table.

Good thing Metis is always around to fight your battles.

I straightened. "Metis—"

"I need ya in the lab, Red." The old man turned from the Director. "You can talk to the Director later."

Flames seemed to burn behind Hoenir's dark eyes, and it echoed the heat flushing my chest and cheeks. I scowled at all the controlling men in the room before storming past Metis and out the door.

———

I was sitting outside of Metis' lab when the cyborg man ambled down the hallway.

"We need to get ya a Skies-damned key," Metis mumbled as he dug through his pocket.

I shrugged. "I only need access to the lab when you are here." I followed the hobbling old man into the laboratory as the motion-censored lights flickered on. "Plus, it will be more sentimental when you die, and Hoenir reads your will to find you left the keys and laboratory to me."

"Cheery," Metis grumbled.

"'And to my adopted, pain-in-the-ass daughter,'" I started in my grumpy, old-man voice I sometimes used to mock Metis. "'I give the key to my laboratory in hopes she will finally get some damned work done now that I'm dead.'" I threw my bag, still heavy with medicine, on the floor, plopped in my chair, and swung my feet atop my desk.

"Do ya understand how serious this is?"

"You dying? Yes. But you have at least a good two to five years left, right?" I mumbled, chewing on a fingernail.

Metis slammed the door shut. "Do I look to be in a jokin' mood?"

"Well, considering your only emotion is grumpy hard-ass, I thought I would lighten things up from time to time."

"Are you tryin' to get kicked outta the Resistance?" Metis grumbled as he sorted through the papers on his desk.

"What are you talking about?"

"How many Skies-damned tantrums are ya gonna throw this week, Red? How hard are ya gonna pull before yer lead finally snaps?" Metis hit my feet with his metal cane until I removed them from my desk.

"Well, maybe if people actually listened to me or decided to tell me the truth, I wouldn't have to throw so many *Skies-damned tantrums*." From my bag, I pulled out my father's journal and slammed it on the desk before me. Metis's eyes snapped to the notebook.

"Where did ya get that?" His voice was low, urgency clinging to his words like syrup.

"You know where I was."

Metis was quiet as he approached my desk, his eyes never leaving the journal. As he leaned on my desk, his eyes slowly met mine, and I felt like his mechanical one was scanning me—analyzing me.

Metis cracked his neck and exhaled slowly, just like he had the other day.

He quickly looked away.

I swallowed. This was the research journal he was looking for.

"Where in the Shed did ya find this?"

I matched his low voice. "Next to my cot, on my nightstand."

"Have you seen this before?"

I shook my head. "Never."

Metis straightened and paced around the laboratory.

"Metis, is this what you were looking for the other day?"

His greasy grey strands swayed as he shook his head. "I don't wanna lie to ya, Red."

"Then don't."

He paused, rubbing his hand over his face. In that moment, in the slump of his shoulders and in the pause of his hand over his eye, I knew. My skin convulsed, a chill running down my spine.

"Someone in this Base stole my father's journal from you and planted it in my Shed so I would find it."

Metis cleared his throat. "It appears so." He returned to his chair, grunting as he sat back down.

I leaned forward. "Why did you have this? Why didn't you tell me?"

He was quite for a moment, not meeting my gaze as he fidgeted with his cane. "You remind me so much of him, ya know?"

"Do not dodge my questions, Metis," I ground out. I didn't need to ask who he was speaking of. "Why didn't you tell me you knew my father?"

The scientist sighed heavily. "I didn't know how much ya remembered him—if ya wanted to remember him. And I certainly didn't want to change how ya remembered him."

I tried to wrap my mind around my mentor's words, but feelings of betrayal crept into my heart and mind, making everything fuzzy and distant. Metis, the man who, in many ways, replaced my father, kept the knowledge about my *real* father from me. I could have learned so much about him. Maybe I could have gained more closure if Metis had talked about him. All this time, I could have felt closer to my family—to my parents—despite them being gone. I could have felt like I belonged to something.

"What is this journal?" I asked as Metis paced back and forth.

Metis swallowed. "It's yer father's life-long work. Well, part of it anyway."

"And you helped him…"

He nodded.

"Why didn't you tell me?"

"Need to know," he shrugged.

"Fuck that! I needed to know!"

"Knowin' what is in this journal will get ya killed! Do ya need to be dead?"

I scoffed. "There is nothing important in there. Just a bunch of equations and data charts—no conclusions."

"That's the point. The Coalition is still workin' on Janus' research." Metis cracked his neck and leaned forward, his voice low. "But they don't have the equations to finish. They have the final products, but no way to replicate the process because they don't have those equations." Metis pointed a metal finger at the journal that lay on my desk.

"Yer father left the Coalition 'cuz he didn't wanna finish his research. Janus saw how it could be abused, saw the chaos it would create, 'n started to despise his work. So, when he fled, all of his research disappeared with him... All of it, except that journal. I thought he would have burned the Skies-damned thing. I sure as blazin' Hell would've."

I eyed him suspiciously. "Where did you find it? Why didn't you burn it?"

He shrugged. "Didn't have the heart. Only a couple days after yer plane crashed, I found the damned thing wrapped up 'n stowed in the enrichment corner of my lab. Don't ask me how it got there. I don't know why yer father would leave it with me." Metis' eyes met mine, and his right eye glistened. "Maybe he felt like he owed it to me as a colleague, or as a friend."

"Metis, what was he working on?"

"I can't tell ya. I was sworn to secrecy."

I slammed a fist on my desk. "For fuck's sake, Metis! My father is dead!"

"And in honor of his legacy, I won't break my word, Red. Not even for you. "

I stood up, crossed my arms, and faced the man.

"How did the journal get from your desk to my Shed, then?"

Metis leaned back. "That's the question, isn't it?"

"Someone here is a Coalition spy?" That one was rhetorical, but Metis answered anyway.

He slowly nodded. "I have had that inklin' for some time now."

"Who?"

"Well, who knows 'bout the Shed?" Metis asked with a grunt as he sat back into his desk chair. I remained standing across from him.

"Only you, Niahm, and now Reign. But it can't be Niahm!" I hated how the words tumbled from my mouth. They were breathy and pathetic. Pleading. I didn't want to think I was so foolish as to befriend a Coalition spy.

Metis shook his head. "Nah. I don't think it's the Owens boy. That whole family is too wholesome to be spies. They're good shit. So, it's possible someone else trailed ya to the Shed before. They know ya. They know yer family. And placin' this journal there was a message."

I turned his words over in my mind. "And it would have to be someone that wasn't on the hit. No one but me leaves Base for extended periods of time, and having me out on a mission would have been the perfect opportunity to sneak into the Shed without me noticing someone was missing. Was anyone gone for several hours during the hit?"

Metis slammed his cane against his desk. "How the hell should I know? I am no one's keeper."

I rolled my eyes at the old man. How such an intelligent person could be so obtuse was beyond me. "Where were you keeping the journal? "

"Locked in my desk. What's that look for, Agent? What are ya thinkin'?"

I tapped a foot. "Locked? You didn't want the wrong people to get their hands on it."

Metis shook my accusation away with a wave of his hand.

"If you've had an *inkling*, why didn't you tell Hoenir?"

"What makes ya think I didn't?" Metis raised a bushy grey brow.

"We would have all been brought in for questioning."

"And what if I just don't have enough evidence?"

"If you didn't have evidence, you wouldn't have a suspicion."

"Gut instinct?"

"That would mean you would have to feel something for once in your life." I half-heartedly joked. The scientist smiled, but just slightly. "You don't trust Hoenir, do you?"

"I don't trust anyone."

I let his words linger in the air for a moment. "And what if you're the spy."

Metis chuckled. "Oh, I've taught ya well, haven't I?"

"You didn't answer my question."

Metis leaned in closer to whisper. "Let's just say the moment ya stop trustin' me is the moment we're all undone, Red." His metal eye whirred.

We stared at each other for a long moment, the air tense with his cryptic words. Metis leaned back in his chair. "So, what are ya gonna do, Agent?"

"What do you mean?"

He shrugged. "Y'aren't the type of person who does nothin' when encounterin' new information. Ya wanna act." Metis pointed a crooked finger at my head. "I see those wheels turnin'. 'N whatever you're plannin', ya can't do it alone."

"I don't know what you're talking about." I pulled dead skin from my cuticles.

"Don't play coy with me, Red!" Metis slammed a palm on the table, drawing my eyes up toward him.

I pursed my lips, stood up from my desk, and started pacing again to get my blood flowing. "Did my father destroy all of his other research?"

"As much as he could. But I dunno if I would call wipin' a

hard drive destroyin'. In my humble opinion, Janus should have lit the whole bloody Laboratory ablaze."

"So, why would he keep the journal? Why didn't he just burn it?"

"He spent his whole life on this one project. It's hard to fully separate yerself from somethin' ya dedicated yer life to."

"He obviously didn't want the Coalition to have it."

"Correct. He didn't want anyone to have the ability to replicate his research."

"But if we have a spy"—I glanced to Metis—"or two, in our midst…"

"Then they know about the journal and could have sent pictures of its contents to whomever in the Coalition," Metis continued my thought.

"What would happen if the Coalition replicated my father's research?"

He shook his head like he was trying to rid himself of an unbearable thought. "Nothin' good."

"What was he working on?"

"A weapon. A very dangerous weapon." His eyes rolled over me, and I felt stripped naked.

A weapon? I couldn't imagine my father making a weapon. He was the most gentle, compassionate, and kind soul I had ever known.

Metis' elbows rested on his desk. "Red, ya need to realize somethin' before ya go makin' outlandish plans." I turned to meet his stare. "Your father leavin' his job was quite an atrocity —more of how he left than him actually leavin'. It was on the news for over a year." Metis gestured for me to sit down. "Ya see, the day after yer father resigned, he packed up yer family 'n put ya on a plane. Within minutes of the hovercraft vanishin', all of his research, all of his data, everythin' he had worked on for decades disappeared. No trace. At the time, not even the best technical teams could recover the files. You 'n yer family were supposed to arrive in Imperium, but the hovercraft never made it. Search teams were sent out 'n found yer plane destroyed, nothin' left but the skeleton of that hovercraft—everything else was burnt to a crisp. No black box, no remains."

"That doesn't make any sense. Our craft landed it safely in a field—"

Metis held up his metal hand, light glinting off the titanium alloy. "The news covered it endlessly. The public was warned to keep a lookout for Janus 'n his family. Pictures of you, yer father, 'n yer stepmother were posted everywhere. Search parties were sent into The Wastes to find y'all. Friends, family, and even acquaintances were questioned by Government Agencies and News Networks. Eventually, word spilled 'bout yer father 'n his position, how all his classified information was lost, and rumors spread fast. The media went nuts, creatin' absurd conspiracy theories, diggin' into Government Resources, and causin' huge problems that eventually led to the dismantlin' of the media as we knew it."

"What were the rumors? What was the truth?"

Metis sighed and rubbed his right knee. "I don't know specifics, Red, 'n sharin' rumors wouldn't be fair to the memory of yer father. I wish I could give ya the truth, but I'm not sure I know enough of it to give it to ya."

"So, what's your point?" I asked impatiently, staring at my own hands as I tried to stuff down the hurt and anger boiling up into my heart.

"The point is that the whole damned Coalition knew Rowyn Eloise Darrow and her father, Dr. Janus Cornelei Darrow. And in case you didn't notice, ya stick out like a sore thumb." Metis pointed to my head. "People aren't just born with hair like that anymore."

I tucked a loose strand of wavy, crimson hair behind my ear, evidence of the recessive trait I seemed to have acquired despite its extinction from the population a hundred years ago.

"You weren't worried about my hair before?"

"Not when it was going to be a one-day mission 'n there were no Coalition Civilians around."

"What makes you think this will be any different?" I asked mischievously.

"Look at me, Red."

I met his gaze.

"There is no information about yer father in the Coalition. What yer father didn't destroy, the Coalition did. Officials erased anythin' that ever pertained to Dr. Janus Darrow. They wiped him from the database like he never existed—even his coworkers were forbidden to ever mention him. All of his history, his work, his name, it's all gone."

I rolled my eyes.

"Don't put yerself or anyone else involved in this mission at risk for yer additional interests," Metis growled. "Ya won't find anythin'."

"But we have already found something!" I jabbed my finger into the journal still on my desk.

"No. You found somethin' of mine."

"That somehow ended up in my Shed. At the very least, we have to figure out who the spy in our Resistance is!"

"'n we can do that from the inside."

I gave my mentor a mischievous smile. "Why don't we just call it research? You have trained me to be an inquisitive little scientist, after all."

"Scientists let logic decide what to ask 'n how far to go. Whether ya like it or not, you're driven by yer feelin's, not by logic. And by the Skies, I've tried to train it outta ya, but ya still don't know when to stop, especially if somethin' is unresolved. So—" Metis grunted, lifting himself up from his chair. "Before you go on and try to make a half-assed plan by yerself, you're gonna need somethin's…'n then a plan C amount of thin's."

"Plan C?"

"Yes." Metis hobbled over to a cupboard. He unlocked it and pulled out a cardboard box. "Plan A is the mission,"—he met my eyes—"which *you* should stick to. Plan B is yer alternative mission, which is idiotic, 'n Plan C is when yer Plan B goes to shit because ya didn't follow Plan A."

"You don't even know what my Plan B is."

"Probably involves the Owens kid usin' his technical genius to extract any information pertainin' to yer father, which is idiotic 'cause that would force Owens to spend more time than ya have available to you and yer team."

"Ye of little faith."

"Oh, shut it." Metis sat back in his desk chair and motioned for me to lean closer to him. "The objective is to make you somewhat plain lookin'." He started pullin' out smaller white boxes with his liver-spotted hand.

"Oh, Metis, you think I'm pretty."

The old man let out an awkward grunt but overall ignored my quip. "First off," Metis started, handing me a white box, "ya gotta get rid of that burstin' flame atop yer head." The box held two bottles, each half full of liquid, one liquid colored dark, muddy brown and the other an opaque white color. "Before ya leave, mix the contents of the small bottle into the large bottle 'n dowse yer hair in it. Leave the solution in yer hair for forty-five minutes, then rinse. Make sure ya get yer eyebrows too, but only let the solution sit on them for fifteen minutes."

Metis handed me another box. "This is for hair maintenance." I opened the box to find a small, unlabeled orange bottle filled with tiny white pills. "Created it myself back in the day. It will alter the proteins produced by yer follicles so yer hair will grow brown instead of that red beacon coverin' your skull. Take one pill a day."

I lifted my brows. "I am starting to think you have been planning this longer than I have."

"When I fled the Coalition to join the Resistance, I brought some supplies I thought might help with undercover operations. When *you* stumbled upon our Base 'n I saw that flaming hair of yers, I knew it would come in handy. We just didn't need it 'til now." He handed me the last box, which contained four pairs of contact lenses.

"Thank you, Metis, but I can see just fine." I pushed the box back toward the old man.

"They aren't for seein'," he said and pushed them across his desk toward me again. "They will change the color of your irises."

"Even my eyes will give me away?"

He shrugged. "We just wanna ensure no one will give ya a second glance. Like your blazin' hair, yer golden eyes were everywhere once." Metis waved a wrinkled hand at me. "Go ahead, put 'em in."

"Metis, I have never put in contacts before, and I am not going to do it without a proper mirror."

"Have it yer way, but do it before ya leave to make sure ya don't have any irritation. Oh, 'n watch the tutorial."

"Tutorial?"

"Yeah, they also record 'n transfer data through an encrypted satellite signal straight to here." Metis tapped his metal eye. "The tutorial will explain how to use the contacts properly," he explained nonchalantly.

I analyzed the lenses, their brown tint hiding the tiny nanochips.

"And probably probe my deepest thoughts and cloud my vision with my darkest nightmares."

"Only if yer darkest nightmares include me talkin' yer ear off."

I shrugged. "Sometimes." I stared at the contacts and the hair-dyeing kit. They felt heavy in my hands.

Would I even recognize myself?

"Any questions?"

I shook my head. "Not yet, anyway."

Metis gave me a slight nod. "Well, if ya do, those"—he pointed to the contacts—"will show ya how to ask me."

I glanced up at the old man, his mechanical eye emitting a green light. "Thank you, Metis."

"Don't mention it," he grunted, lifting himself from his seat.

"Metis, if something goes wrong, will you take care of Reign?"

"Red," he tapped the cold metal handle of his cane against my chin. I eyed him carefully. "Everyone looks after that 'lil nugget of yers. She'll be safe. Besides, she's just as smart 'n independent as you."

I swatted Metis' cane to the side. "That's what I am afraid of."

My mentor hobbled around his desk to stand behind me. I felt his hand pat me awkwardly, trying to comfort me the best way he knew how. "She'll be safe 'cause you've taught her to be as strong 'n as brave as you."

CHAPTER 7

My team was small—a few specialized agents to get us into the city, erase all the information they had regarding the CRF, quickly install a virus that would set the Coalition's systems back one week, and get the hell out.

Much to his chagrin, Niahm was the key to our mission since he had more technical skills in his pinky than the rest of our team combined. And despite his injury, Balor was also essential for his experience and wicked aim. As for me, I was leading this mission—and I prided myself in besting my comrades in hand-to-hand combat.

If I had sole control over the matter, it would have just been the three of us. However, Hoenir insisted Ulysses was crucial for his knowledge of the city and his uncanny ability to gain access to pretty much anywhere. Then Balor threw Clay Dawson in the mix because he 'never had any luck with even numbers,' though even I had to admit the thirty-four-year-old man was extremely handy with a knife.

And to just completely fuck over my mission, Sirius decided to sneak out of the CRF Base and track us all the way to our campsite last night. I almost killed the hybrid when I found him gnawing on squirrel bones from the ashes of our campfire dinner.

The stubborn canine refused to go back to Base, though even if he did, I doubted Hoenir would have let him back in—he hated the mutt.

So, my team was small…ish.

We crouched in a huddle, hidden from view in a brush line about twenty miles west of the CRF Base. The night sky was clear, and the moon shone bright, casting eerie shadows in the wooded bluffs beyond the Great River. It was quiet. The only sounds the rustling of leaves and our steady breathing as we waited for the electric train to slow to a stop.

I checked my watch.

Nearly twenty-one hundred.

I worked my feet and toes, readying to run.

Almost showtime.

We had rigged a small EMP device about two miles up the tracks from where we waited. Once the train ran over the device, it would detonate, rendering all the electronic systems on the train, including video footage and COM-devices, useless. Of course, we needed to make sure the train would run again, so Niahm engineered a device so small that it wouldn't fry the electric engines, just shut them down until someone rebooted the system.

"Remember," I whispered to my team, "spread yourselves throughout the train. If you are found, do not engage. In your packs, you have syringes with sedatives that Metis concocted for us. They will knock a soldier out for two hours and erase any memories of the previous twenty minutes. I would suggest keeping one handy." Everyone started shifting through their packs to pull out the syringes. Everyone except for Ulysses. "Aim for the thigh or bicep if you can."

I glared at Ulysses. "Remember, do not engage." A small sneer widened across his face. "Dismissed." As everyone turned toward the train rail, I grabbed Ulysses by his collar and pulled him toward me. "Kill anyone, and there will be consequences," I growled in his ear. He smelled of cinnamon and black pepper.

"Screw up this mission, and I will make sure you never see the CRF again." I tossed him off, but Ulysses quickly grabbed my hand and pulled me back to him.

"I like it when you're feisty, Red." Ulysses' gaze darted from my lips to my eyes. "It's fun to watch those flames of yours spark to life in your eyes. It's like watching you burn from the inside."

My gut wrenched. *My contacts. I completely forgot.*

Ulysses dragged a lazy finger down my cheek to the corner of my mouth, and my cheeks burned. I hated myself for it.

His finger started to trail down my jaw, but I slapped it away before it lingered down my neck. I turned from Ulysses.

Focus, Red. I commanded myself. *This is exactly what Ulysses wants—to get into your head so you fuck up the mission.*

I shook the thoughts away, set my pack on the ground, and used my tube light to look for my syringes. I pulled two of them out, sliding them into the slim pocket on my bicep. I tugged on my fingerless, black leather gloves, and with a flex of my fingers, I could feel electromagnetic energy flow through them. Sirius nudged my elbow with his snout, a silent beg for scratches behind his ears. I obliged before working my way down to his Military harness and looping a hand around a strap. "Follow my lead," I whispered to my canine companion, and he cocked his head. "I hope that's a yes, ma'am," I said, giving him a quick pat on the head.

I whistled the call of a Wilson's Snipe Chick. My team bolted at the signal.

I followed behind them, taking up the rear with Sirius flanking my right, silent as a field mouse despite his large pads. One by one, my team hopped on the train. Ulysses jumped on car three, Balor climbed on car eight, and I had to stifle a grin when Niahm slowly and awkwardly crawled into the car after his father, with Balor eventually needing to haul Niahm aboard. Even injured, Niahm's old man was more agile than him. Clay brought up the rear, sneaking onto car thirteen, and I… Well, I changed my mind last minute.

Only several feet from car two, I rubbed my hands together, and the gloves buzzed with friction. The subtle smell of hot rubber flowed from the gloves as I charged up their electromagnetic force. I jumped, reaching up to the tall ladder attached to the back of the car, and climbed.

Peeling one hand off a rung at a time, I climbed up the ladder and onto the car platform. Once I reached the top, Sirius started in a full sprint before jumping onto the platform with me. A spark of light gleamed in his emerald eyes as I patted the canine on the head.

I tried the handle on the car door.

Locked.

Since the whole train was electric, Niahm predicted the doors would automatically lock if the system were to turn off. The only other way in or out was the manual top hatch on each car, but with Sirius, I no longer had that option.

I pulled out the Damascus Steel knife from my left boot and jammed it into the thin gap between the door and the car. Carving the knife down the crack, the door gave, and I pried it open. The knife held strong against the pressure. When the gap was big enough for my hands, I shoved the knife back into my boot and rubbed my hands together again, charging up my gloves again. I grabbed the edge of the door and pulled it open, my shoulders and core straining with the force. Once the split was just wide enough, I stepped through the threshold and into complete darkness.

A faint click of a handgun welcomed me.

"Yield," a deep, stern voice commanded. Slowly, I faced the shadowy figure to my left, and lifted my hands high in the air. "Down on your knees, dreg."

I obeyed, my knees finding the cool metal floor of the train car, and my eyes fixed on the dimly illuminated crate before me, the American Coalition Emblem—a triangle topped with a star and surrounded by three-tiered rings—taunting me as I knelt helplessly before this soldier and his gun. I shuddered as the cool barrel pressed against the back of my head and cursed silently.

The last thing I was going to see was the damned Coalition sigil and 'Ex Ordo Fortis'—

Sirius leaped through the door, bounding over me. He landed heavily atop the soldier, and the gun flew from his hand. Sirius snarled in the soldier's face as I bounced back to my feet, raced to the soldier's gun, and picked it up. I aimed the pistol between the soldier's eyes.

"Communication device. Now." I demanded, lowering my voice to sound more intimidating. Stupid but effective. The soldier looked at me as though I was from another planet. "Give me your damn communication device."

"You mean my COM-tab?" the man grunted, Sirius' whole body still pressing into his chest.

"Yes," I growled, one hand outstretched.

He reached into his pocket and pulled out a small, thin device completely foreign to me.

"No good that's gonna do ya'," the soldier scoffed, voice worn and raspy. "It was torched when the damned EMP went off."

Good, I thought to myself as I tucked it in my pants pocket. *I wouldn't know how to work it anyway.*

From my left bicep pocket, I pulled out a syringe with my right hand while my left had the gun still aimed at the soldier's head. His eyes grew wide as I pulled the cap off with my teeth, revealing the three-inch-long needle. I didn't bother with words as I plunged the needle deep into the muscle of the soldier's thigh. His hazel eyes fluttered before unconsciousness claimed him.

I pulled the syringe from the soldier, recapped the needle, and then tossed it out the open door. My hands balled into fists, and as I looked down upon the limp man. I wanted to choose the easy way out—I wanted to drag the older man outside and dump him off the car. If he survived and remembered, it would be a while until he told someone that a Rebel snuck on the train. It would have been so easy. Instead, I pried open one of the crates to find it filled with blankets and sheets. I tore long strips apart, then cleared him of all his weapons, identifications, and clothes.

"Well, Corporal Bishop," I muttered to the incoherent man as I held his I.D. in my hand, "now that I know your name, let's get you naked." I replaced my clothes with his, the soldier's strong, musty cologne assaulting my senses. After puncturing a new notch with my knife, I pulled the belt tight, then laced the boots and replaced my hat with his, tucking my newly dyed brunette hair under the Military cap. I bound his hands and feet with the strips of fabric, tossed him into the crate, and secured the lid over the metal container.

"Good night, Corporal," I cooed, dusting off my hands.

A breeze tickled the back of my neck.

"Shit," I mumbled as I turned around to find the door still open, but Sirius sat in the car entrance, standing watch. I rubbed my hands together, still sheathed with my electromagnetic gloves, and pulled the door shut.

"Phase One complete, Sirius," I grunted as the solid metal door latched shut. I sent up a small prayer to whatever God my father believed in that the others were safe. My heart tightened at the thought of Niahm in trouble—

Focus, Red. I chastised myself, forcing the feelings edging up inside of me into a deep pit I used for missions such as these.

I started rummaging through the pockets of the soldier's uniform and examined all of the weapons. Most of them were dead due to the EMP. The only weapons that were useful were the knives I brought along with me and the pistol I obtained from the soldier.

In the front pants pocket, I found an earpiece. I placed it in my ear and tested the device.

Nothing. Not even static.

I studied the COM-device the soldier had given me. It was a

thin, transparent rectangle made of glass or acrylic. On the bottom was a black strip with two small holes and three flat, black buttons, nearly invisible against the frame. I tried pressing them. Nothing.

As I slid the device back into my pocket, the two lights at either end of the car blinked to life, casting eerie shadows throughout the metal box I was stuck in. I hunkered down in a dark corner, and Sirius snuggled up next to me with his snout on my lap. I scratched behind his ears as we waited. Thirty minutes passed before the quiet rumble of the train engine started to purr.

————

The rest of the train ride went off without a hitch. Even though it was dark, and I had no mirror, I decided to apply the contact lenses Metis gave me and watched his tutorial during the rest of the ride into Imperium. Instructions panned through my vision as I sat in the dark.

Press right temple for three seconds to turn on, left temple for three seconds to turn off. Two quick taps to right temple to start and end a recording. Slide finger over right brow to scroll through options. Tap right temple once to select options.

For the most part, the instructions were pretty straightforward.

When the train finally pulled into Imperium's Tenth Ward station, I uncurled myself from the dark corner. The doors hissed open, letting early morning light and crisp, cool air pour into the car. I straightened my borrowed jacket and squared my shoulders before I stepped through the threshold and climbed down the train ladder. Siris hopped down and fell in step beside me. My pulse thundered loudly against my eardrums, and I willed my body to fill out the too-large Military uniform. Hopefully, the ambling train station workers wouldn't bother to stare too long as I marched toward our rendezvous point—hopefully, they wouldn't notice how I filled out a man's uniform in all the wrong places.

I found my team huddled behind large metal crates near the end of the train. I crouched beside them. "Everyone good?"

In unison, they all whirled around, and Clay, the swift and strong agent that he was, had a knife pulled out and at my throat, before I could even flinch.

I held my hands up. "It's me. It's Red."

As if I wasn't proof enough, Clay studied Sirius, who was crouched and snarling at my side, teeth glinting in the LED lights of the train station.

Ulysses crossed his arms and eyed up the Coalition Military uniform. "Well, that wasn't part of the plan."

"I had to improvise." I shrugged, noting a red crust under Ulysses' nails. The more I studied him, the more red specks I saw dotting the back of his hands. Before I could ask, Balor blew out a low whistle: the signal. Within twenty seconds, a man appeared with a very large metal cart, a black tarp draped over it. The man was as plain-looking as a stick. Sandy hair, white skin, and no real distinguishing features except for a slight limp when he walked. This must have been our guy. I nodded to him. He winked, scratched the back of his head, and winked again. *Yup. This is our guy.*

The cart was pulled tightly between two stacks of crates, and we snuck into the cart one by one. Sirius was the last of us to board the cramped cart, and his thick fur made the limited air in the covered cart unbearably hot… and incredibly pungent. The stench of man sweat and dog breath had me gagging as we were wheeled off, and my heart began to race as every inhale felt even more suffocating. Silently, I counted the uneven steps of our internal operative, willing away a foreboding panic rising in my chest.

After about twenty paces, the cart came to a sudden stop,

jerking us forward. I felt an elbow jab into my kidney, and I stifled a grunt.

"Hey, Tim!" A bright male voice chimed. "Ya' need a hand with that?"

"Ah, nah, brother." Our guy, Tim, his name must have been —though I didn't think we were supposed to know that— hollered back. "I've got it. Good for the ol' joints to keep them movin'."

"If only we had those hover carts like they do in Media!" the other man shouted, his voice fading as he walked away.

Tim laughed. "Oh, ya' know them are just rumors. They work just as hard as we do." We all fell backward as the cart started moving again.

"Always the optimist," the other man yelled back. Tim chuckled lightly but kept walking.

The cart slowed to a stop just as my muscles started to cramp from the uncomfortable crouch I was stuck in. My heart thundered as a muffled *clang* and *click* of a metal door and latch echoed beyond our cart before the tarp covering us was ripped away to reveal a bright and airy garage. I nearly gasped in relief as fresh air hit my lungs, and as I glanced around—blinking my eyes as they adjusted to the lighting—I half expected to find my team surrounded by Coalition soldiers. Instead, we were surrounded by long shelves lining the walls with various supplies. There was a solid metal door at one end of the space and an aluminum garage door on the other. We crawled out of the cart and stretched our cramped muscles as Tim grabbed a backpack similar to my own. He rummaged through it, pulling out folders of papers before passing them out.

"These are your papers," Tim started. "They will get you all to Ward Eight for your exit. If any soldier pulls you over and asks to see anything, give them these. You will have your identification booklet, your day pass, and your trading licenses. Though I have to admit"—Tim glanced down at Sirius, who sat patiently next to the crate—"I didn't plan for the mutt. You might have to get creative." Tim's brown eyes met mine, my folder of papers still in his hands. "You can look at these, but you cannot keep them. Your keeper will hold onto them."

"My keeper?" I asked, taking my folder and opening it to examine the contents. The smell of parchment greeted my senses.

Tim nodded. "All women have a keeper here in Humilis. It is either her father, her husband, or her…" He trailed off, choosing his words carefully. "*Guardian*," Tim finally intoned. I knew what he meant.

Her panderer.

I glanced through my file. My alias was Adellaide Stevens. She was twenty-two, brunette, brown eyes, and my height. Tim even had a black-and-white picture of my profile in my identification booklet, which he must have obtained from Hoenir, who handled all the dealings with our internal sources.

Tim glanced back to the rest of my team. "You are not in the electronic directory, so do not give them a reason to double-check your identification. Oh, and memorize your Coalition ID number. If any soldier stops, detains, or interrogates you for any reason, they will ask for your ID number."

I found my number on the first page of my booklet.

IH0782403

I repeated it several times in my head. I also took several snapshots with the contacts Metis gave me and stored them in the contacts data file.

My name is Adellaide Stevens. IH0782403. I work on my husband's farm in Ward Eight and have three kids.

Shit… My stomach churned. *I have three kids already?*

Wait, who is my husband?

"Who is Samwell Stevens?" I asked after a quick glance at my papers.

Balor's head snapped up. "Me."

My eyes widened. "Balor is my husband? He is old enough

to be my dad!" *Not to mention the father of the only guy I've ever slept with.*

Ulysses snickered. Niahm choked on a cough.

Tim just shrugged, clearly unaware of the awkward energy surrounding my team. "It is not uncommon for women to be married to older men. Gives the men more time to perfect their trade, and then they have someone to care for them in old age."

"Gross," I muttered. "No offense, Balor."

Balor chuckled. "No offense taken. I find it just as distasteful."

"Appropriate clothes for the men are in that box in the corner." Tim pointed to the far corner near the garage door—the only box not dusty and laced with cobwebs. "I would suggest depositing all of your weapons in the box since you will not be able to take them with you when transferring to a different Ward."

I was pulling my various knives from the Military uniform and throwing them in the box when Tim handed me a bundle of dull linen clothes. "These are for you, darling." I took the bundle after handing my folder to Balor.

A gray, shapeless dress, black, worn leather boots, charcoal stockings, and a large cowl shawl. The men pulled out clothes from their box as I slipped out of my Military Uniform.

Tim blushed and turned from my indecency, but I didn't care. Obviously, there was no private dressing room, and modesty was a leisure for those with an abundance of time. We had a schedule, and I wasn't going to wait for the boys to be done so they could hold the tarp around me as I dressed.

Once I was clothed in Humilian attire, I looked up to see all the men, besides Tim, staring at me.

"What?"

"Y-Your hair. A-and eyes," Niahm stammered.

I brushed back my hair, my gut twisting into a knot. This was exactly why I kept my hair tucked in a cap the whole first phase of the mission.

Ulysses let out a long whistle. "Would you look at those chocolate locks!"

"Will you shut up Ulysses?" I whispered sternly. "The last thing we need is your big mouth giving us away."

"Just saying, you should have warned us before you put out that fire!"

I rolled my eyes.

"How'd ya do it?" Clay asked as he straightened out the Coalition Military Uniform he now donned.

"Metis."

Clay nodded like it explained everything.

Niahm's eyes were fixed on my head.

I had waited until the last possible moment to color my hair. Tears stung my eyes as I applied the dye, and not because of the chemical fumes. I sat in the bathroom for a good thirty minutes after witnessing the final product. It's not like I hated the color, but it wasn't me—I felt like I was staring at some brunette clone version of myself. Skies above, Red was my name! Red was, well, my identity. And now, with the contacts, I couldn't even begin to imagine how different I looked.

"You are going to want to pin your braid around your head," Tim suggested. "And I would probably take the harness from the dog.

I nodded, unstrapping the harness from Sirius and shoving it into my pack.

"I don't have any pins."

Tim held out a hand. I opened mine to accept the few metal pins and did as he instructed, swirling my French braid around and pinning it at the nape of my neck. Tim nodded in approval.

We all gathered around in a loose huddle.

"Okay," I started. "Everyone have their shit memorized?" My team nodded. But just to be sure, I quizzed them all on their names, birth ward, identification number, and their business in Ward Ten. They all aced it, though Niahm stumbled through the answers.

I nodded to Tim, signaling we were ready. He gestured to the cart. "There are cameras around the building. I just need to get you in the blind spot, then I will let you out. Use the map in your packets. They will get you to the market. From there, you will be able to see the security post you need."

My team hopped into the cart, and I climbed in last after directing Sirius to jump in before me. Tim pulled the tarp over us, and we started moving again, entrenched in utter darkness.

Phase Two complete.

CHAPTER 8

The morning was gray and bleak. A thin layer of frost covered the gravel beneath our feet, and a chill nipped at my nose. Everything seemed frigid in Imperium, or at least down here in Humilis.

As we emerged from the dim alley adjacent to the market square where Tim had unloaded my team, I glanced up toward the rest of the city. A dense fog concealed the two other Circulums, but their shadows, cast down from above, were a reminder of their presence.

Coalition city-states were divided into three distinct Circulums, or social rings. Humilis was the lowest. It consisted of Wards eight through twelve, each Ward comprised a different agricultural zone. Media was the second ring. Built upon an enormous concrete structure that held the city's prison, Media was divided into Wards four through seven and focused on industrial work like sanitation and textiles. Floating high above the second Circulum was Excelsis. The highest Circulum was divided into Wards one through three and was home to the elite.

In Media and Excelsis, there were stores that provided goods, but here in Humilis, the citizens depended on barters and trade in the market square. It wasn't unusual for people from other Wards to participate in the different markets. With the proper paperwork, one could access goods and produce not available in other Wards, so our different faces here in the Tenth Ward would not be seen as suspicious.

My team spread out among the market, and a little piece of me relaxed each time one of them reached their position. Balor and I remained on the perimeter of the market. I hooked my left arm around his elbow and hunched my shoulders, keeping my gaze down at my feet, like the rest of Humilis' citizenry. Balor led the way. His gait was uneven as we walked, his leg still injured from our hit just a few days ago.

Guilt coiled around my abdomen like a python.

Sirius seemed excited as he wove in and out of the crowd. There were other mutts trotting around, most, if not all, of them malnourished, their coats thin and wiry, and ribcages exposed as they wandered around the market looking for scraps. They were all ignored or shooed away from the trading stands with sticks. Sirius, larger and more well-fed than all the other dogs, stuck out like a sore thumb.

I must have been gravitating toward my dog because Balor's arm grew taut in mine, and my RAC gently pulled me back in. His eyes darted from stand to stand. They all looked the same—dim, splintered planks of wood nailed together with various goods perched atop them. Some merchants were selling bread, others meat, a few sold vegetables, and one merchant sold candles and soaps, the floral scents from his wares miraculously cutting through the usual musty, barn smell that coated Imperium's lowest Circulum.

I glanced at Balor, whose left hand grasped a beaten-up leather sack slung across his shoulder like it held precious goods perfect for bartering.

Niahm and Clay were still in sight, donned in Coalition Military Uniforms and glancing from citizen to citizen as if scrutinizing each of them. My undercover comrades slowly meandered toward the Security Station, precisely the reason we chose the market in Ward Ten—it was adjacent to the largest Security Station in Humilis, the key for accessing the Imperium Database. However, if something went wrong, there would be an instant influx of guards surrounding us.

In order for our plan to work, we needed to pull as many soldiers as possible away from the station. The market was the perfect place for a diversion. If we could cause a big enough distraction, the soldiers would flood out from the Security Station, and Niahm and Clay could then proceed to access the Coalition's Database and Server from the Station's computer. Once the job was finished, we could all fade easily into a large, chaotic crowd.

While the rest of us were paired up, Ulysses was solo. His job was to sow discord amongst the citizens in the market, to set them on edge. For this, I gave him free rein because I personally knew pissing people off was Ulysses specialty.

Balor nudged my shoulder and nodded toward Clay, who was chatting up a Coalition Soldier. Niahm stood behind him, his fingers nervously tapping against his left thigh.

I stifled a groan.

That was precisely why I suggested Clay take the lead. In addition to Niahm's inability to lie, he twitched and stuttered when he was nervous.

I stared back down at my feet.

"They're in," Balor whispered in my ear. Balor glanced around, then set his eyes on the merchant closest to the Security Station—a thin, scraggly old man, the only merchant selling soaps and candles made of goat milk. Beneath his white, bushy eyebrows, the merchant greedily eyed up Balor, then quickly glanced away as if not to look too eager.

Balor scanned the booths again. "I have noticed Ulysses engaged with several tradesmen, each becoming more perturbed than the last. He has sown the seeds well." Balor finally looked me in the eye and tucked a loose strand of hair behind my ear. "Your job should be easy." I met his eyes, willing 'tentative adoration' to be painted across my face. But behind him, a group of about seven men marched into the Tenth Ward. My eyes flicked to the group of men. Not just ordinary men or a gang, but a small force of soldiers—an impending black and plum storm cloud, the colors of the Coalition. The leader of the small Military Patrol wore black, marching tall and commanding as the dim sunlight glinted off the three stars that stretched across each shoulder.

"Fuck." I dropped my head down.

"What is it?" Balor asked, moving his hands down to hold mine, still playing his role as my husband.

"Lieutenant General," I breathed. "What the fuck is a Lieutenant General doing in Humilis?"

A man near us did a double take as I cursed. Balor must have noticed, too, because he quickly gripped my chin hard, forcing me to look at him. "Watch your mouth," he demanded. I knew Balor was just playing his part and far better than I was—a woman from Humilis would never swear.

I whimpered and cowered but stared into his blue-grey eyes as he held my chin. "It will be fine. You just need to hurry."

Balor pushed my chin away, causing me to stumble. I rubbed at the hurt. He pointed at a rugged boulder for me to sit on, and I obeyed like a good wife. Right as Balor hobbled over to the soap merchant, positioning himself closer to the Security Station, a shadow darted through the crowd, its feet light and swift. Sirius was keeping an eye on me. My anxious heart steadied a little.

I twiddled my thumbs and picked at my fingers as if nervous, but through my lashes, I glanced up to survey the Lieutenant General and his team. They were closing in on the Security Station. My muscles burned, preparing to run.

Come on, Ulysses.

A shadow hovered over me.

"Looking for some business in the daylight, whore?" I never thought I would be so thankful to hear that voice.

I avoided eye contact, though I knew it was Ulysses looming

over me, probably donning his usual mirthless smile. I didn't respond to his taunt.

A dark figure darted between the feet of civilians again, no more than twenty feet from where I sat.

"Oh, you're quiet now, but you will be screaming when I take you." Ulysses pulled the hood of my cowl down and caressed the shell of my ear with his finger, his skin warm against the autumn wind's chill. I couldn't drag this out much longer when I noted the band of soldiers edging upon the station. I batted Ulysses' hand away.

"I'm afraid you're mistaken, sir." I cowered, still staring at the gravel beneath my feet.

"Oh, am I?" Ulysses grabbed my hand firmly.

I grunted daintily, trying to pull my hand away like a powerless woman.

"Sir, please. M—my keeper…" I started, my voice pitched to a whine.

Then, a grey-haired stranger grabbed Ulysses' right shoulder. "Is this man bothering you, miss?"

"This is none of your concern, old man." Ulysses shrugged off the man's grasp.

Head after head started to turn in our direction. Males started to gather, either to defend me or to get a piece of the man who had been harassing people all morning.

My fellow agent gripped my wrist and pulled me up. "Come on, whore. Let's finish what we started." Ulysses started hauling me away when another man stepped in and shoved my perceived abuser away from me.

"I've had enough of you today," the robust stranger spoke sternly. He was a large man with protruding pectorals. His hair was dark and full around his scalp and jaw. "First, you go around trying to force shit deals, then you harass poor girls as soon as their keepers turn away." As the stranger chastised Ulysses, I glanced around nervously as though I was searching for my husband. I couldn't find Balor, but the patrol of Military soldiers had taken an interest in the scene unfolding. The Lieutenant General turned, the rest of his group also diverting their course from the Security Station. He stood tall and foreboding as he approached. The Lieutenant General wasn't as large as most of his team, but there was an aura about him that commanded respect and deference. My gaze swept up his broad shoulders to his light stubble, and my heart burned as our eyes met. There was something familiar in the Lieutenant General's eyes, but—

The stranger who was yelling at Ulysses growled like a vicious beast. As I turned, I vaguely heard Ulysses' mumbled response, though I couldn't quite process the words before punches started flying, and the repeated song of ripping flesh and breaking bones filled the air. I ducked and backed away from the full-out brawl that had ensued. Ulysses was taking down every man that came after him, and soldiers started pouring in from every direction, a large mass of men flowing from the Security Station like bees fleeing their hive, including the Lieutenant General and his patrol.

Good. Now, all Ulysses and I had to do was escape the scene.

I flung my bag over my shoulder, pulled my hood up, and whistled for Sirius to find me, then darted toward the square entrance. Sirius caught up, flanking my right. As I was twenty paces from the entrance, I saw Ulysses come at me from my left. A malicious grin was painted across his face as he winked at me —a taunt. A warning. My mind screamed, but before I could stop, Ulysses flung an arm out, nailing my chest. I flew into the sharp gravel-covered streets, my back landing heavy on the ground and my lungs struggling to grasp air.

Ulysses towered over me, straddling my legs. "Good luck, Red." A mocking tone cradled his words. Ulysses stomped on my right heel, his booted foot flattening my ankle to the ground. A sharp *crack* shattered through my right leg as gravel crunched beneath my foot. I cried out in agony, but I couldn't hear my screams. Blood pounded in my eardrums as the echo of bone and tendon snapping reverberated through my body.

My vision wavered.

I felt the shift of feet on gravel as Ulysses darted from me.

A tide of cold rushed through me as I tried to push myself up. The wave crested and crashed like hot, sharp needles into my ankle, and the blood drained from my head, leaving me dizzy and nauseated.

Through my watery vision, I found Sirius. He stood just inches from me. His snout worked like he was barking and growling, but blood still pounded in my head, denying any sound from entering my mind.

Women and children darted around me, their feet threatening to trample my body, and I tried to regain Sirius' attention by grabbing at his paw, but a black boot crunched the gravel mere inches from my nose. Slowly, I lifted my gaze to meet a pair of sparkling emerald eyes staring down at me, but they weren't Sirius' eyes. No, above the eyes was an onyx Military cap stitched with three gleaming stars.

I've seen those eyes before. They were from my childhood. From Militum.

The Lieutenant General squatted before me. "So, you're the one who caused this mess."

CHAPTER 9

Cold. That was all I felt as I came to. Icy cold nipped at my forearms and coiled around my wrists. Cold sweat licked my back, and cool, crisp air kissed my cheeks, and the air was stale as I deliberately inhaled and exhaled through my nose. Slowly, my eyes fluttered open to reveal a painfully bright concrete and steel room filled with little more than the steel table before me and the chair to which I was bound, iron shackles tight around my wrists. Two aluminum chairs stood across from me, and behind those chairs, on the far wall, was a mirror. I stared at the brunette woman in the reflection, surprised when she mimicked the slight cock of my brow. My mind surged.

The mission.

My team.

Fuck. My eyes darted around the room. *Where the hell is my team?*

I took a deep breath. *I will worry about them later. I need to focus on where I am and what is happening right now.*

The mission.

My team.

Ward Ten.

Ulysses' sabotage.

My ankle.

Oh yeah. I inhaled sharply and stifled a wince as my ankle throbbed, pain shooting through my right calf like sharp needles.

The pain made it difficult to think.

Okay. I gritted my teeth. *How did I get here?*

The mission.

My team.

Ward Ten.

Ulysses' sabotage.

Skip over the ankle part...

Green Eyes.

Callum's eyes.

The Lieutenant General.

I forced my face into a mask of indifference as I realized the room I was in was most likely an interrogation room, and the mirror across from me was most likely a one-way window. Based on the crick in my neck, whoever was behind that window had been watching me for hours—I was a lab rat in a maze.

Stretching out the tight tendons, I rolled out my neck and rotated my shoulders forward, then back. My strong frame slowly loosened, tension exiting my body in soothing waves, and as the tension left, my blood began to flow, clearing the fog from my mind.

I was trained to be a soldier, not a spy—I was never trained how to handle interrogations. Panic settled into my chest as I realized I was in way over my head. I cursed Balor, Hoenir, Ulysses, Metis—damn it, I cursed the whole lot of them while I sat alone, chained to a chair in a cold interrogation room.

Breathe, Red. Just breathe and think. How are you going to play this out? Who are they expecting to interrogate?

My papers detailed Adellaide Stevens as a lowly woman from Humilis who worked on her husband's farm. If they believed that, then maybe I was just here for a few questions.

Though, the shackles tight around my wrists proved that to be very unlikely.

Most likely, they suspected I was Resistance or the instigator of the brawl that broke out in the market. I was hoping it was the latter. I could work with the latter.

Footsteps echoed outside the door to my left. As they drew near, my pulse quickened, my sympathetic nervous system preparing every muscle, every neuron, for fight or flight.

I am Adellaide Stevens, and I am a farmer's wife from Ward Eight.

Keys jingled in the lock, and the door opened, swinging wide for two men. The first was tall and beefy, his hair light in color, a stark contrast to his cold, onyx eyes hidden in the shadow of his protruding brow bone. The second man was not as tall or muscular but somehow more intimidating in the way he carried himself. All this man needed to command a room was to stand up straight and stare everyone down with the stone-cold features that made him look as though he was carved from granite. His jawline was strong, his nose straight as an arrow, and as he looked down upon me, I couldn't look away. While his face seemed carved of granite, his eyes looked as if they had been hewn from emeralds.

As they drew closer, the second man swung a black pack off his shoulder. *My pack.*

My eyes followed my property all the way down to the floor.

"Hello," the second man greeted—the same man who found me crippled on the market gravel. My eyes shot up to meet his. Metal scraped against the concrete floor as the men took their seats across from me. "I am Lieutenant General Osouf, and this" —the man gestured to the other at his right—"is Major General Clausen." The Commanding Officer reached down into a pocket, pulled out a small communication device, and placed it on the table.

Osouf. Why does that name ring a bell?

My head began to pound.

Osouf. Osouf. Dr. Freyja Osouf.
Callum Osouf.

I felt my eyes flicker to him at the realization. There was no way. He lived in Militum. Osouf can be a pretty common name, right? And green eyes… I'm sure there are a few Osoufs with green eyes in the Coalition. There has to be.

The Lieutenant General must have seen the shift in my eyes, because his brows pinched slightly, the wheels in his head turning. Then, in a blink, I watched him mentally push the moment aside, probably choosing to dwell on it later. Osouf waved a hand to his comrade, and Clausen handed over a tan folder. The Lieutenant General flipped through the file. It was the paperwork from my backpack.

Shit. My pulse quickened. *What else did they find? My contacts? My medicine?*

The Lieutenant General cleared his throat. "According to your paperwork, your name is Adellaide Stevens. Is that correct?" He didn't glance up for a response.

It was hard to find my voice. Shock curled around my throat like a serpent. "Yes," I finally croaked.

"And you are from Humilis?"

"Yes," I intoned again, this time stronger yet soft, like a woman who has been submissive to men her whole life.

Osouf finally looked up to meet my gaze. "Do your friends call you Addie?"

I couldn't help but cringe at the name. "No."

The man grimaced. "Shame. I kind of like the name Addie. Adellaide is such a mouthful. You must have some sort of nickname."

"No."

"Okay…" Osouf drawled and typed something into the COM-device on the table. "So, if you live in Ward Seven—"

"Ward Eight," I interjected.

The Lieutenant General raised his brows. "Excuse me?"

"You said I lived in Ward Seven, but I live in Ward Eight." He was testing me.

Osouf glanced at my paperwork again as if double-checking. He nodded, one brow arched high. "Ah, right. Ward Eight. Still, that begs me to ask why you were in Ward Ten?"

I nodded toward the paperwork. "It should say in there, sir. We were granted permission to trade in Ward Ten's market. It is nice to have a change of pace, to see different faces and different merchandise, especially in the winter when pickings are thin."

The Lieutenant General cocked an eyebrow. "And you were there with your keeper?"

Keeper? What the hell is a keeper? It took a moment for my memory to jog before recalling the small text on my paperwork.

"Yes." I nodded. "My husband, Samwell Stevens."

The larger man, Clausen, snorted. Both the Lieutenant General and I considered him. "Sounds like a storybook name," Clausen defended, crossing his large arms.

Osouf shot his comrade a glare, clearly not amused by Clausen's joke. He stacked my paperwork into a neat pile, picked it up, and tapped it a few times on the metal table.

"And where is your keeper, Ms. Stevens?"

"I-I don't know, probably wandering around Ward Ten looking for me."

The Lieutenant General gave me a small, amused smile.

"Do you know why you are here, Ms. Stevens?"

I shrugged. "I am assuming it has something to do with the brawl that occurred in the market. I assure you, sir, I didn't try to instigate anything. I was just minding my own business—"

"No, Ms. Stevens, that is not why you are here." Osouf ran a hand through his sandy hair, a gesture that, if I were standing, would have made my knees buckle.

"Because I lost my keeper?" I guessed again.

"You think two highly ranked officers in the Coalition Military would be here interrogating a Humilian woman for being separated from her keeper?"

I picked at a loose thread on my dress.

Osouf cleared his throat again. "We are here, Ms. Stevens, because my canine was found *guarding* your unconscious body."

Shit. I forgot about Sirius!

I hid the panic from my face. "Canine, sir?" I tried not to swallow.

"You know, the big black beast wandering the market?" Clausen clarified for me.

I laughed. "You mean the mutt? The hybrid? I had just given him a scrap of food, sir, and he took a liking to me." I shrugged. "But that is all. I had never seen him before."

Osouf's jaw tensed. "Then why was this"—the Lieutenant General whipped out Sirius' harness and slammed it on the table—"in *your* bag?"

I flinched, then glanced from the Lieutenant General to the harness—three gold stars, and *Sirius* flickered in the fluorescent light.

My mind whirled, recalling the three stars looming over me as I lay on the gravel street.

Well, fuck.

The blood drained from my face as I stammered. "I… Uh… I saw the hybrid wandering around the market, and I did notice the harness. I thought we could trade it, or pieces of it, for a little extra food or wool this week." I glanced down and fiddled with my bound hands. "The beast looked like he was abandoned long ago. I didn't think anyone was missing him or the harness."

The Lieutenant General leaned in closer, and the metal table creaked. "You don't understand, Ms. Stevens." Under my lashes, I met his harsh stare. "The last time I saw my companion was three months ago. I was performing a perimeter check with him along the wall when he spotted a hare and darted off."

For a Lieutenant General, this man was not a very good liar. He was close enough that I noticed his pupils dilate, and I heard his finger tap the table—a tic. Why he was lying, or what part exactly he was lying about, I didn't know. But some part of the story was wrong, and if I were to make an educated guess, it would be the part about Sirius darting off—he was better trained than that. Some unforeseen circumstance separated them. I was almost sure of it.

"Even if there was a way he could get back through the wall," Osouf continued, "he knows how to return to me, to my Base in Excelsis, from any Ward in Imperium." This time, the Lieutenant General slammed a finger into the metal table, deliberately.

"I apologize, Lieutenant General, but I am telling the truth."

"And you don't think that any Humilian soldier who saw *my* canine trotting around wouldn't try to lure him or alert me?"

I shrugged. "Maybe the mutt just broke through the wall today. Maybe he was on his way to find you in Excelsis."

The Lieutenant General's expression was unreadable.

"Listen, Lieutenant General, if you were to bring my keeper in, he would sort everything out. His name is Samwell Stevens. He is about six-foot, salt-and-peppered beard—"

"Look, Ms. Stevens, we do have other problems." Osouf tapped a finger angrily on my paperwork. "First, your CCD Number is IH0782403. The 'I' stands for Imperium, the 'H' stands for Humilis, and the first two digits always indicate to which Ward you live in. Your two digits are Zero-Seven, not Zero-Eight, which doesn't even make sense because Ward Seven is located in Media, the Circulum above Humilis."

I opened my mouth to protest, but the Lieutenant General ignored me.

"Second, we took the liberty of running your DNA." Osouf nodded to his comrade.

Clausen tapped a few fingers on the communication device on the table, then swiped two fingers up the digital screen. A three-dimensional image of a twisting double-helix projected from the device. In glowing red letters above the image were the words: *DNA Not Matched*

My heart dropped, and I glanced between the two men in confusion.

The Lieutenant General gestured to the image. "You're not even in the CCD. We tried searching your name, and still nothing." He stared me down, his eyes cold and unyielding. "According to our records, neither Adellaide nor Samwell Stevens exists."

I chose not to say anything—nothing I could say would have helped. The only obvious reason I wasn't in the database would be because I was Resistance or eliciting some other sort of illegal activity.

Osouf shifted in his seat, back pressed against his chair. He propped his right ankle on his left knee and folded his hands in his lap. "We can play games all day, Ms. Stevens, but in the end, you will lose. So, just help us along and tell us something useful."

"I am sorry. What is it you want to know?"

Osouf pinched the bridge of his nose. "Let's start with why you had my canine."

I sighed. "Like I said, he was begging for food, so I gave him a scrap of meat. He must have thought the kindness made us best friends. And I took his harness to make a nice barter. Honest. What the mutt did while I was lying unconscious is not my problem."

"And why don't you show up in the CCD?"

"CCD?"

Osouf sighed. "The Coalition Citizenship Database."

I shrugged. "I don't know."

The Lieutenant General rose from his chair with an annoyed grumble. He paced back and forth while his counterpart remained seated, eyes fixed on me. Osouf ran a hand through his hair. "What can you tell me about the virus released on the Tenth Ward's Security Station this morning?"

My eyes widened, feigning naïve surprise. "Like an illness, Lieutenant General?"

Osouf scoffed. "No, Ms. Stevens. A computer virus. What can you tell me about the computer virus?"

"I have no idea what you're talking about, sir."

"Today"—the Lieutenant General crossed his arms—"around zero-eight-hundred, a computer virus was introduced directly into the Tenth Ward's Security System."

I painted a blank look across my face despite the thundering in my chest.

Did the virus work? Did they catch anyone else from my team?

"You really know nothing?"

I shook my head. "Why would I?"

"Because, Ms. Stevens, it's oddly suspicious my lost canine shows up, you are found with inaccurate, thus illegal, paperwork, and a computer virus was installed in a Security Station. All around the same time. All in the same Ward."

"Sometimes, coincidences are just that, Lieutenant General."

Osouf sucked on a tooth. "So, you aren't going to tell me anything."

"Sir, I have nothing to tell."

Clausen crossed his arms. "We can always do this the hard way, Ms. Stevens. We are used to handling Resistance spies."

I cocked my head. "Is that why I'm here? You think I am Resistance?"

"I thought that was quite plain, Ms. Stevens," Osouf replied.

"I can assure you—"

Osouf held up a hand. He stood from his chair and walked to the one-way mirror, leaning on the ledge there. His ribs expanded and contracted.

"You see, Ms. Stevens, I don't know what to do with you. From our past experiences, all the Resistance operatives we've detained have matched with a Coalition Citizen, or we have been able to trace their DNA to a family member in the CCD."

Damn. How many of us have they caught? I couldn't think of one person that I knew falling into enemy hands. *Maybe there were people here on the inside who were caught, and Hoenir just didn't tell us?*

"But you? Nothing." Osouf turned to face me, hands crossed behind his back in Military fashion. "So, until we know what to do with you, or until you start giving us some answers, you will be incarcerated. Maybe a few days in Imperium's prison will loosen your lips." The Lieutenant General waved a dismissive hand at his companion.

"Clausen, please see to it that Ms. Stevens is properly detained."

CHAPTER 10

I stifled a groan with every uneven step as Major General Clausen led me from the interrogation room and through the concrete corridors of Imperium's prison.

There were no windows in the halls, only small vents to filter out the scents of stale sweat and wet stone that hung thick in the air. Every breath was heavier than the last as humidity clung to my lungs like tree sap on pine branches. Clausen towered over me, and his fingertips bruised my skin as he gripped my left bicep. My ankle throbbed, though the familiar thrumming was settling into the joint and tendons—my body had already started the healing process.

I wondered if any of my fellow agents had walked through these halls—been carried off into a room behind the steel doors we passed. Did any of them know that our mission failed? That if they were caught, their torture was for nothing? And how would Hoenir know if the virus worked or not? Obviously, if no one came back, they would know we were captured—or worse. Would they just assume our mission failed and move the whole Base? Even if Balor, Ulysses, Niahm, and Clay returned, how would they know Niahm's computer virus didn't work? How could I contact them?

My contacts. I stumbled, my feet tripping over themselves at the realization of my stupidity. Pain wrapped around my ankle as it gave out completely, and heat shot through my body in waves. Only Clausen's iron grip kept me upright.

"Keep walking," the Major General grunted.

I kept my eyes trained on my feet and recalled the contact tutorial I'd watched on the train. Hands still shackled together, I reached up and pressed my right temple for three seconds with the pad of my forefinger until my contacts blurred to life. Two quick taps to my right temple and a red light blinked in the far right corner of my vision.

"What are you doing?" Clausen jerked my bound arms toward him.

"Sorry. I had an itch," I lied, trudging alongside the soldier. We rounded another corner and were met with three doors.

"Where are you taking me?"

Clausen pushed a button. "To your jail cell, you idiot."

A door slid open, and we entered a metal carriage. It jerked upward, and another needle of pain shot through my injured ankle. I ground my teeth.

"Will I have an inmate?"

"No."

"Is the jail separated by sexes?"

A cruel smile twisted at Clausen's thin lips. "No."

The carriage stopped. My stomach churned as Clausen pulled me out the door and down equally damp corridors, ironically reminiscent of the CRF's halls.

"When will I be able to leave?"

Clausen scoffed. "What makes you think you will ever leave? Once we prove you are Resistance, you will be executed for treason."

"But I'm not—"

He yanked at my arm. "Even if we can't prove you are Resistance, we will try and execute you accordingly. You will serve as a reminder to the Coalition citizens."

"Then what is the point of imprisoning me?"

Clausen clicked his tongue. "So many questions for a Humilian rat." He pulled me in close, and his breath caressed my ear. "Protocol, *Carissima*."

I stepped away, and his cruel chuckle raked down my spine.

"Not to mention, Osouf is a softy. If it wasn't for his damned dog, he would have let you off the hook. But if it was up to me…" We stopped before a steel door, and Clausen turned to me. "…you'd be unconscious in a pool of your own blood by now."

A lump formed in my throat at Clausen's crooked smile.

Eyes still locked on mine in a predatory gleam, Clausen pressed a thumb to the scanner on the right of the cell door, and the cell entrance screeched open. I made sure to get a good look at the cell number before he pushed me through the threshold.

4152.

I tapped my right temple twice to end the recording as I stumbled into the room and fell to my knees.

A message scanned through my vision. *Save. Send. Delete.*

I slid a finger over my brow until 'send' was highlighted, then tapped my temple once.

Message sent to Dr. Metis Barnes.

The contacts flickered once as they entered standby mode.

Clausen's clunking footsteps echoed off the bare walls of the jail cell before his hand grasped under my arm, and he hauled me to my feet. "Cot, latrine, sink, desk." The Major General pointed around the dim cell. The only glimmer of light seeped through a small, barred window about ten feet above my cot. Clausen turned, and I thought he was going to leave, but he slammed the door shut, the metal clang near deafening. "And now it's time for initiation."

I met his eyes. They were glazed over with a dark lust. A deep, unsatiated hunger seemed to emanate from every bob of his Adam's apple and lick of his lips.

I stumbled back, my hands still bound together and hanging uselessly in front of me. "What do you mean?"

Clausen stalked toward me as he unbuckled his belt, his teeth bared in a predatory gleam. "Get on the cot."

My heart thundered, and the thick air that once clung to my lungs now seemed distant—absent. My mouth worked, and I shook my head.

"Get. On. The. Cot." Clausen's command was a low growl as he prowled closer, one hand reaching between his legs. The Major General herded me into a corner, my calves now pressed against the cold metal of the cot. I did not dare sit down.

He worked himself, a hand pumping between his legs.

Frantically, I looked around the room for something—anything—to aid in my defense against him.

Wrong move.

As my eyes darted away from his, Clausen seized the opportunity to grab my hair with his other hand. I grunted as he pulled me to him, my stomach flushed against his pumping hand.

"You're definitely not the first woman I have had the pleasure of initiating, but you sure are the prettiest." Clausen loomed over me, and his breath was hot against my brow.

I spat in his face. "Even my darkest nightmares are filled with creatures more beautiful than you."

Clausen's pumping ceased. Both relief and terror swirled in me like a rip tide. He reached for his cheek and wiped my spit off with two fingers. He considered the gleaming wetness, smiled, then returned his dark, crazed gaze to me as he reached down and spread it down himself. He grunted in pleasure, and my stomach churned.

"Let's put that pretty little mouth of yours to some more good use." My skull burned as the Major General yanked down on my hair. I screamed. Clausen pulled me down to the cot, and my eyes were now level with his cock. It twitched, and I tried to look away, but Clausen's fist held tight to a tangle of my hair, anchoring my head where he willed it.

Clausen's hand started to brace my skull, readying to force my mouth around him. Before he could pull me toward him, I jerked my good leg up, nailing my knee right between his legs. He crumpled forward, and Clausen's thick hand released. I pushed him over and bolted toward the door.

"Help!" I slammed my bound fists into the cold metal. "Someone! Please, help!"

I yelped as my head yanked back, hair ripping from the follicles. Clausen pulled me to the ground. Air was propelled from my lungs. I coughed as stars clouded my vision.

"No one is going to help you here, *Carissima*. They all know the drill." Clausen's face was crimson, brows pinched in fury as he straddled me. The concrete floor raked against my clothes and skin as I tried to scramble away, but my efforts were useless as Clausen's whole-body weight fell onto my hips.

My eyes stung with tears. "Please, stop!" I wriggled and writhed under him, but his smile only grew more feral—a cat toying with a mouse.

Clausen's large hand reached for my tunic, ready to tear the fabric from my body when the steel door to my cell slammed open.

A tall, lithe woman stood in the threshold. Her hair hung in dark coils around her shoulders like tendrils of shadows against the Military camo she donned. "What the fuck is going on in here?"

"Initiation," Clausen growled. "Would you like to join?"

My lungs seized. My head reeled. Would this woman be my savior or just another assailant?

The woman crossed her arms and leaned against the door frame. "You know damn well 'initiation' practices have been banned, Clausen."

"That is Major General to you. And I don't give a damn—"

"Oh, but I bet my brother gives a damn. You know Sancus is such a stickler for the rules." The woman examined her sharp black nails, stark against her smooth, light-brown skin. "Oh, and then there is Osouf." She huffed a bemused laugh. "You know, the one who is standing in the way of your promotion. Yeah, this"—she gestured vaguely to where Clausen straddled me in the cell—"would definitely be a setback. If Osouf were to find out, that is."

Clausen shot the woman a glare.

She shrugged. "Your choice."

With a heavy grunt, Clausen stood. I remained lying on the floor, my body frozen.

The woman shielded her eyes. "Oh, for fuck's sake, put that thing away."

"Oh, I know you want a piece of this—"

As Clausen made to move toward the woman, manhood still exposed, I sliced my good foot across, kicking Clausen's legs out from under him. I jumped back up to my feet as the soldier fell face-first to the floor.

"You bitch!" Clausen turned and lunged for me, but I tumbled out of the way.

"Second Lieutenant Gillian and Lieutenant General Osouf, I request your assistance at jail cell 4152," the woman chimed in a communication device.

Clausen whirled. "What did you just do?"

The woman's dark brows flicked upward. "I would get the fuck out of here before Osouf shows up."

Clausen glanced from where I stood—hands bound but ready to grab for the aluminum desk chair—then to the other woman. She shrugged.

"I am not finished with you." Clausen pointed a thick finger at me before bounding out the door and through the hall.

My savior—who introduced herself as Private Aletheia Gillian but insisted I call her Aletheia—remained perched against the door frame, picking at her black nails as Lieutenant General

Osouf and the other soldier, Second Lieutenant Gillian, bickered about what to do with me outside of my prison cell. I remained seated on the thin cot in the far corner of the dank room, bound hands shaking in my lap as my mind tried to process the assault.

I didn't let it.

"I'm gonna kill him. I'm gonna fucking kill him," the Lieutenant General whispered, his harsh words distracting me from the trauma that clawed at my mind.

"We will deal with him later. We need to focus on what to do now. You have an undocumented person close to shock in that jail cell."

My throat grew tight.

"I don't know what to fucking do, Sancus!"

"Well, she can't stay here." Aletheia countered, eyes still fixed on her cuticles. "She's not safe. You saw the footage. She made an ass outta him, so he's gonna come back and finish what he started, promotion or not."

"Will you both keep it down?" the other man, Sancus, growled.

The men's voices turned into hushed, indiscernible whispers. My ears strained, but it was no use.

I closed my eyes and tried to breathe. *I am so fucked.*

When I opened them again, a message panned across my vision.

One(1) New Message(s). Would you like to play New Message(s)?

With a swipe over my right brow and a quick tap to my right temple, I selected 'yes.' Video footage began playing, and my surroundings were replaced with an image of Metis' face in his laboratory.

"Red." His rough voice eased my aching heart. "I have no idea what the bloody damn is going on. Yer team has not returned to Base yet, so neither Hoenir nor I have been debriefed on the status of yer mission. Hopefully, they'll arrive soon so we can get some damned answers, or we'll have to plan for the worst. In the meantime, stay alive. I've attached a file…" Next to Metis' cyber eye appeared a blue folder. "…which'll indicate a new cover story for ya. I am hopin' it'll buy ya more time until we are able to extract ya from Imperium's prison. If it contradicts too much with falsified information you've already given, you'll have to adapt accordingly. I'll get an extraction plan to ya as soon as I am able, but it could take some time." Metis pursed his lips, and his good eye softened. "I'm aware ya were not trained for this, but yer smart, Red. If anyone can survive this, it's you."

Metis' face and surroundings faded, replaced by the surrounding jail cell and another prompt.

Open file?

Yes. I selected by tapping my right temple.

I scanned through the file containing Metis' utterly absurd cover story, and bile rose in my throat at the irony. I was nearly raped, and now Metis wants me to pretend I'm a—

"You could just throw her into the Excelsisan Integration Program."

I flicked my eyes toward Aletheia.

"What?" the two men questioned in unison.

The Private shrugged. "She is obviously not safe here—no woman is—we don't know for sure that she is Resistance, so we can't torture or kill her, and we don't know where she is from." The girl looked to me, brown eyes assessing. "Place her in the Integration Program."

"What's the Integration Program?" I asked, pretending to scratch at my temple while I prompted the file displayed on my retina to disappear.

Osouf finally walked through the door, pushing past the woman, and the man—who I presumed to be Second Lieutenant Sancus Gillian—was on his heels. He was a dark-haired and freckled-skinned soldier, shorter than both the Lieutenant General and Aletheia.

"It's a program usually for Media and Humilis minors who are gifted enough to climb the social hierarchy. It is very difficult to be accepted into the program, and the application process is long and tedious," the Second Lieutenant answered.

Osouf crossed his arms. My pack was strapped over a broad shoulder. "And I can't just let some woman we know nothing about into Excelsis. I have a city to protect. How about you give us some real answers, like why you have contraband material in your backpack."

"Contraband material?"

He stepped closer, and I flinched. Osouf's green eyes softened, probably noticing the trauma reflected in my eyes. He swung the pack around, placed it on the wooden desk across from the cot, and pulled out a white box. "The *three* pairs of brown-irised contact lenses—they are prohibited in Humilis."

I looked away.

"My keeper prefers the color."

"What?" Osouf leaned in closer. The Second Lieutenant shifted, standing at attention while the Private still leaned against the doorway.

I rolled my eyes. "My keeper prefers my eyes to be dark brown."

He crossed his arms. "And what is your natural eye color?"

Shit. I couldn't lie to him. What if he asked me to take the contacts out? What if he demanded to see the real color of my eyes?

I bit my lip. "An odd amber color."

The Lieutenant General's brows furrowed. "Let's see." He stepped closer to me and held out a hand.

One by one, I plucked the contacts from my eyes and placed them in the palm of his hand. There was a shimmer of recognition that flickered across his features, but it was quickly replaced by his soldier's mask of stern authority. "Interesting…" he muttered.

My heart stammered in my chest. There was a part of me that wanted him to recognize me—to see the small girl he used to run around manors with and terrorize his nanny. But if he did recognize me, then what? There would only be more questions. More problems.

Osouf started closing his palm when I stopped him with a hand, our fingers touching, and my skin burned. "If you don't mind, Lieutenant General," I started a little too eagerly, "I would like to continue wearing them. My keeper was able to get a small prescription in them to assist my vision."

Osouf looked down his nose but uncurled his fingers. I plucked the contacts from his palm to cradle them in mine.

Osouf continued to rummage through my pack, and he pulled out the orange medicine bottle filled with the pills Metis created.

"What are these?" Before I could open my mouth to spout some lie, he shook the bottle to stop me, the pills tapping along the side of the plastic bottle. "I would tell the truth, we took samples. Our lab is processing them as we speak."

Then why the hell do you need to ask me, Lieutenant General? I wanted to snap. Instead, I swallowed the retort and looked Osouf in his beautiful eyes. "It's medicine to change the color of my hair."

"Why?"

I shrugged. "Again, my keeper prefers this color." I fingered my dyed hair, glancing up at the Lieutenant General through my lashes.

His eyes softened slightly. "What is your natural hair color?"

"A muddy blonde." I stifled a scoff. The Lieutenant General couldn't verify unless he stripped me down.

"And why would your keeper care so much about how you look? Humilians hardly care about such things."

I bit my lip and took a deep breath, preparing myself for the lie Metis had concocted for me. "Because Lieutenant General, you are correct. I am not a Humilian woman, and my keeper and I were conducting illicit activity."

The whole room seemed to still, everything hanging on a breath at my confession.

"The truth is, sir, I am a brothel worker from Media, and we were in Humilis to find new—" I swallowed the lump in my throat. "To find new recruits."

The two men stared at me.

"Well, shit," Aletheia murmured.

Sancus shot Aletheia a glare, but Osouf's eyes remained fixed on mine, searching.

"Forced or by choice?"

"What?"

Osouf sighed. "Are you a sex worker by force or by choice?"

My cheeks heated. "Not by choice, sir."

"And the people you were 'recruiting'?"

I looked away, as if ashamed. "Not by choice."

Osouf's face drained of color as he shoved my belongings back into my pack and threw it on the cot. "You may keep your things, but you are still under surveillance. You will remain here until—"

"Sir, hasn't she been through enough?"

The Lieutenant General and I both snapped our attention to Aletheia. Osouf and the Private exchanged knowing glances.

"She would be a good candidate for the Excelsis Integration Program."

Osouf glanced over a shoulder, and our eyes met. Electricity seemed to spark in the air between us, and his eyes flickered from the energy. The Lieutenant General ran a hand through his sandy hair before he glided toward me and knelt at my feet. He pulled out a key, and in a few swift movements, the Three-Star General unlocked all my chains.

He closed his eyes and took a deep breath. "My apologies. Believe me when I say Major General Clausen will be reprimanded for his actions and will receive adequate punishment for his deeds." Osouf's voice was flat, distant.

I nodded, my heart still racing, my chest heated to a flush.

"It's fine." My voice was brittle. "It's nothing I haven't dealt with before," I lied.

Our eyes were locked on each other, breaths dancing in the

empty space between us. Finally, he rose and turned toward the Second Lieutenant and Private.

"Take my speeder and bring her up to First," Osouf explained as he pulled out a small black object from a pectoral pocket and tossed it to the man.

The Second Lieutenant glanced at me. I rubbed my wrists, raw from the handcuffs.

"Take Sirius with you. You know the code. Make yourselves comfortable."

The man grabbed Osouf's shoulder. "Sir, I don't think—"

"Sancus, take her to First. That's an order."

With a tight salute, the Second Lieutenant Sancus Gillian relented. After a dismissal from his commander, Sancus gestured for me to follow him.

I rose from the cot, pack clutched closely to my chest, and hobbled toward the Second Lieutenant.

As I passed Osouf, he gripped my arm. I turned to meet his gaze, and my heart dropped to my stomach as his eyes turned cold. "Do not think for one second you are out of the woods, *Ms. Stevens*." He emphasized my name like he knew it was fake. "Every move you make is being watched. Every breath you breathe is a gift I have given you. Any step deemed out of line, and the Second Lieutenant has orders to incapacitate you in whatever measure he deems necessary."

I swallowed—my only response before the Lieutenant General released me, leaving me breathless. His scent of wood and earth still lingered in the air, and his green eyes were still pierced on my retinas as I exited the cell.

CHAPTER 11

Sirius sat in the back of the vehicle, tail wagging and tongue out like he got an early start on vacation as Second Lieutenant Sancus Gillian and Private Aletheia Gillian led me onto a landing pad jutting out from the huge prison complex. Sancus opened the speeder's back door for me while Aletheia climbed in the front. The stench of wet dog hit me as soon as I entered the vehicle, which was not as welcoming as Sirius's sloppy kiss across my nose. I wiped away the saliva, smearing it away with my forearm, and scratched him behind the ears. Sirius' fur was damp like he had just received a bath, but it was still a comfort that eased my soul. I stifled the urge to hug the beast, to use his comfort to forget about my pain, which was all-consuming.

My ankle.

My heart.

My mind.

I felt like I was splitting at the seams from all the hurt and betrayal in the past few hours.

The 'speeder' Osouf mentioned was nothing short of a small aircraft. It was different than the hover vehicles I recalled from my childhood—leaner, not quite as boxy, and it had wings that popped out when Sancus switched it over to flight mode, so instead of just levitating over the ground, the speeder actually flew. I was jerked backward as we shot higher and higher into the sky.

We soared over rural Humilis, then bounded over industrial Media, until we finally reached the shining beauty that was Excelsis. Sancus steered the craft around the Circulum in the Clouds. He pointed to various buildings that glittered and gleamed like they were made of stars, a stark contrast to the brick and concrete buildings I noted as we shot past Media. Parks were littered among the sleek buildings, the grass bright green despite the impending winter. Various birds flew to and fro, but as I studied them more closely, I noticed there was a strict pattern they kept. No, not a pattern—a boundary—like they were fluttering from end to end in an invisible domed bird cage. I remembered Metis informing me about the atmosphere controlling force-field surrounding Excelsis. It was similar to the walls surrounding Imperium's boundaries, but it stretched like a bubble, completely encasing the highest Circulum.

I felt Aletheia's dark-brown eyes on me through the wing mirror as Sancus aimed the speeder at a large, glowing purple rectangle within the forcefield. I didn't meet her gaze as we zoomed right through it, my eyes burning from the bright, amethyst flash as we entered Imperium's highest Circulum. Sancus drove the vehicle on a small runway before switching it back over to hover mode. There was a quick jerk, and then we cruised through the streets of Excelsis. Sancus rolled down his window. A light, balmy breeze kissed my cheek as I peered out my window, entranced by the soaring buildings and the Excelsian people strolling down the *trames*.

It had been so long since I had seen so many people.

I gaped at the citizens and their ornate clothes. Most wore Coalition plum, white, or black, but all were heavily embroidered with metallic threads or intricately bejeweled—so different from the dull, scratchy clothes back at Base.

The vehicle slipped to a smooth stop before a tall, glass building.

I met Sancus' golden-brown eyes through the rearview mirror. "Where are we?" I asked sheepishly, my hand instinctively gripping Sirius' black fur. I had kept my hand on Sirius' back throughout the ride, his coarse coat and familiar musky scent keeping me tied to reality instead of slipping into a dark pit whose shadows already clawed at my mind and scratched at my soul.

"Callum's flat."

Wait.

"What?" I leaned closer to the soldiers, but Aletheia was already crawling out of the vehicle.

Sancus turned to look at me, his freckled brow crinkled. "What?"

"Who's flat?"

"Oh, sorry." Sancus shook his head. "Lieutenant General Osouf's. We go way back, so I am used to calling him by his first name."

Aletheia's door shut, and Sancus extended an arm to open his own.

My eyes widened. "Which is…" I needed to hear him say it one more time.

"Callum…" Sancus paused. "Why?"

Impossible. As much as I tried to deny it to myself in the interrogation room—as hard as I tried to push away any possibility—the reality was that the Lieutenant General was once my best friend.

My vision blurred into a memory of a huge mansion and a small boy welcoming me through an ornate wooden door, his eyes shining in the sun. In my memory, I glanced upward to see a stone wolf.

Direwolf. The word rang in my mind.

The legendary beast was carved on a large marble crest. Its eyes were made of large emeralds, and it appeared to be snarling down on me, teeth bared and threatening, and below its maw were carved letters. *Osouf.*

I blinked. "Nothing. I apologize. It's just—" I stammered. "It's just such an odd name for an Excelsian, don't you think?"

Gillian's eyes narrowed, flicking to the rearview mirror to look at me. "I suppose."

———

I was given no tour of Callum's flat, which was perched at the very top of the sleek, glass complex.

Callum's flat.

I only found out mere minutes ago, but his name slipped back so easily to the forefront of my mind. It felt surreal as I stood in the entrance, pack folded tight in my arms as Sancus raided the refrigerator, and Aletheia plopped herself on the couch. She switched on a very large COM-device, similar to the device Callum had used in the interrogation room, but at least ten times larger. Images popped from the screen in a three-dimensional rainbow of colors showing miniature people in their miniature homes, talking to each other.

Is it some sort of recording device?

The sound of laughter boomed around the room, but it wasn't from any of us—it was from the COM-device.

"Oh, no. We are not watching one of your dumb reality shows again." Sancus yelled from the kitchen. "There is a huge Hover Ball Match in twenty minutes."

"Great. We can watch this until it starts," Aletheia replied cooly.

As the siblings bickered, I scanned the open flat. The kitchen was closest to the entry hall, and it flowed openly into the dining room, which then flowed into the room where Aletheia was lounging. Everything was sleek—there was little adornment on the walls. Pale blues, grays, and whites colored the rooms, and they smelled of cedar and dark spices.

Sancus pushed past me, food and drinks stuffed in his arms. "Well, make yourself at home!" He sat next to his sister, and they proceeded to bicker over food as Sirius nudged my right hand with his cool, wet nose, silently encouraging me to move.

"Maybe you want to take a shower?" Aletheia asked around a mouthful of chips.

I took a deep breath. "Yeah, a shower would be perfect, actually."

"Here," Sancus grunted as he set a bottle down on the glass coffee table right next to where Aletheia's feet were propped. "I'll show you the bathroom and get you some of Cal's clothes to change into."

Heat rushed to my face. "Oh, I really don't need his clothes. I can change back into these." I glanced down at the blood-stained sack I was wearing, then back up and Aletheia. She arched a pristinely groomed brow.

"He won't mind. Come on, Cal's bathroom is right this way. " Sancus motioned me along.

———

I stood before the bathroom mirror, and all I saw was someone I didn't recognize—someone with brown hair and brown eyes. Dirt still clung to my skin and clothes; bruises marred my face.

Lungs shuddering as I tried to take deep, controlled breaths, I pressed my right temple for three seconds. My vision blurred to focus on the retinal display projected from the contacts. There were no messages waiting for me, but I decided to send one. I tapped my right temple twice to record. My normal vision returned, but there was a blinking red light in my right periphery.

I stared at the new version of myself and whispered to Metis in the recording. "I'm fine," I lied. "I am still in Imperium, but I think I'm now in the First Ward. I know for certain I'm up in Excelsis. I am at the home of Lieutenant General Callum—" I swallowed, still not able to process the soldier I met today as my childhood friend. "Osouf. I have no idea why they want me here. They mentioned something about the 'Excelsian Integration Program.' Right now, I am being kept in his company with his soldiers. Do not pursue."

I fell forward, my hands bracing the cold marble counter.

"Metis, I'm so scared. I don't know where I am. I don't know where my team is. I was almost—" I closed my eyes, unable to finish the sentence. How could I possibly explain to the man who was like a father to me that I was almost raped? "I need assistance. I need an extraction plan—I need to get the hell out of here. Please, Metis. Please help me. Oh, and Metis, don't trust Ulysses—he is the reason I'm here. I don't know if he sabotaged my mission to secure his promotion or if he is a Coalition spy, but he ensured I would be captured."

I tapped my right temple twice to end the message. My vision blurred to a prompt.

Send. Send and Save. Save. Delete. Using my forefinger, I rubbed down along my eyebrow to select send and tapped once.

Message Sent to Dr. Metis Barnes.

I pressed my left temple for three seconds to turn the contacts off, then stripped down and tiptoed into the shower. There was no door, no curtain. I was exposed. I was vulnerable. Just like I was in that prison cell.

I tried not to think of Clausen's thick hand grabbing my hair or preparing himself. I tried not to think about what would have happened if Aletheia hadn't barged into the room. But it was all I could think about.

I was assaulted.

I was molested.

I was nearly raped.

I sucked in a deep breath, but the steam was suffocating me, and my throat grew tight, cries threatening to burst from my lungs.

I had never felt so out of control, so powerless.

The thought sent my head reeling. I slid to the shower floor, my back pressed against the cold tile, and I cradled my head between my knees. The water stung my eyes, and I wrapped my arms tightly around my stomach as my will gave out, and convulsions broke over me like waves with every desperate sob.

———

"Still alive in there?" Aletheia called through the bathroom door.

I didn't know how long I was in the shower—long enough for my body to stop shuddering and for my fingers to prune.

"Yes, I am fine," I choked out.

"Uh, okay…" she responded through the door, clearly unconvinced.

Thoughts of my assault had brought me to my knees, but the dubiety of my team's mission had me curled up in the corner of the tiled shower. I stood, shoving away the quandaries of the computer virus and the lives of my fellow agents. I quickly washed my hair, face, and body with a bar of soap that sat on a ledge along the shower wall. I dried myself and stood exposed as I thumbed Callum's clothing, and thoughts of the little boy I knew flooded my mind.

My best friend, my kind and gentle friend, grew up to be a soldier in the Coalition Military. Did he recognize me? I stared at myself in the mirror, at my brown eyes and my brown hair.

No. There is no way. After all, he probably thinks me and my family are dead, nothing more than burnt bones long buried beneath the dirt and leaves in the middle of The Wastes.

I started to pull on the clothes, a simple t-shirt and grey sweatpants. The sweatpants fit surprisingly well, but the shirt was large, hanging loosely on my shoulders. I wiped the condensation from the mirror to get a good look at myself.

Yeah, there is no way Callum could recognize me, and that was a good thing, I told myself, *because here, in Imperium, I am Adellaide.*

"She's alive!" Sancus shouted as I dragged my feet into the living room with one arm wrapped around my waist, Callum's cotton shirt a small comfort. The siblings sat on the couch.

"Sorry, I must have lost track of time. Usually, I can determine how long I have been in the shower by the slow cooling of the temperature and the sputtering of the water pressure."

"Welcome to the Excelsis, dearie!" Sancus replied, his eyes still fixed on the three-dimensional video.

"Do not call me 'dearie'."

Sancus carefully glanced over, his face stricken from the shock of my bitter tone before a small apology slipped from his lips.

Sirius hopped down from the couch to greet me, his tail wagging gently, and I patted him on the head.

"So, you both live here in the First Ward?"

"No," Aletheia answered this time. "We live in the Third Ward."

I crossed my arms. "How can you cross Wards?"

"In Excelsis, there are no strict Ward boundaries. You can live in a Ward you don't work in and travel freely," Sancus answered.

"And we're Military—we have to go to all Wards for work, so we can go to all Wards for play. One of the 'perks,' I guess," Aletheia explained, sarcasm sticking to her words like tree sap.

"But we still have to be home by curfew if we are off duty," Sancus chimed in. "Unless, of course, good ol' Lieutenant General permits us to stay longer or overnight.

The front door groaned. "But then you are late for duty in the morning." Lieutenant General Callum Osouf walked through the door, chiding Sancus. Callum's Military uniform was already unbuttoned, and his black cap was shoved under his arm. "And you have to answer to an angry Major General Anderson." His voice was light with jest.

"Major General Anderson is always angry," Sancus grumbled.

The Lieutenant General chuckled. "I am going to tell her you said that." Osouf walked behind the couch and flicked Sancus on the head.

The Second Lieutenant rubbed the spot and scoffed. "No, you won't. You know Bellona always shoots the messenger."

"Touché," he said, green eyes glancing over to me, finally acknowledging my presence in the room. "Huh." The Lieutenant General eyed Sirius, who was now sitting at my side, before returning his gaze to mine. "Sirius always greets me at the door, no matter who is around."

I shrugged.

"It looks like you took a shower. *And* found a change of clothes." The soldier's eyes rolled over me, assessing, and I felt exposed under his gaze. "I'm glad you have made yourself at home."

"Sancus insisted," I said flatly, folding my other arm over my torso.

He nodded once, then ran a hand through his hair in the way that stole the breath from my lungs. "Please follow me."

Callum, hands in his pockets, led me back through his bedroom and into his bathroom. He shut the door behind me, and we were alone.

My heart stopped.

Callum cleared his throat. "I am sure you, of all people, already know, Ms. Stevens, but the Coalition is not a perfect place. Not even our Military avoids corruption, but I am working hard to remedy the faults within our system. Obviously, you are here for your safety, but I will do whatever it takes to keep the Citizens of the Coalition from any harm. So, if I detect the slightest threat from you, I will return you to Imperium's prison, where you will be dealt with.

"In the meantime, I am preparing your application for the Excelsis Integration Program. This will be…a challenge since there are no records of you in the CCD. It will be extremely difficult to find not only a job placement but a foster home to aid in assimilation. Until we can find a volunteer to welcome you into their home, you are to stay with me. Under my watch. Under my protection." The Lieutenant General cleared his throat. "What happened to you in the prison will not happen again. Not to you."

Osouf's hand twitched like he was reaching out for mine. Instead, he stopped himself, hand flinching away to grab something from his left bicep pocket. He pulled out two syringes. One was lean, thin and long. My eyes bulged at the sight of the second. It was huge. The needle itself was as wide as a pen.

My eyes grew wider. "What is that?"

"This"—the Lieutenant General held up the large syringe—"is your chip. Every Excelsian citizen has one. We are working on implementing them into Media and Humilis."

I took a step away from the soldier. "And what does it do?"

"This small device is a new form of ID—the chip holds virtually all your identification data: who you are, how old you are, your occupation, medical information. It even balances your hormones and alerts medical officials when your blood pressure spikes or heart stops. It can access your bank accounts and track your whereabouts. When programmed, it can access your clearance for points of entry in various buildings and rooms."

"How does it work?" I swallowed the hard lump in my throat. The Coalition could control every aspect of my life via one tiny chip.

"It uses the electrical impulses created by the firing of neuron signals as energy. With that energy, the chip acts as a mini-computer, inputting and outputting information into your nervous system." The Lieutenant General pulled out a solution and cotton pads from his cupboard. He gestured for me to sit on the toilet. I hesitated, glancing from the toilet to the syringe to his face. He gestured again, and I complied, slowly sitting down. Callum tugged on my left forearm and stretched it over the cold, white marble. Chills danced up my arm as it rested on the countertop.

"So, the Coalition can do whatever they want to me through a chip?"

Osouf shook his head as he poured the solution on the cotton pad and swabbed a small spot in the middle of my left forearm. The scent of alcohol stung my nose and eyes. "It's not like that. The chip is to help you, not control you. It will make your life easier."

I knew propagandist bullshit when I heard it. "Don't I have to sign a waiver or something?"

"Chip is mandatory. Only I need to sign a document indicating I was the personnel who performed the procedure."

I rolled my eyes. *Of course.*

He prepped the small syringe, uncapping the needle and flicking the tube to release any air bubbles.

"And that does what?" I nodded to the small needle in his hand.

"This is a numbing agent."

How kind. At least I wouldn't have to feel it when Callum placed a preverbal leash inside my body.

Osouf pricked me with the small needle. I flinched, but the Lieutenant General held firm, his strong, warm hand grasped tightly around my sore wrist. His right thumb pressed the fluid into my arm.

The numbing agent worked instantly. My left arm felt tingly as Callum pulled the needle back out, and then I felt nothing when he pressed a cotton pad over the same spot—even my fingers felt slow and distant as I tried to flex. The Lieutenant General removed the cotton pad from my arm and replaced it with the large needle. I watched as the wide, hollow needle sank into my skin, and though I prepared myself for the pain, none came. I only felt the erratic thundering of my heartbeat when the

Lieutenant General pulled out the large steel object, blood pooling. I was officially trapped in the Coalition.

Callum quickly placed the cotton pad back over the new wound and I held it while he rummaged for something in a vanity drawer. He pulled out a bandage and dried the wound, wiping away alcohol and blood, then quickly adhered the bandage to my skin.

"There you go," he grunted. "Your arm will probably be sore tomorrow. I will remind you to ice it tonight."

I tried to wiggle my fingers, but they only slowly twitched.

The Lieutenant General laughed. "Yeah, you won't have feeling for at least a few hours."

"Great," I mumbled before glancing up to meet Osouf's eyes. They sparkled brightly, shimmering like light bouncing off the waves of a windy lake. "So, now what, Lieutenant General?"

"Now"—he released a large breath that seemed as though it was tightly wound around his lungs—"I pour myself a drink and order us some pizza." He turned and made his way to the door. Before he opened it, Osouf looked over his shoulder, a hand still lingering on the doorknob. "And you can call me Callum. Or Cal. Whichever you prefer."

My heart throbbed.

Callum opened the door and gestured for me to walk through first.

CHAPTER 12

The flat was quiet. Too quiet. Since Sancus and Aletheia left, the silence between Callum and I was a taut string ready to snap. I sat in a grey, tufted armchair, my stomach full and bloated from the pizza, while Callum sat on the leather couch with Sirius curled up next to him. Callum had hardly stopped doting on his canine since he got home, and I couldn't help but feel guilty. Though I had nothing to feel guilty about—it wasn't my fault the Lieutenant General lost his mutt.

"Well," Callum grunted as he stood up, "I'm going to start on dishes."

"Let me help," I chimed, pushing myself up off the chair with only my right arm considering my left was still useless.

He held a hand out to me. "No. I got it."

I hovered over the chair. "Are you sure?"

Callum nodded and started picking up plates and untouched silverware. "Positive. But feel free to look around. Make yourself comfortable."

I nearly laughed. I was a Resistance Agent in the presence of one of the most powerful people in the Coalition, and he wanted me to make myself comfortable.

With a handful of dishes, Callum made his way to his

kitchen. At the large kitchen island, Callum plopped the plates in the sink and turned the water faucet on. It was odd watching such a powerful man scrub and dry used dinnerware, but he looked so serene as he flowed through the motions, his eyes glazed over in contemplative thought while his strong arms, exposed from his rolled-up sleeves, worked at such a menial task.

Through his lashes, Callum's eyes met mine. I jerked my head away, blood already rushing to my cheeks, and scanned the room for something—literally anything else—to stare at. My gaze stumbled upon his mantle, where a small stone was perched. It was the only object adorning the mantle, yet it was inconspicuous. With the naked eye, there was nothing special about the rock. It didn't seem carved, painted, or particularly beautiful.

But it called to me.

"What's this?" I asked as I picked up the rock. It was cold and rugged between my fingers.

Callum looked up from the dishes he was working on and gave the object a quick glance. "Just a little piece of home." The smallest smile lit up his features.

"Where is home?" I asked, though I knew the answer.

"Militum. Down near the Severing Sea."

I rolled the stone in my hand, and it seemed even more lackluster as light refused to bounce off the dull grey and brown tones. "What's so special about it? Was it a stone from your house or yard?"

Callum chuckled. "No. Actually, it was from a friend. She threw it at my head because she thought I was acting 'dumb.' We were young. I was about seven or eight. She was a couple of years younger."

I suppressed a smile. "Sounds like she liked you." I set the rock back on the mantle.

When I spared a glance at the Lieutenant General, I saw a small, innocent blush blooming on his sharp cheekbones.

I walked over to Callum, and every step closer felt like I was stepping into a natural hot spring, my body unwinding and relaxing.

"Well, I sure liked her. I gave her a rose. That's how I ended up with a rock thrown at my head."

The memory flashed across my vision. The garden. The scent of rosewood and lavender. The rock flying through the air, and a hard *clunk* as it slammed into Callum's head. His hand slick with blood as he pulled it away from his new wound. My taunt.

I blinked, and the memory was gone. Only the lingering guilt remained.

And the rock.

Callum stood, one brow arched high, and his sudsy hands braced the sink.

"I would, too. Roses are cliché flowers with thorns that make you bleed. You might as well have thrown a rock at her head." The words came out before I could stop them.

Callum's lingering smile dropped as his brows creased together. "Funny, that's almost exactly what she said." We stared at each other for a moment.

Stupid, Red. You complete idiot. I swallowed, searching for words in an attempt to switch the subject, but they were far from me as I found myself lost in his eyes—in our past.

The Lieutenant General cleared his throat, breaking the silence. "Well," he sighed, "it's in the past." Callum returned his attention to the soapy dishes.

"Yeah." I turned and glanced around the apartment. "I suppose you have tons of girls coming through this bachelor flat, anyway. No need to think on your little childhood crush."

He looked at me, his mouth set in a hard line. "What is that supposed to mean?"

"Well, I don't see a ring." I glanced over my shoulder to his hands. "And since you so graciously invited me into your home without needing to check with anyone, I assume you live alone." I raised an eyebrow to him. "You're a single, highly ranked

Military man—I'm sure you don't have any problems procuring women."

Callum's eyes narrowed as he grabbed a towel and roughly dried his hands. "This might come as a surprise to you, *Ms. Stevens*, but I have plenty of other things to worry about than women." He threw the towel on the counter and turned to pour amber liquid from a large, clear container into a crystal glass. The sharp scent that danced in the air proved the liquid to be some sort of alcohol. Callum walked back toward the living room.

"I'm sorry, I didn't mean to insinuate women. Do you prefer men?"

Callum sat in a chair near the balcony doors, opposite from the one I sat in earlier. "No." He ran a hand through his hair. "I do not prefer men."

I returned to my chair and crossed my legs. "Do you not prefer men or women? I have heard rumors that some Excelsians do not find pleasure in sex, so they do not participate."

Callum choked on his drink, covering his mouth as he coughed. "And why are you so curious about my sex life, Ms. Stevens?"

"Because my whole life has been about sex, Lieutenant General." The lie was smooth as it slipped past my lips.

Callum's eyes darkened as he glanced down at his glass. He took a sip.

I sank deeper into the armchair, Sirius curled up at my feet, and the blanket of silence covered us once more. Though I loved the quiet and the peace, it seemed out of place between Callum and me. I wanted to dive in—I wanted to ask him more about his life after I left. I wanted to find out everything I could about him, but more than anything, I wanted our friendship to pick up exactly where it left off.

And that was the danger to this mission—a danger I couldn't have dreamed of in a thousand years. I never thought I would find myself sitting across from my childhood best friend, who was now my number one enemy.

"He seems to have really taken to you." Callum gestured to Sirius with his glass, now empty.

I nodded.

Callum leaned in, elbows resting on his knees, glass grasped in both hands. He kept his eyes on a single drop of liquid as it swirled along the bottom. "Sirius trusts you, which makes me think I should too, but trust starts with honesty and vulnerability. I want you to feel free to talk with me about your past. Can I ask how you ended up working in a brothel?"

I bit my lip. I had never been so thankful for my photographic memory as I recalled the file I had read earlier that day.

"My mother was a brothel mistress in Media. She became pregnant, but no one knew which of her clients could be the father—she simply had too many, and no one would keep their bastard daughter, so I was raised in the brothel. The Keeper of the House told me that my mother was traded to another house shortly after my birth, but I knew that was a lie. We all know what happens to a mistress after they give birth. They are deemed spoiled, then they are killed—probably dumped in some rubbish bin. The Keeper of the House raised me with my 'brothers and sisters.' I was taught the trade from a young age, and I had my first client at twelve."

Callum's hands seemed to tighten around his glass as he studied me. There was no concern or pity—only a face devoid of emotions as the wheels turned behind his eyes.

I cleared my throat. "It is very rare for a mistress to leave the House, but when she can, she is drugged and blindfolded, so she doesn't know how to get out or back in." I glanced down and fidgeted with the strings of Callum's sweatpants. "It is an honor to see the outside world, even though you know what your job is when you are escorted out.

"Today, when you found me, I was at the market with the

Keeper of the House to—" I took a deep breath. "To *recruit*. Well, that's what Keeper called it, anyway. Though it's more of a trade. Mistresses are only brought along to calm the new girls. Keep them quiet. Soothe them."

"And why did you volunteer for this?" Callum leaned forward.

"I didn't. We are chosen. But a mistress would be stupid to say no, not only because she gets to see the outside, but if she declines, she is severely punished. The girls who do decline cannot work for weeks after their punishments, and if they don't work, they can't eat, drink, or enjoy any comforts."

Callum closed his eyes and inhaled sharply. "Then why were you chosen?"

"I look the healthiest, so I don't raise any questions when out in public."

"What do you mean the healthiest?"

I shrugged, giving myself a second to weave a lie. "I am good at my job. My clients are always satisfied, and I get a lot of requests from new clients. I am also the most expensive, so the more profit I bring in, the more food and luxuries I am given."

The Lieutenant General paused and rubbed his jaw like he was trying to massage questions from his mouth but wasn't sure where to start.

"Can you give me any details on the whereabouts of the brothel? I could shut them down and free the other workers. I could give you justice." Callum's voice was strong and reassuring.

I shook my head. "It was dark. Probably underground or in the basement of some building. There were hardly any windows. And like I said, if a mistress is escorted out, the Keepers take every precaution to ensure the secrets and safety of their property." I pursed my lips. "Even if I did know, even if I could tell you, how could you possibly help them?"

"We could create a system, find them places to live or families to adopt them. We could find them other jobs."

I turned over his words in my head. On paper, his plan could work. *But would people of Media actually take prostitutes into their workplaces? Into their homes?* According to Metis' research, brothels in the Coalition were real—nearly a dozen operating in Media alone—but I had no idea where they were or how to find them.

After a long moment, I sighed. "I'm sorry, Callum." My heart thumped at his name on my lips. Even Callum's eyes flickered. "I want to help them. Of course I do. But I have no information to offer."

He nodded.

"However,"—I leaned in close—"if there is any way to help them, I want to be a part of it."

And I meant it. That was what the Resistance was all about, right? Creating a better country for everyone.

CHAPTER 13

Apparently, it took a lot of people and a lot of delegating for a Lieutenant General to get a day off. Callum was making calls when we sat down for breakfast the next morning at a nearby *prandium*. Even outside with a balmy breeze, the café's garden smelled like freshly baked bread and lemon zest. Callum wore black boots with deep blue jeans, a grey shirt, and a black leather jacket. His hair was combed in its usual style.

I couldn't help but notice, as I gazed upon the other patrons, how different Callum styled himself. While most of the Excelsians' clothes were heavily embroidered with gold filigree or adorned with heavy and ornate beading on top of vibrant jewel tones, Callum wore clothes free from any intricacies, seamlessly blending into the world like a shadow with his dark, fitted clothes.

However, I certainly stuck out like a sore thumb. All Callum gave me to wear were my boots from yesterday and more of his loungewear, which still hung on me. I felt embarrassingly underdressed in the *prandium* as we dined at a white linen table in the garden. I wrapped my arms around myself, hoping to seem smaller and unremarkable, as I sank deep into my chair.

Glass lanterns floated among the garden, reflecting the sunlight into rainbow facets along the smooth marble lawn tiles. My silverware gleamed, and the glassware sparkled in front of me. Robotic servers wheeled around the garden, filling water glasses, serving food, and taking orders. Their voices were smooth and melodic, matching the tone of the restaurant. Sirius, quietly lying under our table out of the sunlight, was the only animal in sight. I assumed it was a special privilege of the Lieutenant General for his hybrid to be allowed in the *prandium*, even if we were technically outside.

Finally, after nearly fifteen minutes of sitting at our table, Callum stowed his COM-device into his pocket and released a heavy sigh.

"Everything sorted?" I asked.

Callum nodded before taking a sip of water. "Yes, much to my subordinates' chagrin. But I guess they should be thanking you for the extra workload."

I grimaced. "I could have just stayed in your flat all day."

"No. I hope your paperwork will be processed by the end of the week, and you will find a host by the beginning of the next. If I help you gain your bearings around Excelsis, then you will be less of a burden on your new host." He ran a hand through his hair, and my throat went dry. It was hard to believe that the awkward little boy I left all those years ago was now sitting across from me…*and he is*…I swallowed…*a man.*

My eyes lingered on his strong jaw, the way his broad shoulders pulled slightly at the seams of his black leather jacket, and how his hands flexed on the table. Callum looked like a Greek god in modern dress.

I crossed my legs and took a sip of cold water.

"That's quick," I murmured around an ice cube.

Callum shrugged. "I imagine you will have a few host options. When you're the Lieutenant General, you find that a lot of people want to help you when you are in need."

"So you don't shoot 'em?"

Callum scowled. "No. Because you're an important authority figure."

"That can shoot people."

"I am not going to shoot people just because a job couldn't be done in a timely fashion."

"Well, it's certainly not going to make you not want to shoot people."

Callum leaned forward. "Is that all you think I do?"

I shrugged. "I guess I haven't really thought about it."

"Well, it's not."

I swirled the water in my glass. "Why couldn't I stay with Aletheia?"

Callum examined the menu. I had already made my decision while he was 'delegating.' "She lives in the Third Ward. I don't think you would find the Military barracks very accommodating for you—it's already difficult for my female soldiers."

I smacked my lips. "So…what do we do in the meantime?"

Callum sighed. "We are going to eat. Then, I guess I will show you around Excelsis to officially start your integration process."

"Oh, how exciting."

He chuckled. "Very. By the way, how is your ankle? You seemed just fine on our walk here."

"Oh, it must have just been a little twist," I lied. I stuck out my leg from under the table and rolled my foot back and forth, testing the motion—it moved fluidly.

Last night, before I crawled into Callum's guest bed, I dared a peek at my injury. It was swollen, colored in gruesome shades of yellow and green, which told me all I needed to know—it was healing rapidly. When I woke up, nearly all the coloring and swelling was gone. Nothing left but a small yellowish circle hugging the ball of my ankle. The snap I heard when Ulysses stomped on my joint was most likely the snapping of tendons. If it had been bones and I hadn't set them properly, my body would have used its rapid healing in a less than beneficial way, rendering my foot useless until I re-broke the bones and set them properly.

Callum's glance was a quick flick of his eyes meeting mine. "Mmhm. And your arm"—he nodded to my left forearm—"it doesn't appear to be bothering you."

I didn't dare lift my arm to show him the injection site. There was no sign of yesterday's procedure. I had already checked. "Thick skin." I shrugged.

He sucked on a tooth. "Do you feel lethargic or irritable today?"

"What?"

"Do you feel tired or grumpy?" Callum clarified.

"Not more than usual. Why?"

Callum pursed his lips. "The chip has some side effects during the first few days due to the readjustments of hormone balance. This can prove to last longer or be more difficult for women because of their longer hormone cycle. Studies have shown an increase in lethargy, irritability, appetite, depression, anxiety, as well as an increased chance of strokes, suicidal thoughts, heart attacks, stomach ulcers, brain aneurysms, and a few other minor complications."

I gawked. "Those sound like *major* complications!"

"I wouldn't worry too much about it." Callum waved a hand. "Your chip will contact the medics if it detects any significant problems."

"Right," I mumbled, glancing around the garden once again. The rose hedges were immaculately trimmed—not a stem or thorn out of place—and the lilac bushes near the east exit were still in bloom, which amazed me. Sparrows and finches played in the shrubs, their chirps and tweets filling the garden with their songs. No one paid us too much attention, though there were the occasional disapproving glances from a few old ladies across the way, clearly looking for their fix of gossip for the day.

"So, Lieutenant General," I trilled.

"My name is Callum."

"Okay, *Callum*, where are you taking me today? What are you going to show me—your favorite spots in Imperium?"

He huffed a laugh. "Most of my favorite spots in Imperium are forbidden to a civilian like you. While your paperwork is being processed, the purpose of today is simply to give you an idea of Excelsis' layout, show you some of the major sites, and help you gain your bearings here in the Circulum."

"Are you sure we can get that all done in one day? You might have to delegate more chores tomorrow," I teased.

"Oh, Ms. Stevens, I would not underestimate me." He smiled mischievously, eyes glinting in the early morning light, and sipped from his water glass.

———

Callum walked me and Sirius around the entire Circulum. Though Excelsis was the smallest of all the Circulums, its diameter still stretched about five miles. During the tour, Callum showed me various memorials, statues, and landmarks erected by or for important people who 'contributed to the Prodigious American Coalition.' The words etched on the Coalition memorials and Callum's own words were nothing short of pure Coalition propaganda. I wasn't exactly sure if the Lieutenant General was trying to educate me or if he was simply trying to bore me to death.

I was so exhausted when we returned to Callum's flat that I told him I was going to lie down for thirty minutes.

I didn't wake up until I heard the soft *pat pat* of footsteps outside my door the following morning. I rose in a panic, heart thundering as I shrugged on a white sherpa robe and matching slippers that were kept on a warming rack. I examined myself in the mirror. My brown hair was tossed up in a bun that had shifted to the left during my sleep, but I didn't care.

I unscrewed the caps of my contact container and slid a lens over each eye, blinking them into place. The retinal screen twitched and grained before the contacts flickered to life. There were no new messages.

My heart sank.

Tapping twice, I started a recording.

"Metis, I don't have much real intel, just some footage of Excelsis I took yesterday. I will send over the files. Do you know if our virus was successful? Have you heard from my team? Are they safe? Please let me know soon, Metis."

A hot tear crawled down my face as I turned my contacts off. I stared into the mirror, but this time, I didn't blink curiously at the woman in the mirror, nor did I panic at the sight of her. I was starting to get used to seeing Adellaide as my reflection.

Callum was leaning against the light marble counter, sipping on a hot cup of coffee as I entered the kitchen. Not a thread, fuzz, or pin was out of place on his Military uniform, and his hair was slicked to one side, though I knew it wouldn't look kempt for very long because of how often he ran his hand through it. But for right now, Callum was the epitome of a Coalition soldier.

"You're returning to work?" I asked by way of greeting.

"You're alive!" Callum feigned astonishment.

"Yeah, sorry." I rubbed at my neck. "I guess everything has really taken a toll on me."

"Do you feel rested?"

I nodded.

"Good." Callum's porcelain coffee cup clinked as he placed it on the black granite counter. A sweet, warm earthiness still lingered in the air from his morning brew. "Yes, I am returning to work today. As much fun as it was dragging you around Excelsis yesterday"—a sarcastic air filled his voice—"duty calls. Coffee?"

I nodded silently, stifling my excitement. I didn't know how often Excelsians had coffee, or Medians for that matter, but on Base, it was a rare treat. I thought it better to feign apathy as I rested my elbows on the cool island countertop. Callum turned toward the kitchen command panel next to the fridge and pressed a few buttons. Within seconds, a mug full of the deepest brown liquid emerged from a panel in the wall, and a nutty aroma wafted through the room.

"So, am I staying here all day?" I inquired, taking the cup from Callum. It was hot to the touch, burning through the calluses layered on my fingertips.

"No." Callum leaned back against the countertop. "The Major General will be taking care of you."

I felt the blood drain from my face.

"Shit," Callum said, realizing who I was thinking of. "No. This is a different Major General. *Anderson* will be your own personal hell today." I sipped my coffee and then smiled as warmth unfurled through me like a liquid blanket.

I relaxed. "Oh"—I raised an eyebrow at my host—"and what will the Mr. Major General and I be doing today?"

"That's *Ms.* Major General if you care to know." Callum smiled knowingly. "And you two will be shopping, which will be her *own* personal hell. When she walks in, please remain quiet about the shopping. I haven't told her yet, and I would like to be the one to break it to her."

Ms. Major General Anderson?

The name finally clicked. I believed Major General Anderson was the same commanding officer Sancus was complaining about the other night.

Great.

"Why bother torturing both of us?"

"Because, Ms. Stevens"—Callum's brows rose, almost in challenge—"that is what Coalition soldier scums, like me, enjoy the most about our job."

My heart stopped.

Was this a trap? It felt like a trap. Was he trying to get me to show any amount of disdain for the Coalition Military? Would that be enough proof of my Resistance ties? At the very least, I could be incarcerated for treason.

And when a knock sounded at the door, I nearly curled over in relief.

Callum pushed himself off the counter and walked over to open the door, giving me a quick wink as he breezed past.

Was it a trap? Or was he just messing with me?

I relaxed, releasing a deep breath.

As soon as the door opened, a woman, who I assumed to be the Major General, walked through the entrance. Our eyes met instantly. She was an inch or two shorter than I, but she looked far more deadly. Though, it wasn't her eyes or her height that got my attention.

It was her hair.

Half of her head was shaved, revealing a beautiful, black, and grey barn owl inked into her scalp, perfectly crafted to look as though it was whispering the secrets of her enemies into her right ear. The left side of her head donned beautiful cocoa hair, straight as an arrow and brushed to a shine. It fell like a silken curtain of onyx right below her ear.

Her brown, almond-shaped eyes narrowed beneath her thick brows as if wondering if I was really this troubled girl Callum had told her about. I stared, unable to move, as she shook Callum's hand in greeting.

She was strong and formidable in her uniform—a boulder in a stream—and for the first time in my life, I felt small. Not vulnerable, like I felt with Clausen, but like a mouse standing in the presence of an owl.

I found myself standing up straight as she completed her entrance into the room, my coffee mug still hot against my palm. The woman glided into the kitchen until she stood on the other side of the island, and she reached out her hand.

"Major General Anderson." Her voice was husky and commanding.

I cleared my throat and took her hand in mine. "Adellaide Stevens."

Anderson's grip was firm and cold, mirroring her hickory eyes as they scanned over me.

I released her grip, not wanting whatever coldness that was in her soul to be transferred into mine. "So, I hear we are going to be shopping buddies today," I drawled, giving Callum a coy smile. A glimmer of shock and dread shimmered across his sharp features.

Anderson turned to Callum. "Can I see you in the other room, Lieutenant General?" Her voice was hushed and strained, teeth gritted to hold back a snarl.

Callum glanced at me, eyes narrowing, then he dipped his head toward his room. Anderson followed her commanding officer. Hearing the door click shut, Sirius just lifted his head off the couch and cocked his head at me.

I tiptoed over to the door and then quietly sat down.

Sirius must have been curious about my behavior because he jumped from his comfortable spot on the couch and trotted over to where I was perched. He nudged my hand with his snout, begging for pets, but I was busy. I shoved the brute away, pushing on his chest, then ribs, then bum as the hybrid huffed and moped back toward the couch.

I returned my attention to Callum's bedroom door and picked at my nails as I listened to the soldiers' muffled voices. I didn't catch everything, but the gist of the conversation was that Anderson—whose first name turned out to be Bellona, confirming my suspicion that there was a sense of informality between the two soldiers—*didn't make it this far in her career to be a babysitter.* But Callum didn't trust me to be alone with Aletheia…something about how he was still concerned I could be a Rebel spy and Bellona could be more useful than Aletheia at slyly extracting information.

I was about to softly crawl away until I heard Anderson laugh spitefully.

"You know what I think? I think you are worried you're getting too close to her," she accused. "I think you need me as a backup to catch anything you miss because you might be getting *emotionally involved.*" The Major General's words were venomous. Though I wasn't in the room with them, warmth rushed to my cheeks in embarrassment.

"That is ridiculous. It's been two days! I *need* you because I *trust* you," Callum said tersely. "Because I *need* to make sure any information we obtain gets released when and to whom I decide. I *need* your help as a woman because if she has been abused her whole life, she won't talk to me or any other man she comes across, and she won't get the second chance she deserves."

"The second chance she *deserves*?" Bellona laughed at the idea. "Because you happened across her at some market in Humilis? Because you gallantly saved her from her 'keeper,' you think this sex worker from Media deserves a new life here in Excelsis?"

"No." Callum sighed, and I could picture him running his hand through his hair. "Adellaide is rational, curious, and kind. She is intelligent." If I didn't know any better, I would have thought his words kind and compassionate. But I did know better. To a Lieutenant General of the Coalition, I was nothing but a pawn in his own Military strategy or political game.

But all those thoughts dissipated as Callum said, "And...I think I know her. Somehow. From somewhere."

My mouth went dry.

"Do not tell me you actually visited one of Media's brothels."

"No, of course not!"

"It doesn't matter. She won't fit in here. She doesn't have a place."

"You don't know that."

"Fine. Fine!" Bellona shouted. "If you want to play 'fixer-upper,' if you want to be her knight in shining armor, fine. But if I sense any foul play, anything wrong with her, you better listen to me because I will take her out *regardless* of your orders." And with those jarring words, hard footsteps clopped toward the door. I remained seated, leaning against the wall next to Callum's bedroom door, and picked at my nails. The door opened, and Bellona towered over me, arms crossed and eyes cold as frozen winter mud.

"Well, you couldn't honestly believe I was just going to sit on the couch like a good little girl while the grown-ups talked, could you?"

The Major General growled.

I dared a glance upward and smiled darkly. "In my profession, secrets are the highest form of currency."

CHAPTER 14

Callum may not have trusted me alone with Aletheia, but the Private still joined Bellona and me on our shopping adventure. Honestly, I was relieved Aletheia was joining us. Since she was the one who stopped Clausen from seriously harming me, there was a strange connection between us —an understanding or maybe even the start of some odd friendship.

Aletheia met the Major General and me outside of a building made of dark glass with a bright green sign above the door that read "Paradigm." Obsidian doors opened automatically for us as we walked through the threshold, and I was immediately underwhelmed. The store was small, dark, and not a single scrap of clothing was in sight, only curtained-off booths lining the dark walls.

"This is Paradigm." Aletheia gestured with a dramatic flair. "It's my favorite store because you get to shop without having to try things on." Aletheia glided across the room, her lean legs stretching even longer with black high-heels. The clacking of her shoes against the marble floor ceased as she stopped before a booth and pulled open shimmering dark blue and purple curtains. With a wave of her arm, she welcomed Bellona and me into a rectangular booth no bigger than a small closet. At its center was a circular platform that stood before a large, blank screen about the size and shape of a floor mirror.

"I cannot wait until we are able to do this from the comfort of our own homes," Aletheia said rather straightly as she pulled me onto the platform, her long fingers tight and cold against my wrist. The screen before me turned on, and a soft but deep female voice bounced off the walls of the booth.

"Welcome to Paradigm—a new way to view fashion. Please stand still as we take your measurements," the sultry voice commanded. A small, white circle spun around and around in the center of the long screen.

"Aletheia…"

The Private hushed me, pointing to the screen. An image of myself popped up on the display like I was looking into a mirror. Except I was naked.

"Holy shit!" I screamed, immediately crossing one arm over my breasts and a hand over the apex of my thighs in an attempt to cover myself. The Rowyn in the screen was, in fact, a mirror image, arms and hands crossed over her body to retain modesty, her cheeks turning red.

Aletheia tugged my arms down. "Oh, stop it. We are all girls."

"Aren't you used to people staring at your bare body, Adellaide?" Bellona asked, her arms crossed tightly over her chest. I couldn't tell if the Major General was being sarcastic or not—testing me or not.

I let Aletheia tug down my arms, and I stood a little straighter to feign confidence.

"Yes, Major General. Though, I usually know when I will be undressed before someone—even a prostitute hates a stalker."

Bellona snorted as she sat on a stool in the front left corner of the small booth and crossed one leg over the other. Her foot bobbed like she was already done with the endeavor despite it just beginning.

I returned my attention to my bare image on the screen while silently reminding myself that my person was not actually naked. What I was seeing wasn't actually real. Bellona and Aletheia couldn't see the beauty mark on my right breast, the hair on my unshaven legs, or the scar above my left hip. It was like the Rowyn on the screen was painted over in some fake flesh.

"So, how does this work?" I asked.

Aletheia cleared her throat. "This platform and that camera" —she started pointing to a small red light above the screen— "use low-level electro pulses in addition to infrared and normal light spectrum to create a realistic picture of you on the screen. Paradigm has calculated your total body fat, water, and muscle mass. It also calculated your measurements like your bust, waist, hips, leg, and torso length and analyzed your hair and skin tone, texture, and type. So, the Adellaide reflected isn't exactly a mirror image, but it's pretty damn close." Aletheia scanned the image of me up and down, then turned her head over a shoulder, her dark coils bobbing, and winked at me.

I tried not to blush. "Ok…now what?" I asked, hands on my hips. It startled my senses to see the image of me touching bare skin while my hands felt the soft cotton of Callum's shirt.

"Well, what do you want to shop for?" Aletheia's tone was direct and to the point, edged with a hint of apathy as she inched over to the right side of the screen. She waved her hand over the panel, and a menu popped up. "We can shop for care products best suited for your skin and hair needs. We can look at tops, pants, skirts—"

"She needs a dress," Bellona sighed.

"We will start with undergarments—"

"I think I can do that on my own," I interrupted. Bellona shot me a look, piqued with curiosity, probably wondering why a prostitute would again ask for modesty. "I just don't want to waste your time," I added smoothly.

Aletheia leaned against the wall. "Training was a waste of my time. This"—she gave my body another look-over—"is definitely not. And trust me, once you get the hang of this, I will leave you be. Then I have an excuse to do some shopping of my own." She cocked a half smile, but Bellona rolled her eyes.

Aletheia pressed buttons on the screen, not moving from her casual stance against the wall. "Let's try this on, Adellaide."

A red, lacy bra and pair of underwear donned the screen version of myself.

A rock settled deep in the pit of my stomach.

"Oh, that's nice." Aletheia winked at me.

"Okay." Bellona shot up from her stool. "I am not going to sit here and watch you flirt with your fantasies, *Private*." Bellona started shoving Aletheia out of the booth. "I think Ms. Stevens can figure it out from here."

"I was just trying to help," I heard Aletheia mumble through the curtain as I glanced at Bellona in confusion. But she wasn't paying attention to me as she shut the shimmering curtain behind her.

I glanced back at myself on the screen and smiled. "But wait!" I yelled after the two soldiers. "How do I add this to my cart?"

The only response I received was a sultry laugh from Aletheia.

———

We finished our shopping in about two hours. Aletheia eventually stepped back into my booth to help me with personal care products. She switched a setting on the screen that basically detailed every single flaw on my body that needed to be remedied and what products would fix them. I had never felt so overwhelmed and insecure in my whole life.

"Are you sure you don't want to get that mole removed?" Aletheia grimaced, pointing to my right breast as we left the store. "Some would say it's not very beseeching."

I battered her hand away. "I'm not looking for perfection. Besides, some have called it sexy."

"Well, you're not a little Median whore anymore, Adellaide. You're an Excelsian angel." Her voice was a dark, smooth caress as she hooked an arm through mine. I stopped myself as I tried to jerk away from the Private, her gesture catching me off guard. Aletheia must have noticed my hesitation because she gave me a small, reassuring smile, different from her usual feline grin.

"Don't say things like that, Private." Bellona rolled her eyes. "She is not some pet you get to keep."

"No, but maybe she will be Callum's." Aletheia's voice was a taunting song as she nudged me with an elbow. Heat burned my chest, and suddenly, I did feel like a mistress—using my person as a currency to get whatever I needed to survive, shoving whatever feelings I had down deep to get the job done.

But isn't that what you've always done, Red?

My stomach lurched in discomfort at the reality.

You don't have time for this, I reminded myself, willing the emotions away. Willing them deep down again, in the bottomless pit—the dark abyss into which I tossed all my uncomfortable feelings, memories, and even dreams.

My pain, or numbness…whatever I was feeling…must have been written across my face because Aletheia shoved me gently with her hip. "Oh, I am just ribbing you, Adellaide."

I faked a laugh. "If Callum keeps paying for everything, I might just have to follow him around like a little fox."

Bellona grunted before picking up her pace to walk ahead of us.

I glanced sidelong at Aletheia.

"Oh, don't worry about her. She is just a buzzkill." Aletheia pulled out a small pen-like object and took a puff from it. I had seen the Private do the exact same thing all day. Inside or outside, it didn't matter, and she must have done it at least a dozen times. I had no idea what it was or what she was inhaling, and I didn't bother to ask.

Bellona stopped about ten feet in front of us and tapped impatiently on her COM. When we caught up to her, the Major General informed us she had called a lift to take us the rest of the way to Callum's. I kept quiet for most of the ride as I gazed outside my window, memorizing street names and buildings, trying to map out the city in my head. Bellona and Aletheia were quiet too, perhaps tired from a long day of shopping and babysitting. Or maybe they were just sick of each other.

———

As we strode through Callum's door, we were welcomed by boxes and bags of all my latest purchases, which was probably the closest thing to magic I had ever seen. Sirius wagged his tail excitedly as his tongue hung out the right side of his mouth. Aletheia helped me bring everything into the spare room and organized my closet as I stored my toiletries in the bathroom.

"Aletheia, I think I bought too much stuff!" I yelled to her as I struggled to find room for the last few items I had left to stow.

"Theia," she corrected, "and no, you did not! Honestly, if you do stay in Excelsis, you will need more."

I sat on the bed when I was finished, and Sirius jumped up to sit beside me, nudging my hand with his wet nose, a silent request for a scratch behind his ears.

"Do you know how to do make-up?" Aletheia asked, placing the last item of clothing in the closet. I shook my head. That was one detail I could not lie about—I would be caught as soon as I stepped out of the spare room looking like a complete idiot or with tears running down my face from accidentally stabbing an eye.

"Of course not," she murmured under her breath. Aletheia sauntered over and plopped herself on the bed, crossing one long leg under her. "Look." Her voice was a stern whisper. "I don't give a damn where you came from. Honestly, I don't give a flying fuck if you are a Rebel spy. Not my problem."

The shock across my face was genuine because she should care—Aletheia was a Coalition soldier. Then again, as I stared into the Private's brown eyes, I realized that besides clothing and fashion, Aletheia didn't give much of a damn about anything.

"But if you are going to sell this ruse, you have got to be better because she…" Aletheia pointed to Callum's living room, where Bellona worked remotely from her COM-tab. "She's not buying it. Any damn prostitute in Media would know how to do make-up. I know for a fact there is a black market down there for the stuff we use up here, and most of it goes straight to the brothels."

I opened my mouth to say something, but she lifted a hand to silence me.

"Don't. Whatever the fuck you're going to say, do not say it. I don't want you to think you can trust me, because you can't. So don't.

"However, I am in a good mood from ditching training all day, so I will help you. But tonight, you use that holo"—Aletheia pointed to the screen in the corner of the room—"and you do some damn research on makeup. And you better fucking believe Callum and Bellona will be surveying your search history, so if either of them asks why, you tell them you want to know the latest trends to fit in better." She studied me. "And do not erase anything you search for. That is a red flag. They *will* find out everything and anything you do on any holo or COM-device. And you *will* get caught and questioned."

For the first time, I wondered if Aletheia was a Resistance agent—if she really did want to help me but couldn't because that would put her own mission at risk. The question formed on my tongue, but to even ask if she was Resistance would only confirm her suspicions of me.

Aletheia stood up, uncurling her long, lean legs in a fluid motion, then leaned down. Her lips were to my ear and her dark coils tickled my neck as she whispered, "Do not get comfortable, or you will slip up, and we will take you down."

We.

Her words were as much a threat as they were a warning. No. She wasn't Resistance. She could be messing with me, but her tone was too real. Too raw. It was the truth. Aletheia never did anything unless she was ordered to or if it suited her best interests, so I assumed, for whatever reason, turning me in right now did not suit the Private's best interests.

"Now, go sit down at the desk," she said loudly. "I'll show you how to not look like a Median Mistress."

Light footsteps tapped outside of the guest room and into the living room. Bellona was listening. And Aletheia knew. She had timed everything perfectly—she knew exactly when Bellona got curious, when to start whispering, and when to end the conversation.

"I'm not sure you're the one for the job, Private," Bellona quipped loudly, her voice echoing through the walls, probably trying to cover up her footsteps.

Aletheia turned to me and flicked her brows up. Yes. She was exactly who I should watch out for.

———

"Don't you have anything, ugh, I don't know, more revealing?" Aletheia called from my closet as I sat at the guest bedroom's vanity. Powder and the scent of burning hair hung thick around me.

"I thought I was supposed to put a damper on the 'Brothel Mistress' aesthetic."

"This will do, I guess." Aletheia pulled out a black dress and ordered me to put it on with a pair of tights she threw at me. I complied. The sleeves of the dress reached to just above my elbow, and each side of my waist was cut out to reveal bare skin opening to the back. An intricate golden embroidery stretched across my breasts, curling down to just above the knees, forcing eyes to wander along my curves. Aletheia helped me button up the back of my dress and picked out black booties to wear that laced up to my ankle.

"Just one more thing." Aletheia poked through her purse and pulled out a deep crimson lipstick. "Perfect," she purred after she swiped the color across my lips a few times. My skin felt heavy from all the makeup she'd painted on my face.

She pulled me toward the door, and my knees buckled under the odd pressure of walking in heels, but my body was fit and adjusted quickly.

Opening the door, Aletheia chimed in only a way her low, caressing voice could, "One date for the General."

Date? My pulse pounded in my chest.

Callum turned on his stool. He was sitting at the kitchen island, a crystal glass in hand. His emerald eyes twinkled a little, brows lifting in either surprise or awe.

My cheeks heated.

"Great," Callum croaked. He cleared his throat before continuing. "We are expected soon." The Lieutenant General stood up and swung his drink back, draining the glass in one easy gulp. After setting the empty glass down on the marble counter, one ice cube clinking gently in the glass, Callum straightened his white button-up shirt and black jacket.

I glanced around the flat. "Where is the Major General?" I asked gently.

"Gone. She had work to do and didn't want 'to waste any more of her time,'" Callum mocked. "Theia, can you grab Adellaide's coat, please?"

She rolled her eyes, mumbling something about not being his mutt, but acquiesced. When Aletheia came back, I shrugged on my ebony coat and glanced down at myself, noticing my lack of color. I felt a little more like Rowyn. Though, I wasn't sure how Adellaide felt about it.

"I must look like a shadow," I said.

Callum shrugged his shoulders. "I don't care much for color, anyway."

I smiled slightly. "Me neither."

Callum held out an arm for me to take. It was strong and hard and steadied me as I wobbled on my heels.

"Okay, have fun, kids." Aletheia waved us off as she lounged on the couch.

Callum halted, turning his head back to her. "No. You are leaving, too. Go home. Do something productive with your life."

"Well, there is this guy I met today that wanted to hook up…" she trailed off.

"Not what I meant," Callum said in a stern voice, but Aletheia's eyes remained focused on her nails as she picked at them. "Whatever, just don't have him over here." Callum turned back toward the door and whistled for Sirius to follow us.

The hybrid snuck out the entrance like a ghost escaping the light.

"Sirius is coming?"

Callum nodded. "He's been cooped up all day. Besides, he loves to chase the squirrels through my parents' garden."

My heart stopped—my whole body stopped, pulling Callum to a halt. "That's where we are going? To your parents'?"

Excitement should have been what rattled my bones. Instead, terror struck my body like lightning.

"Yes," he said matter-of-factly. "I have dinner with them every Friday."

I knew if there was any information about my father, it would lay with the Osoufs—specifically Callum's mother—but meeting his parents would greatly increase the chance of someone discovering my real identity.

"I can just stay here." I dug my feet into the hard floor. "I promise I won't try to leave or anything. I will just watch the holo with Aletheia or something."

Callum gave me a wicked smile, and my heart stilled. "I don't think so," he said and led me out the door.

CHAPTER 15

Sirius bounded ahead of us as we strolled up the walkway lined with bare cherry blossom trees, and my mind whirled from dejá vu.

The grand, white stone house stretched before us, magnificent steps yawning up to the opulent Lyptus front door intricately carved with whorls and knots like streams of water. It also bore three glass panes, each covered with vines and flowers molded from iron and matching the door knocker and knob. However, what caught my eye was perched above the door. Looking down upon us and every other guest who had entered this home was a stone Direwolf. The beast's teeth were bared—its maw open wide to reveal large canine sabers—and it looked as though it was bounding out of the woods in attack. It was surrounded by knots, similar to those on the door, and shining from the marble animal were two emerald eyes.

"It's our family emblem," Callum said and then clanked the iron knocker three times.

I nodded. I remembered staring at a similar Direwolf in Militum. It scared me as a child, but now it felt more nostalgic. Somehow, it felt like home. I turned toward Callum, and his eyes seemed to dance in the lantern light, similar to the sparkling jewels that loomed over us.

The door opened, a stout butler greeting us with a silent nod as he swung the door wide. Callum led us into an ornate foyer with marble flooring made of all different colors that twisted and twined in more vines and branches. Above us, light bounced off an opulent crystalline chandelier with a gold-flaked frame carved into leaves and flowers of impeccable design. I felt like I had wandered into an enchanted forest from a storybook.

The butler helped remove my coat for me, and as I finished peeling off my outer layer, I noted the windows with long velvet curtains of forest green and gold and the enormous staircase matched in color and patterns to the front door. I was entranced by the beauty and wonder of this manor. My heart fluttered each moment I noticed something new, and my breath kept escaping me in waves of awe.

I was brought back to reality as a light but sturdy hand rested against the bare skin of my back. I looked to my right to see Callum staring down at me intently, his slight smile burning into me like a brand. The curve of my spine grew warm and tingly at his touch, and I fought the blush that threatened to bloom on my cheeks.

The Lieutenant General nodded his head to the right and pressed his hand more firmly into me, leading us to the next room. We walked through glass French doors into a dining room as equally exquisite as the foyer but in a different way. Deep blue covered the walls, and dark wood was the choice for all of the furniture. Little accents of gold and deep green flitted around the room, finding themselves in vines on the curtains, branches on the plates, flowers flowing from vases, and gilded leaves on the fixtures.

"Oh, Callum, dear! Hello, hello!" An old woman chimed from across the room. Well, not old…but not exactly young either. The woman's hair was the color of sea salt and cracked pepper, long, with gentle waves pulled back at the nape of her neck. Her eyes were blue and bright with wisdom, but where I expected wrinkles to deeply crease along her eyes and mouth, there were none. Her voice warbled with years of use, though the woman who greeted Callum looked no more than forty-five.

"Amma. You are looking stunning as usual." Callum greeted the woman with a peck on each cheek. Her smile was pure and genuine, a light blush kissing her cheeks at his compliment.

She patted his left cheek softly. "Oh, my boy. You are too kind." The woman peered behind Callum to meet my gaze. "And I did not realize you were bringing a guest!" The woman nudged Callum out of the way, nearly shoving him over to get to me. "And a beautiful one at that." She winked at him while passing.

I held out a hand to the woman. "Adellaide." I forced a gentle smile onto my lips despite the thundering of my heart deep in my chest that reverberated through my whole body.

"What a lovely name! So very lovely." She grasped my hands gently, and hers felt cold against my skin, but they were soft as satin. The scent of mulling spices and rosewood fluttered in the air around me as she pecked my cheek. "I am Callum's grandmother, Rheamarie, though you can call me Amma if you would like. I know a couple of Callum's little friends do. But it is whatever you prefer, dearie."

Rheamarie removed her hands from mine and turned to take Callum by the shoulders, shaking him a little. "Oh, this is so exciting! Your Afi will be so happy!" She clapped her hands together, the several rings adorning her fingers glittering in the candlelight before she pushed through a swinging door adjacent to the foyer's entrance. Through the wall, I heard Callum's grandmother talk to who I assumed was Callum's grandfather. Something about a 'young lady,' and I started to wonder if Callum had ever brought a girl to a family dinner before.

I sucked on my bottom lip when Callum turned to me. "That is my Amma…"

I quietly nodded, glancing around the room. "Your parents have a beautiful home."

"Thank you. Before we moved to Imperium about eight years ago for my father's job, my parents built this manor as an exact replica of their home in Militum."

"Do they still own the property?"

Callum nodded. "Yes. My mother's parents live there now, and we visit them on occasion. It kind of serves as a vacation home. Though, since it looks exactly like this one, it doesn't feel like much of a vacation, and when I do go to Militum, I usually have work to attend to."

"And what does your father do?"

"He sits on the Council of Delegates. Look…" Callum combed his fingers through his hair. "I know you didn't expect this…"

I eyed him wearily. "I just don't understand why I am here."

"I—" The door behind Callum swung open softly, cutting him off. Another woman strode into the dining room, a woman I vaguely recognized. My mind started pulling at the strings of memory, trying to match this woman's face to a name.

"Ah, Callum, nice to see you." The woman's voice was cold and indifferent as she breezed by Callum, her straight white hair shifting gently with her brisk movements. She adjusted a glistening table setting, slightly tapping each piece of flatware this way and that as if arranging them to perfection. She then proceeded to walk around the dining room, modifying the bouquet of flowers and the ferns in the middle of the grand table.

And as the word started to form on Callum's lips, the name clicked.

"Mother…" Callum started.

Dr. Freyja Osouf. This was the woman who worked with my father.

I tried to make myself small, not wishing for this woman to see me, but to my delight, Callum's mother was far too preoccupied at the moment.

"Eunice! Eunice, are these really the flowers that were ordered? They look absolutely horrendous!" The stiff-backed woman shouted curtly in no particular direction and to no particular person as she stood across the table from me. Her hair was platinum and cut at her shoulders, framing her oval face and high cheekbones. She wore a white dress with gold buttons, and her shoulders were covered with a gold lace caplet.

"Mother," Callum tried again, his voice deep and stern now. Her eyes darted up toward me instead of to her son.

I swallowed the knot in my throat.

"This is Adellaide."

The woman's quick-silver eyes bore into mine as she straightened. My skin went cold. She tugged on her dress and swiped at the fabric to loosen the wrinkles she may have caused by bending over before she strode around the table and back to her son's side. She looked me up and down, then extended a hand.

"Freyja." Her introduction was hard and short, but there was no glimmer of recognition in her eyes.

I relaxed. It seemed that fate had dealt me a hand I couldn't throw away. "Pleasure," I said, taking her hand. Freyja gave one short shake, then promptly removed her hand from mine.

The mother turned to her son. "I thought I told you Laurunda would be joining us this evening." She chided her son, her voice tight and quiet but just loud enough for me to hear. I stiffened.

Callum smiled. "I thought since you were bringing a friend," —his arm curled around my waist—"I could bring one as well." I felt the heat rise from my neck to my cheeks, leaving the rest of my body chilled and clammy. Freyja's eyes returned to mine as she offered a cold smile.

"Eunice!" The matron of the house yelled, again to no one and nowhere in particular. "Eunice, set another place at the table! It seems we have another dinner guest!" Freyja looked me up and down one last time before marching out of the room.

———

Rheamarie was correct. Callum's 'Afi,' Odin, was indeed very excited to meet me. Odin seemed even more kind than his wife, though a bit more reserved. He emanated a grandfatherly peace, and I was grateful to be sitting next to him at the dinner table. A woman named Laurunda arrived at the door very shortly after the maid, Eunice, had finished resetting the table. She stood two inches shorter than I in her golden heels that were strikingly similar to the luminescent color of her hair, half of which was pulled back, showcasing her graceful neck and bright, sapphire eyes. Her full lips were light pink, complimenting the soft blue of her dress, which was made of near-see-through material that hung from a thick bronze collar around her neck.

Freyja greeted Laurunda enthusiastically and with a kiss on the cheek as she handed the young lady's coat to the butler. "Ah, Laurunda, donning blue as usual," Freyja observed.

"Oh, you know Senator Osouf." Laurunda's voice sounded like wind chimes on a summer breeze. "He prefers me to wear blue. It soothes him." She smiled sweetly to Freyja, and Callum's mother returned the sentiment, though it didn't quite meet her eyes.

"Oh, Callum!" Laurunda chirped, embracing him tightly. "It is so good to see you again." Callum hesitantly wrapped an arm around the small woman, patting her gently on the back.

"You too, Laurunda," he said through tight lips.

"Oh, you know to call me Auri."

And I want to hurl.

Laurunda stepped back, both hands lingering on Callum's biceps. "Wow, you have gotten so strong!" Callum tried to keep her at a distance with both his hands propped on her small hips an arm's length away.

"I saw you three weeks ago, Laurunda." Callum gave a quick glance in my direction as if silently pleading for help. And suddenly, I knew why I was here.

Well, fuck him. Callum was willing to take a girl out of slavery just to make her a pawn in his games.

Little does he know I have my own game to play.

"Auri," she corrected.

My stomach heaved.

"Laurunda…" Callum said pointedly, grabbing my waist and pulling me to his side. The urge to shove him away surged through me, but I resisted, not yet knowing how I wanted to play my part. "This is Adellaide." Laurunda's bright smile faltered a millimeter before growing even larger.

"It's so nice to meet another one of Callum's *friends.*" She held my hand so gently I barely registered what was happening until she moved it up and down in a handshake.

I smiled. "Likewise."

"Wow, that lip color is splendid! It really takes the attention off your luxuriant eyebrows." Before I could respond, Laurunda floated across the dining room to greet Rheamarie and Odin.

Blankly, I stared after the young lady, fingers hovering over an eyebrow. Callum seized my hand and squeezed it once. "You will get used to it."

"Used to what?" I shook away from his grasp.

"That." He nodded toward Laurunda. "A backhanded compliment. Though, I thought you would be used to them, given your"—he leaned in closer—"profession."

Right. I supposed there would have been a lot of pettiness between women in a brothel.

"It just *sounded* so genuine."

"Oh, you should hear her and Aletheia get at it. It's like a passive-aggressive catfight." For a second, I thought he sounded amused, but not a glimmer of humor was written on his face.

"I wouldn't think they would run in the same friend circle," I said, noting the differences between Laurunda and Aletheia. Theia was so dark and moody, while Laurunda was bright and…annoying.

"Not at all." Callum pulled my chair out to seat me next to his grandfather. "But if I am out and Laurunda sees me, she has to say hello, even if I am with company such as Sancus and

Aletheia. I think they knew each other from primary school, if I remember correctly. They were in the same grade. The feud has been long-lasting." His voice was a caress against the shell of my ear before he took his seat on my other side, and I was left cold and haunted.

When I glanced around the table, I noticed one seat remained empty. It was the seat at the head. Callum must have noticed as well because he asked Freyja if his father would be joining us tonight, nodding to the empty chair.

"Yes," she said curtly. "He will just be a little longer." Freyja glanced at Laurunda. "Work kept him late." Before Callum could ask any more questions, Freyja rang a small bronze handbell placed by her wine glass.

Immediately, a door that was seamlessly part of the wall opened, and out flowed maids carrying bowls of soup, steaming and filling the room with a rich, earthy scent. The maids placed each of our soups down simultaneously, and the head maid, who I presumed to be Eunice, announced the course as a pumpkin sage bisque with a traditional French baguette. My mouth watered instantly, though I had no idea what any of those food items were, except for pumpkins—there was a patch that grew wild near the Shed.

The maids silently left the way they'd come, and as soon as the wall clicked shut, Callum's father entered through the foyer doors.

"Sorry I am late, everyone." He walked over to Freyja and bent down to give her a quick kiss on the head. "Work kept me." The man sat in the empty spot at the head of the table between his wife and Laurunda. His eyes lingered on the latter.

"Perfect, now we can open the wine!" Freyja said, averting her eyes from her husband's lustful gaze, which was not directed at her but Laurunda. Freyja's expression was stony as she rang her little bell, and Eunice appeared a moment later through the wall with a bottle of wine in tow.

The maid presented the wine as a Viognier, and after

allowing Freyja to taste and approve the wine, she poured a small glass for everyone.

"Father," Callum said, interrupting his father's sip of wine, "this is Adellaide Stevens."

Callum's father looked at his wife sidelong. A flick of her eyebrows was her only response. "Adellaide," Callum's father tested my name on his tongue as his hazel eyes met mine. "Senator Erebus Osouf," he introduced himself.

Callum's eyes rolled at the title.

In my childhood, I had only met Erebus a handful of times. From my understanding, he wasn't around much, too busy running the Coalition from whatever governmental role he had wormed his way into.

"Pleasure." Then, the silver-haired man raised his glass of wine before I could respond. "A toast to Adellaide!" I noticed the Senator's left hand slip under the table. Laurunda shifted, a seductive smile creeping across her face. "It's always a pleasure to have new company in our home and at our table."

"*Salularia!*" everyone called out in unison. Everyone except for me. I merely nodded and smiled softly at the patriarch before sipping from my wine glass. The white wine was exquisite—light and refreshing. It filled my nose with the scent of roses and sweet fruit before it passed over my lips. It tasted of honeysuckle and spices, and it was almost oily as it flowed across my tongue.

"Adellaide," Freyja started, "I have not heard *anything* about you. What do you do for a living?"

"Actually, Mother," Callum interjected before I had a chance to open my mouth, "Adellaide has been selected for the Excelsis Integration Program. Currently, her paperwork is being processed, but she will be able to find a suitable host and job soon."

"Oh, it is so nice that you are volunteering despite your busy schedule, Callum," Rheamarie said as she looked adoringly at her grandson.

Freyja pursed her lips. "How did you come into hosting this young girl, Callum?"

Callum's throat bobbed. "It was an unusual circumstance, but it is necessary that Adellaide stays in my care right now. As we wait for her acceptance into the program, I have taken on the role of host for the time being. Actually, Adellaide will be shadowing me in a couple days to see if the Military would be a good fit." Callum turned to me. "But, of course, we will need to schedule other shadowing opportunities so we can find you a good career to fit your skills."

Freyja's white brows were arched high in contempt. "And what are your skills?"

"Well…"

"Did you not just fire someone the other day, Freyja?" Odin chimed in, ignoring Freyja's question or perhaps not even hearing it.

Freyja's quicksilver eyes grew wide. "Pardon?"

"Yes," Rheamarie stepped in. "I believe you did say that yesterday. You fired one of your Laboratory assistants. Or was it your Laboratory assistant's assistant?"

"Um, yes. That is true." Freyja gripped her spoon tightly. "But a Laboratory assistant requires years of training."

I took a sip of wine, enjoying the cards fate continued to deal me. If I was going to be stuck here, I might as well get what I came for—some information on my father and his research. And what better place to uncover his secrets than in his former colleague's lab? "What is required of a Laboratory assistant?"

"They take detailed notes, clean equipment, and have a working knowledge of cellular and molecular biology, as well as genetics and biochemistry."

"Sounds right up my alley," I gloated.

"Adellaide—" Callum started, and a hand fell on my knee. I pulled my leg out from under his grasp.

"Biology was one of my best subjects during my meager Median education." I gave Freyja a sweet smile.

"Adellaide—" Callum warned through his teeth.

"I can start on Monday if that is all right with you, Dr. Osouf."

"Well, Ms. Stevens, there is usually a résumé submission process, then an interview process, and of course, you will need to be compatible with—"

"Oh, Freyja, throw the girl a bone," Odin insisted, waving his fork in the air.

"Yes, but—"

"I am sure you will do wonderfully, dearie!" Rheamarie clapped excitedly. "To your new job, Adellaide!"

Odin followed with a *"Salularia!"* Everyone raised a glass and toasted to my new job. Everyone except for Freyja.

During the rest of the dinner, I looked my enemies in the eyes, drank their wine, and shared their food. I memorized every bit of personal information they decided to share and planted seeds of trust so as to encourage them to share more over time. I eyed Laurunda wearily as if I really was a jealous lover and sucked up to Callum's parents and grandparents like I desired their approval. And most importantly, I remembered who I really was. I felt it in my bones.

I was a part of the Coalition Resistance Forces.

I was a secret agent deep inside Imperium to obtain information.

I was Red.

And I tapped my right temple twice.

CHAPTER 16

Callum and I didn't speak to each other as he drove the hover through Excelsis. Even Sirius remained quiet in the backseat, though I assumed it had less to do with his tiredness from chasing squirrels around the garden and more to do with his acute animal instincts sensing the taut string of tension connecting Callum and me. At twenty-two hundred, it seemed the night was still relatively young for the highest Circulum. The *trames* were teaming with people ready to start their Friday night adventures, which apparently was common within Excelsis, and there were lines of people outside various buildings with brightly colored lights and signs. Most patrons were dressed in slight, scandalous clothing that looked more like the undergarments I had bought earlier that day than real clothing to wear in public. I spent most of the ride to Callum's apartment mesmerized by the different colored lights and groups of people, a nice distraction from the anger that had settled beneath my rib cage.

Upon entering the flat, Sirius trotted in, glanced to Callum's room, then to the guest room where I was staying, almost like he was debating which bed to curl up in—who to curl up with. The hybrid looked back and forth again, before releasing a strangely human sigh and trudging to the living room. Sirius then proceeded to step onto the couch and curl up in the pillows.

I walked straight into the guest room and shut the door. I was done with people. I was done with Laurunda, I was done with Callum's family, I was done with *him*. I couldn't wrap my head around the fact that he would… No, that he *did* put me in such an uncomfortable situation. I was forced to meet his family while apparently pretending or at least alluding to being his little charity case. I threw my coat on the bed in frustration.

But now I am one step closer to uncovering information about my father's research, a small voice inside me whispered.

My anger drowned out that small voice.

He used me. He made me a pawn in his own stupid little family games. With no warning. No briefing. Nothing.

I started pulling out all the pins in my hair and placed them in a jar on my vanity. They tinkled gently against the porcelain in satisfying little clinks as my chestnut hair fell in billowing waves.

Callum took advantage of my vulnerable position.

I tugged off my tights and threw them at the closet door.

That's what you get for trusting him, Red. That's what you get for thinking he was the same caring little boy you once knew and not the Coalition Military dog he has become. I chastised myself as I reached between my shoulder blades to unbutton my dress. The brass was cold against my skin, the buttons smooth and small, and the loops they were bound by were even smaller. I tried to look in the mirror while unbuttoning them, contorting my body every which way to attack the problem from multiple angles.

"UGH!" I screamed in frustration, throwing my arms down at my sides. I shook them out, forcing the aches from my muscles, then tried again, tugging at the dress, at the buttons, at my hair, which kept getting tangled up in the obstacle.

"You have got to be fricken kidding me!" I yelled.

A gentle knock sounded at my door.

No. No. I do not need his help.

I tried to unbutton my dress again, but the Skies-damned brass buttons were so small and so slick.

Knocks echoed again.

I marched toward the door and swung it open.

"What?" I snapped.

Callum peered in. "I half expected your room to be destroyed by all the huffing and grunting going on here."

Your room.

A smile played at his lips as his gaze returned to me.

I started to shut the door, but Callum stopped it with his palm. "Can I help?" he asked quietly, gently, before glancing over my shoulder and nodding toward the back of my dress.

I couldn't help but roll my eyes as I turned my back to him, sweeping my hair over one shoulder. Callum's hands were warm and gentle as they worked the buttons on my dress. Each one popped effortlessly, but all I could focus on was the heat of Callum's breath caressing the nape of my neck and the back of my ear. The feeling sent chills down my spine, forcing my skin to shiver despite the heat rising to my cheeks and palms.

"I'm sorry. Are you okay?"

"I'm fine," I choked.

I heard Callum puff hot air into his hands, then the rubbing of skin on skin.

If he only knew what the real problem was.

No. I corrected myself. *There is no* real *problem.*

The last button released, exposing my back fully to him. We both lingered there for a moment, then I felt a hard finger drifting down my spine.

There is no problem at all, Red.

Shamelessly, I flipped my hair back over my shoulder, and it smacked the Lieutenant General in the face before it flowed freely down my back.

"Sorry," I quipped and turned to face him. I tried not to look at Callum—oh, how I tried—but he was a solid force in front of me. His black jacket was removed to reveal his white button-up with the top four golden buttons unfastened, exposing his bare chest. As my eyes lingered there, a breath escaped me. Before I could meet his eyes, I grabbed the door and started to push it shut, but his arm reached out again, palm flat against the white wood door.

"What?" I finally looked up. Callum's cheeks were flushed, and gold flecks flared to life in his eyes.

"I didn't mean to…"

"To what? To embarrass me? To lie to me? Was this all some test to see if I would be welcomed into your precious society?" I dug a finger into his chest, and I felt his heart beating rapidly under the pad of my forefinger. The Lieutenant General merely stood, straight and solid as an oak tree, ready to take whatever storm of fury I was about to unleash.

"Or do you get your jollies off watching Laurunda paw for you like a jealous cat? Or maybe you like the whole 'forbidden love' cliche? Is that what does it for you?"

"No," he protested, face hard. He gently removed my finger from his chest.

"Then what was all that? Because I did not enjoy becoming a pawn in your family Olympics. I was quite terrified, in fact, becoming a lead role in your familial drama."

"Well, what is it?" Callum mocked. "Are you a pawn or a lead role?"

He was trying to throw me off guard—to catch me in a hole.

"I don't know what I am!" I threw my hands up in the air. "I simply do not like the fact you forced me into any part to play!"

"Then choose, Adellaide." The name sounded like a plea on his lips—the name that was not my name. But, *oh*, how I wanted Callum to say my name like that. The thought of it caused my knees to buckle. "What part do you want to play?" He took a step closer to me, and the air we breathed danced in a forbidden melody.

"I do not desire to be a part of your game." I stepped

backward, but as I did, the light in his eyes flickered, like my words caused him pain.

"If you don't *desire* to be a part of my *game*, then why did you play along?"

A harsh laugh escaped from my chest. "What choice did I have?"

"Do not play at that, Adellaide. Do not make yourself a damsel in this narrative. You are better than that."

"And what do you know of me?"

Callum's smile was canine as he stepped forward so that we were nose to nose, but I stood firm, not allowing myself to back down. "I know that you are a force to be reckoned with, *Ms. Stevens*. And..." he trailed off.

And what? I wanted to shout.

But Callum took a deep breath and closed his eyes. "I didn't know what *game* I was playing tonight, Adellaide, but I knew you could handle it. And you did. Spectacularly, in fact." He ran a hand through his hair. "But I do apologize. I should have warned you. I was merely afraid you would refuse. And my parents... Well, they are..." I watched as his gaze shifted from my eyes to my lips, then back up. "Difficult to say the least. I wanted the attention to be elsewhere for once. Which was selfish..." He kept speaking, so I couldn't. "I was selfish." His hand moved toward mine, like he wanted to take it, but he stopped himself. "I am sorry." Callum's eyes were earnest.

"I thought, coming up to Excelsis, I wouldn't be used any longer, Lieutenant General."

His lips pursed. "I... I didn't mean to use you, Ms. Stevens." There it was again, the flick of his eyes to my lips.

"And I do not enjoy being taken advantage of."

"I apologize."

"Nor do I appreciate being lied to." Our breaths intertwined.

"I know." A whisper. Another flick of his eyes.

Then why did you do it?

"I know because of my *profession* that you must think I have little standard, but quite the opposite is true, Lieutenant General," I explained. "You see, in my *profession,* I get to choose which of my vulnerabilities will be exposed. I get to choose how I react and feel." I couldn't help but glance at his lips when I heard his breaths quicken. "You crossed a line tonight, and I suggest you do not do it again." Callum's eyes lazily rolled over me—all of me—and my hip burned as his hand hovered over it like he was ready to pull me into him, like he was ready to claim me.

I shoved the Lieutenant General over the threshold, swiftly closed the door in his face, and sighed deeply, though not quietly. I turned and slumped against the door as a warm chuckle sounded from the other side of the wood. I couldn't hold back the smile.

"So, I can't make you a pawn in my game, but you can make me one in yours?" A light thump reverberated through the wood separating us, and the gentle baritone of his voice sounded so close I wondered if Callum was resting his forehead on the other side of the door, longing to be close to me.

"That's right," I purred.

He laughed again, a deep baritone song that resonated in my bones—in my soul. "Well, what if we played the same game, Adellaide?"

Indeed, Lieutenant General. What if we played the same game?

Despite having a job lined up, Callum insisted I still shadow him for a day. He thought it best that I knew all my options and not jump into anything.

I got the feeling Callum did not want me to work with his mother, or maybe it was the bio lab in general. Perhaps he thought a potential Resistance spy could glean more top-secret information in the laboratories than the Military Base. Or perhaps there would be more oversight in the Military fields.

After a shower, I pulled my hair up into a tight pony and tugged on a set of athletic clothes—a shimmering gold sports bra, tight black leggings with mesh cut-outs all down my left leg, and a matching cropped sweater. Once I was dressed, I plucked my contacts out of a small container with a special cleansing liquid Metis had concocted specifically for them, and I placed them over each eye. I blinked a few times, and once the contacts were adjusted, text appeared across my vision.

1 Unread Message, Blink Twice to Open

I blinked twice.

Metis' image appeared in front of me, but it was fuzzy and broken, like it was a poor recording. His voice boomed, but not in my ears. In my head.

"Red. I trust you're all right. I apologize for takin' so long to contact ya again. We've had some…complications here on Base. Everyone got back from Imperium all right, except for you 'n Ulysses, 'n Hoenir's fuckin' gripey about it. He's been sittin' everyone on yer team down individually 'n debriefin' them. Made me sit in every single one of the bloody damn meetin's, too. Hardly had a moment to myself, or to work with Mr. Owens, for that matter. But no one knows what happened to you or Ulysses, 'n we have received no word from any of our contacts about the two of ya. Hoenir's best guess is that the two of ya are captured or dead."

Dead?

"Anyways, I know this mission of yers didn't start as planned, but yer exactly where ya need to be. Turns out, the computer virus didn't work. The Coalition still seems to be functionin' normally on a technological level, so we are preparin' for an attack any day. What I need ya to do is keep yer eyes and ears open for any information pertainin' to the Resistance—any captures, any press releases on the whereabouts of our Base.

Hell, even if the average Joe is chattin' about the Resistance, I want to know about it.

"I'll do what I can get gather some dirt about Lieutenant General Osouf 'n his family—hopefully, I can find somethin' to use against 'em. I see where ya are as an opportunity and, honestly, somethin' we should have done years ago. But seein' as Hoenir thinks differently, yer mission is our little secret."

Metis glanced over his shoulder before looking back at the recording device…or was he looking into a mirror and recording with his eye? "Your sister is safe. Niahm is safe. The rest of yer team is safe. Just focus on yer mission." He glanced over his shoulder again. "And be careful, Red. I don't think Ulysses is captured or dead. Hoenir's spent hours by himself, locked up in that fuckin' office of his, 'n during those hours, I've heard whisperin'. I think Ulysses is up to somethin'. Just a hunch. I'm preppin' an emergency exit strategy, but it'll take a few weeks." Metis' mechanical eye whirled. "I assure you, I will keep your sister safe."

Metis' face disappeared, and another message paned over my vision.

To Delete Message, Close Eyes for Three Seconds

I squeezed my eyes shut, tears pricking at my lids.

One. Two. Three.

Message Deleted

To send current footage saved to Metis Barnes, blink twice

I blinked twice, and a tear crept down my cheek.

Files sent

My vision returned to me, and I found myself staring into the bathroom mirror, my face contorted in confusion.

I thought about recording another message, but I didn't know what to say.

Captured. Or dead.

Reign thinks I am captured or dead.

My breaths came unevenly.

Calm down, Red. I told myself as I forced air through my nostrils. *You are not in this alone. Metis knows what he is doing...I hope.*

I shoved my fear and anxiety down deep as I hurriedly brushed my teeth and applied a thin layer of jet-black mascara to my lashes. When I entered the kitchen, black trainers in hand, Callum was leaning against the kitchen counter, examining his COM-tab in one hand and holding a steaming cup in the other. He donned his Military uniform; every brass button and medal was polished to a shine, sparkling gently in the warm morning light peeking in through the windows, and his hair was slicked up and back, flowing like he had just run his hand through the sand-colored strands. His green eyes snapped to me for a moment, then returned back to his device.

"Perfect." He took a large swig from the white cup he grasped, then set it in the steel sink. "Put on your coat, and we will head out." Sirius stood up from where he was lounging on the couch and stretched, yawning deeply.

"You sure you want me to shadow you today? Think of all the Military secrets I could learn if I really am a Rebel spy." I winked at Callum.

He pinned me down with his eyes, brows creasing. "You bring up a good point. Maybe I should just set you free amongst the city so you could wreak havoc among the Circulum."

I lowered my head as a lie formed on my tongue. "I just don't want to be an inconvenience."

He didn't make me look at him. He didn't try to comfort me. Callum merely pulled on his black gloves with shimmering brass buttons. "I think of you as more of a challenge, Ms. Stevens. And I do enjoy a good challenge."

CHAPTER 17

I peered out the window of the black hover as Callum drove us through Excelsis to the Third Ward, which mostly consisted of the enormous Military Base. We flew past long, grey barrack houses while Callum explained how each city within the Coalition had a Military Base in the Third Ward, and this one wasn't even the largest. Since we were in the Capitol, Imperium had the largest First Ward—the Governing Ward—whereas the Coalition's city of Militum had the largest Military Base because it was the Coalition's Military headquarters.

"Then, shouldn't you be in Militum if you are training to be General?" I asked after we had parked the hover and strode into the Military Base's large training complex.

"No. The general position I am to fill sits on the Coalition Council of Delegates, as well. I will be representing the entirety of the Coalition's Military when it comes to passing laws, offering assistance, and giving advice to the other delegates."

"So, what are we doing here?" I gestured to the empty, white-washed hallways.

Callum ran a hand through his hair and stopped in front of two large steel doors. "I'm checking in on some training today."

Callum opened the door easily, revealing an enormous gymnasium. It was grey and dim but easily three times the size of CRF's gym. In the middle stood a square, raised platform with roped fences on each side. Callum entered first, and as he marched into the gym, every soldier stood at attention. I followed behind as the Lieutenant General looked everyone over, hands folded together behind his back. I spotted Aletheia among the squadron, though there was no hint of the usual feline grin she favored. Instead, her jaw was set, and her eyes…well, her eyes screamed in an eternal fury. Callum stepped before the captain, and he looked the soldier over, scrutinizing every detail of the stern man's uniform and person. Captain Rickert, according to the golden nametag glinting on his left pectoral, had slate grey eyes, his hair identical in color, and a scar marring his left eyebrow.

I tapped my right temple twice, and the familiar red light blinked in the corner of my vision.

"Lieutenant General," the captain greeted Callum, still standing at attention. He was the only soldier besides Callum in full Military Uniform. His squadron was dressed in black fatigues, their ranks and full titles stitched in gold on every soldier's left pectoral and right arm.

"At ease," Callum commanded, his voice clear and confident. Then, he addressed the captain. "I am here to oversee hand-to-hand combat training. Ms. Stevens is shadowing me for her Integration Program."

"Yes, sir."

On the far wall of the gym, there was a screen, like a giant COM-pad. Each of the soldiers had their first initial and last name on the board, ranked from highest to lowest, followed by specific achievements they had earned.

I turned to Callum. "Aletheia's in last…" I whispered.

Callum nodded knowingly.

"Is it because you and Bellona had pulled her out of training a couple of times?"

He shook his head. "She claims 'unfair treatment.' Aletheia thinks she is being cheated, and she gets placed in a year."

"So, you want to see for yourself?"

Callum nodded again. "The captain knows I am friends with her and Sancus. Since I am here, he will try to 'prove' Aletheia's unsuitability."

And like clockwork, the captain's voice boomed, echoing throughout the gymnasium. "Gillian, Bridges! In the ring!"

Aletheia climbed through the ropes, followed by a huge brute of a man, Bridges. He was close to seven feet tall and as broad as an ox, muscles nearly ripping the seams of his combat uniform. His dull brown hair was cut short, accentuating his protruding brow bone and strong jawline.

"That man is massive!" I whispered.

Callum raised his head knowingly.

It was like the captain paired a mutated grizzly bear with a cheetah.

I glanced at the ranking board to find Bridges at the very top.

Before I could protest the disparity, Callum stepped forward. "How did you decide on this pairing, Captain?"

"Weakness is only rooted out by strength," the captain boomed.

Aletheia's ebony eyes sparked in rage.

Callum walked forward to the ring and turned to the brute, Bridges. "How much can you bench, Soldier?"

"Four-twenty-five, sir!"

"And to get better, you just kept throwing on four-twenty-five until you could finally lift it off your chest?" Callum quipped. A couple of soldiers smirked at his remark.

"No, sir!"

Callum crossed his arms. "Then how did you do it, soldier?"

Bridges glanced to the captain. He knew it was a trap for his commanding officer, and, like a dog on a leash, Bridges answered Callum only after a nod from the captain. "By slowly adding weight to the bar over time, sir! I started at one hundred as a lad, then kept adding by twenty-fives once I mastered a set."

"Incremental strength training. Right, soldier? That is how you were taught?"

"Yes, sir!"

"So, tell me, Captain"—the Lieutenant General climbed through ropes and entered the ring—"how do you justify this paring?"

The captain remained silent.

"Surely Bridges needs a little more of a challenge than Gillian here." Callum started to unbutton his jacket. "And Gillian should fight someone similar to her rank, correct?" He tossed his jacket in the corner.

Captain Rickert lifted his head.

Callum turned to Aletheia. She stood at attention, eyes fixed on the ranking screen. "Private, exit the ring and wait for your next orders from *me*." Callum turned to Bridges, who was still standing at attention in the middle of the ring. "Now, let's give you a real fight, boy."

Callum pulled his shirt over his head. My mouth went dry as his back muscles flexed while he stretched his arms. Callum wasn't massive like Bridges, but he was every bit as chiseled—a marble masterpiece.

Callum held his fists up, readying himself, and the soldier followed suit. The men started to circle each other like wolves.

Callum swung first. Bridges dodged, sidestepping out of reach from the Lieutenant General, his face just missing Callum's fist.

Bridges jabbed right toward Callum's jaw.

Callum dodged, then hooked one fist after the other into Bridge's kidneys. The soldier grunted in pain.

Bridges turned toward Callum, rage finally forming on his face, almost like Callum flipped a switch.

"There we go. Finally gonna let the beast out, huh?" Callum taunted again. Bridges jabbed—hard—connecting with Callum's jaw. Callum took the hit with ease, letting the contact reverberate through his body, channeling the momentum into a set. Like a viper, Callum struck with two quick jabs to the face and a left hook. His opponent dodged the first jab but walked right into the second, stilling himself enough for the hook to his ribs. Callum backed off and let Bridges shake off the hits before the Private ran straight toward the Lieutenant General like each hit triggered something primal in the man. Callum rolled out of the way and swung a leg at the end of his roll to trip the soldier into the ground. Bridges hit the mat hard while Callum circled back around, balancing on the balls of his feet, fists up and ready to block his face. Bridges got back up to his feet, shook off his embarrassing plunge, and took three deep breaths like he was trying to center himself. Indeed, when he turned back, his head was low and eyes narrowed.

"Good. Good, Bridges. Feel that? That's your sweet spot." A smile tugged at the Lieutenant General's lips.

Bridges nodded.

"Okay, let's have a real fight."

The fight turned from a schoolyard scuffle to an intense brawl. I knew Callum was still going easy on the boy, but the point of training wasn't to completely obliterate your opponent, but to practice moves and countermoves. The fight finally stopped when Callum caught Bridges in a tight chokehold, and the younger soldier tapped out. As Bridges caught his breath, Callum patted him on the back and praised him for a good fight.

"Now," Callum said as he grabbed a towel from a corner of the ring to pat sweat from his brow and chest glistening under the fluorescent lights. "Gillian and"—the Lieutenant General glanced up to the ranking board—"Bowers," Callum decided, choosing a mid-ranking soldier. "Get in the ring!"

The men climbed through the ropes to make way for the two women Callum called into the ring. Callum resumed his spot next to me, still shirtless. The scents of salt and earth lingered in the air around us, ebbing in waves with every rise and fall of Callum's chest. My head reeled.

"Why not pair her with another lower-ranking student?" It took all my willpower not to breathe him in, to control my wandering mind from pondering the taste of his pursed lips or glistening neck.

Callum smiled gently. "To make a point."

Sure enough, the two soldiers were in the ring for three minutes before Aletheia knocked Bowers out cold. Instantly, the board flickered, and the ranks changed, Aletheia moving up a few slots and Bowers falling down one. A badge of accomplishment appeared by Aletheia's title.

Callum climbed into the ring to help Bowers from where she was sprawled on the floor. He pulled her to a chair in the corner of the ring and poured water on her face. Bowers woke with a start, but Callum pushed her back and started checking her vital signs. He mumbled a few care instructions to her and clapped her on the shoulder.

"Good job, soldiers," Callum yelled, gaining the attention of the room. To my dismay, he donned his shirt and jacket previously strewn in one corner of the ring, then walked toward the captain and climbed out of the ring to stand in front of the stern man.

"For your sake and the sake of your students, pair them up according to rank, Captain. Do not make me interfere again," Callum commanded. As he stepped past the man, Callum stopped and muttered a few more things in the captain's ear as he nodded to Bridges. Once Callum was finished, he nodded once in the direction of the gym entrance, and I followed the Lieutenant General out.

"What else did you say to the captain?" I asked after the metal doors shut behind us.

Callum shoved his hands into his pockets, cap now secured on his head. "I told him to adjust Bridges' testosterone levels.

His T2's need to be higher, so he is more aggressive and dominant without getting shaded."

"Shaded?"

"Did you notice how Bridge's eyes glazed over when he started to get angrier?"

I nodded.

"We call that 'the shade'—it keeps you from thinking clearly and acting purposefully. His hormones would be sorted out eventually, but it needs to be done quicker."

"He didn't seem very keen on fighting you."

"Bridges is not very dominant. Especially for how big he is, Bridges needs to progress further and faster. Adjusting his T2's will help with that as well. Too much T1 and you get big brutes, but they're not very smart. Great for soldiers who are not very bright to begin with but know how to take orders and how to beat someone up. However, Bridges has empathy—he has emotional intelligence, perfect for climbing the ranks and becoming a good commanding officer. I need him to be powerful, assertive, smart, and empathetic."

"That's why you helped him."

"I help every single one of our soldiers. They all have different needs, though, so it can be difficult sometimes. Captain Rickert just wanted to build Bridges into a killer. That is one of the reasons he kept pairing him with Aletheia and other low-ranking soldiers so that all Bridges would know is dominating people physically. What the Captain doesn't understand is how it's killing the poor kid inside."

I recalled how Bridges had looked at Aletheia when they entered the ring. His brown eyes were filled with pity and remorse. He didn't want to be paired with her because he didn't want to hurt her again. I wondered if Aletheia knew how he felt.

"If things do not change within the squadron, he will commit suicide, probably within the year. Bridges empathizes with each of his comrades, feeling what they feel. On Captain Rickert's path, Bridges will become depressed and discouraged by how he lets the captain use him. He won't ever find purpose in hurting people, and people like Bridges need purpose, and they need a good one."

"Some soldiers kill themselves?"

Callum sighed. "Unfortunately, yes. We breed—or nurture—them that way. Either way, we create it. Big brutes are needed to some degree, but it should not be the default. However, people like the captain think so."

I glanced at the Lieutenant General. "What do you mean 'breed?'"

"More so *select* than breed," Callum admitted. "We keep the big brutes up here in Excelsis while the weak go down to Media and Humilis—when they are placed, that is. Then, we are able to edit and change hormone levels from their chips." Callum pointed to his forearm.

My heart stopped. "You can adjust anyone's hormones just like"—I snapped my fingers—"that? The soldier doesn't get a say?"

Callum shrugged. He actually *shrugged*. "When a person enlists in the Military, they are beholden to the Coalition. Their superior officers can code for changes in a soldier's gene expression for a more desirable outcome. It's for the greater good of the Military, if done for the right reasons."

"And who decides the *right reasons?*"

"Well, me. Anyone with the rank of captain or above can make chip modifications. I can execute changes for Bridges myself, but I want to see if Captain Rickert will follow orders."

"What about outside of the Military?"

"The American Coalition has a whole branch of Medical Experts dedicated to managing Citizenship Well-Being. They monitor an individual's health through chip data and code for alterations in gene expression if necessary."

"Do they at least notify the individual first?"

"No."

I shook my head in disbelief. "And everyone is just okay with this?"

"What is best for the individual is what is best for the Coalition," Callum responded like it actually answered my question, which it did not. "The Oversight Committee of Citizen Well-Being has created standards of living those medical personnel must enforce. It's one reason why the Senate passed the Controlled Birth Bill about ten years ago, a bill my mother constructed—all marriages and procreations must be approved by the Oversight Committee of Citizen Well-Being to ensure that only the best progeny are produced."

I stopped in my tracks. "What?"

Callum turned to meet my gaze, his brows set in confusion like he couldn't understand what I didn't understand. "It ensures that healthy babies are born by greatly reducing genetic abnormalities from incompatible partners and aids in population control."

I examined the man before me. His words were logical, but the humanity was gone from them. They weren't his words. I knew from the shadows they laid behind his eyes they did not belong to him. "And what if a woman does get pregnant without petitioning the Oversight Committee?"

A shadow cast over Callum's face, but he covered it quickly with a mask of indifference. "Before the chips were implemented throughout the Coalition about five years ago, the woman would undergo a procedure to abort the child. Now, the Citizen Well-Being Medical Experts code the woman's chip to abort the child. However, more often than not, a woman's fertility is controlled by the medical experts anyway, prohibiting her to ovulate until the Oversight Committee grants permission."

"So, the woman has no choice in the matter."

"By not having to deal with the burden of children, her choices have grown exponentially."

Every answer was carefully crafted. Every answer he gave me made sense. I mean, what could be better than having a child exactly when you expect to and with minimal health defects at that? What is more empowering than focusing on who you are and what you want to do and not having to worry about the responsibility—or the possibility of the responsibility—of having children?

Or is the Coalition just eliminating choices to get their desired outcome?

"What will happen now?" I asked as I took a step forward. I couldn't dwell on this subject any longer.

Callum cleared his throat as he kept pace beside me. "I will check up on Bridges—make sure the captain adjusted his testosterone levels. In theory, it should propel Bridges enough to move up the ranks. If nothing changes, I will move him to a different troop with a different captain who will channel Bridges' potential."

"And Aletheia?"

Callum laughed. "She would kill me if I moved her. She wanted to deal with this problem on her own, for the most part, but she needed her squadron to see her differently, so I gave her the opportunity. Now the rest is up to her."

I nodded in understanding. "Will the captain prove to be more difficult for you?"

"He already was."

"But don't you need him as an ally?"

"I always have at least one friend and one antagonist in every platoon. It gives you a fuller picture of the team and how it works. Aletheia is my ally; the captain, not so much. I hear the good and the bad from both sides. I prefer to have an adversary for each ally and vice versa. Keeps things even. But today, I just made Bridges a friend, and probably a good one at that. But since Captain Rickert is higher ranking, he's worth at least two, despite Aletheia's sheer sass and wit."

I nodded, then noticed Callum smiling at me—it was a playful and mischievous thing.

"What?" I paused.

"Nothing." He smirked and started walking away.

I started jogging to keep up with him. "No, you have to tell me."

"I was simply curious if you enjoyed the show."

I scoffed, stepping in front of him. "You just wanted me to see you shirtless, didn't you?" I poked at his chest.

"Ms. Stevens, you couldn't expect me to put up a good fight in my uniform, could you?" Callum mocked.

"You knew what you were doing today." I cocked a brow. "Why didn't you just wear your combat suit?"

"I couldn't let the captain think that I knew what I was going to do during his training lessons today."

"Oh, right." I crossed my arms. "Well, it doesn't matter. I was watching Bridges the entire time anyway."

"I didn't realize you were interested in massive *underage* brutes."

I blushed. I hadn't realized he was *that* young. Aletheia certainly wasn't. I assumed squads were based on age brackets.

I turned, eager to change the subject. "So, does every soldier have their testosterone levels adjusted?"

"Yes, it is part of our supplementation regimen." Callum walked in step beside me.

"And what does that do to the…" I pointed down toward the groin area.

Callum's chuckle bounced off the walls. "That side effect has been remedied. Don't worry. Your friend Private Bridges will be naturally endowed."

I shoved Callum with an elbow. "What is next on your agenda, Lieutenant General?"

"Media. I have some business I need to attend to down there."

"Finally taking me home?" I teased.

Callum looked at me side-long. "No. I think I have other plans for you, Ms. Stevens."

CHAPTER 18

allum brought us to the *Vectio* or the Transport Building—the hub of the Third Ward located in the center of the Excelsian Military Base. Military men and women bustled around to secure transportation to their designated patrols. There were garages housing all Military vehicles and rail stations to send larger groups across the Circulum. But Callum brought us to the heart of the Transport Building—the *Militia Attollo*—connecting Excelsis to the center of Media, where its Military Base was located, which, in turn, was connected to Humilis' Military Base.

Soldiers patiently waited in lines throughout the bright corridor for carriages to become available in order to make their descent into a lower Circulum. As we waited in line, slowly shuffling along toward burnished steel doors, Callum described Media and Humilis' Military Bases.

"They really are more like security Bases. One of the soldiers are particularly skilled, especially in Humilis, despite all the soldiers and security personnel Excelsian produces. To be assigned either Media or Humilis is extremely shameful, the latter especially."

I glanced around. "So, all of these people—."

"Oh, no. Median and Humilian soldiers live in their respective Circulums. Every soldier in here is a higher-ranking officer who has business or Privates that have rotational duties. No, you'll recognize a Median or Humilian soldier when you see one—they are real pieces of shit. Once soldiers are demoted, they seem to change for the worse. There tends to be a general, overwhelming need for lower Circulum soldiers to hurt or manipulate the civilians in order to gain power or make themselves feel better."

I thought of Balor, and my heart panged. He was never a piece of shit, but he had told me plenty of stories of his cohorts and commanders doing despicable things merely because they had the power, and no one would blink twice.

"Why aren't the officers punished?" I asked as we entered a weird carriage. The steel doors shut tight behind Callum, and we were encased in a clear acrylic cylinder with steel walls beyond us. Callum pressed a few buttons on the transparent panel next to the door we walked through. Below our feet, metal parted to reveal a small light in the distance, and our carriage started to descend. Quickly. I grabbed for the steel railings lining the carriage as my heart flew up into my throat. The light beneath my feet grew closer and larger until it engulfed the carriage and blinded me, sunlight permeating my retinas for a few brief moments. As I blinked my eyes into focus, Callum grabbed my shoulders and turned me toward the blinding sun. Beyond our small acrylic tube was a large expanse of land stretching for miles and miles, and right below our feet was the cityscape of Media rising toward us, growing larger and larger. I thought we were going to crash into an enormous industrial building when all went dark again. The carriage lurched to a stop. My heart plummeted down into my stomach, and my head swirled alongside nausea.

"Yeah, you'll get used to it." Callum patted my back softly.

"What in Skies' name was that?" I swore as I exited the carriage.

"That is a *Militia Attollo*. Well, one of them. We usually just call them 'The Tubes.'"

I took a few deep breaths and clutched at my stomach. "Yeah, the puking tubes."

"Charming." Callum led the way into a white hallway with grey concrete floors. "To answer your previous question, no one cares what the officers do down here," he said, speaking of Media now that we had descended down to the middle Circulum. "Mostly because no one cares about the lower rings. It's quite disappointing, actually. If anyone else would have come across you in the Tenth Ward a few days ago, they could either have left you there to let you fend for yourself, brought you back to Media, and returned you to your slavery, or they could have charged you as a Resistance spy, and interrogated you for weeks only to be executed in the end."

My palms grew clammy at the thought of execution.

"But soon, it's all going to change," Callum assured.

"How?"

"Me." The Lieutenant General nodded. "Once I get promoted, I'm changing all the programs down here. Actually, the whole Military will get turned upside down."

"That's an enormous task. That wouldn't just turn the Military on its head, but the whole Coalition."

He nodded. Callum seemed so confident, so sure of himself. I stared at the Lieutenant General's profile, noting the gleam in his eye.

"So what? You want to turn everything into one giant Military State? General controls everything?" I asked, still following Callum through a labyrinth of hallways that reminded me of the Resistance Base. The overwhelming dread of grief washed over me like a rushing waterfall—cold, sudden and sharp. I missed my friends. I missed Reign.

"Oh, Skies, no. That's not what I want at all."

Callum's response seemed far away, my mind pushing away the real world around me, not able to take in new information as anxiety coiled around my neck and shoulders.

I inhaled deeply. *Focus, Red.*

With a slow, smooth exhale, my presence returned to the world, and I tried to recall all the turns we had made, making a mental map of the Median Base.

"I want soldiers like Bridges and Anderson to be in charge instead of people like Captain Rickert and Clausen," Callum continued. "Not only in charge of the Military but in charge of themselves. I want smart, capable, and good soldiers in all Circulums, including Media and Humilis, and I want justice for all men and women, not just those who are lucky enough to get what they deserve."

For a moment, I agreed with the Coalition's Lieutenant General—I felt in sync with the Coalition soldier walking beside me, but what surprised me the most was that I could see myself living in his dream world.

"The Coalition Government won't allow it. They will stop you before you have a chance to make a lasting change."

Callum's shoulders slumped just a millimeter, but enough to tell me that I was underscoring the doubts in his mind. The Lieutenant General released a large breath as he straightened himself. "But at least I can say that I tried."

"Why?" I didn't know exactly what I was asking. Maybe : *why* go through all the trouble in the first place? Maybe: *why* he wanted to make the changes? Maybe: *why* he wanted to die? Because dying was inevitable if he continued to implement his plans.

"I have seen too much injustice to let it all go unpunished."

I hadn't realized we'd stopped until Callum broke away from my gaze. We stood outside of the security compound, and on the door behind us, there was a large '6.' Before us stood a hover vehicle, jet black except for the gold lettering that read 'Sixth Ward Patrol.'

The Industrial Ward. And it smelled like it. The air was thick, and billowing clouds of iron, charcoal, and sweat clung tightly to the brick buildings and concrete streets.

Callum opened the door for me, and I climbed into the vehicle. "What's going on here?"

He clicked on his seatbelt. "Some group causing trouble."

"Rebels?"

Callum shrugged. "Could be. Most likely a gang turf war."

"Gangs?" I didn't realize there were gangs in Media, but as soon as Callum shot me a suspicious look, I knew it was something I should be familiar with. "I...I just thought the normal security patrols should be able to handle them."

"Yeah." Callum chuckled. "One would think." He pressed a button and the hover roared to life, and he drove us north.

"How many gangs are in Media?" I kept my eyes on the industrial roads and buildings in front of us.

"I don't remember exactly. Somewhere between twelve and fifteen."

"And how often do they cause problems?"

"At least one gang causes trouble every day."

"That's astounding!"

"Yeah, but it's their culture." Callum rubbed an eyebrow.

"Violence?"

"Not exactly. Really, gang culture is primitive. It's a derivative of tribal cultures, similar to that of early humanoids. Not saying these people are less developed; that is far from the truth, but when resources are limited, any little amount of anything that is yours needs to be protected. Land, food, energy, people... That has all been claimed by the tribe or, in this case, the gang, and you only share with your tribe or gang because there is barely enough to go around as it is. Any time anyone threatens the resources of one tribe, that tribe will retaliate."

"And there is no way they can just get along?"

Callum shrugged. "They see each other as different in some way, and anything different is not trusted. Once primal instincts are triggered, it's hard to shut them off. Not to mention, the family dynamics are extremely harmful psychologically. When you have single parents who work all day to keep food on the table or even two parents who are absent either because of work or drug addictions, kids tend to look toward adolescents in their communities, which is fine. Actually, it's encouraged, but adolescents have poor living conditions, too, picking up poor habits and coping mechanisms, including destructive behaviors, as a way of dealing with emotional and physical pain. Those habits inevitably get pushed onto the younger kids, and it becomes an endless cycle."

"Do you think any of the gangs are part of the Resistance?"

Callum pursed his lips and shook his head. "No." He said it firmly, like he'd thought about and debated the idea plenty of times before. "They have enough to worry about internally, and to some extent, I think that is the point."

My brows furrowed. "How do you mean?"

Callum took a deep breath. "If the government were to step in and give more resources, give more opportunities for Medians to live more successful lives, or information to free them from their bad choices and habits, then over time they would accumulate more wealth, thus having more resources. Then they could look to external problems instead of internal—they would become more unpredictable in their thinking patterns and be free to choose."

"And that would be a bad thing?"

"For Medians? No, of course not. For the government? Yes. Because when people gain more freedom, they accumulate more power. They could demand change—they could break the chains —and for the people who hoard the power, that would be the worst thing imaginable."

"So, the government just lets this happen? They let the gang turf war go on, costing innocent people their lives?"

"Lets…makes…it's all the same thing."

I couldn't help the judgment emanating from my expression. "But aren't you a part of the government?"

He stared straight ahead, a small, disappointed smile pulling at his lips and eyes. "Yes." Callum breathed. "Yes, I am."

Then the ground shook.

CHAPTER 19

Callum swerved the hover to a stop as fire and smoke erupted in the distance. The Lieutenant General exited the vehicle as I started to unbuckle my seatbelt.

"No. Stay in the hover!" Callum ordered, holding a palm out.

I rolled my eyes. "Over my dead body." I whipped off my seatbelt as Callum darted toward the explosion. As I stumbled out of the vehicle, another explosion rocked the ground beneath me, and I clutched the hover door to stay upright. Towering brick buildings trembled around me as I ran toward Callum, weaving in and out of the panicked Medians. Screams and wails bounced off the quaking buildings, and when I finally reached Callum and grabbed his arm, a third explosion rocked through the Circulum. Callum's arm wrapped around my waist, and he tucked me into his chest.

"Where are they coming from?" I called out through the roar of screams and sirens.

"I have no idea." Callum glanced around, eyes searching for something before he pulled his COM-tab out of his pocket. "We need a squad down on Six ASAP," he commanded, still keeping me close to him. Then Callum pressed another button, bringing up a holo of Sancus sitting at a computer. "Sancus. Give me details on Media."

"Looks like we got central thermal readings four blocks east of your location," the Second Lieutenant explained, eyes scanning like there was a screen in front of him. There probably was, but it looked unnatural in the glowing light of the holo. "Another reading six blocks north, and a final reading two blocks south."

"All the explosions happened in Six?"

"Yes, Sir."

"What are the fucking odds?" Callum mumbled, and his arm tightened as another shock ran through the ground, not quite as intense as the last.

"Was that another?" Callum asked Sancus.

The Second Lieutenant shook his head. "No readings. Maybe a collapsed building."

"Fuck." Callum glanced around. Debris scattered the street, and the air around us grew thick with smoke and dust. "Change my order. Give me a platoon down here now! One squad at site one, another at site two, a third squad at site three, and the final squad organizing a medical site for all the Medians. Then, send another platoon down to Humilis. I want to make sure these explosions have not impacted their Circulum, and I want to make sure this doesn't initiate Rebel riots down there."

"Yes, sir!" Sancus saluted before his image disappeared.

Callum stowed his COM-tab back in his pants pocket, then ripped off a piece of his undershirt. "Use this to filter out the smoke." He handed me the torn piece of fabric, and I put it to my face. His scent of earth and wood filled my nose, instantly soothing me. "Keep close!" Callum ordered before he grabbed my hand and sprinted south. The Lieutenant General snaked us through the stampede of people running away from the explosion, screams and cries growing louder as we narrowed in on the southern site.

A large man barreled into me. My right shoulder was jerked

back, and Callum's hand broke from mine. I stumbled to the ground and rolled on the concrete street, trying to dodge the charge of people. A pregnant woman nearly stepped on my ankle, and a lanky man kicked my ribs, tripping over me and stumbling to the ground himself. He was not as lucky as I was. After I scrambled to my feet, he was kicked in the head by a boulder of a man, rendering him unconscious. I lost track of the fallen man in the chaos, but I heard faint, repeated sounds of boots on flesh.

"Callum!" I shouted as I pushed the trampled man from my mind. "Callum!" I knew we were heading south, but I was disoriented—smoke and debris hung heavy in the air, blocking my view of the sun. "Callum!" I searched for a Military uniform, for three bright stars on a shoulder, for his sandy hair or emerald eyes, but there was no sign of the Lieutenant General. People continued to barge into me—men shouldered past while women rushed by, some carrying children in their arms.

Focus, Red. Focus. I shook my head and forced myself to breathe deeply, but when I inhaled, my chest constricted and burned as smoke coiled around my lungs, like a snake suffocating its prey. I brought my fist up to my face to use Callum's shirt to filter the air, but my hand was empty. *I must have lost the cloth in my tumble.* I scanned the ground, but I knew even if I found the cloth, bending down to retrieve the fabric would render me vulnerable—someone else was bound to trample me, and the chances of me getting up a second time were thin.

I ripped a piece of my black sweatshirt away, then brought it up to my mouth, whirled around, picked a direction, and ran. I was bound to run into a soldier or officer or security guard at some point. I would tell them who I was and that I was with Callum. And I hoped they would believe me.

While most Medians avoided the buildings, afraid the brick structures would topple over at any moment, I stayed close because they were clear of people, making it the fastest route to find Callum. Before I even made it a block, a hard hand clasped around my mouth and an arm wrapped around my waist. I was pulled tight into a strong, large man and hoisted off my feet. I kicked and screamed, but the ambusher held firm. Though the streets were filled with people running about, either no one noticed in all the chaos or no one cared. No one yelled at my attacker, no one tried to tackle him to the ground, no one tried to stop my assailant as I was carried into a dark alley and thrown on the ground. My palms burned as they slid on the concrete, and my knees ached in pain as they hit the alley floor, instantly bruising. I turned sharply to look my assaulter in the eyes, but a hood covered all of their features besides a cruel, crooked smile—a smile that had tormented me every day in training.

"Was that really necessary?" I spat as I stood to my feet.

"No, but it certainly was fun," Ulysses crooned. He slid off his hood to reveal his face.

I dusted the dirt off my pants. "Why didn't you just grab my arm or something? Like a normal human being..."

Ulysses laughed. "There is no way you would have gone with me." He was right, of course. He had to keep the disguise, and I wouldn't have let any hooded man drag me away by the arm, not when I could so easily take him down that way.

I just crossed my arms. "Why are you here, Ulysses? How?" I knew I should be glad my fellow agent wasn't captured or dead, but something didn't feel right as Ulysses stood in the dark shadows of a Median alley. *How did he find me?*

"What? Not happy to see me?" Ulysses pouted.

"You sabotaged my mission! You are the reason I am fucking stuck here! And how did you even get to Media from Humilis?" I glanced around. I had half a mind to turn him in, but that would be a security risk to everyone I love. *If he's a double agent, what would it matter, anyway?* My heart sank at the thought.

"I have my ways." Ulysses cracked his knuckles one by one.

Annoyed, I shoved his vagueness to the side. I knew our time was limited. "Have you talked to anyone from Base? What do you know?"

Ulysses shrugged. "What do *you* know?"

I ground my teeth. Of course this was how he was going to play it. "The mission didn't work. Lieutenant General Osouf said—"

"Not what I heard," Ulysses interrupted.

"What?"

He shrugged. "Niahm checked. He said it worked."

But Metis said—

I shook my head, confusion clouding my thoughts. "So, if you're not here to finish the mission, you must be here to extract me?" I glanced around. "The explosions…were they all you?"

Ulysses leaned against the bricks, one leg propped against the alley wall. "Extract you? No. I am here to obtain your intel. The explosions?" Ulysses shrugged. "Maybe."

"H—how? How did you do it? How did you know I would be here?"

"Again,"—Ulysses gave me a cruel smile—"I have my ways. Now…" He held out a gloved hand. "Contacts."

How did he know about my contacts? Metis said he wasn't going to tell Hoenir, but did he tell Ulysses? Did someone else? I shook my head. "Not until you tell me how."

Ulysses sighed. "Well, thanks to you, we knew you were with the Lieutenant General, and we had Intel indicating he would be in Ward Six today. Rigged an explosion, crept around until I found you. Now, here we are." Ulysses wiggled his fingers, silently urging me to give him the contacts.

"Three."

Ulysses furrowed his brows. "What?"

"Three explosions. You rigged *three* explosions."

Ulysses shrugged, still holding out a hand. "I had to have backup plans."

"And you still decided to detonate your backup plans?"

"Mistakes happen."

I glanced toward the opening of the alley. "They were safe explosions, right? Like no one got hurt? They were all detonated in abandoned buildings or something?"

A wicked smile tugged at his lips again. "There is no such thing as a safe explosion, Red. You, of all people, should know that."

Memories from a couple of years ago sparked to life behind my eyes.

I blinked them away, then grabbed Ulysses' wrist, wound him toward me, and spun him so I could pin him against the brick wall of a building, my forearm pressing hard into his windpipe. "You killed innocent people just to meet up with me? How did you even know I was going to be here? How did you *know* the Lieutenant General would take me with him?"

"Come now, Red. We are supposed to play nice."

I pressed my arm harder into his throat. "Since when do you play nice?"

"There's a first time for everything," Ulysses choked.

I exhaled and let him go. Ulysses folded over, leaning on his knees as he took a deep breath and held out a hand. "Now, be a good little agent and hand over the contacts. Don't let all those innocent lives be lost in vain, Red."

I spat at him, my saliva landing on his left cheek.

And then it hit me—Metis never told me he had notified Hoenir or Ulysses about the contacts, about the intel I was gathering. Plus, I was able to download all of my data into encrypted files in Metis' cloud. Something wasn't adding up.

Ulysses flicked my spit from his cheek and held out his open palm again. "Failure to hand over Resistance intel is treason. Punishable by death. I have my orders. I was told if you hesitated or if you seemed like you were suddenly a Coalition sympathizer, I am to take you out. And I will. But if you hand over the contacts, you're good to go—set to continue on with your mission.

"Why do you need to retrieve my contacts? I can just transfer my data to—"

"Cloud's been compromised."

"But Metis didn't tel—"

"If he sent a message to you directly, the Coalition would be on your tail, and you'd be dead in minutes."

My stomach knotted. "I received a message from Metis earlier this morning. He said you did not return to Base, so how could you have possibly known about my contacts or if the server was compromised? How could you have possibly gained that intel?"

Ulysses' dark eyes rolled. "You think you are the only one with special communication gear?"

Well, yeah, kind of.

I glanced around the alley. Panicked people still ran by the entrances, oblivious to the two of us slinking in the shadows.

Something didn't feel right.

"Come on, Red," Ulysses urged. I glanced back to his hand, still outstretched. "I don't got all day."

"You have never wanted to help me a day in your life. Why now?"

He shrugged. "I got what I wanted—your mission was fucked. Now I get to be the one to fix your mistakes."

I gritted my teeth, remembering Metis' warning, recalling my father's journal that mysteriously appeared in my Shed. "And how do I know you're not a double agent?"

Ulysses' features shifted, and—for once in his life—his face looked earnest, almost like he was letting his guard down. *Almost.* "If I wanted you gone, if I wanted to turn you in, I would have already. If I wanted the Resistance destroyed, why wait all this time?"

I turned his words over in my head. Every fiber of my being was screaming at me to run to find Callum and tell him about Ulysses. But that might raise more suspicions; it might garner more questions that Callum would ask of me.

I grunted. "You better tell Hoenir that next time he needs a better fucking plan," I demanded as I plucked out each of the contacts. Despite himself, Ulysses was right; if I didn't give him the contacts, all these deaths, all this mess, would have been for nothing. I placed the contacts into Ulysses' palm. He smiled at me, then pulled out a contacts case and placed each contact gently inside the two compartments. Ulysses tucked the case back into a pocket on the inside of his coat, near his heart, and pulled out an identical case. However, this one was black, whereas the other was white.

Ulysses handed it to me. "Here. These lenses store slightly more data. Again, do not transfer data to the cloud. It's been compromised. Store whatever you can in these lenses, then we will trade during my next pick-up."

I plopped the new contacts in my eyes and blinked them into place.

"When is the next pick-up?"

Ulysses shrugged. "Whenever I can get up to Excelsis."

Skies knew how long that could take.

"And what should I do with the other lenses?"

"I don't know. Throw them away, burn them, dump them down a sewer drain. I don't give a flying fuck. Just do not use them."

"Couldn't you just take me home now? I have obtained a decent amount of information." I handed Ulysses the case since I didn't have anywhere to stow it.

Ulysses laughed. "You think the Lieutenant General has trusted you enough to give you any good information?" He shook his head like I was a child who believed in unicorns. "No. We need *real* Intel, Red, and Hoenir thinks you can get it." Ulysses winked at me. "Nice cover story, by the way. Really intriguing. I didn't think you could actually pull it off, but you're still alive, so you must be doing something right in order to convince the Lieutenant General of your lie."

"What exactly are you implying?" I crossed my arms.

Ulysses trailed a finger down the side of my face. "I'm sure a good fucking would loosen the Lieutenant General's lips."

I swatted his hand away before his finger reached my neck. "You are a pig."

Ulysses shrugged. "This is your mission, Red. I just want you to succeed, that's all." His voice was mocking, but he might be right. I mean, my alias was a brothel worker, and it's not like I hadn't thought about it before…or earlier this morning when sweat glistened on his abs from the training fight with Bridges.

"I don't need to fuck the Lieutenant General to charm information out of him." I shoved Ulysses. "Now, get out of here before you get caught."

Ulysses stumbled back a step, his face aghast and a hand to his chest, looking for all his life like he was truly offended. "Oh, Red. I thought you enjoyed our time together."

"On the contrary," I sneered.

Ulysses donned his hood again as he stepped closer to me. "I bet I can fix that." Ulysses grabbed both my wrists with one of his hands and turned me around so that I was pinned against the wall—my right cheek flushed against the cold brick of the alleyway, stomach, and chest shoved so hard into the wall that I could barely breathe.

"What the fuck are you doing? Get off of me!"

"Oh, come on, honey," Ulysses whispered in my ear. "Give him a real show."

I writhed. "What are you talking about? Let go!"

A shadow appeared against the light from the bustling street. "Adellaide?"

Callum.

"Help!" I shouted to Callum, understanding now what Ulysses meant. "Callum, help me, please!"

Callum darted toward us. I couldn't see his face, but every step was hard and angry against the concrete. "Get off of her!"

Before Callum reached us, Ulysses fled down the alley into

the shadows, and I crumpled to the ground, holding onto my uneasy stomach.

The Lieutenant General kneeled beside me and gathered me into his arms.

"Did he hurt you?" Callum asked softly after a few moments.

I shook my head.

"Did you know him?"

I shook my head again, remaining quiet as I played my part as the unnerved victim.

Callum pulled out his COM-tab and started ordering men to track down a hooded figure heading toward Busch's Cannery, but I stopped him, saying it wasn't worth it and convincing the Lieutenant General that the lives of those in the explosion sites were more important.

Callum nodded, canceled his orders, then swept loose strands of my hair back to get a good look at my face. "Are you sure you didn't know him? He wasn't a previous client or something?"

A test. Callum was testing me.

"No," I whispered. "At least, I don't think so. I couldn't see his face, and I didn't recognize his voice."

Callum brushed back my hair again. "Well, let's get you home."

Home.

Callum helped me up and looked me up and down, probably looking for scrapes and bruises. One finger grazed my right cheek. It stung. Ulysses must have scratched it up when he shoved me against the brick wall, but I didn't recoil from Callum's touch.

Then he took both my hands in his, examining the scrapes from when I fell in the street and when Ulysses had dragged me into the alley. Callum's eyes turned cold, his expression hard.

"I'm fine," I reassured him.

Callum's green eyes met mine, and something flickered in them—something I couldn't quite read. "I will have Sergeant Phillips take you home. I need to stay here."

I nodded.

"He's a good soldier, I promise. He won't touch—"

I took Callum's hand in mine and squeezed. "I trust you."

A small smile tugged at the corner of his mouth. With his other hand, Callum pulled my head to his lips and gently pressed them to my forehead. He lingered for a second, breathing me in, and I couldn't help but do the same.

Earth and wood.

When he stepped back, Callum kept my hand in his and led me away from the dark alley and into the light and chaos.

CHAPTER 20

I was alone in Callum's apartment—the first time I'd been allowed to be alone since I was unconscious in the interrogation room. But even then, I wasn't truly by myself. As I laid on the guest bed, staring at the ceiling and Sirius curled up by my feet, I knew I should be doing something productive— gathering intel, snooping around Callum's apartment, literally anything—but I couldn't move.

Screams echoed in my mind, and my chest still burned from the debris stuck in my lungs. And when I tried to focus on the white, orange-peel ceiling, my eyes only saw the Median man trampled to death in the street.

I bit back a sob as a tear trickled down my cheek and over my ear.

All those people, dead and hurt, because of Ulysses. Because of the Resistance. Because of me.

The Resistance was supposed to help people, but today, hundreds were injured, and dozens died at their hands. What kind of Resistance was that? What kind of a rebellion burns a whole Ward?

Sirius' black snout nuzzled under my elbow, and I tucked the canine close to me. His tongue swept across my face, brushing away the streams of tears.

———

My eyes shot open when the front door thudded shut. Boots thumped across the floor to my door, then knuckles tapped on the white, wooden door to my bedroom.

"Come in," I croaked as I sat up. Sirius uncurled himself from me and scooted to the edge of the bed as the door creaked open, his black tail fanning my face as it wagged back and forth.

Callum strode through the threshold. "Oh." His eyes met mine, probably noting the puffiness there, which felt like thick down pillows under my eyes. "I didn't realize you were sleeping."

I wiped at my eyes, and when my hands came away slick, I knew it wasn't just the swelling Callum noted. "Oh... ummm... I was just resting."

Callum sat on the edge of the bed, a strong hand scratching behind Sirius' ears, but his eyes remained fixed on mine. My heart rushed under his gaze.

"Do you want to talk about it?"

I shook my head.

"Well, whenever you're ready to, let me know."

I nodded once, glancing down to my hands. The small scrapes from my tumble already healed. My heart stopped, and I clenched them tight, not wanting him to notice.

Callum shifted to stand.

"Do you need to talk?" I blurted.

He half turned, a light smile playing at his lips. "No. I did my fair share of talking today."

I smiled, but it faltered as he turned away again.

"Callum."

"Yes?"

I looked away from his gaze, cheeks burning. "I don't really want to be alone right now."

He shoved his hands in his pockets and nodded to the door. "Let's order some food and put up a holo. Sound good?"

"Sounds perfect."

———

"That movie was awful!" I practically screamed at Callum once the credits started scrolling. I must have startled Sirius because he quickly raised his head, ears perked up and jaw slightly ajar like he was ready to bark at whoever dared make me scream. The gap Sirius had crawled into had grown smaller and smaller during the movie, with half of the hybrid now laying atop Callum's lap, and his butt—still on the couch—was pressed against the outside of my thigh.

"What do you mean? It was awesome!"

"There was no plot!"

"Sure there was. There was a bad guy and a good guy who defeated the bad guy. Plot."

I shook my head at his simple, male mind. "Okay," I conceded. "There was a thread of a plot, but it was mostly explosions and guns."

"That's what made it awesome! And what do *you* know about holo movies, anyway?"

I couldn't help but glare at him. "Any intelligent person can detect a good story when they see one. And you are a Lieutenant General! You should find the movie appalling because it's never that simple."

Callum cocked an eyebrow. "Maybe that's what I like about it—the simplicity of it all. Besides, how do you know my job is never that simple?"

"Because people are never that simple!"

Sirius finally jumped off the couch in a huff, clearly annoyed by our disturbance.

"Agree to disagree," Callum declared with a definitive click of the holo remote.

I tried to ignore the small gap between us, empty now that Sirius had left for a cooler spot on the concrete floor next to the glass balcony doors. "No. There is no disagreement. No one is ever that simple." I pointed to the holo like it was going to prove my point.

"You are wrong," Callum said as he turned to face me, bringing a knee up to rest in the space between us, near inches from my thigh. Something pulsed between us. "Clausen is that simple," he stated.

I laughed ruefully. "I cannot believe that— that—" The words were lost to me.

"Deplorable pervert?" Callum suggested.

I laughed again. "Yes! I cannot believe that *deplorable pervert* is up for your position!"

Callum scoffed and ran a hand through his hair. "Trust me, if it was only my choice, I would choose Bellona. Hands down. No further questions. However, the current general *insisted* I have a backup option, and that option should be Clausen."

"Why is that?"

"Oh, because he is incredibly sexist."

"Really?" I thought sexism was such an archaic ideology. It was crazy to me how some people could actually believe that men were more capable than women, especially in leadership roles.

Maybe that was Hoenir's problem with me...

Callum nodded assuredly. "I can choose whoever I want, but I need good reasons to back up my decision. My personal preference or bias isn't enough. I'm just waiting until I get some good dirt on Clausen to prove he is not qualified for the job."

I grimaced. "Wasn't sexually harassing me in my jail cell enough?"

Callum shook his head. "No," he sighed. "It is truly awful how soldiers treat imprisoned citizens. Anyone taken in by security or Military personnel is property of the Coalition until they are released, and since Military personnel are, in essence, the Coalition, they can do with prisoners whatever they please. Especially since you were a brothel worker, no one will see it as a crime that Clausen forced himself on you. If anything, they would have demanded you gave Clausen what he wanted as payment for your crime."

My heart throbbed at the thought of other people, men and women in prison, who endure similar treatment—or even worse—every day.

Callum shifted, inching closer to me, and the gap turned into mere centimeters, sparking with electricity. "Once I am General, that will all change." Callum seemed so certain. Could I deny the fact he could change the regulations within the Military? No. Not one bit. But I knew enforcing those new rules would be a hard, uphill battle, and Callum might not see the victory in his lifetime.

I wanted to tuck my hair behind my ear, tapping my right temple twice in the process, but something about our conversation seemed personal, and a part of me thought if I saw that little red dot in the corner of my vision right now, the little trust that had been built between Callum and I might dwindle into oblivion.

There will be other opportunities, Red.

Instead, I smiled at him. "You seem to have a lot of aspirations for your upcoming promotion, Lieutenant General," I noted as I mimicked his position, our knees grazing each other.

"You have no idea," he muttered as our eyes locked.

I wanted to ask what else he wanted to do as General of the Coalition Military. Again, the urge to tap my right temple twice and record all of his plans needled at my brain, but his eyes were mesmerizing—entrancing—and I couldn't seem to move. I couldn't seem to breathe as I took Callum in—as I studied his sandy hair, his straight nose, and his lips; his bottom lip plump, while the top was narrow, like it was begging for a mate to complete it.

"What about you?" Callum asked, drawing my attention back to his eyes. "What are your aspirations now that you will be living here in Excelsis?"

The words shocked me. "I—I don't know. I guess I haven't really thought about it."

"Well,"—Callum rested his cheek on his fist, arm propped against the couch—"what are your interests?"

My interests? *I have a lot.* But none that Callum could know about. None that Adellaide would have actually acquired. *Am I just supposed to tell the Lieutenant General that Adellaide knows how to hunt and she loves to kickbox? How could I possibly tell him that I am knowledgeable in genetics or I can disarm an assailant in five seconds?*

I shrugged. "I don't know if I really have any."

"There isn't anything you enjoy?" Callum pressed, brow furrowing.

I brought my other leg up on the couch to sit cross-legged. "I didn't have access to anything that would count as a hobby."

He looked me up and down. "You look pretty strong. You don't run or workout?"

"Well...my job did keep me pretty active." I winked at him, and Callum's eyes grew wide. *Probably not the answer he was looking for...* "But yes," I conceded. "I did train a little. Had to make sure I was appealing for my clients." I gave him a half smile. He returned the gesture, and like mine, it didn't meet his eyes.

Callum cleared his throat. "Do you like to read?"

"Yeah." I shrugged again, trying to play it cool because I actually *loved* to read. "But I am not very good," I lied. "I didn't have access to many books."

"Well," Callum grunted as he rose from the couch, and my chest felt like there was a string connecting our hearts that grew taut as the distance between us increased—it felt like I was losing something. I had the urge to follow him, but I stayed on the couch as Callum walked over to the large fireplace. He placed a hand on the wall above the mantle, and right before my eyes, the opaque white wall turned into transparent glass, revealing a bookshelf filled to the brim. Some books were even laid upon the tops of other books.

I had never seen so many books in my life. Well, not since my father fled our family from our estate in Militum.

I found myself standing up from the couch and gliding toward the books, eyes transfixed on beautiful leather bindings and gilded lettering on the spines.

"They are beautiful," I whispered. Callum slid the glass open, pulling it up so that the glass disappeared into the top of the bookcase. I gently fingered the spines as the dusty smell of parchment and leather filled my nose.

"Which one do you want to read?" Callum was leaning on the mantle, but his question was so soft, so lyrical, it was like he was whispering in my ear. I glanced over to him, and a gentle smile lit up his face, perhaps mesmerized by my bewilderment.

"Umm, what do you recommend?"

"Hmmm…" Callum turned to examine his collection, though I wagered he knew every book strewn between the shelves. "If you are in the mood for Epic Poetry, you can never go wrong with *Beowulf* or *The Iliad*. But if you like gossipy romances, then I would recommend *Anna Karenina* or *Jane Eyre*. My personal favorites are *Red Rising, 2001 Space Odyssey,* or *Frankenstein.*"

"*Frankenstein?*"

"It's a classic," Callum explained, mistaking my sarcastic annoyance for genuine interest. "It's hard to come by. All of my favorites are, actually. Banned by the Coalition."

I studied him. "Why would the Coalition ban books?"

He ran a hand through his hair. "Books can be dangerous. They give people thoughts and ideas. They provoke thinking, which is the enemy to people in power. That's why they 'encourage' other distractions, to keep books out of reach."

Callum was right. Books often changed my mind or my way of thinking—they challenged me and molded me. Granted, there were some thoughts or ideas authors expressed in books that I didn't agree with, but that was the beauty of ideas—we could accept other people had them, but we didn't have to take them ourselves.

I continued to scan the books, touching each spine as I read the titles. "*Winnie the Pooh Bear*?" I asked in wonder. It looked just like my copy in the Shed. I plucked the yellow book from the shelf, careful not to disturb any surrounding companions. Sure enough, the book was an exact replica of mine—the same little boy with a raggedy bear drawn on an oval in the middle of the cover, etched into a sea of a mustard yellow binding and gold filigree.

"It was one of my favorite faerie tales when I was little," Callum replied. "Well, not really a faerie tale. Rather a collection of children's stories about a boy and his adventures with his stuffed animals who all suffered from mental disorders." A small laugh escaped Callum's lips. "My mother always chided me when she saw me reading the book. She said that Christopher Robin, the little boy, had serious issues if the only friends he could conjure up all suffered disabilities."

"Any child that can conjure up dream worlds to help them cope with reality is brave in my book. Extremely brave," I said, and Callum's eyes lit up in the corner of my vision.

"Some would say those children are foolish."

"They are wrong. People who say such things are the fools." I half turned toward my host. "What is your favorite faerie tale, Lieutenant General?"

"My mother discouraged such things."

I nodded, my heart thumping hard as I remembered that tidbit of information I thought was lost forever. I remained silent, not wanting to say how I thought his mother was a cruel fool who didn't inspire her child to dream, though the words were implied already if Freyja indeed thought kids were foolish for conjuring dream worlds.

Callum pointed to the yellow book I clutched between my hands and cleared his throat. "This was actually a gift from the father of one of my childhood friends. Her nickname was Wynnie." I snapped my head up to meet his eyes. I tried to hide the shock from my face, but his furrowed brows and slight grimace told me I was doing a very poor job. "What?" Callum asked rather defensively.

"Oh," I feigned shock. "It just seems like an odd nickname. You know, being called a fictional stuffed bear."

"Wynnie was short for Rowyn," Callum stated. "Rowyn Eloise Darrow." The sound of my name, my real name, on Callum's lips was like honey drizzling into a hot cup of tea. "Her dad called her Wynnie for short."

"She must have been a real sweetheart if she was nicknamed after a stuffed bear."

Callum chuckled. "Quite the opposite, really. She had enough sass to shame a Sasquatch."

I glanced sidelong at Callum and cocked an eyebrow. "Lieutenant General, was that a joke?"

A bright smile lit up his face. "I can be funny." He snuck an arm in the small space between me and the mantel. Heat ran through me at the nearness of his touch. When he pulled his arm back, his strong fist was clutching something. Callum opened his palm to reveal the rock I had inquired about the first night here. "Wynnie is the girl who threw this at my head."

I nodded. I stared at that rock every time I was in this room, replaying that day when we were kids over and over again.

"Because you gave her a rose, right?" I asked, playing my part in the game.

He nodded, not meeting my eyes. Instead, Callum stared at the rock as he rolled it gently in his palm. "She, her father, and her stepmother died years ago. Her dad got a huge promotion in the department my mother actually runs now, so they were moving here from Militum for her dad's job when their hovercraft crashed. It was tragic."

My throat bobbed. "And there is no way they could have survived?"

Callum shook his head. "No. The crash site was found and searched, nothing but hovercraft debris and charcoaled human remains." His fist clutched the stone tightly.

I reached out to him and curled my hand around his fist. Heat rushed into my palm. "I am so sorry, Callum."

His tear-lined eyes met mine.

After all these years, over fifteen, my death still pains him. And to think, with one sentence, with a few words, I could heal all that grief.

I took a deep breath. "You must have really loved her. And her family."

Callum nodded. "They were better than mine."

After a few silent seconds, I broke my eyes away from his and released my grip on his hand, my heart and mind feeling as cold and empty as my palm now felt. The temptation of telling him all about me, about Rowyn, was tearing at my insides—eating me alive. I had to let go before I made a mistake I could never undo—before I confessed truths I couldn't take back. Before I endangered my mission and my sister.

"I'm sorry," Callum breathed. "I always seem to find exactly how to ruin our time together."

I shook my head. "You didn't ruin anything. You don't owe me anything. Skies, I just dropped into the middle of your life— perhaps the most important part of your life with this big promotion and everything. I am just happy to be here. I am happy you've let me into your life." I bowed my head, averting my gaze as I chewed on my lip, not quite sure how to form the words I wanted to speak. "I know we just met, but I'd like to be your friend, Callum. I'd like to know all your past—all your hurts and all your loves. I want you to feel comfortable enough to tell me."

Callum shifted uncomfortably at the word 'friend' like he didn't like it. Though Callum and Adellaide just met, Callum and Rowyn have known each other forever. I knew there was a deep, slumbering part of him that recognized my soul. It wasn't sparks between Callum and Adellaide; it encompassed Callum and Rowyn. I couldn't help little parts, important parts of the real me, seeping out into who Adellaide was, into her life. Callum was most likely grasping onto the traces of Rowyn I wove throughout Adellaide's story.

I couldn't help but wonder how one little girl—how I—could have left such a hole in his life.

Didn't he do the same to you?

Callum was silent as he stuffed his hands into the pockets of his grey sweatpants. His chest rose and fell as he released a deep breath. "Feel free to read this and any other books you would like. But maybe check with me before you leave the flat with one in tow. Again, most of my collection are banned books. I don't want you to get into trouble, but most importantly, I don't want them to get confiscated." He winked at me.

With a smile, I nodded and held the book close to my chest. "Thank you."

"Of course," Callum said softly. "We should retire. It's getting late."

I nodded again. "Goodnight, Callum."

Callum hesitated for a moment, lingering, the emerald ocean in his eyes churning. Slowly, he leaned close and kissed my cheek. "Goodnight, Adellaide." His lips were soft as silk, and his words smooth as polished silver, and I couldn't fight the blush that burned under my skin all the way to my bedroom.

I quickly got ready for bed, excited to read the book I already had memorized. I knew whenever I read the copy we had in the Shed, I could hear my father's voice in my mind, but I wondered if it could still happen with Callum's version. It looked similar, but mine was well-worn while this book looked brand new. I crawled into bed and opened the front cover. In my father's scrawled handwriting, there was a note that read,

"To Callum, You have always been like a son to me. Thank you for being the light in our lives and the joy in our souls. You are always welcome in our home, wherever we are. Love Janus, Aura, and Wynnie."

My heart warmed at the words, and tears threatened to pour from my eyes. I flipped through the book, trying to pick out an adventure, when something caught my attention on the back cover. There was a map of the Hundred-Acre Woods, but under the sketched map was a hidden flap. Carefully, I pulled it open to reveal another note in my father's hand.

"And to my darling Wynnie, May this help you when you find yourself lost in the woods. Love Dad."

CHAPTER 21

Faces moved in a blur around me—strangers all donned in lab coats flitting between laboratory hoods, centrifuges, and incubators. They worked eagerly, micro petting solutions, recording data on their COM-tabs, and centrifuging blood samples.

But whose blood?

I sat in the middle of the room, my legs dangling on an examination table.

"How are you feeling, Wynnie?" My father's face came into vision before me. His lips were drawn tight, forehead crinkled in worry.

I glanced at the tube in my forearm, a bead of blood dripping from where the needle had entered. "Dizzy. My head is tingling." I felt for my skull, but wires were in the way.

He smiled gently, but it didn't meet his blue-grey eyes. "That's normal." My father cupped my cheek. "Now, I will be in the other room. Callum's mother will be with you the whole time."

My heart sank in my small chest. "What's going to happen?"

My father's Adam's apple bobbed. "Nothing you will remember."

"Dad?" My voice was no longer a child's, and I saw my face reflected in my father's gaze. "What did you mean in the book inscription? What woods? How did you know I would be lost? Why did you leave the message for Callum to find and not for me?"

"The woods are a place where all seems lost—where you can't determine what is wrong or what is right." His hand fell from my face and gripped my shoulder. "We all find ourselves lost in the woods at some point, Wynnie. But I'm going to get you through."

I wanted to yell, but I kept my voice even. "How? You left me. You left us. And don't you dare say that you are always in here." I pointed to my heart. "Because that lame-ass shit is not going to cut it."

His face shifted, like it was made of clouds, and his words rumbled like thunder from his fading figure. "May this help you when you find yourself lost in the woods."

I felt the weight of a book in my hands, but I couldn't look down, not as a new face formed in the space before me.

Her hair white as snow, and her eyes empty as an abyss, Freyja appeared before me. Her mouth opened, but I knew she wasn't talking to me as she held a small microphone to her lips. "Beginning procedure—"

"No. Daddy!" I screamed, my voice a small child's again, but it was quickly drowned out by the excruciating pain that wracked through my skull. My spine arched, and an unearthly scream escaped my lips before my whole world went dark.

———

To say I was anxious about my first day of working in Dr. Freyja Osouf's lab was a massive understatement. I woke up with my palms slick with sweat, my heart racing, and the sheets of my bed strewn about the floor—even the fitted sheet was no longer tucked into the top two corners of the mattress.

And though I had grown used to seeing Adellaide in the mirror, even I couldn't recognize myself with the massive bags under my eyes. I reached for the new contacts Ulysses had given me, but I hesitated. I wanted to grab the old ones—the pair Metis had given me—and tell him about the note I found in Callum's book and the terrible dreams that haunted me last night.

Why the fuck should I trust Ulysses, anyway?

I opened the drawer and reached for a pair of the old contacts. But as my fingertips pressed into the smooth plastic of the case, Ulysses' words echoed in my mind and coiled around my heart.

Cloud's been compromised.

Should I really risk my friends and Reign just because I detest Ulysses?

The Coalition knows where the Resistance Base is, anyway. How much more of a risk could it be?

But they don't know that I am Resistance.

Cloud's been compromised.

I released the old contact case, slammed the drawer shut, and cursed Ulysses as I plopped in his contacts.

———

Callum prepared everything I needed for a successful first day at the laboratory—a large breakfast with a steaming hot cappuccino, a new outfit—white slacks and a white jacket heavily adorned in geometric patterns with fake jewels and brass studs, a modest, sweeping neckline, and shoulder pads. He even included an armchair full of gifts such as a brand-new COM-tab —larger than the current pocket-sized one I had—state-of-the-art nano-vision safety goggles, a holo-stylus, books on genetics and nanobiology, a lab coat, and a work bag. But my favorite gift was a leather-bound journal. It reminded me of my father's Prometheus Project Journal, and when I paged through it, aromas of parchment and musk filled the air around me.

Once I was ready and my work bag was packed with my new gifts, Callum drove us to the center of the Second Ward, where five glass towers gleamed high into the Circulum. Callum called them the Cultivation Towers, which were essentially extremely large greenhouses where all the vegetation for Excelsians was grown. The Cultivation Towers conserved land, which was extremely important in the smallest Circulum, but it also allowed cultivators to control all the variables like weather, soil, minerals, and water. Callum also briefly explained the intricate ventilation systems that brought in Carbon Dioxide for the plants, then distributed the oxygen released by the plants into Excelsis' contained atmosphere. Because Excelsis was so high in the earth's troposphere, it was important to utilize any bit of extra oxygen and pump it into the Circulum.

Nestled in the middle of the Cultivation Towers was the Research Facility—where I was to meet Freyja's assistant. White and angular, the Research Facility wasn't as beautiful as the towers, but it was the center of an intricately carved web—an elaborate network of clear acrylic corridors connecting not only the research building to the Cultivation Towers but the Cultivation Towers to each other. The corridors were already teeming with busy scientists—spiders balancing on their crystalline web.

"All of this is relatively new," Callum explained as we parked outside of the Research Facility and exited the hover. "When my family and I moved here about ten years ago, this was one of my mother's first projects—her very own Research Facility." The Lieutenant General gestured to the building. "After years of hard work and several successful experiments, she was finally going public with a top-secret government research project."

"But why the capitol? This city isn't known for its scientific and technological advancements. It's known for being the political center of the Coalition."

"My father needed to move here for his new position as

Senator, not to mention it's where he grew up. I come from a long line of politicians. And my mother, clever as she is, insisted our nation's most esteemed leaders needed the highest quality of food energy available, and she was able to create a system just for them." He rolled his eyes. "Freyja always gets her way, but it worked out very well. So well, in fact, that similar systems are being built in other Excelsian Circulums across the Coalition."

Gently, Callum took my hand and led me toward the Research Facility. His hand was hard and warm as my fingers gently brushed against his skin before trailing down his wrist to his pulse, thumping gently.

"What was the project called?"

"I think it was named after Gaia, the Grecian Earth Goddess."

"Hmm." I nodded, familiar with Greek myths and legends. I thought of the titan Prometheus and my father's journal. It must have been a theme they kept.

Callum squeezed my hand. "I am sure my mother will tell you all about it. You might veritably learn of a few secret projects I can't even know about."

"Really?"

He laughed at my disbelief. "Of course. I'm not nearly important enough to know or have access to everything, certainly not top-secret biological experiments."

"But what about when you are promoted to General?"

Callum shrugged. "I doubt any of it will be necessary for me to know."

"What about secret biological warfare projects, bioweapons, or crazy genetic manipulation experiments to create terrorizing beasts?"

Callum paused mid-step. He slowly turned to look at me, a single brow raised. "Adellaide Stevens, are you a spy?"

My heart stopped, and the breath in my lungs was gone like the air was a rug pulled out from under me.

"No," I managed to sputter out. "No. Of course not!"

Callum's face relaxed into an impish smile, and he nudged me with an elbow. "I'm just ribbing you."

Callum started walking again, and I took a moment to silently regain my breath, forcing my heart to pump back into a normal rhythm.

"But you do realize that's how Sirius was created, right?"

I nodded, matching his pace once more. "I mean, I've heard rumors about canine hybrids. Sirius is so massive, I just assumed he was a wolf-dog."

"Sirius isn't technically a hybrid. A hybrid is created by breeding two compatible creatures together to get a new creature and then breeding the new creature with another new creature to get the desired traits. It's really how most standardized dog breeds were created, but Sirius is different. My mother created his genome from scratch to create a creature very similar to a Direwolf, the symbol of our family line. He was a birthday gift to me when I was sixteen.

"He does kind of look like those hybrids…but he is taller and broader—all around larger and more powerful. Since my mother designed his genome from scratch, she was able to pinpoint specific characteristics that were able to make him more domesticated and willing to work with humans. While most hybrids have blue, brown, or yellow eyes, Sirius has green to match mine—to match our family crest."

"Do green eyes run in your family?" I asked, not bothering to look where I was going as I studied Callum's emerald eyes.

Callum paused, like he had never really thought about it before. "No. Now that I think of it, I do not recall any other family members with green eyes."

"Strange." I stared at him, and it wasn't until he tugged at my hand that I realized we had stopped in the middle of the busy walkway, strangers shoving past us and walker-bys confused by our standstill.

I shook myself from my trance and started walking toward the Research Facility's entrance. "What floor are we going to?"

"I…" he corrected, pulling the door open for me, "am just walking you in, but you are going to the eleventh floor." Callum walked us up to a large, solid marble structure. "I cannot go past this desk." He tapped the cold, black marble and turned to the old woman behind the desk. "Lydia, this is Ms. Adellaide Stevens, and she is here—"

"Yes, yes," the older woman interrupted, waving a hand in dismissal. "She is here for Dr. Osouf." The woman's chin-length salt and peppered hair whirled as she turned toward me. "And you're late," she *tisked*.

"She is precisely on time," Callum interjected.

Lydia whipped her head toward Callum, clearly unafraid of the Lieutenant General and getting whiplash. "Which makes her late. You, of all people, should know the difference between the two, Lieutenant General."

Callum stared the older lady down, teeth clenched in frustration. "Just see to it that she gets to where she needs to go, Lydia." As he turned to me, Callum forced a smile onto his face. "Good luck," he said tersely before he tucked his hands in his pockets and strode off.

I faced the crotchety woman. "So, Lydia—"

"You"—she pointed at me with a crooked finger—"do not call me that. You call me Ms. Martinez." *Ms. Martinez* then proceeded to slam a steel wand onto the black marble desk. It was long, with two prongs protruding from one end. "Now, place the prongs on your forearm so that your chip is between them, and press the button there." She pointed to the middle of the wand. I did as she instructed, and a small, short jolt pulsed through my arm.

I jumped back in shock. "What was that?" I seethed, cradling my arm.

"That"—Ms. Martinez grabbed the wand from my hand— "has now authorized you to certain parts of the building. You are allowed to enter the first, second, ninth, eleventh, and twenty-third floors of this complex and the exact same floors of each of the Cultivation Towers and Research Centers." The woman explained things quickly, tapping the screen of her COM-tab. "The elevators will not let you pass through the doors unless you are authorized for that particular floor. There are exceptions, of course. If you are given a temporary code for a floor, with floor-authorized personnel, or in case of an emergency."

Ms. Martinez continued to tap on her COM-tab, never looking up to meet my eyes. She made a large sweeping motion over the surface and a three-dimensional image shown bright over the large screen—a blueprint of a building. "This is where we are…" The woman pointed to a three-dimensional desk that sat right in front of the large doors. "And this," she continued, moving her finger toward an elevator corridor, "is where you will be meeting Dr. Yong. She will escort you to your research floor." Ms. Martinez made another large sweeping motion over the COM-tab, but in the opposite direction. This time, the three-dimensional holographic image collapsed back into the screen. "According to my clock…" She swiped again and revealed the screen of her COM-tab. In bright green, the time blinked zero-eight-zero-five. "…you are late." Ms. Martinez pointed to her left toward the elevators. "Haste!" the woman urged me.

I quickly gathered my belongings and rushed toward the elevators—again, strangers looked upon me with judgment and confusion in their eyes. When I arrived at the elevator corridor, a young woman stood in the middle, white suit stark against her dark hair pulled back into a strict tail, and her small, narrow eyes were crinkled in worry. She clutched a thin COM-pad to her chest, arms tightly crossed, and her back so straight she looked as though she was tied to an invisible wooden board.

"Ah, thank the Skies above. I have been waiting for you. You are very late." The young, worried woman sharply turned toward an elevator that had no door but a transparent light screen that glowed a dull, dark purple. She shuffled through the light and into the elevator. "Dr. Osouf will not be impressed by your tardiness on your first day." She turned to face me. I was still outside the elevator, transfixed by the light that may or may not have been a doorway. "Haste!" the young woman urged me in her stern yet quiet voice.

Why does everyone keep saying that?

I scampered through the entrance, afraid that the door might shock or fry me.

When I made it through the doorway unharmed, I released a breath. "My apologies for the delay." I reached out a hand. "Adellaide Stevens." My escort hesitantly extended her arm. I grabbed her hand and shook, closing the space between us. Her hands were soft, cold, and...well...weak. I had to glance down to make sure her hand was actually in mine as I squeezed it gently, which apparently wasn't gentle enough because she winced at my touch. If I was Rowyn, and this girl was my Reign, I would have yelled at her right then and there to strap up and push out. I had no tolerance for weakness, let alone feeble handshakes. But I wasn't Rowyn, not right now. So, I gave her a bemused smile and leaned forward like I was expecting her name.

"Dr. Hlín Yong." The slight woman nodded before quickly releasing my hand and returning to clutching her COM-tab.

A soft bell rang overhead before the elevator shot upwards with such force I nearly fell to my knees. Glancing over to Dr. Yong, I noted how she stood still and straight as a boulder in a hurricane, unphased by the abrupt disturbance. In preparation for the stopping elevator, which I assumed would be just as virile as the start, I set my feet farther apart and clenched every muscle in my body. And just as soon as the elevator shot up, it came to an abrupt stop. My body shook and swayed, but I remained fully erect.

Dr. Yong proceeded through the gleaming door. "The eleventh floor is where we will be spending most of our time."

"Will Frey— I mean Dr. Osouf be working with us at all?"

"Oh, no, no, no. You will be working under me as my assistant. Dr. Osouf is far too busy managing many projects to be bothered by the day-to-day research."

My shoulders instantly relaxed.

We passed rooms and rooms full of biochemical hoods, large incubators, and centrifuges, each teeming with researchers hard at work. I also noted how each room entrance had a light screen similar to the elevator door, though some were different colors, mostly blues and greens.

"Then how will she know I was late?" I asked.

"Because I will tell her," Yong said flatly.

"Or it could be our little secret…" I said in a sing-song tone.

I watched Dr. Yong as her eyes grew wide. "Oh, we do not keep *secrets* from Dr. Osouf. Next thing you know, we would be keeping data, notes, results, whole research projects!" I think the poor thing was about to start hyperventilating. "We keep *nothing* from Dr. Osouf."

I held one hand up in surrender. "Okay, okay. I am sorry. No secrets from Dr. Osouf."

Dr. Yong gave one firm nod.

"So…you're going to inform Fr— Dr. Osouf that I suggested for you not tell her I was late, huh?" I pursed my lips.

Another firm nod.

Perfect.

We passed a few more rooms before I asked, "What projects will we be working on?"

"Today, we will be working on some Gaia research." We rounded a corner, and Dr. Yong passed through a doorway that glowed deep blue. She glided through with such ease, whereas I couldn't help but pause outside, unsure of what *this* color could do to me. Dr. Yong continued into the room, unaware of my hesitancy, as I slid a toe through the screen to 'test the waters.' When my big toe wasn't singed off, I proceeded to take a full step through the light and then another.

"Will I be able to access all the rooms on this floor?" I asked curiously, looking back at the doorway I had just walked through.

"Most of them, yes. Though, some are restricted. They will have yellow, orange, or red ray-doors. The colors indicate certain clearances. You will be able to access Amethyst, Lapis, and Emerald but not Heliodor, Clinohumite, or Ruby."

"And what would happen to me if I tried?"

"It depends, really." Dr. Yong placed her COM-tab on a stand, and a large single strand of DNA three-dimensional hologram image popped up. Every atom of the DNA was displayed with each type of atom, whether carbon, hydrogen, oxygen, phosphorus, or nitrogen, glowed a different color. A key glowed brightly below the image, designating each atom to a color.

"You could experience a near debilitating shock or receive second-degree burns." Dr. Yong's nonchalance broke me from my trance.

"Second-degree burns? Isn't that a little excessive?"

The young doctor turned sharply to me, small eyes narrowing into dark slits. "Not when the research inside could be put at risk. Unauthorized personnel could do untold damage, possibly ruining decades of work and advancements!"

I pursed my lips, stifling a laugh.

Metis would love this girl.

The thought made my heart tighten. I missed Metis so much, and the thought of not being able to debrief him anymore was nearly debilitating. Was I still upset that he never told me he knew my father? Of course. But I had too few friends, and I couldn't afford to push him away, especially when he has always supported my endeavors and ideas.

"So, what are we looking at here?" I asked, nodding to the holo.

"Our cherry trees have been a little picky with the

horticultural lights we have been using for them in our greenhouses." Dr. Yong sighed. "There are some things nature is just better at, I suppose. But we are trying to target change in the chloroplast DNA of *Prunus Cerasus,* so it will utilize the light we give it more efficiently."

"Why not just change the lightbulbs?" Seemed like a simple enough solution—some plants thrived on different lights within the spectrum.

The doctor sighed in frustration. "Do you not think that is the first solution we tried, Ms. Stevens? Nothing has made them happy enough to bear much fruit."

"What do you need me to do?"

"You get to take notes." Dr. Yong handed me a thin COM-tab and a needlepoint stylus.

"Take notes?" My heart deflated.

She nodded, shrugging on her lab coat and buttoning it closed. Before I could tell her that I could do more than just take notes, a ringing emitted from her COM-tab.

"Oh, dear," she whispered as she swept over the screen. A giant hologram of Freyja's stern face appeared directly in front of Dr. Yong.

"Dr. Osouf."

"Dr. Yong, I noticed you enrolled later than usual today. What was the delay?" There was an edge to Freyja's voice. Then again, there was always an edge.

"Ms. Stevens' escort, Lieutenant General Osouf, was apparently a delay. I made sure to inform Ms. Stevens of the inconvenience and opprobrium of tardiness. It will not happen again." Dr. Yong's hands shook as she fidgeted with a holo-stylus behind her back.

"See that it doesn't." With a *blip,* Freyja's face disappeared, and the holo of the cherry tree DNA fragment reappeared.

Several moments of silence passed between us as Dr. Yong wiped her hands on her lab coat, mindlessly straightened the buttons, and pulled strands of hair behind her ears.

"How does she know we were late?" I finally asked.

The frazzled Dr. pointed to her forearm—the same spot on her arm where the chip was placed in mine. "Every time we enter or leave a laboratory room, our chip is read, and the data is recorded. It determines our pay."

"And what if you need to leave for the bathroom?"

"Oh, you can use the washroom, but you certainly will not be paid for it."

"What if we need to access a different research lab?"

Dr. Yong pointed to the back of the room where another Lapis doorway gleamed. "There are small corridors that connect the laboratories. There are even a few small storage or shared corridors you can walk into."

"But what if we need to go into another research or greenhouse building?"

"You do not get paid for walking, Ms. Stevens. Only for work."

But you are walking for work, I wanted to reason again, but I knew the point was moot, so I nodded once to let her know I understood these rules.

"Now, enough dawdling, we have a lot to get through today." She pointed to my COM-tab and stylus with a smooth, pale hand. "I will talk. You must record."

"Couldn't your COM-tab do the recording for you?"

Dr. Yong stiffened, probably growing annoyed with my constant questions. "For academic integrity, it is best for there to be more than one person examining and accessing research materials for any given project," she explained tersely.

"But I don't even know what's going on."

"Be patient, and you will."

I released a sigh of frustration as I picked up my COM-tab and fingered my stylus.

"Yesterday, we used our Gene-Sim software to alter the methylation in the chloroplast DNA to alter gene expression for three different ribosomal proteins," the young doctor started as I tapped my right temple two times.

Honestly, I had no idea if the cherry tree chloroplast research would be important. But maybe there would be something the Resistance could learn from their experimentation. A red dot appeared in the corner of my vision.

CHAPTER 22

When Dr. Yong and I finally finished up our work for the day, it was twenty-hundred, and I was starving. I locked up my lab COM-pad in the safe provided in the room, as Dr. Yong explained how only we could access the safe in this laboratory due to our chips, but the data we recorded and utilized today would be seen by others on the projects, including Freyja. However, they would not be able to edit the data or notes—we were the only researchers who could do that from our authorized COM-tabs.

Nothing came up about the Prometheus Project, or my father for that matter. I didn't really expect it to. If Metis was right and all his research was destroyed, I was going to need to do some digging or ask some questions, but that did not seem like a bright idea on my first day.

I started packing up my bag when I noticed a message from Callum on my smaller, personal COM-tab.

Something came up at work, the message read. *I won't be able to drive you home tonight. Let me know when you are finished, and I will send a hover to take you home.*

"Perfect," I said to myself as my stomach grumbled in protest. I needed food. *Now.*

I knew the drive wouldn't take long, and Callum's flat was my home for the time being, but I still felt uncomfortable rummaging through his cabinets and fridge. And quite frankly, I was too tired and lazy to make a whole meal.

If I walk to Callum's flat, I'll probably stumble across a popina *or someplace to eat. Even if the walk is far, breaking it up with dinner in between won't be so bad.*

I tapped on Callum's name on the messaging screen. Sure enough, his contact information popped up, including his address. When I tapped on the address, a holo map projected up from my screen, showing me the fastest route from the Research Building to Callum's flat about a mile away.

I could make that in twenty minutes, easy. I need to learn more about the layout of Excelsis, anyway.

"I could call you a hover," Dr. Yong offered as I studied the map.

"That's all right, it will be nice to stretch my legs."

The slight woman nodded once and finished packing her things.

"Actually," I started, turning toward her, "would you like to grab dinner with me?"

Her eyes grew wide, and I could finally see that her irises were not black at all, but they were the color of hickory nuts I often found in the woods.

"Oh, no, no. I still have much work to do at home." Dr. Yong started to pack her things more quickly.

"More work?"

"Yes."

"Would you like help?" I offered, regret sinking deep as soon as the words left my mouth.

Dr. Yong shook her head anxiously. "No, no." She slung her bag over her shoulder and started walking out the ray-door.

"Dr. Yong!" I called out to her. She turned, not meeting my eyes. "Your lab coat?"

The young doctor glanced down to see her white lab coat still buttoned. "Silly me," she chuckled to herself, walking back through the doorway. Her laugh was a bright, innocent noise—beautiful in a simple sort of way, just like her. Not simple-minded, of course, but in her appearance.

Once she hung up her lab coat in the corner closet of the room, she nodded to me and left the laboratory, not bothering to escort me back down to the lobby of the building. As she disappeared down the corridor, I thought about taking my lab COM-tab home. There were probably files I could access that might prove to be beneficial for the Resistance, though everything I would do on there could be monitored. And right now, patience might be key in order to gain trust. After a few weeks, it might not seem suspicious for me to be taking work home or looking into other research.

I left the complex with a pit in my stomach. I felt as though I had forgotten something, but I had no idea what it could be, especially since Dr. Yong did not go through any closing procedures or exiting information. So, I continued walking south toward the First Ward. Though the night sky was a looming pit of obsidian, the buildings and walkways of Excelsis gleamed in the darkness. The fresh air was crisp and rejuvenating after a full day stuffed in a laboratory.

My COM-tab, which was safely stowed in my black leather bag slung across my back, chimed faintly after I had walked a block. I ignored it, too focused on finding a place to eat.

After walking eight blocks, I had not found a single *popina* or *prandium.* My stomach was starting to ache from its emptiness, and my head started to feel dizzy from the lack of sugar in my system. I reached into my bag and pulled out my COM-tab. A message from Callum was displayed across the screen, but I ignored it, too eager to find food. The three-dimensional map informed me of a *Chorus Clava* just a few blocks ahead. A dance club wasn't exactly what I was looking for, but it still advertised food, and I was desperate. I checked the time, and it was only twenty-thirty. *Who would actually be clubbing this early, anyway?*

I kept my map open as I followed the route it highlighted to the *clava*. Excelsis' controlled climate usually kept the evening around eighteen degrees Celsius, so the air felt cool on my skin as sweat beaded at my brow and lower back as I marched along the *trames*, my feet throbbing from the damned heeled boots I had been wearing all day.

I glanced up at the neon blinking sign above me. *Bacchanalia.*

Thankfully, there was no line outside of the club, but there were a few Excelsians smoking something that smelled like lilacs.

I started for the entrance, but when I grabbed for the handle, a large brute of a man appeared in front of the door. I hadn't noticed him standing there a second ago, though I should have— I always noticed everyone, everywhere. I glanced up at his massive face, his bald head shown brightly in the neon lights, but not from the shine of his skull, but the gleam of gold piercings dotted throughout his scalp. His small eyes narrowed, nearly hidden by a protruding brow bone.

"Chip."

"Excuse me?"

The towering man bent down, arms crossed tightly over his bulging pectorals. "Chip," he demanded again.

"Oh," I stammered. "Of course." I extended my left arm, and the brute scanned my chip with a wand very similar to the one Ms. Martinez had used. However, this one glowed green when meeting my chip instead of shocking me.

The hulking bouncer nodded toward the door. I started to step into the club when I heard, simultaneously, my COM-tab chime and a pleading scream from around the corner of the building.

"What was that?" I asked the bouncer, ignoring my device.

"Your COM-tab?" the man grumbled.

I shoved the man. "No, the screaming!"

He shook off my shove and shrugged.

"Shouldn't you go check it out?"

He shrugged again.

"Are you serious?" I moved to stand right in front of him. The huge man kept his gaze tight and looked over my head as another scream sounded, grating down my spine like a lion's claw. "You have to do something!"

The man slowly looked down at me. "Not. My. Job." His voice was a low grumble—callused and hard, just like his heart.

Another plea echoed from around the corner. I dropped my bag at the bouncer's feet and bolted into the alley. Through the darkness, a flickering light shined dimly on two figures. One smaller, lither figure with long, flowing hair was pinned against the wall. Her wrists were held above her head, both of them bound by the massive hand of the second figure, and even in the dim light, I recognized the golden hair and the man's strong, dimpled chin.

"Fuck off, Clausen!" Slowly, I stomped toward the brute and his victim.

Major General Clausen turned his head toward me, and his eyes widened hungrily as he took me in. "Well, if it isn't the Lieutenant General's little pet. I was getting there—to the fucking that is," he purred. "Come back for more? Is little Osouf not satisfying you enough, *whore*?" Clausen's lips were etched into a smile that was neither feline nor canine, but of a creature more deadly than both combined.

I kept my eyes fixed on the girl who was trembling as tears streamed down her face, smearing her dark makeup. Her blouse was torn, breasts exposed and peaked in the chilled air. "Let. The girl. Go." I spat. To my shock, Clausen released her wrists and threw the girl to the ground. I ran over to her, whipping off my coat before I crouched over her small body and covered the girl's exposed chest. I tried to comfort her, but the hairs on my neck stood on end as a shadow loomed over us.

Hot breath crawled into my ear. "You're the one I am really after anyway, Adellaide," Clausen whispered. "And I want you all to myself."

Before I knew it, something solid impacted my stomach, and I was sent flying. A rock stabbed into my right kidney as I landed hard on my back, my vision blinded by phosphenes. A large pressure fell onto my hips, and as my vision returned, I found Clausen straddling me. I turned my head to where the girl was previously, and, in the distance, a small figure darted through the alleyway, heading for the other end. A small wave of relief passed through me as the girl escaped, but as my gaze returned to my assailant, all my muscles tightened and my jaw clenched. I readied myself.

Clausen started to open his mouth to speak again, but now was not the time for talking.

I thrust my hips forward and leveraged myself to whip my right leg up despite the spot where the rock barbed, protesting. I jabbed my foot right into the back of Clausen's neck, and the force sent him forward enough that I pulled myself from under him and curled over into a solid crouch. I whipped my head around to see Clausen rising to his feet, grunting as he rubbed the back of his neck.

"Bitch has a bite."

I stood up to face him. "How about you cut your losses and go home to grope yourself?"

Clausen sauntered toward me, eyes narrowed in a predatory gleam. "Because, *Carissima*," he purred, "I came out for a ride, and it just so happens that I found the prized mare." Clausen jolted for me, attempting to grab my hair, but I ducked under him and turned to give him two quick jabs, one to each kidney.

My attacker grunted while he stumbled forward and turned. "Looks like Osouf still hasn't broken you yet." Clausen grabbed for my wrist. He clenched down tight, and it took all my willpower to stifle a cry. Pulling me close, Clausen flushed his front into my back. "Maybe we should start with a bit so you learn how to keep your mouth shut." His mouth skimmed my left ear. "Or should we start with a rope so I can keep you exactly where I want you?" He released a tight, ragged breath. "Right. Between. My legs." I felt Clausen pulse against my back, and my stomach whirled in disgust.

"Your metaphors are really getting annoying," I replied, as I leaned forward, then shot back to nail my skull into his nose. Warm liquid flooded down my neck, drenching my white blouse as iron and salt filled my nose.

Clausen's hand bound my wrists like steel cuffs, but I twisted and turned to knee him in the groin, after which he finally released his grip and crumpled forward. I grasped my hands around his ears and pulled his head down as I drove my right knee into his nose again. More blood poured out onto my white pleated pants.

He was kneeling on the ground, hands clutching his nose, when I turned to leave him there, collapsed and bleeding in the dark alley. But as I started to walk away, a hand gripped my ankle and pulled me down onto the concrete. My chin bounced off the ground with a hard *clunk*. Clausen dragged me through the blood and gravel toward him. I flipped over onto my back, and I used my other foot to kick my attacker in the jaw. I was free again, but I was done running. I got to my feet and tackled the beast. We were a twist of limbs and flesh, and I couldn't help but smile at the irony as we tumbled in the dirt and dust of the alley. Clausen had finally shoved me off, chest heaving, but anger contorted his face into something I had never seen—the cunning smile was gone, replaced by a feral grimace that reminded me of horrifying beasts in faerie tales my father used to read to me as a child.

Staring at me, Clausen wiped the blood gushing from his nose with his forearm, blue eyes dark in the shadows of the night.

Run. A small part of me thought. *You are faster; you can run.* I was faster, and though I was strong, compared to this hulk of a man, I was a small sparrow, and he was a golden eagle looking for his next meal. But I was faster—I could maneuver around him until I eventually got the better of him. I just had to get him in the right hold—I could render him unconscious if I could wrap my legs around his torso and get my arms around his neck.

Just run, Red.

NO. I was not running. I never ran. And I wasn't going to start now.

We squared off, each of us waiting for the other to make a move. But Clausen's anger wore his patience thin. He charged for me, taking aim at my waist. I sidestepped left to avoid his collision, and then I swung around to give him two hard hooks in the ribs, but he anticipated my attack. I was caught off guard when he extended an arm, catching my left side, and shoved me down onto the ground. All the air was forced from my lungs, and I was under him once again, but this time my arms were pinned under me. I couldn't push up; I couldn't move as Clausen's full weight crushed into my hips, forcing me into the cold concrete. His knees pressed tightly into each of my sides as I tried to wriggle and writhe, but with each movement, Clausen would render an opposing force to mine tenfold.

Dark blood dripped from his nose onto my face.

"That took a little longer than I had planned, but here we are again." He cocked a cruel smile. "I do like a challenge." Clausen reached down to slide a thick finger down my jaw and to my neck, spreading his warm, slick blood across my skin. He didn't stop as he reached my collarbone, where my blouse started.

No.

He continued down over my blouse and grabbed my right breast with his bloody hand.

"To think, you have let so many other men—and women"— he smiled at the thought—"touch you, yet you refuse to let me."

Another drop of blood fell. It landed on my lower lip, its warmth sliding down the side of my mouth. "Why is that, *Carissima?*"

I spat in his face.

Clausen was not phased. He simply wiped my spit off with a finger and sucked on it. He smiled viciously.

This is it, I couldn't help but think to myself. *Clausen will rape me, and no one will care because they think I am a whore anyway.*

My assaulter clutched the fabric around my breast, pinching my nipple. A small noise escaped my lips, something between a whimper and a scream, and the creature smiled down at me in pleasure. He started to tug at my blouse, but before he could tear the fabric, exposing my breast to the cool night air, a black figure toppled him to the side and clubbed his left temple with the hilt of a blaster. Clausen tumbled to the ground as I lay frozen on the concrete. A single tear fell from my right eye, crawled down the side of my face, and dripped onto the ground.

"Get up." I recognized the tight female voice.

"Bellona?"

"Get up and get moving!"

I stood up, but I took a moment to glance back to find Clausen strewn across the concrete ground, unmoving. When I glanced back at Bellona, she was sprinting around the corner—a wraith in the night. I tried to catch up to the Major General, but the heel on my left boot was broken. When I entered the light of the *trames,* Bellona stood by the entrance of *Bacchanalia,* and I hobbled to her side. The massive bouncer was still standing in front of the door, arms crossed and his expression sober as a dark hover with tinted windows pulled up beside us. Bellona shoved me in the back seat. Every bone in my body ached at her touch, but I didn't bother protesting despite not knowing who was driving the vehicle.

The hover was dark, the only light emanating from the windshield display screen. I strained to get a good look at the driver, but he was wearing all black with a cap covering most of his face. As soon as Bellona climbed into the passenger seat, the vehicle bolted forward.

No one spoke. As minutes passed, I recognized the route we were taking—it was the same route I would have taken to get back to Callum's flat. Sure enough, a few minutes later, the hover stopped under the tower of condominiums. Bellona, smooth and quiet, slid out of the hover and opened the door for me. I crawled out, not making a sound. The driver opened their door and left the vehicle as well. Once we were all on the sidewalk outside of the complex, the hover beeped a few times, then zoomed away, not a single person in the vehicle.

"Shouldn't someone be driving—" I finally got a good look at the driver, and I realized I was in a lot of trouble.

Callum, stone-faced and jaw set into a tight line, stood between Bellona and me. He glanced at his Major General. "Did you at least get the footage?"

CHAPTER 23

Callum led the way into the complex, the black leather work bag he had given me earlier that day—the same one I'd thrown at the bouncer's feet—slung over his shoulder. Bellona, dressed in all black, looked like death's personal assassin. She nodded me toward the entrance, a silent command. I rolled my eyes as I removed the white leather torture apparatuses called shoes, clutched them in my right hand, and strode after Callum, keeping my back straight and my head held high despite the knot forming in the pit of my stomach. I had no idea why I felt guilty, but it was there—settling deep in my abdomen and tightening around my chest like a constricting snake.

What footage was Callum asking about? Is it footage of me? Do they know I'm Resistance?

The elevator ride was long as I mentally scrolled through everything I did today, trying to find an error—a moment when I might have given myself away. The air was stale and silent, and as we strode into Callum's apartment, even Sirius must have sensed something tense swirling around the soldiers and me because the canine rose from the couch. As soon as his gaze met

Callum's, Sirius' ears and tail fell in apprehension, and he changed his trajectory from us to Callum's bedroom.

Bellona closed the door behind us, pressed a few buttons on the keypad adjacent to it, and a quick gleam of blue light lined the perimeters of the whole flat before returning to normal. Casually, the Major General leaned against the door, a small smirk crawling across her lips as she looked at me. Her brows flicked up in— *Warning? Expectation?*

Callum whirled on me. "What, the FUCK, Adellaide?"

My heart stopped. "Um, excuse me?" I gawked at the Lieutenant General as we stood nose to nose.

"What. The. FUCK. Were. You. Thinking?" Callum enunciated every word. "Why didn't you message me when you were leaving? Why didn't you take a hover home? You didn't even look at the messages I was sending you! You didn't take my call! You ignored my every attempt to contact you!"

I couldn't help but laugh at his audacity. *He doesn't know I'm Resistance. He is just upset that I didn't heed him like a trained canine.* "Are you seriously making this my fault? I was nearly *raped*, then left for *nothing* in the dust and dirt of an alley, and you are making this *my* fault?"

Callum inched closer. "I told you to take a hover." His voice was a low, commanding rumble.

I looked him dead in the eyes. "I am not a soldier that you can just command about, Lieutenant General."

I shoved past him. I couldn't stand to breathe the same air as him, but Callum grabbed my wrist.

"Do not touch me!" I growled and jerked away from his grasp. "I have been assaulted enough for one night. I don't need *your hands* all over me either." A flicker of hurt flashed in his emerald eyes. *Good,* I thought. I wanted him to hurt.

I turned my back on him and walked into the living room.

"Tell me why, Adellaide. Tell me why you didn't message me. Why you didn't want to take a hover back home." Callum followed after me, but Bellona moved to the kitchen, keeping her distance from the altercation.

She's probably enjoying the show. I thought of the flick of her eyebrows before Callum started yelling.

I turned with an exasperated sigh. "Because I was hungry! I was hungry, and I was stuck inside all day. I just wanted some fresh air!"

"And you thought a good time for that would be at night? In a Circulum that is still very new for you?"

"I wanted to clear my head after a very long and exhausting day."

"Not all that exhausting if you were still up for a walk." Bellona nearly yawned, arms crossed in boredom.

"Excuse me? What exactly are you implying?"

"It's just a little suspicious." The Major General's eyes were iced over.

"Bell—"

"Oh, no. Let her speak." I gestured to Bellona.

She shrugged. "Either it's your first day off-leash, and you decided to test your boundaries, or you were waiting for an opportunity."

"An opportunity for what?"

The Major General leaned her elbows on the kitchen island, and her feral smile gleamed in the Imperium city lights streaming through the windows. "I don't know. You tell us. What I do know is that you're hiding something, Ms. Stevens, and tonight you slipped."

"The only thing I am hiding, Major General, is the pleasure I would have pummeling you into the ground."

"Aggression will not help your case." Bellona arched a dark brow.

I started for her, but Callum used one hand to push me back. I used that momentum to turn in a circle, pacing in an attempt to get my head straight.

"How did you even know where I was? Why were you even there?"

The soldiers exchanged glances, Bellona taking a second to look at Callum.

Then I remembered what Callum had told me days ago. "It was a setup. You need dirt on Clausen so he doesn't get promoted."

Callum sighed. "It wasn't a setup. It was a stakeout."

"Sir—"

The Lieutenant General waved Bellona off. "We have been tracking him. We know his patterns and predicted something like this"—Callum waved to nothing in particular—"would happen tonight."

"But I—"

"You were not a variable we thought we would have to worry about," Callum said flatly.

"So, what? You were just going to watch him rape that poor girl tonight?"

Callum sat on the couch and rubbed at the stubble around his jaw. "He was going to whether we were there or not."

I stood over him. "But you were there! You could have stopped it!"

Callum leaned on his knees. "With that footage, we could have prevented many other occurrences. With that footage, we could have saved many more women."

"Could have?" I asked.

"We're not sure if the footage we have of *you* will be good enough," Bellona replied.

I crossed my arms. "And why not?"

"Because he didn't actually rape you." Callum stared at his feet.

"Well, he certainly implied he was going to. Many, many times."

"That's not good enough."

"Why not?"

"Because," Callum started, "you would be surprised how many people can talk their way out of trouble."

I couldn't believe this was happening. "But he assaulted me!"

"It doesn't matter."

I stared at the Lieutenant General, then at the Major General. "This has happened before?"

Callum nodded. "And not just with him."

Bellona sighed. "This type of thing has become a serious problem inside the Military ranks."

"Why?"

Callum shrugged. "We have our theories."

"Well, what about that bouncer? Why didn't he do anything?"

"We are looking into that." Callum breathed deeply and rubbed at his chin. "If he really didn't care, claiming that it wasn't his problem, there isn't much we can do. But if he was paid off by Clausen or even his boss to ignore these types of things, we can charge him and whoever else is involved for bribery."

I nodded, taking in all this new information. Then I realized I forgot to turn my lenses on and cursed myself silently.

Silence lingered before I finally asked, "So, why didn't you let him rape me?"

Callum's eyes widened and his jaw fell slack.

"Well, if you needed the proof so badly, maybe you should have." I glanced at Bellona, and she shrugged. Maybe she had suggested that in the first place—they thought Adellaide was a prostitute after all.

Callum stood up and walked over to me. "Do not"—the Lieutenant General growled, index finger pointed right at my chest—"*ever* suggest *that* again."

I slapped his hand away. "What's the difference, Osouf?" What is the difference between me and that poor, innocent girl?"

"The difference is I know you."

"Well, someone knew her!"

"You are under my protection!"

"You are going to be General of the Coalition's Army. Everyone is under your protection!"

Callum turned away from me and ran a hand through his wavy hair. "We are done with this conversation."

"Just admit that either way, you were in the wrong! Just admit your plan was bullshit from the get-go, and you were going to make a very poor decision!"

He whirled on me. "I was making a hard decision. That's my job, Ms. Stevens. I have to make the hard calls, and I was sticking to my decision because the benefits outweighed the costs!" Callum's shoulders fell. "Then I was going to stay up all night, wondering if I actually did make the right call, playing whatever horrible things happened over and over in my mind, wondering if *one girl* was worth all the rest." He shook his head. "I couldn't even guarantee there would be more, but the chances were very high, so I made the call. And Skies-dammit all, I was going to deal with the consequences. But you"—Callum pointed another finger at me—"came along and fucked everything up! Because if there was one thing on this Earth I couldn't deal with, it would be watching the horrible things Clausen has done to countless other women being done to you!"

Tears brimmed Callum's eyes, and his chest heaved. "So that's why, Adellaide." His voice was just above a whisper now. "Maybe I was weak. Maybe I made the wrong choice—forsaking the mission for your safety—and maybe I will regret not retrieving you myself right after I castrated that poor excuse of a man right there in that fucking alley, but I am willing to deal with those consequences." He turned from me again and rubbed his face between his palms.

In my periphery, I saw Bellona cross her arms as she studied her Commanding Officer. I had almost forgotten she was in the room with us.

"Cal—" I reached for him, but he stepped away from me.

"Ander—" Callum's voice cracked. "Anderson and I need to discuss a plan of action not suited for civilian ears." He took a deep breath. "And you need your rest. The last thing we need is for you to be late to work again tomorrow morning."

I glanced over to Bellona, and she gave me a single nod. I knew there was nothing I could do, nothing I could say to—to—I didn't know what I was supposed to do. Comfort him? Talk with him? Smooth everything over? I knew I was completely helpless in this mess. So, I padded toward my room.

Clicking the door shut behind me, I took a deep breath as tears stung my eyes. I didn't exactly know why. All I knew was I hurt. Everything hurt. My muscles, my fingers, my heart. It all hurt. And the best thing to do when everything hurt was shower.

———

I scrubbed every inch of me raw in an attempt to remove the feeling of Clausen's hands on my skin, and I think I might have been crying because the water that dripped into my mouth tasted of salt.

Hand-to-hand combat was something I had experienced a lot —nearly every day of my life since joining the Coalition Resistance Forces—but today was different, though I couldn't put my finger on exactly how. Today, I wasn't just fighting for rank or my survival. I was fighting for something so much more. *Was it my virtue? Or sexuality?* Whatever it was, it was deep—it was some innate part of me. Besides Ulysses, I had never been bested by anyone before, and it terrified me. I felt like a part of me was torn away. I had always been good at fighting. That was me. That was Rowyn. But without that part of me, I didn't know who I was.

When I stepped out of the shower, my skin was beet red from the intense heat of the rushing water. Slowly, I dried myself off, savoring the softness of the plush white towel over my sensitive skin. I had changed into a long nightshirt and towel-dried my hair as I put my ear to the door and strained to listen for any noises in the living room. All was quiet. Yet, as I silently pushed the door open, I heard Bellona's voice, her normal voice, loud enough I should have been able to hear her through the door. Then I recalled Bellona punching a code into the screen-pad by the front door and the strange blue light that flickered over the walls of Callum's flat.

She must have entered a code to make the flat, or maybe just the living room, soundproof.

I was about to shut the door when I heard my name. Well, my alias name.

"Adellaide is hiding something," Bellona said like she had told Callum the same thing a million times before. "You saw the way she moved today. You saw how she fought. No one outside of the Military can move like that."

"She is a prostitute. They can be…bendy…"

"Bendy? She held her own against Clausen for over *four minutes*. That is better than any soldier Clausen has been up against, aside from the two of us."

Four minutes? It felt like a lot longer than that…

"What are you saying, Major General?"

"I am saying," Bellona's voice sounded strained and frustrated, "that the odds of her being a Resistance spy just increased greatly." Callum must have made some gesture in disagreement because Bellona continued. "For Skies' sake, get your head out of your ass! You are letting your feelings for this *girl* get the better of your judgment."

"What are you talking about?"

"Look, Adellaide is attractive and intriguing, but she is not one of us. Whether that's because she is from Media or because she is a Resistance spy, I don't know, but she is not compatible."

"You are overstepping, Major."

"With all due respect, sir," Bellona snapped, "I am advising you to switch your perspective. We saw tonight that she has the potential to be a threat, and we *both* need to take that seriously."

"She couldn't take down Clausen. You actually think she could take on one of us?"

Bloody damn right I could.

"If she gets in your head and catches you off guard, she very well could. And based on your actions tonight, I question whether you could pull the trigger."

"Major General." Callum's voice was edged with venom.

"Cal— sir," Bellona corrected herself. "I am just trying to—"

"And I appreciate it, Major General. I will take your *opinions* into *consideration.*"

Bellona released a frustrated sigh. "Fine. But if I have to save your sorry ass because you miscalculated—"

"Then the sky would have caught on fire, and aliens would have invaded Earth because that is not going to happen!"

I heard rustling from the couch, and I shut the door softly before someone could walk by. I turned off my overhead light, crawled into bed, and clicked on the reading light on my nightstand. I picked up *Winnie the Pooh Bear* and flipped through the pages once again. I had devoured the book last night, scanning through every line and searching for more hidden pockets, but there was no indication of further clues or messages my father had left for me or Callum, for that matter. I doubted I would find anything tonight after such a thorough search, but maybe a fresh set of eyes...

Blue light flickered over every inch of my room, and I heard the front door shut. Footsteps padded outside the guest room, then a knock sounded at the door. I quickly covered my lap with my comforter and ran a hand through my hair, still cold and damp from the shower.

"Come in."

Callum opened the door and slid into the room, Sirius sneaking in behind him. The Direwolf trotted past Callum, jumped on my bed, and curled himself on my left, his head on my lap as he nudged my hand with his muzzle. I petted him but kept my eyes on Callum as he sat at the foot of the bed.

"I know you were listening. Bellona did, too."

I nodded. *Of course they knew.*

"The panel next to the door flashes green whenever a door opens in silencer mode," he explained.

Of course it did.

"So, I only heard what you two wanted me to hear?" It wasn't exactly a question, but Callum nodded, glancing down at the bedspread. "I am not a spy," I lied as I kept my gaze on the Lieutenant General.

Callum glanced up, assessing me. "Spy or not, you would say that. Only time will tell." Callum looked—well, I didn't know how Callum looked. His eyes seemed heavy, and his lips were pursed into a tight line. "But Bellona will be keeping a close eye on you."

"I figured." I stared at my fingers as I fidgeted with a piece of white string torn from the blanket.

"I knew where you were by your chip," Callum admitted. "Just as it tracks which rooms you enter in the Research Center, there are scanners throughout the city that track people every day. I was keeping tabs on you during your first day of work, and I received updates on all your movements."

I nodded, not knowing what to say. Honestly, I had figured as much. The possibility of him tracking me via my chip had occurred to me while I was in the shower.

Callum sighed. "Adellaide, there is more."

I glanced up at him.

"I have told you about the medical data your chip tracks, like metabolism, heart rate, and the like. Well, with that data and through your blood samples, we found some interesting things."

I arched a brow.

Did he find out who my father was? Did he discover I was Rowyn?

"You have an unusually high metabolism, in addition to an advanced immune system and unique healing capabilities."

"So?"

His eyes grew cold. "You knew about these? When I asked you about your wounds healing quickly before, you said Aletheia applied something to speed up the healing process. Was that a lie?"

"I didn't want to scare you." I shrugged.

"So, you are aware you have accelerated healing capabilities?"

I nodded. "I have noticed my wounds healing faster than others."

"You see, that's the thing, Adellaide." Callum pursed his lips. "Your genetic make-up is not consistent with other humans.' We can track someone's lineage based on genetic markers—we can even do that if we don't know their parents' genetic information —and we can chart how closely two people are related based on their DNA. You are not more closely related to anyone than a scorpion is to a spider. You are not more closely related to a human than you are to an ape."

I gawked at him. "What does that mean?"

"I was hoping you could tell me."

"Callum, I—"

He took my chin between his fingers, fixing our eyes together. "I don't know what you are hiding, but *now* is your chance to tell me."

"I'm not—" I tried to interject, but Callum wouldn't let me.

"Because if you want me to, I can fix it. *Right now*. I can make whatever it is right. I can cover up whatever you need me to. Adellaide, you *can* start over here." *With me*. Those were the unspoken words that seemed to fall from his lips as Callum's eyes pleaded with mine. "But you have to tell me now."

His offer was tempting, like Eve offering Adam the forbidden fruit. I have only been back in the Coalition for a week, and I have seen the corruption; I have experienced the horror of this society. Yet this man in front of me, a highly ranked official in the Coalition Military—my enemy—has been nothing but kind and gentle toward me. I couldn't imagine him purposefully hurting anyone but himself in an attempt to save someone.

Except for that poor girl in the alley. The thought crept into my mind like a serpent.

But even his friends are good and honorable people, soldiers trying to do their best to keep the Coalition safe.

I thought of the chip in my arm. I thought of Clausen's hand around my throat, the violence in Media Callum talked about, and the gaunt faces in Humilis.

I thought of Reign.

I looked Callum dead in the eyes, took a deep breath…and lied. "I am not hiding anything." I lied like I had done ever since that day in Humilis. I watched Callum as his eyes turned to stone, as his jaw set into a tight line, and his throat bobbed as he took in a deep breath and nodded once to me.

"Okay." He didn't believe me. I felt it in my bones. We both knew I was lying. And I lied anyway.

Callum clapped his hands together and uncurled himself from the foot of my bed. "Goodnight, Ms. Stevens."

Callum snapped his fingers. Sirius leapt from the bed and followed his master out of my room.

And everything we could have been cracked beneath the force of the door Callum slammed behind him.

CHAPTER 24

I arrived to work on time, early actually, and I was waiting for Hlín in the laboratory we worked in previously, which apparently was the wrong place to wait for her.

"Oh, no. We are not working in here today. We are working on floor twenty-three," she chastised once she found me in the lab fifteen minutes after I had arrived.

"Well, maybe that's something you should have communicated, Dr. Yong."

She cocked her head, dark hair unmoving in its tight bun. "Did you not look at the weekly itinerary, Ms. Stevens?"

My heart dropped into my stomach. "You didn't tell me there was a weekly itinerary."

"Yes, yes. It is on your COM-tab." Dr. Yong pulled me from the room and started leading me toward the elevators.

"I wasn't sure if I was supposed to bring it home!"

"Yes, Ms. Stevens. How else do you work on the research at home?"

We entered an elevator unit. "Dr. Yong, you saw me put the COM-tab in the safe. You should have said something. I am supposed to do additional work at home?"

The woman shrugged, her eyes fixed on the elevator door.

I sighed. "Is there anything else I should know about?"

She shook her head, but I didn't believe her. I had a feeling this was either a 'need-to-know-basis' job or she was a 'need-to-know' kind of person. Or maybe she simply hated confronting people.

"So, what is on floor twenty-three?"

"Behavioral Observation."

"For what?" The elevator came to a stop, and Hlín walked out, her footsteps so controlled they were nearly silent on the linoleum floor. She didn't answer my question. I stomped after her in a huff, and maybe it was the lack of sleep that wore on my patience, but I yelled after her, "Are you going to tell me anything?"

Dr. Hlín Yong continued to shuffle forward down the brightly lit hallways, turning this way and that down long corridors. We finally arrived at room 2325, its ray-door glowing green. I followed Dr. Yong into the laboratory, and as soon as I had both feet through the ray-door, excited high-pitched chirps filled my ears. I looked back toward the entrance, stunned I couldn't hear the boisterous chirping from the elevator corridor.

"The ray-doors are soundproof, too?" I asked Dr. Yong as she unpacked her bag.

"Not exactly. Embedded in the doorways of some laboratories are frequency cancellers. They are quite specific, so one device will cancel out a set of frequencies, and another device will cancel out another set. It doesn't catch all sound, but it catches most of it."

"Interesting." I studied the door, searching for any evidence of the devices, and sure enough, there were small, flat, black disks all around the trim of the doorways. "Lieutenant General Osouf's flat can soundproof the walls and rooms. Does it work in a similar manner?" I turned back to the doctor. She had slid on her lab coat and started to slip on brown leather gloves.

"Oh, no. Silencers within homes work much differently. They adjust with the frequencies of the molecules within the walls, stabilizing the atoms. Sound travels by atoms and their components vibrating at a certain speed. If the atoms do not vibrate, sound cannot transmit."

I nodded. "But we cannot use that here because of the ray-doors?"

"Correct." Dr. Yong handed me a pair of gloves, the twin pair to hers, and as I slid them on, I took a moment to observe the noisy laboratory. The room was filled with tall, acrylic enclosures, and in them were brightly colored creatures. They flittered around their cages, chirping and singing to each other. I slowly walked over to enclosure number four as I buttoned up my white lab coat, fumbling with the buttons through the cumbersome leather gloves.

"What are they?" I gawked at the tiny, beautiful creatures. They had the wings and head of a small bird and bore feathers all over their bodies, but they stood on four mammalian legs with long, tufted tails whipping from their backsides.

Yong stood beside me, admiring the creatures as I did. "These are *Aurum Leo Fringilla*."

"Gold Lion Finches," I whispered because I didn't want to scare them. They looked like miniature griffins. I was mesmerized by how their wings seemed to glisten as they flitted around in their cage, and their tails seemed so tiny and fragile I couldn't imagine how practical they would be. But on a much larger creature, it would be powerful.

Callum did say that his mother created Sirius, a Direwolf. Could she—or her team—have created huge griffins? What would be the implications of that kind of experimentation?

Dr. Yong nodded. "They are one of our species in *Fringillinal Felidae*. This species was our first successful experimentation in creating a whole new species of animal that can reproduce."

I glanced around the room. "Well, it looks like breeding has been successful."

"Extremely."

"What exactly needs observing? It seems like they are thriving."

Dr. Yong nodded to the opposite side of the room, and we walked over to an enclosure closest to the window—enclosure number nine. "These are our troubled members. They tend to be more aggressive."

Even at first glance, I understood what she meant—feathers littered the bottom of the enclosure, most likely torn out due to fighting—and these small creatures didn't flit around like the rest of the groups. Instead, they segregated themselves into small flocks, puffing up and emitting a high-pitched clicking sound when a different member got too close.

"They have obtained more lion behaviors than the rest?"

Dr. Yong nodded. "Most likely. Though, we are still not sure if the aggression is something that can be trained out of the individual or if we need to eradicate their genes from the pool."

I stepped closer, thinking about the options she laid out. "I think it depends on their purpose. If you intend to merge them into an ecosystem within the Coalition, having aggressive birds —lions—Lion Finches wouldn't be the worst thing because it would keep population numbers down. However, if you intend for people to keep them as pets, for the safety of the civilians, it would be better to weed out the aggressive birds."

"Yes, yes," Dr. Yong nodded. "These are all things we have considered. These creatures could be beneficial in Humilis Circulums throughout the Coalition. *Leo Fringillia* are omnivores, so if we introduced them into Humilian ecosystems, they would help disperse seeds for crops, just like finches, in addition to aiding in pest control in fields and barns, similar to small cats." The doctor sighed. "But Freyja is certain these creatures would be a hit in small pockets of Excelsian high society. She thinks we could make a profit selling them to collectors and oddity enthusiasts."

Odd. This was a government facility; this was government research. Why would Freyja need, or even seek, to turn a profit?

I walked over to enclosure eight, observing the other flock of happy Lion Finches. "Well, if you released them into Humilis, that could potentially harm the ecosystem. They would be in invasive species—they could take over."

"Potentially."

"That doesn't worry you?"

"It's just Humilis, Ms. Stevens. Either the ecosystem will adapt, or the people of Humilis will. Some things in science can't be predicted. You just must run the experiment and record the data."

My blood ran cold. That's all this was to Dr. Yong. Humilis didn't matter. The lives of citizens did not matter. The lives of these Lion Finches did not matter. The only thing of value to Dr. Yong was her data and probably the paycheck she received every week.

Was this how my father thought? Is this the type of work he would take part in? Creating unnatural creatures for the hell of it, not bothering to think of the consequences? *Is this why he left?*

I swallowed my resolve and played my part. "I don't see why they can't be both." I shrugged. "Send the more aggressive ones to Humilis, planting flocks on farms, while the docile creatures can be sold as pets."

The young doctor paused. "Yes," she said thoughtfully, "that might be a great solution, Ms. Stevens."

I shrugged. "Who knows? It could be another experiment to see how the two different groups adapt over time. They might even evolve to be separate species one day."

Hlín's eyes lit up. "Brilliant."

I kept my attention on the creatures in enclosure eight. One Lion Finch flew over and perched on a branch close to the habitat's door. It stretched its wings wide and cocked its little head. The Lion Finch's golden eyes grew wide in bemusement, like I was the one in the cage. Its little tufted ears twitched as its friends chirped and sang around him, but its eyes never left mine.

"May I?" I asked Dr. Yong, not daring to look away from the curious finch.

Dr. Yong nodded slightly then reached to unlock the enclosure. Once the door was open, I slid my gloved hand between the slip of the screen and slowly placed it before the miniature griffin. The Lion Finch hopped on the leather glove with a chirp, and its tail twitched back and forth in either nervousness or excitement, I couldn't tell. Slowly, I pulled it from the enclosure and tucked the feathered creature close to my chest. I examined every inch of the small beast as the doctor clipped a leash to a cuff encircled around his back leg and wound the leash around my fingers. Yong must have startled the little guy because the Lion Finch stepped away from her hand, chirping loudly.

"I see you added a hook to its beak." Normal finches had large protruding beaks that came to a small, fine point, perfect for cracking open seeds.

"We figured that if they gained a hunting instinct from their lion DNA, we should equip them like a bird of prey."

"Smart." Though I didn't see how it would encourage them to be omnivores—if their beaks are made for cracking open seeds, they are going to eat seeds. I turned my hand over, wanting to get a good look at the Lion Finch from every angle. He—or she—was bigger than a normal finch but no larger than a robin, and its golden feathers glinted in the fluorescent lighting. The Lion Finch's molten-gold eyes followed my every move, and they reminded me of mine. Of Rowyn's eyes. I felt like I was staring into my own eyes.

"I would be careful, Ms. Stevens. They can be temperamental when you stare at them for too long. They see it as a challenge."

I ignored the doctor's warning. But then the Lion Finch stretched up on its hind legs, chest puffed, and golden wings spread wide. It bellowed a loud *KAW*, and dark claws jutted out from its back paws. Due to the heavy leather glove, its sharp nails did not puncture the skin, but it was still an impressive sight. I didn't cower from the bird, and it was perplexed by that, eyeing me suspiciously, like it didn't realize it was only the size of a small squirrel but instead saw itself as a large mythical beast.

I let the Lion Finch finish its little fit in peace, not showing any sign of emotion, and once it had finished, it settled back onto my hand and cocked its head to the right. I tilted my head in return. Then the Lion Finch cocked its head again, but this time to the left. I mirrored his movement, which must have excited the beast because it fluffed his feathers, bobbed its golden head, and chirped a few notes of a short song.

"Do they lay eggs?" I asked the doctor. Slowly, I crept an index finger toward the Lion Finch's cheek. It leaned into my touch, allowing me to pet it.

Dr. Yong's jaw fell slack. "Umm…yes."

"How many?" Now I scratched the top of its smooth head.

"Three to four." The young researcher continued to observe me and the Lion Finch, possibly taking mental notes to record later.

The Lion Finch let me slide a finger down its spine, and it even pushed its butt up, urging me to scratch the base of its tail. "I would limit the number of eggs to two," I said nonchalantly. "They do not have any natural predators to keep their population in check."

"But that would bring us back to square one! And we have all these birds we already do not know what to do with."

I shrugged. "Just my advice, if you don't want their flocks to fly out of control in a few years." I brought the Lion Finch up to my right shoulder. He—at least I thought it was a he—hopped on, singing in my ear as he did so.

"I do not know if that is the best idea, Ms. Stevens," the doctor warned.

I simply patted the small head of my new friend. "I think he would love to help us with our work today." I sauntered over to my bag and pulled out my COM-tab. At the jostling movement, I felt little pinpricks on my shoulder as the Lion Finch dug his claws through my coat to keep stable. "What file should I save my notes into today?" I asked, ready to start working.

"Ummm," Dr. Yong stammered, clearly distracted by my new companion. "There is an *Aurum Leo Fringillia* file within the Epimetheus folder."

My heart stopped. "Pardon. What folder?"

"The Epimetheus folder. It is where we keep all of our research for genetically engineered creatures." Dr. Yong looked confused. "Is something wrong, Ms. Stevens?"

Epimetheus. In Greek mythology, Epimetheus was the titan who gifted animals with positive traits to aid their survival in a cruel world. He was also the brother of Prometheus. *Maybe there could be some sort of link between the two projects that could lead to more information about my father.*

"Ms. Stevens…"

I realized I was gawking at Dr. Yong. I blinked my widened eyes a few times and shut my mouth with an audible snap. The Lion Finch on my shoulder flapped his wings at the sudden sound.

"Oh, no. I'm sorry. I just remembered I forgot to tell Cal— Lieutenant General Osouf a time to pick me up." I quietly released a deep breath. "What time should I tell him?"

The doctor blinked at me. "Umm, around eighteen-hundred tonight."

"Right." I quickly messaged Callum telling him when to pick me up because I really did need to do that, but then I exited out of the messaging screen, leaned on an elbow, and tapped my right temple twice. "Now, I'm sorry. Remind me of the project name again."

"The Epimetheus folder is where you will find the *Aurum Leo Fringilla* file. Now, please pay attention, Ms. Stevens," Dr. Hlín Yong chastised as the red dot in my vision blinked to life.

Callum never responded to my message, so I had no idea how I was getting back to his flat as I left the Lion Finch laboratory.

He had hardly talked to me this morning, and now he wasn't responding to my messages. Was he still mad about last night? Did my fight against Clausen really raise suspicions that I might be a Resistance spy?

I pushed the questions from my mind as I exited the Research Facility, a bright red hover catching my eye. Muffled music and a strong bass emanated from the vehicle as it rocked back and forth. The loud, indiscernible music was unleashed like chaos from Pandora's box as the tinted window rolled down to reveal Aletheia behind the wheel, dressed in something short, dark, and revealing. The lithe woman leaned over the passenger seat. Her lips—the exact shade of red as the hover—moved, but her words were drowned out by all the noise. I rushed over, pointing to my ear to signal I couldn't hear a thing she was saying.

Finally, Aletheia turned down the Skies-forsaken racket and repeated, "Get in, princess, we're going out."

"Is that really necessary?" I asked after sliding into the vehicle.

"Is what necessary?" Aletheia asked before she turned the volume dial, blaring a techno-rock mix once again.

"Calling me princess!" I yelled over the noise. The gold-skinned girl shrugged, then proceeded to bang her head to the beat of the song. "Are you even paying attention to the road?"

"What?" Aletheia screamed over the music.

I turned down the music to a dull roar and repeated my question.

"It's on auto! I'm just here for the ride!"

I laughed. "Aren't we all…"

Aletheia let loose a wicked cackle. "Track that!" She reached for the volume dial, but I swatted her hand away.

"Where is Callum?"

She shrugged her narrow shoulders. "All I know is I am on princess duty tonight."

The word 'princess' grated uncomfortably on my ears. "One —stop calling me *princess*. Two—what aren't you telling me?"

Aletheia's eyes grew wide, and her mouth curved mischievously at my tone. "First of all, it's not always about you. Secondly, I need to blow off some steam, and you need to let loose, so that's what we are going to do."

I didn't know what Aletheia had planned, but letting loose was not on my agenda. I had to figure out the Coalition's weak spots. I had to nonchalantly dig in the research database to find something about the Prometheus Project, and I had to mend things with Callum so I could get more info on how he was connected to my father. *Had he seen the note to Wynnie, too?*

I turned to protest, but Aletheia already had one finger up to silence me, her other hand typing a message on her COM-device. "I already got us into the VIP section of *Bacchanalia,* and all my friends are going to be there. I'm in charge of you tonight, and you are going."

I crossed my arms and sighed in defeat. "So, what am I wearing?"

———

I didn't know what I'd expected, but it wasn't this. Different colored lights bounced around the dark room, off every wall, table, chair, and object in the club. According to the large, bright neon sign that greeted us when we walked in, we were at *Bacchanalia.* Aletheia said it was the most exclusive club in Imperium, but it seemed pretty packed for an 'exclusive' venue.

Music pulsated through my bones as soon as we walked through the doors. Some people were dancing, drinking, laughing, singing, smiling, and talking. Others were writhing, grinding, thrusting, grabbing, kissing, and locking up together.

Sancus and Aletheia most likely thought Adellaide was used to scenes like these, but Rowyn was appalled.

They think I work in a brothel, but Aletheia and Sancus frequent one! Callum, too, for all I know.

The middle of the dance floor looked like an orgy—a heap of nearly-naked bodies sweating, thrusting, and grinding to the beat of the music, skin against skin. It was difficult to distinguish where one person began and another stopped.

Aletheia grabbed my hand like we were best friends and led me up to the bar. She ordered us each a drink from a broad male bartender who ignored everyone else once he saw Aletheia. She looked like a golden goddess donned in gold chainmail with her lips and eyes lacquered in gold paint. I looked like a worm compared to her. My makeup was dark, or 'smoky' as Aletheia called it. My lips were painted a nude color, and golden freckles were spattered across the bridge of my nose and cheekbones. Aletheia dressed me in a white mini skirt covered in gold embroidery, a tight black leather tank, and very tall, maroon boots I could hardly walk in.

Sancus, however, looked very charming. He wore a maroon velvet suit with golden embroidery on the lapels of his jacket and big, black leather Military boots. Simple, yet flashy.

Aletheia smiled and winked playfully at the bartender as he mixed our drinks. When he slid her a bright, almost glowing green drink in a long-stemmed crystal glass, Aletheia leaned over the bar and whispered something in his ear, her lips so close they left a stain of gold on the bartender's tanned skin.

He leaned back, a seductive smile stretching across his face, then turned his attention to me. He winked a blue eye at me as he handed a drink twin to Aletheia's, and I couldn't help the blush that bloomed under my gold-painted freckles. Sancus' drink was in a short, stout glass with one ice cube floating gracefully in an amber liquid.

Aletheia and Sancus clinked their glasses to mine and shouted, *"Dum Vivimus Vivamus!"* Then they sipped. I followed suit, though their words remained lost to me. My drink smelled of citrus and tasted like overripe melon fruit. If there was alcohol in it, I couldn't taste any, a stark contrast to whatever brew Metis usually swigged from back at the CRF Base.

We made our way to the dance floor, drinks in hand, and it wasn't long until I lost sight of Aletheia. I turned around in a panic to see Sancus by my side.

"It's ok, Adellaide," he shouted over the roaring music. "Happens every time. She will be fine." The colored lights bounced off Sancus' golden skin, the dark freckles across his cheeks and nose sharp against the light.

Yeah, but what if you leave me, too? I wanted to ask, but I also didn't want to seem needy. Sancus turned to dance against some blonde girl who wore nothing but heels, a mini-skirt, and pink flowers covering her nipples. He winked at me, maybe reassuring me that he would be there while encouraging me to dance with someone as well. And right on cue, a half-naked stranger started to sway against my ass, his silver-painted hands holding tight to my hips. Despite my utter revulsion, I couldn't help the heat blooming across my chest and the tightening between my thighs.

"How's it going, sexy?" the man growled in my left ear.

I couldn't reply. A sense of shame settled in my stomach, and suddenly, I felt bare, naked, and exposed, despite being clothed. My whole body turned red. I turned from my dance partner and bolted toward the entrance.

The cool air was welcoming as I exited the building. I didn't pause for my retreat until my feet met the curb, and all the strength within me seemed to flee my body. I collapsed to the ground, my head falling between my arms as I still clutched the drink Aletheia had ordered for me. I contemplated calling Callum to come pick me up. Though, I knew he had better things to do—bigger things to worry about than my discomfort and strange men writhing against my body.

How could I even explain to the Lieutenant General that I,

Adellaide Stevens, a sex worker from Media, was uncomfortable with strange men riding up on me?

I closed my eyes and took a deep breath. I tried to focus on the bass still beating against my heart and the cool air whistling in my ears, but four words echoed off the hollow corners of my mind. *Why am I here?*

"Yeah, I didn't think you were ready for this." Aletheia's sultry voice greeted me as she sat on the stoop beside me. The glittering, golden woman took a drag of a joint in her hand, held her breath for a long moment, then released grey smoke to her empty side. "For growing up in a brothel, you seem pretty rattled."

I released a sigh. "Triggering, I guess," I lied, not meeting her eyes. "Plus, it's different when you're working rather than—"

"Playing?"

I gave a small, rueful laugh. "Yeah."

Aletheia took another drag from her joint. As she released her breath, she asked, "Ever tried Bacchus' Bloom? It's available illegally in Media, though I think it's called something different."

I shook my head.

"That surprises me." She took another drag.

I shrugged. "Doesn't help with *performance*," I replied, though I had no idea. I just wanted her gone. Better yet, I wanted her to take me back to Callum's flat so I could do something useful with my life. How was I supposed to 'let loose' when the CRF was in danger—when my sister could be fighting for her life right now? But, of course, Aletheia didn't know any of that.

"You have probably spent so much of your life surviving, you haven't been able to just live." Aletheia held out the joint between two dark, slender fingers, her black dagger nail slicing through the night. "It's time to start, Adellaide."

Looking at the small, burning joint, my hand twitched in hesitation. I know she wasn't speaking to me—she wasn't talking to Red. Still, something true rang in her words. Or maybe, deep down, I wanted her words to be true. I wanted to live like the people in *Bacchanalia*—oblivious to the problems of the world. Or maybe they weren't oblivious, maybe they chose not to care, even just for a while.

Through lowered lashes, I glanced up at Aletheia.

"It will be our little secret." She winked at me, her gold-painted eyes glinting in the moonlight. Shared secrets can make the best friends.

I took the joint from her, put it between my lips, and inhaled.

CHAPTER 25

Aletheia and I went out the next couple of nights—it was a nice reprieve from the burdens of Red. I could just be Adellaide and not worry about my mission, or my father's research, or consequences for that matter. But when Friday rolled around again, I still expected Callum to bring me along to his family dinner if only to keep up whatever facade he desired, so I dipped out of work early to prepare for the Osouf's weekly family dinner.

Callum never came home to retrieve me.

Once my COM-tab blinked twenty-hundred, I gave up. I returned to my room, plucked the pins from my hair, brushed out the curls held in place with nearly half a can of holding spray, slipped off the gold dress I was wearing, and pulled on a pair of flannel pajamas.

Two hours later, I heard the front door open and shut, followed by the clinking of glasses and the bubbling of liquid pouring from a bottle.

I remained in the guest room, tucked tightly in my bed, nose-deep in a book.

About a half hour after that, a knock sounded at my door.

"Come in." I replied over the book I was reading. I was all

curled up in blankets and pillows when Callum opened the door and leaned against the frame.

"*Anna Karenina*? What do you think?"

I kept my nose buried in the old Russian novel and clicked my tongue. "They say you can tell a lot about a culture by the books written at the time." My dad told me that once and my tutor emphasized it in my studies. I remembered learning that in the early twenty-first century, the most popular books were 'self-help' books—people were concerned about their emotional health and the impact it had on the world around them. The irony of it all was that the more inward-focused you are, the less beneficial you become to society. I believe it's when you start looking outward and become concerned about the people around you, society—as a whole—thrives.

A small smile tugged at his lips. "What, pray tell, does *Anna Karenina* tell you about nineteenth-century Russia?"

"They were absolutely horrendous gossips." I fingered the pages of the book. "But I am only halfway through."

Callum's eyes brightened and he bit his lip, almost like he was restraining a laugh.

I closed the book, set it in my lap, and finally heeded the Lieutenant General. It was a mistake. His sandy hair was messy like he had just raked his hands through it because he probably had, his arms were crossed over his broad chest, and he still donned his suit coat, but the shirt underneath was unbuttoned and untucked. This casual and raw Callum was someone I was sure very few people saw, and I was thankful because I wanted him all to myself.

"So, what can I help you with, Lieutenant General?"

My question seemed to jog his memory as to why he'd entered my room, and he took in a deep breath. Callum's shoulders tightened, and all semblance of joy disappeared. "I found you a new host in the Second Ward. She lives in a nice neighborhood and it's close to your work."

"Is there a bad neighborhood in Excelsis?"

"I guess not…" Callum muttered. "Would you like me to set up an introductory meeting for the two of you? I want to make sure you are compatible."

I waved a hand at Callum and picked the book back up. "I'm sure she will be fine." There was a pause. "Will I be able to move in next week? Will Bellona be able to keep tabs on me there?"

Callum straightened. "I think she will manage. But the one hiccup, I suppose, is that the host needs time to adjust her living arrangements to make room for you. She requested three weeks to prepare for your stay."

"Three weeks?" I asked in astonishment. *I don't know if I can live like this with Callum for another full week… Let alone three.*

Callum nodded.

I took a deep breath. Why did it matter, anyway? Hopefully, I would be extracted any day. Even though I hadn't seen Ulysses or heard from the CRF didn't mean they weren't formulating a plan. It didn't mean I would be stuck here for three more weeks. "Alright." Still, silence swept over the room, turning the air stale. I picked at the cover of the book nestled in my lap, and my eyes began to burn.

Callum cleared his throat. "Well, goodnight, Ms. Stevens." He turned and walked through the guest room door.

"Goodnight, Lieutenant General," I whispered as he shut the door behind him.

———

The following days were filled with Laboratory work from dawn until twilight, then clubs, drinking, and dancing from dusk until morning. Sleep eluded me. And so did Callum. Yet another Friday passed that I was not invited to his family dinner, and when I arrived at Callum's flat that night after spending hours at various clubs, I found the Lieutenant General tangled up with some blonde on the couch. At first, I thought it was Laurunda, but as I crept by, Callum broke away from his companion to introduce the blonde girl with brown eyes as Calista. *Callum and Calista.* My stomach churned. Her eyes were glazed over, and she didn't even bother fixing her dress which was askew. Callum's lips were stained with her pink gloss. I gave her a curt smile as I breezed on by, trying my best to ignore the disgusting display as I stumbled into the spare suite I dwelled in and retched my guts out in the bathroom. The sickening was probably from the poisoning of my stomach and liver, but seeing Callum and *Calista* together certainly didn't help my stomach feel any less queasy.

I had heard nothing from my Resistance counterparts. I recorded any information I deemed important, which usually consisted of Laboratory research I was certain Metis would find useful, though I knew I needed more information on security, the Military, and the structure of the Coalition itself in order to please Hoenir. However, I didn't have access to any of those things, and the way everything was going down with Callum, I probably never would. If Niahm was here instead of me, he could use his technological skills to access secret files from the Coalition databases from his COM-tab, maybe even without the ability for the Coalition to trace him. But I was the one stuck here, not Niahm, and I didn't have any fancy tech skills.

I thought about abandoning the mission—I wasn't any closer to finding information about my dad or his research than I was to gathering important Military details. I probably would have if I had any idea how to get out of this fucking place, but with the damned chip embedded in my forearm, there was no way I was getting out of this city without getting tracked.

"Ms. Stevens, are you paying attention?" Dr. Hlín Yong snapped her fingers in my face. Startled, I jerked away from her hand and shook my head.

"Yes, sorry."

"What has gotten into you?" It was the Monday after I saw Callum and Calista together. *Ugh, I could just stab myself. I am a*

Resistance agent—I am Red—and I am letting some low-life Coalition soldier get the better of my emotions.

"Nothing." I avoided eye contact with the young doctor.

"Then pay attention!" Dr. Yong chastised before she continued to point at the three-dimensional DNA projection glowing in mid-air. She was adjusting another segment of chromosomal DNA from the cherry trees because the previous simulation did not yield the results she had wanted. I was recording her changes and her train of thoughts on my COM-tab: *why she was changing this particular segment of DNA, how she thought the sequences would be expressed, etcetera.*

Once our work for the day was finished and we were packing up, my mind kept slipping back to Callum.

"Are you married?" I asked the young doctor, though I wasn't sure where the question came from or why I cared.

Yong's dark brows knitted tightly across her pale skin. "Yes."

"For how long?"

She took a moment to think, stowing her COM-tab in her brown leather bag. "About five years now."

"Wow! You must have married so young!"

Dr. Yong's eyes tightened into slits as she smiled. It was a sweet, genuine smile, and a glow seemed to kiss her cheeks. "Yes, I was twenty."

She is only a year older than Callum. I stuffed my COM-tabs into my work bag. "How long did you know each other before you got married?"

"We met in school when we were children," the doctor explained as she unbuttoned her lab coat. "We started seeing each other after we were placed. He was placed as a bureau and I as a geneticist. We missed seeing each other so often, we decided to make time for each other, at first in little ways like movie nights or coffee. Then he became intentional about meeting two times a week and started treating me to dinner or theatrical shows."

"And over time, you just realized you wanted to spend your life together?"

Dr. Yong nodded.

I slung my bag over a shoulder. "How have you stayed together and happy for so long?"

Dr. Yong pursed her lips, taking a second to think about her answer. "Honesty," she said after a moment, "we never lie. We tell each other everything. We are honest about who we are and our intentions."

I picked at the beds of my nails, and my heart sank into my stomach as her words rang true in my mind. I could never be honest with Callum—not anymore. I had my chance, and I wasted it.

"Is that what all this has been about, Ms. Stevens? A lovers' quarrel?"

I was starting to see a side of Dr. Yong I never knew was there—she seemed almost compassionate in this moment. She was showing interest in something besides her work, and I didn't think it was possible, though it had to be if she was happily married.

I huffed a laugh. "You can't have a lovers' quarrel without a lover."

The young woman looked me straight in the eyes. "You are a liar, Ms. Stevens."

My cheeks heated at her accusation.

"I can see it in your eyes. There is a darkness in the upper right corner of each eye, and that is where lay your lies."

I wasn't sure if that darkness was actually there or if she could see the small chip in the contacts, but I didn't dare interrupt.

"I don't know if you are lying to yourself, to me, to your lover, or to the world—maybe you are lying to all of those things —but you are a liar. If you want to stop being a liar, you must tell one truth a day. Only one truth a day. And you must stick to it. If you are lying to more than one person, you must tell each of them one truth a day. And you tell one truth to every person every day until there are no more truths to tell. That is the only way you will find peace."

For a moment, I felt like a wrinkled old sage sat across from me—and I was some paladin seeking guidance for a mysterious mission.

I bobbed my head slowly.

"Good." She nodded once as she carefully placed her pack on her shoulder. She wagged a finger at me. "Now, you better listen to me because I do not want a distracted assistant. If you mess up my notes, it is my reputation on the line, not yours. And I will fire you before you make me look like a fool, Ms. Stevens."

"Yes, Dr. Yong." I made my way toward the blue ray-door, but she stopped me, fingers smooth and gentle around my wrist.

"Ms. Stevens,"—a smile swept across her face—"please call me Hlín."

I mirrored her gesture. "Thank you, Hlín."

———

I declined Aletheia's invitation to go out. I was tired, and I needed to rest—and I told her that. I told her the truth.

I was laying on Callum's leather couch, reading *Anna Karenina,* when the Lieutenant General walked through the door around twenty-two hundred. I hadn't read on the couch in nearly two weeks. Hell, I hadn't sat in the living room for nearly two weeks—I had confined myself to the guest room whenever I wasn't at work or dancing at the clubs. So, I noticed the brief flicker of confusion across Callum's face before it was replaced by the mask of a soldier.

"What do you think of the book now?" the Lieutenant General said by way of greeting.

"It's okay. Not quite my cup of tea," I responded quietly.

Callum nodded, and his lips pursed, not quite in agreement but in understanding.

"How was your day?" I placed the book on the floor and sat forward.

His eyes narrowed, hooded brows hovering tightly over his emerald eyes. But then he considered. "Fine. Long. Yours?" Callum poured himself a knuckle of amber liquid from a crystalline decanter stowed in his liquor cabinet.

I shrugged. "Same."

Callum ran a hand through his golden-brown hair.

Damn, I thought, not realizing how much I had missed that familiar mannerism.

He walked into the living room and sat in the armchair closest to the balcony. I picked at my nails as he swirled the amber liquid in his snifter glass, observing his choice of liquor.

"I would like to stay here." All the words seemed to fall from my mouth at the same time, bouncing off my tongue as one giant word instead of a coherent sentence.

Callum paused, and the liquid inside his glass settled to a stop before he nodded and took another sip.

Another truth down. I told myself. Though I had the urge to tell another—that feeling of scratching an itch on your shoulder that had moved to the middle of your back. However, I didn't know what truth to tell. I couldn't tell him I was a Resistance agent. It was far too late for that. Two weeks late. He gave me the chance, and I squandered it. I couldn't tell him I was Rowyn —he probably wouldn't believe me. He might get extremely angry that I was tormenting him in some way and kick me out on the street or send Adellaide back to Media.

Maybe that wouldn't be a bad thing.

My heart thumped a hard *no* at the thought.

I took a deep breath as I thought of my conversation with Hlín earlier. "I miss spending time with you, and I would prefer not to move in with a new host. I would like to stay here. With you." My heart pounded. I was too embarrassed to look at him, so I continued to stare at my hand, where blood now pooled in the nail bed of my left middle finger from my picking.

Callum leaned forward, elbows resting on his knees. I glanced up through my lashes, and I caught the glimmer of the Lieutenant General's eyes bearing into me. I willed him to see the truth in my eyes. Or at least this one truth.

Callum finished his glass of amber liquid in one gulp, and his lips pulled back from his teeth in a painful inhale before he set the glass on the coffee table. He stood up from the armchair, and my chest pounded, the anticipation of his response threatening my heart to explode. But Callum walked away—he retired into his room and shut his door with a soft *click*.

My heart sank, and my stomach churned.

I sat there on the couch for what felt like an eternity as tears burned my eyes. I replayed what happened over and over in my head.

Did he not understand what I said?

Did I accidentally say something wrong when my words flowed together?

I repeated the mashed sentence in my mind, but I couldn't think of him interpreting my words any other way.

I picked up his empty glass, brought it to my nose, and inhaled. Aromas of earth, smoke, and spice flooded my senses— they danced in a wholesome harmony. I breathed it in again, willing my mind to focus on just those three things: earth, smoke, and spice, but the more I inhaled, the more I was reminded of Callum—of him just walking away from me. From my truth. A tear crept down my right cheek, and I set the glass down.

Then Callum's bedroom door creaked open. I swept the tear from my skin with the palm of my hand as he reappeared wearing grey sweatpants and a white t-shirt, two books in tow.

"I have a secret stash in my room as well." He handed me a book.

2001: A Space Odyssey.

"Read it next. It's an entirely different genre and era, but it's fun." Callum set the other book on the coffee table and picked up his empty glass that was clearly not where he had left it. "Would you like a bit?" he asked, raising the glass to me.

"Umm, sure. Thank you."

He turned and made his way to the kitchen, bare feet tapping gently on the marble floor. "I didn't pin you as a scotch girl."

I shrugged. "I haven't tried it, but it smells good." *It smells like you,* I wanted to say.

Callum poured a knuckle's worth in each glass, then sauntered back to the living room and handed me a glass of my own.

I sniffed the liquid, and it smelled just like the last. I took a sip, and the liquor instantly warmed my whole body as it slid effortlessly down my throat. The earth, smoke, and spice were still there, but on my tongue lingered on notes of caramel and vanilla.

"What do you think?"

I eyed the liquid. "Good, but I didn't think the Coalition received imports."

"Ah, well," Callum chuckled, "when your father is a Senator, you would be surprised what goods I can get my hands on." Callum settled into his armchair and crossed a leg, book in one hand and scotch in the other.

"What are you reading?"

He simply tilted the book so I could see the cover. *The Adventures of Huckleberry Finn.*

I laughed. "Isn't that a children's book?"

"It's always good to stay young at heart, Adellaide."

My heart fluttered, and I settled back into the couch, sitting up this time so I could sip on my scotch. I was tempted to ditch the Russian novel and start the new book, but I didn't want to disappoint Callum, so I opened the novel, but after a minute of blankly staring at words, I glanced around the room before my eyes lingered on the Lieutenant General. My chest swelled—I felt more joy in that moment than I had all the nights partying combined. Though, there was still something missing.

"Where is Sirius?"

Callum's nose remained in his book. "Bellona needed him tonight."

"Doesn't she know I don't need to be tracked tonight?"

Callum peeked over his book, eyes twinkling in mischief. "You are so vain. Not everything is about you, darling Adellaide."

I rolled my eyes before replanting my nose in *Anna Karenina* as Callum's low chuckle hung in the air.

CHAPTER 26

The next couple of days weren't exactly back to normal, but pretty close. If Adellaide's life could be called normal.

I knew Callum was still holding back, though whether it was to protect himself, to protect me, or to protect the Coalition, I had no idea. It made sense—trust was slow and hard to rebuild after it had been broken. The truth was, Callum shouldn't trust me—but I needed him to. I couldn't leave the Coalition empty-handed, and the only way I could gather valuable intel was through the Lieutenant General.

When Friday evening rolled around, I was curled up in Callum's armchair reading *2001: A Space Odyssey* and I hadn't anticipated Callum returning home until after his family dinner, but at seventeen-hundred, Callum strolled through the front door.

"Hello?"

"Why do you sound surprised? This is my flat."

I turned around, kneeling on the chair so that my eyes peeked over the top to peer at the Lieutenant General. Callum smiled hesitantly as he stripped off his Military jacket.

"I just didn't expect you home until after your family dinner."

He titled his head. "And what were you planning to do for dinner?"

"Thought about ordering pho," I shrugged.

"Oooo," he moaned. "Perfect night for that."

"Hmm?"

Callum checked his COM-watch. "According to the weather widget, it's the coldest day of the season so far. It was negative fifteen degrees Celsius when I woke up this morning."

My thoughts raced to my Resistance family. This was the kind of weather that would stall out the generator, shutting off all the power, including heat. Hoenir and Niahm would have to spend hours out in the cold to fix the problem, and Metis would be cursing up a storm because his incubators and bio-lights would shut off, ruining his experiments.

With a shrug, I forced the thoughts to the back of my mind and returned my attention to the Lieutenant General. "It's a shame that Excelsis is climate-controlled. If it was really cold, we could order some spicy curry with fresh, hot naan."

Callum licked his lips, and the gesture made my heart skip. "Maybe I will just stay home and join you because both options sound amazing." He sauntered into the kitchen, grabbed an amber bottle from the fridge, and popped the cap off with the brass bottle opener nailed on the side of a low cupboard.

"You should probably go," I chuckled.

Callum sipped his beer. "I'm surprised you're back so early." He walked around the living room to plop on the couch.

I followed him, sitting back down in the armchair. "Hlín had some secret work to do for Freyja, and I wasn't invited. But," I sighed, "it was an early day for me. I was done around fifteen-hundred."

"Lucky you." Callum took a swig from his beer, and I picked up my book, eager to get back to the excitement.

"Well," Callum drawled, "if you are going to make *me* go, then you have to come with me."

I peeked over my book. "*You* are the Lieutenant General. I can't *make* you do anything."

A mischievous grin tugged at the corners of his lips. "If I can't have pho, no one can have pho."

"No one gets pho? The Lieutenant General is going to shut down every Pho Popina in the Circulum?"

Callum thought for a second, then lifted a finger in the air. "Correction: if I don't get pho, you don't get pho."

"That is not fair!"

"You are the one who said I had to go," Callum reasoned playfully.

I shook my head. "No, I said you should *probably* go."

With a shrug, Callum sipped from his beer again. "Same thing."

I set my book in my lap. "I really don't want to upset *Calista.*"

"Not my problem anymore."

Anymore.

I smiled at the implication and picked up my book again, but I felt Callum's impeding stare. I glanced up.

"Well, go get ready!" he urged.

"I don't need two hours to get ready."

"You do for tonight."

I shot him an annoyed glare, waiting for him to elaborate.

"The Osoufs are hosting a dinner party, and all the most important people in the Coalition will be there."

———

When we arrived at Osouf Manor, the mansion was already filled with guests—scientists, bureaus, Military personnel, and officials of every flavor. The butler took my fox-fur shawl, baring my shoulders to the foyer's chilly air. Callum had picked a simple jade dress for me, with long sleeves that clung to a sweetheart neckline. A solid gold plate latched around my waist, and I wore matching gold heels. The dress finished off with a deep slit all the way up to my hip. My hair was pulled off my shoulders and rained down in soft billowing curls, framing my eyes painted gold and my lips the softest apricot. All in all, my look was far more Median in nature—a flat color dress, simple lines with basic metallic adornments paired with natural-looking hair and makeup, very different from typical Excelsian high fashion. I told Callum I would be the laughingstock of the party, but he assured me I would be very much the opposite.

Callum wore his formal Military uniform. All of his medals were brightly polished, and his gold buttons gleamed against the obsidian abyss of his jacket. Traditional Baroque embroidery of gold glinted on his shoulders and cuffs. I looked like a mossy oak against his starlit night—a perfect blending into the magical forest that was Osouf Manor.

Callum swiped two glasses of champagne from a waiter's golden tray and handed one to me. We clinked our glasses together, and Callum downed his champagne in one gulp. He grabbed another full glass off the tray before the waiter was out of reach. Shocked, I took a gentle sip from my glass, glancing around at all the finery. Women wore dresses heavily adorned with beads and luxurious silks weaved in and out of expensive fabrics to create intricate designs. Men wore suits of onyx or Coalition Plum embroidered with paisleys and other elaborate patterns.

I had never felt more out of place in my life—not when my team and I were in Humilis, not when Sancus first brought me into Callum's flat, not even dancing in the clubs. I couldn't help but wonder if Callum picked this dress on purpose—to make me feel like I only fit in Media, or maybe to let everyone else know I did not fit in here.

I took greedy sips of the champagne this time, praying to my father's God for it to calm my nerves.

"Careful," Callum whispered in my ear, the sensation

sending chills down my spine. "We don't need you to get sloppy."

I scoffed. "You're one to talk. And why am I wearing this? I look like a Median woman. I will be the humiliation of this party."

Callum clicked his tongue. "Don't you trust me?"

"No."

He cocked an eyebrow—a silent way of asking: *really?*

"Well, last time I was in this manor with you, I was thrown into your little family games."

Callum chuckled deeply while offering me his arm. Hesitantly, I took it, his bicep hard beneath my hand. "Let me be candid with you. Now, you are in a far more dangerous game. In Excelsis, it doesn't matter if the talk is good or bad. It's simply important that the people are talking. You are making an impression."

"What if I just wanted to blend in?"

"You, darling Adellaide"—Callum nodded to people as we weaved through the manor—"are on the arm of an arising Coalition General." Callum gave me a charming wink. "Blending in was never an option."

"Well, next time, I want a different date."

"Oh?" Callum chuckled lightly. "Who said this was a date?"

I shoved him with an elbow. "You know what I mean." Callum nearly toppled over, backing into an older woman who looked so offended he might as well have given her an obscene gesture.

Callum's eyes narrowed. "Has anyone ever told you that you are unusually strong?"

"Yes," I muttered. "You have. Many times. So many times, I am starting to wonder if you aren't as durable of a soldier as you should be."

"No, darling Adellaide. I don't think that's it at all."

"Oh, stop calling me that!"

"What would you rather I call you? I know you don't like 'Addie,' but what about Della?"

I rolled my eyes.

"Darling Della."

I elbowed him again, but more gently this time. "Will you stop that?"

Callum's only reply was a glorious laugh as he weaved us through an elegant sitting room stylized more like a jungle than a North American forest.

"So, your parents have this party every year?"

Callum nodded once. "Yes, about a week or two before the Spring Gala."

"Ooo," I sang. "A Gala. That sounds fancy."

"It is," Callum's voice was light with laughter. He was no longer looking at me but nodding to various officials throughout the room. "And if you're good tonight, maybe you'll get to go to the fancy party."

"Oh, wow. Do I also receive treats if I perform little tricks?"

"Depends on the trick." He gave me a mischievous wink.

"What is *she* doing here?" A growl rumbled from behind us. Callum was pulled into a corner, and I was dragged along, our arms still linked together.

"Nice to see you too, Anderson." Callum straightened his jacket.

Bellona glared, her deep brown eyes flicking between the two of us.

"Ms. Stevens, here is my…" He looked to me, a smile dancing in his eyes. "… *date* for the evening."

"And you thought bringing a Resistance spy to this particular dinner party was a bright idea? Especially after—"

Callum shot her a warning glare. Bellona's nostrils flared, and her jaw clenched as she crossed her arms. She, too, donned her formal Military jacket, but hers was crafted of Coalition Plum.

"After what?" I asked.

Bellona raised a brow at Callum, like she was silently daring him to answer my question.

Callum shook his head.

Bellona cocked her head, her owl tattoo staring me straight in the eye as she addressed her Commanding Officer. "Why don't you tell her? If she can be trusted to be here, surely, she can know that we briefly apprehended a Resistance spy in Media yesterday." Bellona shifted her gaze to mine, her eyes narrowed and piercing as they met mine. "We found him trying to gain access to the Tubes, probably attempting to infiltrate Excelsis."

My heart stopped, and it took all my willpower not to tighten my hand that was strapped around Callum's bicep.

Briefly apprehended? Could they have captured Ulysses, did he escape? Did he make it to Excelsis?

I swallowed my questions and stood straight. "I am not—"

Bellona held up a hand to silence me. "Whatever you say will not help your case," she snapped.

"Major General." I felt the warning in Callum's voice, and it echoed in the knitting of his brows and the clenching of his jaw. "While I appreciate your concern, stand down." His voice was tight and low as he glanced around the room. I followed his gaze. People had noticed the tension rising in our corner. "And while *I* know you are best for my current position, there are people here you are trying to impress, and you are not doing a very good job so far."

"I don't care—"

"You should." Callum nodded to someone across the room. It was Clausen—he looked polished, clean, and honorable as he charmed a couple of important-looking officials.

Bellona blanched as she looked on, and her nostrils flared. "I don't care about politics. I care about the safety of our Coalition."

Callum gave the Major General a tight smile and lifted his glass to her. "They are one and the same."

The Lieutenant General nodded a dismissal to his cohort as

he wrapped an arm around my waist and shouldered past Bellona. Our audience returned to their previous conversations—or maybe new ones involving us.

"I thought you said all gossip was good gossip," I whispered to Callum, my lips meeting his ear—burning with the contact.

He kept a smile painted on his face. "Okay, I may have over-exaggerated. But what I said to you is still true, and what I said to her is still true. Although no politician gets a say when it comes to Military appointments, everyone in the Coalition Government and Military is intertwined. Whether they are a well-liked Military official or not still matters, and Bellona is not very popular. Some people find her…"

"Cold, distant, calculating, frightening," I suggested.

Callum tugged me closer playfully. "Less than personable."

"What does it matter? Aren't soldiers supposed to be everything that is Bellona?"

Callum looked on at the crowd around us. "On Base, yes, of course. Bellona is a perfect soldier. Every soldier should aspire to be just like her. However, off Base, the people want someone they can relate to—they want to think we care for them on a personal level. People want to believe that we would still choose them over the greater good of the Coalition."

"But you don't. That's not your job."

"Of course it's not, but everyone wants to believe that if they were strapped to train tracks, a soldier would choose to save them, one person, over everyone else on that train."

"That's horrible."

"That's comforting."

We had found a wall, and we stood silently as our eyes locked, like garden flowers alone in the sunlight.

"What would you do?" I asked after a moment.

Callum's brow crinkled. "What would I choose?"

I nodded. "Would you save the one or the many?"

Callum contemplated the question, but his eyes were fixed on mine when he answered. "Depends on who the 'one' is." His hand found mine, and our fingers intertwined. Gravity seemed to pull us closer, like a string that tugged at our stomachs and lips—at our hearts.

"Oh, thank goodness!" I nearly jumped back as Sancus approached our quiet corner. Callum's eyes, which were previously glazed over in a sweet sleepiness, were now squeezed shut in annoyance. "Cal, Senator Richards, and General Daniels are at it again about the Foreign Policy Summit this spring. Can you please go interject?"

The Lieutenant General cleared his throat. "Lovely." Callum handed Sancus his unfinished glass of champagne before straightening his jacket and fixing his lapels. "But promise to give me back my beautiful date once I am finished with them."

Sancus turned to me and whistled. "No promises. Damn girl, you clean up good."

"If he starts sharing embarrassing stories about me, please tell me you will walk away," Callum said.

I smiled. "No promises."

He sighed and ran a hand through his hair. I had expected a sarcastic response or witty comeback, but none came. Instead, he leaned in closer and brushed his lips against my cheek. "I will be right back," he whispered.

Callum's gait was formal and commanding as he walked away and crossed the room. He greeted two men, who must have been General Daniels and Senator Richards, with big smiles and hard thumps to the shoulders. The Senator wobbled a little, nearly spilling his champagne, but the general, in his onyx uniform, stood as a boulder against a windstorm.

"What have you done to him, dear Adellaide?" Sancus sighed.

"Excuse me?"

He raised the glass Callum had handed over to his friend. "I have never seen that man so damn happy."

"I'm sure that is not true." I blushed and sipped from my bubbling glass.

"Oh, not a truer thing has been said."

"He was furious with me these past weeks," I offered.

Sancus shoved a hand into his pocket. "Maybe. But that doesn't mean he wasn't excited to go home after his shift or didn't keep checking on your location every hour."

My spine bristled. "He was just trying to keep tabs on a could-be Resistance spy."

"Nah." Sancus licked his plump lips. "I think he just wants to make sure you are okay. I think he needs to know you will thrive here."

"Well, it's creepy, and he needs to stop doing it." I took a sip from my near-empty glass. I could already feel the effervescent alcohol starting to take hold of my faculties—my head felt light and airy.

Sancus laughed. "Oh, trust me, I have tried telling him with those exact words. But he doesn't listen. He insists on…"

"Being creepy," we said in unison.

We looked at each other, eyes wide for a moment, then burst out laughing. Callum glanced over, a brow arched high in worried confusion. Sancus must have been looking at Callum, too, because our eyes met again, and another laugh erupted from the two of us. Callum then gave me another look that read something like: *Oh, shit. What embarrassing story did he tell you?*

I waved Callum off, encouraging him to continue his conversation with the Senator and the General.

Once we silenced our laughter, Sancus replaced our two empty champagne flutes with two full ones from a passing waiter. I was about to sip the fresh champagne when Sancus grabbed my forearm, preventing me from doing so. "You're good for him, Adellaide. I know you have your secrets, but I like you. For many reasons, but the main one is because you are good for Callum. Not like the 'you complete him' sort of way because he was always complete, but you add to him. You enhance him. He needs that. He doesn't allow many people to see who he really is. Hell, I don't think he does that with me. But he sure as fuck lets you see it all. And I think he has become a better person and Lieutenant General because of it."

Over the course of a month? Sancus thought I *enhanced* Callum that much over just a month? I cocked a brow. "So, where is the warning?"

"What warning?"

"You know. The 'don't hurt my best friend' warning."

Sancus batted the thought away. "I'm not going to bother with that."

"Why not?"

The smile faded from his face as Sancus's gaze pinned me down. "Because you're going to. I know you're gonna hurt Callum."

My heart stopped. *Does he think I am Resistance too? Am I so transparent? Am I a horrible spy?*

Sancus must not have noticed my mind whirling behind my eyes because he continued. "But I think he needs that. Whatever secrets you have, whatever truths you keep, when you decide to tell them, or when they come out, he will need to hear them and accept them. And they will challenge him and grow him."

I couldn't speak. I couldn't even utter a sound.

"So, my warning is this—" Sancus pointed his glass toward his friend once again, and my gaze followed with it. Callum was laughing with the senator and general now, easing the tension the men held between them so they could battle with it on a different day. "Tell those truths sooner rather than later. Control when and how he finds out—it will be better in the long run."

Sancus clinked our glasses together and took a sip of champagne. Hesitantly, I followed suit, keeping my gaze locked on the Lieutenant General. From the corner of my eye, Sancus' hand slid into his pocket, and when I thought he was going to walk away, Sancus leaned in, his sweet, pine scent awakening my senses as his lips brushed against my ear. "I don't think the world can wait for the truth much longer, Adellaide."

Sancus' words sent pinpricks down my spine, and my skin tingled as Sancus kissed my cheek. It wasn't like Callum's that sent heat running through me. No, Sancus' kiss was that of a friend—like he was sealing the warning on my skin, sealing his wisdom with his lips.

And as Sancus strode away, as only a Gillian could, my eyes weren't on the Second Lieutenant. They were fixed on the Lieutenant General of the American Coalition, his smile bright and his head tipped back as he laughed with my enemies.

CHAPTER 27

I missed the stars. Not that I could see many out at the CRF Base with the perpetual smog hovering in Earth's atmosphere from The Demise, but I could see more than none. In Excelsis, the lights of the Circulum were so bright they overpowered the stars, planets, and galaxies—even the moon seemed to shine less brightly in the city among the clouds.

I stood outside on the balcony of my room, leaning on the iron rails as I gazed out over the Circulum. I had never been out here before. I was worried it was too 'suspicious.' But after tonight, I needed some fresh air. I needed some time to myself. Time to think.

I squinted, trying to focus on even the tiniest light out there in the vast, obsidian sky, but only darkness stared back at me. So, I decided to close my eyes and imagine all those nights with Niahm, lying on our backs and gazing up at the stars. We would name all the constellations we'd learned about and recount legends from which their names derived. We counted shooting stars, made wishes, and dreamed dreams bigger than ourselves— dreams of my father's return after all these years—clinging to the hope that he survived. Dreams of Reign finding love and having children, and dreams of Niahm becoming a world-renowned engineer.

And every dream was one wished for someone else.

I always found it difficult to craft dreams for myself. I knew from the gnawing in my gut I was destined for something big, but I couldn't wrap my mind around what it could be. So, I dreamed for others, always wishing for the best story this dark world could ever give them.

When I opened my eyes, I was blinded by the fluorescence from every building, holo-board, and skylight across the city. No wonder the stars didn't shine here—all the distracting man-made light left no room for the true source, covering up the beauty of the universe. Humans had a knack for doing that.

A gentle breeze brushed the loose curls that hung around my shoulders. It was something I didn't feel very often in Excelsis, so I smiled at the hair that tickled my neck and the breeze that kissed my cheeks. My black silk nightgown billowed gently in the crisp air, but the sherpa robe over my shoulders kept me warm. I closed my eyes and wiggled my toes against the cool, polished wood under my feet to refocus myself, to center myself on who I was.

The gentle click of the French door and the reverberation of soft footsteps against the wooden planks beckoned my eyes to flutter open. Callum hesitated before he took another step forward and placed a hand on the small of my back. Chills rippled throughout my body, his touch the epicenter of an icy earthquake.

"What are you doing out here?" He was close. So close. Callum's chest, stomach, and hips were flush to my left side, and his hand threatened to pull me in tighter.

"Thinking," I replied, keeping my gaze on the glowing city in front of us.

"Mmm," his breath kissed my ear. "A dangerous thing."

A small laugh fell from my lips. "Indeed."

"What are you thinking about?" Callum's hand moved from my back to tuck a loose strand of hair behind my ear.

I turned to look at him finally, and my breath hitched. He was wearing the white button-up he usually wore under his Military uniform, but it was unbuttoned, exposing his broad chest, and he still wore his Military pants, but his belt was no longer secured around his waist. "How do you know which way is north without the stars?" I asked, returning my gaze to his emerald eyes.

His brows furrowed in bewilderment at such a simple question. "You use a compass."

"Yes. But they could easily be swayed by another source of magnetic energy."

"A map."

"I guess, but they are man-made. And what if the person who made the map you have made it so you could only go where they wanted you to go, not where you needed to go?" I looked out over the Circulum again. "The ancients," I continued, "they used the stars to find destinations. They were never changing—always constant—but now..." I looked up into the abyss. "How do we find our way? How do we find the truth? Or if you see a star, how do you know you follow that star or another star? How do you know which star is true north?"

Callum's eyes remained fixed on me. "What are you talking about, Adellaide?"

I glanced down at my hands and fiddled with my robe's belt. My chest was tight, and I struggled to breathe as a warm tear tumbled down my cheek. I didn't know where it came from. I hadn't felt the pricking of tears in my eyes until the first drop fell.

Callum wiped it away with a slow, gentle swipe of his thumb. "Adellaide," he breathed, "you can trust me."

Can I?

I wasn't sure. But after Hlín's wisdom and what Sancus told me... After tonight, I couldn't be Adellaide anymore. Not with Callum. He was the one star I saw here in the Coalition, and I had to trust that it was real, and it was there. I grabbed Callum's hand and pressed it tight to my cheek.

"You know that rock on your mantle?"

Callum nodded slowly, perhaps unsure of where I was going.

"I recognized it as soon as I saw it, and that day instantly replayed in my head—but before that, I recognized your eyes."

Callum's brow creased, his lips pursed, and his jaw tightened. I could almost see the wall he started to erect around himself.

Softly, I took his hand from my cheek, kissed it, then set his palm on the railing. I inhaled deeply.

All you must do is tell one truth a day.

"My name is not Adellaide." I paused, biting my lip. "I'm sorry, Callum, but I am not Adellaide Stevens."

I glanced down to find his strong fingers clenching the iron rail, knuckles tight and pale.

"You deserve someone who is honest with you about who they are. You deserve more than I have been giving you. You have known for a while now that I have been hiding something, and this is it: I am not Adellaide."

Callum took a step away from me. "Then who are you?" His voice was a low growl.

Tears flowed down my cheeks. "I am the girl who died in a plane crash when I was seven." Callum's back went rigid, and his eyes widened in disbelief. "I am the girl who ran with you in your parents' gardens in Militum from dawn until dusk." A hard sob escaped my mouth. "I climbed cherry blossom trees with you and held your hand when we jumped into the pond behind my house. And I—" My voice broke. "And I am the girl who threw a rock at you for giving me a rose."

Callum blinked rapidly as his eyes filled with tears.

"I guess that's who I am." I threw up my hands with a sardonic laugh. "I am the girl who throws stones when you offer her everything you can give."

The Lieutenant General shook his head in disbelief. "No, you can't be."

I grabbed his hands and held them tightly to my chest. "Cal." It was the first time I'd ever called him that since we were kids. "It's me. It's Rowyn."

His eyes grew wide, but not in recognition. In anger. Callum ripped his hands from mine, and his jaw was set tight as he ground his teeth together. "Do not play games with me."

"Cal—"

Callum's eyes glazed as he grabbed my shoulders and shook me violently. "Who put you up to this?"

I braced myself. Despite my strength, his fingers dug into my skin. I whimpered in pain under his grasp.

At the sound, Callum's eyes turned sharp again. He let go of my shoulders.

I stepped back from the Lieutenant General and rubbed away the pain, but the bruises would still form. Callum turned from me, not letting me see the sorrow that had begun to take hold of his features.

Silence lingered between us before he finally ground out, "Prove it."

I grabbed his hand and dragged him into the bathroom. One by one, I removed my contacts as Callum watched, eyes unyielding.

I turned around to face him.

"I have seen your real eyes before. It proves nothing."

"Yes, but I saw the flicker of recognition that very first day. I knew you saw me, Cal. You saw Rowyn in my eyes."

He gave a too-tight shrug.

"My fath–" My voice broke again, sobs threatening to escape in wave after crashing wave. "My father was Janus Cornelei Darrow. He was a geneticist from Militum. He married his wife, Aura Darrow, when I was five. And you weren't just my best friend, Callum Orion Osouf. You were my only friend."

Something in Callum softened—his shoulders relaxed, and his hand twitched toward mine.

I couldn't hold it back any longer—I couldn't stop the weeping that expelled from my chest in heaving gasps. I wrapped my arms tightly around my waist in an effort to hinder my cries. "And I have— thought of you—every day—for the past—sixteen years." The words were slow and hard as they escaped between the wracking of my chest.

Callum's expression was still stony—hate and anger lingering in the dark brown flecks of his beautiful green eyes. "But your hair—"

I clutched at my brown tresses, ready to pull them out right then and there. "I dye it, Callum! Remember? I take these fucking pills every day to keep my hair brown." I picked up the bottle of pills Metis created for me and shook it in Callum's face. "But I will shave my head so you can watch it grow back red if that is what it takes to prove it to you—if that is what it takes to make you believe I am Rowyn Eloise Darrow." I choked on my own name. I hadn't said it for so long. "I would do that for you, Cal. I would do anything for you."

Finally, Callum's eyes softened into warm pools of emerald oceans, and his jaw slackened. In one swift, gentle movement, he stepped forward and held me in his strong arms, his voice small and breathless as he whispered my name. "Rowyn?" My name started as a plea on his lips. Then it turned into a gentle coo as my sobs settled.

Callum pulled me up to the bathroom counter once my cries ceased. He wiped away my tears with his white shirt, staining the fabric tan, pink, and black, similar to the stains already setting into his shoulder, which I'd sobbed into for a good five minutes.

"Is it really you?" he finally asked, hands cupped around my damp face.

I lifted my hands to hold his, pressing him further into me. "Yes, Cal. It's me."

He fingered a curled lock of my hair. "But why dye it?"

Shit. I thought to myself. *I told one truth, now what do I fucking do? I still have a sister to protect. Friends who are my family back at Base. If I tell him I am a Resistance spy, they are all dead. And for what? For star-crossed lovers?*

Breathe, Red. One truth a day.

I inhaled, my chest tight. "I knew it was too recognizable. I was never supposed to find you."

Callum's hands fell to my shoulders. "Find me? What do you mean?"

I bit my lip, the lie weaving as I imagined the life my father wished I had—the life he tried so hard to create for me. "The plane didn't crash, Callum. My family didn't die. Well, they did, but not from a plane crash. Oh, Skies, I don't even know where to start, Cal."

His smile was comforting as he tilted my chin up. "We have time."

I swallowed. The lump in my throat felt like the lie itself—painful and hard to shove down. So, I started with the truth. "The hovercraft never crashed. It landed safely in The Wastes somewhere between here and Militum. That's when I knew my father had been planning to leave the Coalition for a while. He and Aura had packed bags of supplies. And then he brought us straight to a decrepit shed, which he fixed up and called our 'new home.'" I could see the *why* forming on Callum's lips. I shrugged. "I don't really know, honestly. There were so many times I asked him if we could go home, so many times I asked him why we left, but he was always so guarded, like there was something he didn't want me to know. My father just said it wasn't safe, and that was that." A sadistic laugh escaped my lips. "But then he ended up dying out there. He and Aura went on a hunt, and they never came back. I went out looking for them, and I followed their trail straight to Aura's corpse. My dad wasn't there, but I saw the tracks—he was dragged off by a mutant bear from the looks of it." I ran a hand through my hair. "I don't know how the Coalition could have been more dangerous than that."

Devastation was painted across Callum's features—in the set of his jaw, the flexing of his knuckles—as he asked, "How long were you alone?"

"Eight years." The first lie fell like acid from my lips.

"You had no one?"

I shook my head, my tongue not quite ready to deceive him again. I hoped it was believable. When we fled, it was still very early in Aura's pregnancy. I doubted many people knew. And if Callum asked— Well, he couldn't know about Reign. If I told him I had a sister, he would bring her here tomorrow. Callum would abandon all of his duties to risk venturing into The Wastes just to find my sister.

Callum pursed his lips, his brows creased in disbelief. "Why didn't you come back?"

"What was I supposed to do, Callum? Waltz right in like I was resurrected from the grave? I was so young when we left, The Wastes was pretty much all I knew."

Callum's mouth worked. "But the hair? The contacts? And why were you in Humilis?"

I shrugged, like the gesture would make it more believable. "The dye and the pills, well, my dad had stashes he brought with us when we left—he knew I was easily recognizable. *The only redhead in over five generations.*" I mocked the tone of some holo-caster I heard when I was little. "But a year or two after Dad and Aura died, supplies were running low. I mean, I could hunt and forage, but medicine, hygiene, and vegetables during the winter…I just needed some help. So, I used the dye and snuck into Imperium's Humilis, and learned how to barter. I eventually got connected to the shadow market for the contacts and a few other special supplies, like the forged paperwork, in case I fell into trouble. But that's why I was in the Tenth Ward when you *caught* me. I was stocking up on supplies for the winter."

He cocked his head to the side, slowly realizing something. "So, you never worked in a brothel?"

"No." I shook my head. "But I had heard rumors in the market. The times I had been to Humilis, I had seen girls and boys alike on the street being…*coerced*." I thought of Ulysses' cover on the day of our mission. "And I really was being harassed by a panderer."

Callum's eyes lit up, and a smirk grew across his face. "Are you saying that I saved you, Rowyn?" My name was like a purr across his tongue.

I shoved him back, and he stumbled a step. "No, I am not! I had it sorted."

"Uh-huh. Whatever helps you sleep at night."

I rolled my eyes. "Skies, you are so annoying. I finally take off my mask, and you are too concerned about your shining armor."

Callum stepped back toward me, his movement slow, and his eyes lowered. He moved into me, his hips finding a home between my legs as he placed his hands on my thighs. His eyes were lazy as they roamed up my legs and over my stomach. They lingered on my breasts, now peaked, his Adam's apple bobbing gently before his eyes continued their ascent, migrating up my neck and past my lips until, finally, his hungry gaze met mine.

"Why didn't you tell me sooner?" Callum's voice was a shadow of a whisper, almost like he didn't *want* to believe I was Rowyn. Perhaps he didn't.

"Callum, you were my best friend. As a child, I loved you, but what does that mean after sixteen years apart? What does that mean when you grow up?" I chewed on my lip, trying to find as much truth to put in these words as I possibly could, because even if I wasn't Resistance, even if I wasn't a spy, if I had lived the life I told him and we found each other like we did, would I have told him right away? "You had lived a whole life without me, a good one at that. I didn't want to fuck that up. I didn't want to be that selfish girl who would just waltz right in and expect you to be everything I needed."

His hands tightened on my legs. "But I did that for you—I mean, I did that for Adellaide, and I thought you were a complete stranger."

"And what would you have done if I told you I was Rowyn right away?"

"Well, I would have murdered Clausen," Callum scoffed.

I rolled my eyes. "My point is, Callum, I had no idea where I —where Rowyn—would fit into your life, and I didn't want to demand that of you. I…" I swallowed. "I guess I wanted to know that you would still choose me. Not because of nostalgia or obligation, but because you actually enjoy who I am."

Most of what I said was true, maybe not in the context he was thinking of, but my words were still true enough.

True enough.

The words rang hollowly in my chest. But when Callum's forehead fell to mine, the words fell silent, replaced by the sweet melody our breaths made as they intertwined. Callum's voice was a low, soothing moan. "Oh, my darling Wynnie…" My heart throbbed at the use of my nickname. "Why can't it be all of the above?"

I smiled, lifting my head slightly to dare a glance at him, but then his lips were on mine. It was soft at first, like a question. But as I eased into him, he crashed into me, a hand wrapping around my neck to pull me in closer, like my lips were his lifeline.

I relented. Fully. I couldn't help it. I had dreamt of this moment ever since I saw him in the market, ever since he hovered over me in Humilis, and ever since he sat across from me in the interrogation room.

My hands ran through his hair, pressing him closer to me while Callum's other hand climbed up my thigh to grasp my hip, pulling me closer to him.

I broke my lips away, needing air, but turned my head to allow him access to my cheek. His lips did not part from my skin, trailing across my jaw and to my ear lobe, where he nibbled softly. "I can't believe you didn't tell me sooner," he murmured between kisses trailing down my neck.

I used one hand to sweep my hair over my shoulder, and the other roamed around his arm and down until I snaked it under his shirt. His skin was warm and soft beneath my fingertips. Gently, I raked my nails down his torso, and his soft growl reverberated against my neck. "I didn't think you would believe me." My voice was breathless as he sucked on the skin between my shoulder and neck.

I could feel the smile crawl across his lips. "Who says I do?"

I shoved Callum off of me. Not too much, just enough so I could look at him, but I still felt cold under the weight of his absence.

Callum stood unmoving before me—lips red, cheeks flushed, and eyes glazed over, a hunger lingering there.

I was still in my nightgown, my robe now off my shoulders and hanging around my elbows as I sat perched atop the bathroom counter. A breeze licked at my thighs where the nightgown had previously covered but was now hiked up nearly to my hips.

I lifted a hand to his face, and he melted into my touch. My heart throbbed. "You are Callum Orion Osouf." His eyes flickered, perhaps cherishing his name on my lips—on Rowyn's lips. "You loved summer sunsets and saving roly-polies. You used to be so mad that I didn't have to go to public education like you did, though I never knew if it was because you were jealous or because you just missed me." I winked at him. He pulled me closer again, both of his strong hands grasping my hips. "I could climb cherry blossom trees faster, but you would always climb higher. You were such a sucker for love." I laughed, wrapping my arms around his neck. "When my father and Aura found each other, even though I was so mad, you insisted that they were right for each other, and my father deserved to find someone to make him happy, even though I thought I should make him happy enough. You were the one who convinced me to give Aura a chance."

A slight smile tugged at Callum's lips.

"And your favorite food when we were little was Aura's Beef Wellington." Callum's eyes sparkled in recognition. I raised my brows. "Your turn."

"Only your dad and I called you—"

"Wynnie. I didn't want anyone else to get used to it because I would grow up one day, and I didn't want a nickname to keep me from climbing the Military ranks."

Callum's stomach danced in a light laugh. "And your favorite color was—"

"I couldn't choose. It was either—"

"Red or green. Red for your name and your hair, or green for the new growth of spring and the promise of summer, which was a pretty sophisticated thought for a six-year-old."

"That was a lie." I glanced down at the small bit of space between us. "It was green for your eyes, which made me think of the new growth of spring and the promise of summer."

Callum's shoulders relaxed, and his hips pressed further into mine. "And you loved me because—"

I held up a finger. "I never admitted that. You were the one who professed your love many times. But I—" My voice quieted, "I never said it."

Callum swept his knuckles across my cheek and pushed hair behind my ear in one easy gesture. "And now?"

I nuzzled my cheek into his hand and held my breath for a moment. "Even though I was only seven, I regret every opportunity I had to say it to you but didn't." My voice was a whisper. But it was a whisper of truth.

Callum held my jaw in his strong hand, and he leaned in close, his lips almost touching mine. "I still knew, Rowyn." My name was a prayer on his lips. "I always knew."

———

Callum smelled of earth, wood, and dewy grass—like so many nights of solo hunts with nothing but starlight gleaming through the branches and leaves. He reminded me of wind-kissed nights where the buzz of twinkling star-bugs above me filled my ears, and dewy soil licked my skin. For every moment I was with him, I relived those beautiful nights over and over, but this time I wasn't alone.

This time, I felt more than just a small dusting of cosmos in the universe. When I was with Callum, I felt as though I was the universe. When I was with him, I felt like he was creating the universe in me and through me—like I was a key part in the making.

He made me feel like starlight, but our love was a comet entering Earth's atmosphere, shining bright and fast, then in the blink of an eye, it was gone. A moment of legend and promise, but it was so foreign that few gleaned hope from it.

Still, I smiled, and I laughed as his lips tickled my waist. I moaned as his tongue flicked against the apex of my thighs. I whispered his name softly, then loudly as he sheathed himself inside of me because we were still entering Earth's atmosphere. We were still hoping for a life we could live together and a life we could bring to others.

Though I knew it wouldn't last.

As I gazed into Callum's emerald eyes after we finished together and held each other tightly, I knew it wouldn't last, and I hated myself for it. I hated myself for the life I was giving him, only to take it away.

A stone for a rose.

But there it was, my father's voice—a whisper in my mind.

Beauty is worth fighting for, Wynnie. Even if it's for a single moment.

Slowly, I blinked my eyes open, and I squinted at the light peeking through the curtains. They billowed in the breeze, gently flowing through the open balcony doors. *We must not have closed them last night.*

We.

I looked over to my left side, where Callum lay in my bed, completely and utterly naked. His bare chest rose and fell with each breath, and I memorized how the sun glistened against his golden-brown hair and eyelashes. Crisp morning air awakened my senses, and I started to replay every moment of last night, from beginning to end. His hands caressing every inch of my body, his lips that followed them… I still felt the ghost of his skin against mine—every ebb and flow of our love. His scent of earth and wood still lingered, clinging to my sheets, in the air, to my skin…

Callum.

I could still taste his name on my lips from the countless times I cried out last night, begging him to go deeper, to hold me harder. The thought sent me whirling again, spiraling down so that my heart skipped beats like it had countless times mere hours before when he was hovering over me, plunging himself deeper and deeper.

I struggled to breathe. *This is fucking insanity.* I thought to myself. *This is a Skies-damned tragedy.*

But not to him. To Callum, this was a love story, a faerie tale, something you read books about. *To him, this is when everything falls into place.* I suddenly became his clarity, his remedy, his answer to the question he had been pondering for over a decade.

Oh, sweet fire, how I wanted to be everything for him. That's why I told him who I was, wasn't it? Why I told him the truth? So I could be the very person he wanted most in the entire world.

One truth every day until you have no more truths to tell.

What would it look like to have no more truths to tell? And how long could that take?

I don't think the world can wait for the truth much longer. Sancus' words echoed in every crevice of my mind.

My lungs constricted, cutting off my air supply. Instinctively, I laid my head on Callum's chest and wrapped an arm around his ribs. The pounding of his heart filled my senses, and it was so different from mine. Callum's heartbeat was strong and steady, like the pounding of a drum, while mine was erratic and disoriented. It reminded me of wind chimes, so easily swayed.

Callum sleepily pulled me closer into him and kissed the crown of my head. Silence stretched between us, but it was different, and like our heartbeats, the silence we were emitting was different. His was a silence of waking from a restful sleep while mine was from a wheeling mind and racing heart, but Callum was surely oblivious to it.

His hands started to trace lazy circles on my arm, unknowingly calming my thoughts and easing my heart. He began to tempt me into the moment—into every moment—with him. I wanted to be fully engulfed in his presence, engulfed in him. Again and again.

A deep sigh escaped my lips, my thoughts returning to my multiple releases last night at the touch of his fingers, tongue, and…

"I could stay here forever," Callum whispered into my hair.

I breathed him in. "Me too," I replied, my words automatic. And I believed myself. I really could stay here with Callum forever. *And why couldn't I?*

I could live here with Callum. In the Coalition—a place I was told to hate. But I was told by my father to hate the Resistance as well, and I had found a home there. A family. People worth dying for.

Worth dying for.

Reign.

Maybe I could sneak her in somehow. Ask Niahm to help me. If I told Callum that Reign was my half-sister who lived with me in The Wastes, I know he would welcome her with open arms.

A plan started formulating in my mind, one that would enable me to stay here in the Coalition with Callum and sneak Reign in to be here with us.

But Callum's smooth and intoxicating voice broke over me like a wave hitting the ocean floor. "Do you remember that song I composed for you on my viola?"

I bit my lip and nestled into his chest. "When you were, like, eight? Yeah, I remember. What did you call it again?"

"Rowyn's Requiem."

"That's right." I laughed. "Did you even know what requiem meant at the time?"

My head bounced as Callum's answering chuckle rumbled in his chest. "No, it just sounded cool. But—" He paused. "Once you left, when I heard that you died, it seemed more fitting."

I swallowed. "You still played it after I left?"

Callum tucked me in tighter. "Of course. I play it every year on the anniversary of your disappearance."

I held my breath, hoping the pressure would keep my heart from breaking into a million pieces. "Will you play it for me sometime?"

"Of course." Silence stretched between us, the comfortable silence I only felt with him. He took a shaky breath, like he was recalling a painful memory. "I love you, Rowyn Eloise Darrow."

I smiled into his chest and kissed his bare skin there. "I love you too, Callum Orion Osouf."

"Prove it." There was a light carelessness to his tone.

I rolled over him so that my bare hips were flushed against his.

"Is that an order, Lieutenant General?"

His gaze was feral, and my nipples peaked under his stare. I felt the throbbing length of him grow beneath me.

"Yes," he growled. Callum pulled me in, closing the gap between us.

And I let him.

CHAPTER 28

Callum was already gone by the time my alarm pulled me from sleep. A steaming cup of coffee and a COM message were already waiting for me on my nightstand. I sipped from the coffee, bitter cocoa, hazelnut, and cream, awakening my senses as I opened the message Cal had sent me.

I couldn't justify waking you. You looked too beautiful. Have a good day at work. I'll pick you up at fifteen-hundred. Don't make any plans afterward. It's about time I treat you to a proper date.

My heart fluttered in my chest.

A real date.

I peeled myself from Callum's bed and got ready for work. Every movement felt like trudging through mud.

Skies above, Monday mornings really suck.

I'd never worked before. I mean, I had my duties on Base, and we obviously kept calendars, but the days of the week just seemed different there. I had not really thought about Monday mornings much since living in Excelsis—I just kind of went through the motions and did what needed to be done. However, after the party Friday night and spending the rest of the weekend with Callum in bed, returning to work today felt like an impossible chore. I just wanted to remain at the top of this apartment complex with Callum forever. If he had been here when I woke up, I don't know if I would have let him leave.

———

I arrived to work a full hour earlier than I was scheduled. Callum's flat just felt too lonely without him there, and I wanted to check on my Lion Finch friend, whom I had aptly named Leonidas. As I sauntered through the ray door, the chirping and singing of the mini griffins filled the room, and they were not alone. A woman with white hair stood before the second cage of Lion Finches, a COM-tab in her hand as she jotted down notes.

"Oh." I stopped in my tracks. "I'm sorry, Dr. Osouf. I didn't know you would be in here. I can come back later."

I turned to leave, but Freyja stopped me. "No need, I was just finishing up." She tapped her stylus angrily on her COM-tab before she turned around to face me. Her features were stoic as her eyes roamed over my body. "I did not see you at my gathering Friday night, yet I have it on good authority you were there."

I clutched my bag close to my chest. I felt naked under her scrutinizing gaze, and for a brief moment, I wondered if she could see the marks Callum's lips and fingers had made on my skin the night before. I swallowed, not daring to move. "I apologize. It was such a busy night, and Callum introduced me to so many people…"

Freyja crossed the room toward her bag, which was hanging on a hook in the corner nearest to the door. "I did not ask for excuses, Adellaide. It is quite rude to not even deign the host with a proper 'hello' or expression of gratitude, especially when you arrive to my party on the arm of my son."

I nodded once, trying my best not to avert my gaze. Though

this woman stood shorter than me, she made me feel so small. She was like Bellona in that way. "My apologies. It will not happen again." I stepped aside from the ray door, expecting the woman to leave, but she remained still.

"What brings you to this lab an hour before your scheduled shift?" Freyja asked, her features unwavering.

"I wanted to ensure the Lion Finches had sufficient food and water."

"We have caretakers for that."

"Yes, but—"

"Have you found their work unsatisfactory?"

"No, I just—"

"Do you think you could do better? Perhaps I should switch your position."

I sighed, exasperated. Freyja's brows narrowed in contempt, and the way her silver eyes flashed, I was sucked back in time.

My dad dragging me down the stairs of Osouf Manor. Callum at the top of the steps, his viola and bow at his sides as he watched in confused horror. Freyja slamming the intricately carved wooden door in my face, my father's back, as we left.

I shook my head, and my eyes refocused on the laboratory around me, on the woman before me. "I enjoy their company."

"Their company? They are animals."

"Yes, and I enjoy observing them."

"Then you will enjoy the Circus. I will be sure to get you and Callum tickets."

Something about the smile painted across Freyja's lips told me I would not, in fact, enjoy the Circus, whatever that was.

"Um, thank you," I stammered.

Freyja stepped closer to the ray door, the amethyst glow reflecting off her white hair and laboratory coat. "Some of my best work has been showcased there. If you are going to continue to be a part of my team, then I think it best that I show you personally. I will have Dr. Yong procure your tickets for this Saturday. She will send them over to Callum by day's end."

"That is very generous of you, Dr. Osouf. Thank you."

Her smile was feline as she passed me. "Oh, no. Thank you, Adellaide, for your genuine interest and enthusiasm for my work. Your involvement is much appreciated."

Freyja left through the ray door, and though I was relieved to be alone, my stomach churned uneasily in the wake of her words.

———

"The Circus is the best entertainment in the city!" Sancus shouted over the roar of the arena as we entered. He was leading the way, a slight skip in his step. I glanced back at Aletheia, but her face was donning its usual mask of apathy. We all followed Sancus, my hand grasped in Callum's, as he led us through the crowds of people either trying to find their seats or waiting in lines for unique libations and exotic foods.

"Just wait, Adellaide. Cal's mom and her co-workers have their own suite. We will have our own bar and our own chef. Oh, and the holo screen! It's the best way to watch the matches."

I still had no idea what to expect. Sancus refused to tell me, and every time Aletheia tried, her brother quickly shut her up.

I squeezed Callum's hand, and he turned toward me. "Will your mother be joining us?" I tried to sound nonchalant, but I was petrified. It had been almost a week since I revealed myself to Callum, and it had been like a dream—we had been on a few dates, and we slept together every night. How were we going to explain to his mother that we were now an *item*?

Wait. Were we? We hadn't discussed our relationship. Panic seized my breaths. I tried to focus on Callum's strong hand wrapped around mine and my name on his lips last night. *It didn't matter what we were, right?*

Callum shrugged. "I don't know. She usually forgoes the Circus, forcing one of her assistants to take extremely detailed notes so *Dr. Freyja Osouf* can get as much time in the Laboratory as possible." Callum's voice was mocking as he let go of my hand and slid an arm around my waist. My stomach flipped. "It's quite rare that she is able to make the Circus, but I am assuming one of her new experiments will be participating. My mother expressed how important this project would be for the Military— she even invited two five-star generals, though they will be in a different suite, presumably."

I straightened, my interest piqued. "Yeah, she mentioned something about her work being showcased here." I glanced at Callum from the corner of my eye. "Like experiments from the Epimetheus Project?" My heart seized as the words left my lips. I hoped he wouldn't notice me digging for information, but if it was important to the Military, it was important for the Resistance.

Callum pulled me in tight. "Yes, but don't say it too loudly, darling *Adellaide*," he whispered in my hair before planting a kiss on my temple. "It is top secret, after all." Laughter coated Callum's words like sweet syrup, and it almost distracted me.

At the very least, he knows of some top-secret biological projects.

He must have felt my spine straighten because he held on tighter to my waist. "Don't worry, my mother will be too busy working to even notice our existence if she does decide to come by the suite."

The suite was more like a private viewing lounge. Toward the arena, before the translucent screens, there were two rows of lounge chairs, padded in exorbitantly decorated, lush fabrics, and in the back was a bar complete with a bartender and row after row of various liquors. Velvet curtains wrapped the windows and doors, pooling onto rich wood floors. Along the wall, golden sconces were dimmed low, setting an oddly romantic ambiance to the room.

As usual, Sancus made himself right at home, waving down a cocktail waitress after plopping his ass on one of the luxurious couches. At first glance, it appeared as if no one else had arrived, but then I noticed a small figure in the corner standing at a cocktail table. She tucked a few strands of dark hair behind her ear as she typed quietly on her COM-tab.

"Hlín." I walked over to the young geneticist, Callum trailing behind me. Dr. Hlín Yong gave me a small, quick smile before returning to her typing.

"Hello," she whispered without looking up from her COM-tab.

"I didn't know you would be here today."

She nodded eagerly. "Oh, yes. I am waiting for Dr. Osouf. She expressed great importance for the Circus today and noted that the data will be crucial to our research."

"For the Epimetheus Project? Is there any way I can assist? Should I be working, too?"

"Oh, no." She shook her head, and a dark lock of hair escaped her tight pony. She tucked in behind her ear immediately. "It's a different project. Very top-secret. Well, until today, I suppose. I advised Dr. Osouf against allowing non-essentials in this booth today, but she did not wish to keep her son away from this extraordinary event. This research could prove useful for the American Coalition Military." The young researcher glanced at Callum, who stood behind me, a hand on the small of my back.

"Oh, I am so sorry. Have you two met?" I gestured between Hlín and Callum.

"No, I don't think we have. I am Lieutenant General Callum Osouf." Callum extended a hand.

"Oh, yes. I know who you are." Hlín pushed invisible strands of hair behind her small ears. "Pleasure, Lieutenant General. I am Dr. Hlín Yong." She took his hand, which dwarfed hers, and shook it gently.

"Pleasure is mine, Dr. Yong. I have heard so much about you."

The geneticist blushed, curling in on herself.

"Well, please excuse me, ladies, but I would like to make

sure the Second Lieutenant and Private Gillian are comfortable." Callum gave a slight nod to Hlín before turning to me and kissing my cheek.

Heat flooded through me, and I stared after Callum as he walked away. *I just want to grab that tight a—*

Hlín cleared her throat. "It seems you took my advice, Ms. Stevens."

I jerked my attention back to Hlín, though I didn't dare to look her in the eye, too embarrassed that she just caught me staring at Callum's backside. "Um, yes. Thank you."

Hlín continued to type on her COM-tab, unphased by my embarrassment. "Do not stop, or you will lose it."

"Easier said than done," I breathed as I relaxed into my forearms on the cocktail table.

"My grandmother used to tell me everything hard is worth the effort."

I chewed on my lip.

"What is your truth for the day, Ms. Stevens?"

A small laugh escaped my lips. "That I need a drink before Dr. Osouf gets here." I waved over a tall, lean cocktail waitress. "What would you like?" I asked Hlín.

Her narrow eyes grew wide. "Ms. Stevens, I am working!"

I rolled my eyes. "Oh, like you don't need a drink before Freyja gets here?"

Hlín's cheeks bloomed rosy. "I took a shot before you and your friends arrived," she admitted quietly.

"Dr. Yong! I did not peg you for a shot girl."

Hlín nodded once, ready to move on from this subject. "That is my truth for you today."

The cocktail waitress stood before us, her clothes minimal and in Coalition Plum, matching the curtains. "What would you like this afternoon?"

"What is your name, dear?" I asked the waitress.

She stood there, dumbfounded for a moment before she

blinked. "Um, Selena, ma'am," she stammered, tugging on her too-short skirt.

"Well, Selena, I would like a glass of sparkling rosé, please." I glanced at Hlín, and she donned the same dumbfounded look the waitress had. "Would you care for anything, Hlín?"

She glanced up at the waitress, voice flat. "Mineral water."

Selena turned to leave, but I caught her shoulder. "Thank you." She looked confused, nodding slightly before retreating toward the bar. I watched as the waitress gave the bartender our order and waited patiently, a plastered smile never leaving her face, yet never quite touching her eyes.

I glanced to Hlín, who was shaking her head at me.

"What?"

"You don't need to be so polite. They are just Integrates."

I grimaced. "Integrates? Like part of the Integration program? Like me?"

Hlín's eyes grew wide as she understood how her words came across. "I didn't mean it like that, Ms. Stevens, I just—"

"So, all applicants of the Integration Program just get placed into service jobs?"

Hlín nodded. "You were quite the exception to the rule."

This information settled uneasily into my stomach as the waitress returned with two drinks balanced on her golden tray. She set two full glasses before us, repeating the order as she did so.

"Any other way I may be of assistance, madams?"

"No," I answered, maintaining eye contact. "Thank you very much, Selena. We really appreciate it." The young girl blushed as she retreated, quietly returning to her position as a wallflower waiting to be plucked once someone had need of her.

"*Salularia*," Hlín muttered in obligation as she raised her glass.

I muttered the same and clinked my glass to hers.

Strawberries and freshly cut grass filled my nose as I took a sip of wine, but it tasted sour as it rolled over my tongue—reality tainting my palate as I stared at the poor girl. *This is what she applied to do? She made it to Excelsis only to be shoved in a corner.*

Hlín sighed, and I glanced toward her. "Yes?"

"Don't feel bad. They live a much better life here."

"How do you—"

She cocked a dark brow. "They still receive fair wages, they are given more opportunities, they have a healthier diet, and they have a promising future for their families."

I ground my teeth. I did not feel like arguing with Hlín. It seemed so unfair to me, but I would just be talking to a wall. I took a large sip of my wine before I asked, "So, what exactly is the Circus?"

"It's different every time," Hlín disclosed, her nose planted deep into her COM-tab. She kept the imaging off three-dimensional mode, probably for security reasons. "It's a testing ring for Dr. Osouf's experiments. She uses the data gathered to determine how the individual test subjects react in stressful situations, how they analyze and solve problems, in addition to their fight or flight responses, and how they manage pain or discomfort."

"That seems..." My stomach churned. "...ethically questionable."

Hlín paused, her back straightening and her head tilting to the side like she had never thought about that before. But with a shake of her head, she dismissed it quickly and returned to typing on her COM-tab. "It is science, Ms. Stevens. What is ethical is solving the mysteries of the universe to then share the knowledge with the world."

I resisted rolling my eyes as I looked away from Hlín and took a large gulp of wine. Callum caught my eye and waved me over. *Thank the Skies.*

I politely excused myself from Hlín and sauntered over to Cal. He was sitting on a swiveling recliner beside Sancus, a glass of whiskey in his hand as he extended the other out to me, then swung me onto his lap. Callum pecked a small kiss on my arm as I relaxed into him.

"How's Hlín?" he asked.

"Anxious, as usual."

"I have something that will help with that." Aletheia was lounging on a couch, her entire body rolled out like a sunbathing cheetah.

I pointed a finger at my friend. "No."

"Just trying to help," she sang innocently, but I knew better.

I turned to Callum. "One would think that someone of your repute would not associate with people of this ilk."

"I heard that!" Sancus yelled as he eagerly pressed the remotes to the large holo screen before us. Whatever Sancus was trying to do, it wasn't working because the same small clip of The American Coalition's emblem—a triangle surrounded by three tiered rings—was glitching on repeat.

"What's going on?"

Callum's best friend was leaning on his knees. "I just want to see what the rounds are!"

"We told you they won't tell the crowd for another twenty minutes," Aletheia groaned.

Sancus was tapping angrily now. "But we are in a suite! We should have early access!"

I turned my head and raised a brow.

Callum's laughter skittered across my skin. "The Circus is different every time," he offered, repeating what Hlín had told me. "The Circus Masters do not share their secrets, but they always make it interesting. Sometimes they plan races, other times brawls. Once, they drew random seats from the audience and made them participate in crazy stunts and fighting."

My eyes grew wide. "Did anyone get hurt?"

"Oh, yes. They haven't done a Circus like that since. It was a big scandal."

"But it was by far the most entertaining," Aletheia chimed in.

Callum glared at the private, but her eyes were focused on

her nails as she filed them into daggers. "Anyway, an hour before the Circus begins, the Circus Master announces the set list—that is also when the wagering windows open."

"So, if they don't pick participants from the stadium anymore, then what do they race? Who do they have brawl?" I asked.

"Usually—"

"Stop!" Sancus held a hand up to his friend, eyes still fixed on the holo screen. "Don't tell her. Let her be surprised and amazed."

Callum wrapped two arms around my waist and hugged me tight. "I guess you will have to wait and see."

"First of all, since when is Sancus the boss of you? Secondly, you know I hate surprises."

He kissed my shoulder. "Oh, really? Because I recall you being the master of surprises."

Aletheia and Sancus glanced in our direction. I elbowed Callum in the chest. "Shut up."

Callum laughed, opening his mouth to say something, but he was cut off when the door to the suite opened. Dr. Freyja Osouf strode into the private room, and everyone fell silent as she floated about the suite.

"Oh, well, don't stop the fun on my account." Freyja waved a hand to all of us in the lounge. Her silver eyes fell on Sancus' whose fingers were still on the remote. Without a word, she huffed a sigh and walked over to the front of the room. As soon as her fingers touched the large holo screen, a keypad flickered to life, and Freyja entered in a code. The screen unlocked to display a menu of the Circus Schedule.

Freyja turned around to face us all. "Second Lieutenant, must you always forget the suite code? And Private, remove your feet from the furniture. This is not a Humilian Barn." I noted the shock of hurt behind Aletheia's stony expression as she removed her feet silently—very much unlike the usually snarky woman. Then Freyja's eyes settled on me, my ass still firmly planted on

Callum's lap. Her lips pursed in distaste, like she popped a lemon candy in her mouth. "Adellaide, dear, you are in Excelsis now. It's best you let old habits die."

Freyja moved to breeze past us, and I shifted, but Callum's hands remained tight around my waist, not allowing me to get up.

"Actually, Mother, Adellaide is right where she belongs."

Freyja stopped in her tracks, her head slowly turning to meet her son's gaze, one white brow raised in disdain.

"Adellaide and I are exclusive."

I heard more than saw Sancus and Aletheia shift uncomfortably. Sancus even cleared his throat and muttered something about needing another drink. I didn't dare watch him leave, not when Callum and I were the subject of Freyja's ire.

"*Exclusive?*" The word fell from Freyja's lips like curdled milk. "You are telling me that you have taken up a Median whore as more than your bedmate?"

My heart stopped. *How did she find out that I—Adellaide— was a brothel worker? Or maybe she is just using a derogatory word?*

Callum straightened, his arms still fully wrapped around me. "I am telling you that we are an item. Adellaide is my partner."

Freyja spat, "Partner?"

My head was spinning. Surely, this was not the right time to tell his mother that we were *together*. We hadn't even discussed it yet.

"Surely, you must be mistaken, Callum. Aligning yourself with a Median Brothel Mistress in such a way can have unforeseen consequences on your career path."

I was pushed from Callum's lap as he stood to face his mother—towering over her. "Actually, M*other*, Adellaide is not—"

I set a hand on Callum's shoulder and squeezed. "I do not think now is the best time to discuss our relationship, Callum. Your mother so graciously invited us to this event, and it would be rude to continue stirring trouble and impede our guests with this…familial drama." I couldn't think of a better way to phrase it, and it was too late to take it back now.

Luckily, Freyja rolled back her shoulders and nodded once. "Adellaide is right; we will discuss this matter at a later date."

I was annoyed that Freyja insisted on talking about me like I wasn't there, but I ignored that, too. Right now, I not only needed peace, but I did not want Callum to tell his mother who I really was—she could not know I was Rowyn, not yet.

I glanced between the two. "Now, if you will excuse me, I need to use the ladies' room."

But Callum did not allow me respite for long because he was waiting in the hallway to the suite right outside the bathroom for me. He kicked himself off the wall he was leaning on. "Why didn't you let me tell her?"

I waved Callum off, breezing past him. "We are not doing this right now."

Callum grabbed my wrist and twirled me toward him. If I wasn't so annoyed, I would have thought it charming—I would have laughed. "We are going to have to tell people eventually."

And he said it, the thought that had been terrifying me all week: eventually, he would want to tell the world.

But I wasn't planning on being here long enough for him to do that.

Or was I?

The whole week had been like a dream, and I had only spared my mission a passing thought or two. I was so busy wrapped up in Callum all week I hardly thought about my friends back at Base, or Metis and his experiments. The only person I really missed was Reign.

"Callum, we are still figuring out what this is! You never even told me that you thought of us as *exclusive*. I don't think telling people that I am Rowyn is exactly a priority right now."

"You don't think we are *exclusive*? Do you not want this?"

I rubbed my forehead. "Skies, no, that is not what I meant. I just— I— Callum, I have been out of this society for sixteen years. What makes you think I understand what that means?"

His eyes softened. "I never—"

"I know." I shook my head, cutting him off. I know he didn't mean to hurt me, and I know it never even crossed his mind that our relationship was something that needed to be discussed. After all, he knew my heart. But the Rowyn that he knew had never been in a relationship before. Skies, the Rowyn he knew was probably a virgin before last week. But even the real Rowyn, me, I had only been with one man before Callum—I wasn't exactly experienced in relationships.

Callum wrapped his arms around me. "I'm sorry, I should have communicated better."

I shrugged. "It's fine. I was just caught off guard."

Callum kissed the top of my head.

"Not to mention,"—I glanced up to meet his eyes—"I still don't know why my father left. Your mother worked with him, and I don't want to bring up anything just in case there is bad blood. Not yet. I just need time to figure things out."

Callum gently pushed me to arm's length. "I can help. I would love to help. I am sure I can find something about your father and his departure."

Well, fuck.

"You would do that?"

A smile lit up his face. "Of course."

"Cal, that would mean the world to me."

He cupped my cheek. "Wynnie, I would burn the whole world to the ground to make you happy."

And I hoped he wouldn't regret those words.

CHAPTER 29

Callum and I returned to find Sancus once more glued to the holo screen and Aletheia on the couch, though her feet were planted firmly on the ground this time, and a large glass of wine was poised in one hand.

"Are the sets open?" Callum asked as he sat down in the same chair as before. Our hands were intertwined, but my attention remained fixed on Freyja since I entered the suite. She was standing by Hlín lips pursed tight while one hand adjusted her glasses as she peered at Hlín's COM-tab, the other angrily pointed at the COM screen. My gut twisted. Dr. Freyja Osouf was in a mood, probably because of me, and Hlín would bear the brunt of her ire.

A sharp tug on my hand returned my attention to Callum. His gaze darted from mine to his lap. I rolled my eyes. *Does he have a death wish?*

Unlike Callum, I was not willing to agitate Freyja further. I untangled my hand from his own and sat on the floor before Callum, relaxing into the chair behind my back and resting an arm atop Callum's right leg. Callum rubbed my shoulders, his touch gentle and reassuring.

"Yeah, but…" Sancus kept scrolling on the remote, an

annoying beeping sound emitting from the screen. Sancus cursed. "It won't let me access the stats and summaries of the sixth set!"

Like Sancus had summoned the Circus Masters with his anger, the display screen glitched, and a plump man with a pointed nose and snow-white goatee appeared before us.

"Excuse me for the inconvenience." His voice was a low bellow. "I am Barnabas Torrand, and on behalf of all the Circus Masters, we thank you for attending the Circus today. We know you are all eager to place your wagers and that you are afraid they may be dependent on the sixth set. We would like to assure you that the sixth and final set will be completely different and unrelated to the first five. All of us here at the Circus have decided to let the sixth set remain a mystery for entertainment purposes. No wagers will be cast for the sixth set until the very second the sixth set begins, and the wager window will only be open for one minute. Every wager for the sixth set will automatically be set as double or nothing, so wager carefully. We hope you enjoy today's Circus. *Felicitas*!"

The holo screen returned to the summary of the fifth set.

"Well, they do like to keep us on our toes," Aletheia murmured, then sipped from her glass of red wine.

I glanced at Freyja, who, during the announcement, had slipped to the front right corner of the room near the lounge, and her eyes met mine. I did not look away—I did not dare—because as our eyes locked, a dangerous and knowing smile was painted across her ruby-red lips.

———

The holo screen also served as a viewing window. About twenty minutes before the first set, the screen turned transparent. Statistics, pictures, and diagrams were projected from the window to describe the arena as the game assistants began setting up. The Circus Announcers boomed through the sound system around the room, discussing previous Circus sets and an overview of the wagers from the crowd.

Located at the top center of the window was the short description of the first set.

Set Number 1: Emu Races.

In the far right corner, there was a small screen of a zoomed-in view of the arena where we could see a hover vehicle hauling a long chain of small stalls.

From my position on the floor, I turned to glance up at Callum. "What are emus?"

"They are extinct, flightless birds," Callum answered over a bite of food. The waitress had brought a board of assorted cheeses, cured meats, dried fruits, exotic nuts, flaky crackers, and delectable spreads. The smorgasbord took up the whole gold-flaked coffee table before us.

Callum carefully fed me a half-eaten cracker laden with a soft cheese and a seeded jam. The cheese was pungent as it hit my nose, but my mouth was bursting with flavors of rich butter, dark fruits, vanilla, and orange zest.

"And they are fast?" I asked, a hand covering my mouth.

From the corner of my eye, I noted Freyja's disapproving glare.

But Callum was either completely obtuse, or he indeed had a death wish because he wiped some stray jam off the corner of my lips, then slid the finger in my mouth. Mischief danced in his eyes as he shrugged. "Apparently."

My heart began to race I wanted him to take me home now, but it would be rude to leave. I tried to ignore the throbbing between my legs. "If they are extinct, how are they here?"

Hlín answered this time. She sat straight-backed in a plain chair—that looked very uncomfortable compared to the rest of the lounge—with her COM-tab over her lap, the holo mode still off as she used the stylus to take notes. "The Circus Masters have strong monetary ties with the Coalition's Department of Ancient Historical Artifacts. The Circus will work with researchers, geneticists, and archeologists to replicate the DNA of extinct animals to either grow individuals from the DNA or create a completely different creature. It is the driving factor behind the games, really, and it is why the government agrees to partner with the Circus—some of the profit of every Circus is funneled directly into the AHA, genetics research, and museums. And the tax money from the gambling profits is distributed throughout the American Coalition. It is opportunistic for all parties."

I was sure it was only opportunistic for Excelsis. I doubted Media and Humilis saw any of that money.

Something clicked. "You said 'create.' Is this what the Epimetheus Project research is primarily used for?"

Hlín nodded excitedly. "And not only the Epimetheus Project. Today, we are showcasing the first successful results from our—"

"Now, now," Freyja chastised her assistant. "Let our guests be surprised, Dr. Yong."

Hlín tucked her chin, returning to her favored mode of existence—neither seen nor heard.

Simultaneously, a ten-minute timer began to count down on the screen as Circus assistants began to parade out the emus. Each of them wore a little coat with a number on it, but that was the only way I could differentiate the similar beasts.

"Are they clones?"

"No," Freyja answered when she realized Hlín was not going to chime in. "We start out with one fully replicated strand of DNA, then run it through our simulators to create diversity within the species. That way, we can ensure breeding will be safe and select for the best individuals over time. Though we can deduce diseases and genetic abnormalities in simulations, there is no way we can ensure we have the best DNA from the best individual in a species. We can only do so by testing them in the real world. So, here we are."

I nodded slowly.

The game assistants began filing the emus into their

designated stalls, and each one squawked and ruffled its feathers at the small enclosure. Most of them stomped their feet in agitation, probably preparing their legs for the run. There were no lanes they had to stay in, but the track was lined with clear acrylic fencing to keep them within the boundaries.

The clock continued to click down, the birds growing more agitated with every passing second.

Three.

Two.

One.

The gates to the stalls opened, and the birds shot from their cages.

The holo screen kept track of all the emus and their speeds, arrows, and numbers floating over each bird. Most of the birds stayed on the track, but some deviated toward the fence. What I thought was just an acrylic wall turned out to be electric. Birds began bouncing off the fence with loud squawks, their feathers smoking from the impact. Some birds ignored the first jolt, only to run right into the fence full force. Those birds did not get back up once their bodies bounced off the electric wall and collapsed onto the dirt floor, their lifeless frames trampled by the herd of running emus.

Sancus stood cheering as the bird he bet on, number forty-two, took the lead about halfway through the track. The crowd's cry boomed through the suite's speakers—a mix of objections and cheers—and the announcer's discourse grew more urgent as the emus began to round the second bend of the track.

In a loud roar, the race ended with number eighty-eight taking the title. It was over far more quickly than it took to set up.

Sancus cursed as he plopped back into the seat.

I wonder how much money he lost.

The announcers were still going on about the good race as the Circus assistants dragged the corpses of fried emus from the track, and my stomach churned. To think, Freyja and Hlín created these emus just to be entertainment and then die. And I worked for them. I was complicit.

————

The Circus assistants brought the top three emus from the race into the center of the arena. The whole stadium shook as the racetrack disappeared and was replaced by gravel, and the holo screen changed over, revealing a new title and a new map of the arena.

Set Number 2: Survival of the Fittest

"In set one, we saw the incredible speed these extinct creatures possess," the announcer's voice boomed, filling the whole suite through the speakers. "But in set two, we are taking the three fastest emus, and we will see how they fair against a potential predator."

The holo screen flickered from the emus—which were all huddled together in the middle of the area, feet stomping and wings flaring in agitation—to the east wing. Behind iron bars were narrowed snouts with bared teeth as the beasts growled and barked. To the right of the angry beasts, an image of some sort of wild dog slowly turned, showing the animal from all angles, and the word *Thylacine* floated above the rotating image.

"About five hundred years before the demise," the announcer went on, "emus were natural prey of the Thylacines on the continent of Australia, which is now completely submerged under the Pacific Ocean.

"Though the Thylacine looks like a canine, it is a marsupial. The stripes along the back half of its body were an adaptation to blend into the shadows of the Tasmanian forests. But in an open field like this arena, it might be beneficial to confuse prey and predators when they circle in their pack, similar to the ancient zebra."

Over the holo screen, a countdown flickered, and from the announcer's mic, we could hear the crowd begin to chant "Ten!"

Sancus joined along with them.

"Ladies and gentlemen, a glimpse into the past in three, two, one..."

A loud buzzer blared through the speaker as the metal gates were raised. The Thylacines sprinted.

The three emus' eyes grew wide, and their plumage stood on end as they noticed five snarling thylacines descending upon them.

A split second later, they scattered, each pacing and circling in different directions to find an escape. There were only two open gates—one on the north end and one on the west end of the arena—but the emus were either too dumb or too spooked to notice. The Thylacines descended on one, the emu who placed second—number sixty-four. There weren't many Thylacines— only five total, which was smaller than most wolf packs in The Wastes—and they weren't particularly fast either, but through yips and growls, they communicated between the pack to herd number sixty-four, which was cornering itself to the south. Two Thylacines flanked the emu's left side from a distance of about thirty feet—not close enough to force the emu to dart erratically, but enough to make it steer away from the carnivores. The other three remained in pursuit, their yowls menacing as they gained ground. Sixty-four began to slow as it ran closer and closer to the arena wall, its long neck tossing from side to side as it searched for an escape. I glanced around the arena to find the other two emus—they were each safely tucked behind ray doors in the north and west gates.

How the Thylacines chose number sixty-four, I wasn't sure. Maybe it was proximity, maybe it was slightly slower than the others? I supposed that will be something for Hlín and Freyja to analyze. All I knew was that when the Thylacines descended onto the cornered emu, there was nothing natural about it.

I had hunted. I had witnessed animals in the wild catching and devouring prey. But this was something that made me sick. Maybe it was the spectacle of it all, or maybe it was the fact that these creatures were made in a lab for our entertainment. Or maybe it was the way people cheered and the way virtual coins cashed into a small little pouch in the corner of the holo screen once the Thylacines ripped sixty-four's throat out. No matter what the reason, I forced myself to sip on my wine to wash down the bile rising in my throat.

My back was pushing into Callum's chair, and I brought my knees close to my chest. Callum's arms wrapped around me, finding their home right over my sternum, and his lips were by my ear. "Are you okay?"

I nodded. "Yeah," but my voice was breathy.

"We can go—"

"No." I glanced at Freyja from the corner of my eye. She was whispering to Hlín, who was diligently taking notes, but Freyja must have felt my gaze on her because her cool eyes settled on me after a moment. Her brow cocked in challenge. "No," I repeated, more evenly this time. I needed to prove to Freyja that I deserved to be here, that I could handle the cruel horrors of Excelsis.

But why should you care, Red? It's not like you're going to stay here. I took a sip of wine. *You have a mission to complete. You have friends to get back to. You have Reign, who needs you.* All of my responsibilities and obligations sat heavily in my chest. It was too easy to get caught up in this new life. *In this fake life*, I corrected myself.

Damnit. I forgot about my contacts.

I tapped my temple twice, just in time for the next set to begin.

No one had even tried to remove the Thylacines from the arena. They were still huddled in a corner, feasting on their prize.

"Well, I hope that meal energized our Thylacines for the next round!" the announcer began again. "This time, we will see how the past competes with the present." The screen paned from the feasting Thylacines to the southern arena gate, but now, behind the bars was a snarling Anoka Bear. The three-dimensional holo image of the beast showed off the bear's sharp saber teeth and the large spines protruding from its back. Based on the glowing stats, this mutated creature dwarfed the Thylacines, standing nearly nine feet tall and edging up to eight hundred pounds.

"During the Demise, animals—wild and domestic alike—were subjected to massive amounts of radiation and chemicals. Some species disappeared instantly, and some were changed forever."

As if on cue, the mutant grizzly roared, spittle flying from its mouth as it pounded the iron rails with clawed paws. The iron bent under the sheer force. The Thylacines turned at the noise. One by one, their hackles rose, and they bared their teeth at the threat.

"They don't stand a chance," I whispered, but no one answered, not as the gate opened and the bear stepped into the arena. The Anoka Grizzly Bear raised its thick snout into the air, nose twitching. The holo image zoomed in on the bear, and the footprints it created on the arena's sand floor, and my mind flashed to the day I found Aura lifeless in the woods, her fur-lined boots stained red. I wanted to scream for Aura to wake up, for her to run. Anything. But I knew it was too late.

A mighty roar bellowed through the speakers in our suite, shaking me from my memory, but as the bear sprinted, my throat throbbed like I was still stuck in that field, sobbing over my step-mother's corpse.

I forced myself to take deep breaths as the Anoka's shoulders flexed beneath his heavy fur. As he pounded the earth with his enormous paws, the spikes from his back appeared to grow as he ran on all fours, and a long club tail whipped from side to side at the rear of the beast, beating against the ground as he ran. I expected the Thylacines to stand their ground and protect their meal, but once the bear was twenty feet away, they scattered into two groups of two and one lone pack member. The bear glanced around, confused, but his nose twitched, probably catching a whiff of the emu carcass. He slowed down to a trot, then to a lumbering pace as he approached the carcass, the Thylacines watching carefully from a distance as they reformed their pack. They were still retreating, not daring to pick a fight with the likes of a mutated grizzly bear.

"In the wild, it is not uncommon for mid-grade predators to defer their latest catch to a beast higher up the food chain. However,"—I could hear the cruel smile in the announcer's voice—"we are not here for deference today."

Through the middle of the arena, a solid ten-foot wall rose from the ground, and the crowd cheered. Tucking their tales, the Thylacines backed away from the newly placed wall, their heads whirling as they looked for another way to retreat. The rumbling of the wall also alarmed the bear. His head whipped around toward the Thylacines, shoulders flexed in aggravation. The largest member of the Thylacine pack stood at point, and its mouth opened nearly eighty degrees as it bellowed a warning cry. The other Thylacines echoed in yips and chatter. The Anoka glanced from the wall to the pack of Thylacines. I could see in the shifting of his eyes and the arch of his back how uncomfortable the bear was in such a small space with another threat in the food chain. The bear's tail whipped back and forth, narrowly avoiding the emu carcass and making a complete mess of its meal before he stood on two legs. The Anoka bellowed an arena-rattling roar.

The Thylacines charged first. They took a similar approach as with the emus, two darting to the left and three pressing forward. They did manage to divert the bear as he charged. However, the bear's tail gave the mutant creature some reach. As the two Thylacines tried to jump on the bear's back, the Anoka swung his hips. The bear's club tail struck the two Thylacines in the ribs, and they were sent flying into the far wall. They crumpled to the ground in a heap of blood, bones, and flesh— neither of the marsupials got to their feet again.

The bear continued to slash through the rest of the pack, his paws nearly half the size of one Thylacine. With every impact, either the cracking of Thylacine bones echoed into the crowd or blood and organs spilled from the small pack of animals. As the Anoka swiped again, one Thylacine pounced onto the bear's back. It clawed and bit into whatever flesh it could grab onto, but its jaws were too weak—it couldn't even break through skin. Once the bear shook off the Thylacine, the Anoka's sabers impaled the marsupial's entire abdomen in one quick flash of his maw.

The third set was over in a matter of minutes, with every Thylacine lying limp on the sandy arena floor.

My head was woozy and spinning as the bear began to feast on the flesh of the marsupial pack, his reward for entertaining the masses. I was not weak around blood, and the Skies knew I had seen my fair share of violence, but this was sickening. I tried not to think of Aura's mangled body—of the bear feasting on my father's corpse. I tried not to think of my parents fighting this very creature in this arena.

Past and present blurred together, and my mind saw my parents retreating from the beast like the Thylacines.

They tried to run.

My mind sharpened. Something cold and hard settled in my chest.

That was a sheer element of evolution alone—if a species was intelligent enough to run when a stronger predator came around, it did. This wasn't a test of superiority in the food chain, this was just chaos.

My hands were clenched tight around my empty wine glass. I debated grabbing another, but I was worried that if I moved, I would jostle the tears loose from my eyes.

A shadow loomed over me. My eyes roamed up the figure in front of me with thin legs and a skirt so short that, unfortunately, from this angle, I could see everything. She squatted before me, a warm smile on her face and her hand outstretched, holding a glass of wine.

"Another one, miss?"

I met her eyes and nodded in thanks as I grabbed the filled glass.

As she leaned back, our eyes met once more, and I saw the hopelessness there. I saw her silent plea for help.

This was clearly not the life she wanted in Excelsis. From her perspective, I was just like her—I was her kin—yet, I got the fancy job. I got the handsome Lieutenant General. And I was the one partying in this suite while she had to work and endure this grotesque chaos on a regular basis.

I prayed Selena could see the helplessness in my own eyes. I had no idea what she wanted or what she expected me to do. I was just one person.

Yeah, one Resistance Agent.

But I wasn't here to rescue people, I was here to gather intel —a job I am hardly qualified for. I wasn't even supposed to be in Imperium. I was stuck here by accident. Well, maybe not an accident since Ulysses sabotaged my mission, but it definitely was not a part of my plan.

As Selena left, picking up empty glasses and plates of food, no one seemed to notice our encounter, not even Callum.

Did I imagine the whole thing?

I sipped from my fresh glass of wine as the announcer boomed over the speakers and the holo screen flickered to showcase the next set. "We have seen creatures from the past and creatures of the present face-off, but now, ladies and gentlemen, we give you the *future*."

The arena was back to normal. They must have lowered the wall while I was distracted, and the Anoka Grizzly Bear was still hunched over Thylacine carcasses, his appetite not quite satiated. But as the ground shook, the Anoka glanced toward the middle of the arena, where a hole slid open. Slowly, an opaque cylinder rose, but even the metal couldn't contain the angry roar from the beast within.

"Our best geneticists fabricated a beast never before seen. Something only your darkest nightmares could conjure up."

The cylinder surrounding the mystery creature began to sink back into the arena floor, slowly revealing the new beast.

The crowd was awed by the obsidian horns that curled around a thick, dark skull. The beast roared with the crowd, throwing its head back, and it displayed its large, black tusks protruding from its jawbone, like mandibles. This creature obviously did not rely on sight for hunting—its dark eyes were small with white lines crawling down like tears—but it must have made up for its poor eyesight with a heightened sense of hearing and smell. The beast's snout was huge, with four slits of nostrils and riddled with sharp whiskers as thick as pens. Its ears were pointed and open to the world, placed on each side of its head right below its horns.

Finally, the full beast was unveiled. It stood as foreboding as the night, its four legs long and powerful as it towered over the mutant bear by a good three feet. My jaw dropped when the beast flexed its paws—half-a-dozen spikes jutting out from the back side of each leg and sharp obsidian claws as long as my forearm digging into the ground.

"Ladies and gentlemen, meet the incredible, the ferocious, the deadly...Achlys!" the announcer boomed, and, as if on cue, the Achlys roared.

The mutant bear literally stood up to the challenge, rising on his two back paws to bellow his defiance. The Achlys bound first, its speed unimaginable for a beast of its size.

Holo stats flickered in the corner. I glanced over the height, weight, sex, and speed, my eyes scrolling to the bottom, where it briefly explained the makeup of the beast's DNA. There were at least a hundred different creatures, both extant and extinct, whose genetic makeup and sequences were used to map out this singular creature.

This wasn't a mere cloning and enhancing experiment—the Achlys was built from the ground up.

In a matter of seconds, the two beasts collided—a mutant

created in nature, derived from human error, and a beast from hell, concocted in a laboratory.

The Achlys' mandibles swiped at the Anoka's jugular, but the bear struck at the Achlys' eyes, thwarting the trajectory. As the Anoka Bear's paw fell, he swung around, landing his tail into the Achlys' ribs. It hardly phased the unnatural beast. Instead, the bear's back was left exposed, and the Achlys pounced. Her teeth tried to sink into the bear's neck, but the two-foot spines on the bear's back stabbed into the Achlys' tender belly, and she yelped, jumping off the bear. The Anoka swung his club tail again, striking for the Achlys' face, but with a jerk of the beast's head, the Achlys shielded herself from the blow.

They seemed easily matched, each creature struggling to land a devastating blow on the other. After a few minutes of back-and-forth blows, I noticed the Achlys growing agitated—not angry, just annoyed, like she was done with the game. Her back went rigid, and her black fur seemed to ripple down her spine, through her tail, and all the way to the tip until a sharp barb burst through fur and flesh.

The crowd went wild.

The Achlys roared as it whirled, her tail like a whip before the barb landed deep into the bear's back. The bear cried out in pain. It did not look like a fatal blow until the bear seized, his body shivering erratically and spittle foaming around his mouth. The bear fell, its body still convulsing on the arena floor. The Achlys sauntered over to the seizing bear. She stood towering over the Anoka, glanced up and down the body, and then with a quick swipe of her head, the Achlys' mandibles slit the bear's throat wide open. Thick, crimson blood poured out onto the floor.

The crowd roared in approval, most patrons rising to their feet, fists in the air at the display. The Achlys turned her attention to the crowd, her furred ears twitching at the excitement and tail whipping back and forth. The fur along her spine and tail shifted again, and her barb disappeared back into her tail, like a medieval night sheathing his sword after a duel. I swear I even saw a glint of pride in the Achlys' eyes, and I wondered if, maybe, the beast was actually intelligent.

The Achlys did not bother devouring the bear then and there. Instead, she clamped her jaw down around the bear's neck and dragged him to the middle of the arena, descending down into the hell from where she came, prize and all.

Our suite was silent, Hlín and Freyja whispering as they recorded data, Aletheia was tapping on her COM-tab, and Sancus was just staring dumbfounded at the screen before he jumped to his feet.

"That was so fucking cool! Wasn't that just amazing, Adellaide?"

Sancus' eyes were lit with pure fanaticism until they met mine, and then his eyes went wide, like a kid realizing he made his mother extremely angry.

I averted my gaze from the soldier, staring into my empty wine glass. "This is disgusting," I muttered, but all eyes turned on me, Freyja's glare heaviest of all.

Callum massaged my shoulders. "It's only a little entertainment, Adellaide."

I turned toward him. "Is that all these animals are created for? *Entertainment?*"

"To be fair, the bear was found in The Wastes." Sancus shrugged.

I ignored him. "They are only destined for a life of pain. And how are these creatures kept? How are they fed? Do they have a proper enclosure? Fresh water?" Questions poured into my mind. That bear was probably perfectly happy in *The Wastes,* as they called it. Granted, it could have been the very beast that killed my father, but who knew how long the bear had been in the Coalition? Who knew how many times it had been required to fight."

"Adellaide, it's just an animal. It doesn't know any better." Callum's voice was sickeningly calm, like his small mind couldn't comprehend how barbaric this type of *entertainment* was.

I stood from my place on the floor and towered over him. "But we do!" I glanced around the now silent room as everyone stared at me. "And what? To what end? We are tiny human beings trying to play God."

From the corner of my eye, Freyja's back went rigid. "There is no God. Only humanity."

I turned toward Dr. Freyja Osouf, a red fury casting over my vision. "For your sake, I hope you are correct." On a sharp heal, I turned to leave.

"Where do you think you are going?" Freyja's voice was lethal as it grated against my eardrums.

I didn't bother stopping. "I am leaving."

I heard a chair skid across the floor. "You are my guest. It would be rude of you to leave before the final set, especially when it will showcase my finest work." Her voice turned cold and threatening. "You won't want to miss it."

As I reached the door, I glanced over my shoulder. Sure enough, Freyja was standing with her arms crossed tightly over her chest. "Well, then you will have to excuse my Median manners, Dr. Osouf. I do not find this *entertainment* suitable to my tastes."

———

Footsteps echoed behind me as I marched down the hallway to exit the arena, and they were far more furious than my own.

"Rowyn, stop."

I whirled. "Don't you dare—"

"I will *dare* whatever I like when you are out of line."

"Me?" We stood nose to nose. "Did you witness those atrocities? Did you see the abuse that occurred in that arena?"

Callum's breath was hot as it danced with mine. "You were a

guest. If you wanted to leave, you could have *asked*, not storm out like an insolent child."

I put a hand to my chest. "Me? Your friends and family are like disturbed teenagers delighting in animal torture. For, um, what did you call it, *entertainment*?" I spat. "I am disgusted by you." I turned—I couldn't stand to look at him any longer—but Callum's hand was like a cobra winding around my wrist.

He whipped me around and pinned me to the wall. His right hand was still clasped around my left, but his other hand was flat against the wall, inches from my head. He leaned into me. "Do not use my words in there against me. Do you really think me so cruel?"

I bucked, testing his limits to keep me pinned there, but he pushed back, his hand wrapping tighter around my wrist and his hips grinding deeper into me. I seethed. "How else am I supposed to interpret your words?"

"If you are going to stay here, then there are some things you need to get on board with, because if you let every sickening display in Excelsis get to you, you will go insane." There was a churning darkness that settled behind his eyes, but his words did not give him a pass.

"No, *if* I stay, I am tearing down every sickening thing until there is none left. Unlike you, I have the courage to do so."

Callum's nostrils flare. "I am one man with bigger beasts to take down."

I narrowed my eyes at him. "Maybe I am a better woman than you are a man."

"You do not know the games you play, Rowyn." Callum's voice was dangerously low. "Your emotions, no matter how noble, will do you no good here. You think they are going to wait for you to make a move while you openly protest?" He ground his teeth together. "If you step one foot out of line, they will erase you like you never existed. All that will remain of you are memories."

Metis' words rushed to the forefront of my mind. *Officials erased anything that ever pertained to Dr. Janus Darrow. They wiped him from the database like he never existed—even his coworkers were forbidden to ever mention him. All of his history, his work, his name, it's all gone.*

I swallowed. "And you wouldn't fight for me?"

Callum's hand traveled up my arm, but he wasn't tender as he cupped my face. His warmth burned against my skin. "I will do whatever I can to protect you. I will do whatever I can to keep you by my side. But you need to play the long game—you cannot be dictated by your emotions. This is bigger than you and me and whatever happens in that arena." Callum sighed, his eyes growing softer before he rested his forehead against mine. "I love you, Wynnie, but I have too much at stake for you to get carried away with heroic side quests."

Why does everyone think I am ruled by my emotions? First Metis, and now Callum? And what does he mean he has too much at stake? Does he mean his Military promotion? His position in society? His family?

I opened my mouth to ask, but he straightened and shook his head. "Please don't. Just—" He licked his lips. "Just trust me, okay?"

I nodded slowly. But I wasn't sure if I actually did trust Callum. How could he just sit by and watch this sort of abuse happen? I could tell by the exhaustion in his eyes that he was done with the conversation, and fighting about it now would get us nowhere.

He rubbed his thumb over my cheekbone. "You *are* right, Wynnie. The Circus is atrocious, and I won't bring you back here. To make it up to you, let me show you something beautiful."

I chewed on my lip, thinking. "Okay," I relented.

And the Lieutenant General led us away.

CHAPTER 30

Callum wanted to show me his favorite spot in all of Excelsis. The Labrum was a small park on the south side of the First Ward, and it was easily the most beautiful piece of land I had ever seen in my life. The park was bedded with bright grass and clovers where kids tumbled and played. There were tables where older patrons talked or played games. Trees towered over benches where lovers shared kisses and citizens read books. Lilac bushes were jungle gyms for tiny birds and critters, while small patches of flowers were beds for tanning lizards and lunch for tiny bugs. But the most spectacular part was the waterfall. It flowed from the top of the force-field surrounding the Circulum and pooled down into the park, creating a small lake of crystal-clear water teaming with fish and underwater creatures.

I wasn't sure how I had missed this park in all my wanderings of Excelsis, but I supposed I hadn't been looking for it. Maybe I hadn't expected something so beautiful to exist in a place so cruel and wicked.

Callum's fingers intertwined with mine as he led me down a small walkway that led behind the cascading waterfall. The crashing of the water drowned out all the sounds of the bustling city, filling my ears with the sounds of a summer rainstorm instead.

I reached out to touch the rolling current, and I felt as though the pure water had cleansed my whole body with only a couple of streams flowing over my fingertips. I turned around to look over the city, and I was on the edge of the world. As I looked down onto Media and Humilis beyond, it was like standing on the top of Mount Olympus. My breath hitched at the thought of falling and plummeting to the earth, but my heart panged when I thought of the citizens below who would never be able to experience something this pure and beautiful.

Callum pulled me into his arms, forcing my thoughts away. We stood directly in the middle of the pathway behind the waterfall. Callum's beautiful eyes bore into mine, and his strong arms gently wrapped around my waist as he leaned in.

But before his lips touched mine, I whispered, "Why is this your favorite place?"

Callum pulled back slightly, giving himself space to think. "Although this space is man-made, it feels like the most untouched piece of land in Excelsis—it feels natural."

I nodded. "Yeah, it makes me miss the rain—the gentle rolls of thunder and pattering of rain on the roof, it always relaxed me."

Callum pushed back a strand of hair that stuck to my face, damp from the spray of the waterfall. "So, you like it?"

I smiled mischievously. "It's okay, I guess."

"So picky." Callum *tisked*, uncurling himself from me.

"No, wait." I grabbed at his shirt, trying to tug him back to me, but Callum drew out his COM-tab from a pant pocket and held one finger up. I pouted. A small smile tugged on his lips, but he remained focused on his COM-tab, tapping and swiping at the translucent screen in earnest.

"Now you are just being rude," I protested after a long minute. Again, he popped up a finger, silencing me.

Then, a second finger.

Then, a third.

A large rumble shook through the Labrum. I peered up to where the sound was emanating and watched as the waterfall began to move. I reached for Callum's hand and held it tight. "What did you do?" I yelled over the roar. Callum didn't answer. Instead, he pulled me to his side as the waterfall stretched around us into a large arch, fully enclosing us behind and beneath the tumbling water. Then the ground began to tremble as two panels on either side of the sidewalk disappeared to make way for the new flow of the rolling stream.

Callum pulled me in with his other arm, so my chest and stomach were flushed to his, but I continued to look up and around in wonder.

"You did this?"

Callum nodded.

"It's amazing!"

"Like getting caught in a rainstorm?"

I returned my gaze to him, looking into his eyes and then to his alluring smile. "Better."

———

"Lieutenant General Goody-two-shoes actually fucked you behind the waterfall?"

Aletheia stood before a large floor mirror as a seamstress placed pins in the fabric of the Private's Gala gown. The old seamstress blushed at the words but diligently continued her work.

"Scream a little louder, Aletheia! I don't think the farmers heard you in Ward Twelve."

Aletheia glared at me in the mirror. "You ditched me, remember? You left me alone with Sancus, the creepy silent scientist, and Callum's crazy mother, to go fuck my brother's best friend. I should send out a Chirp right now, so the whole Excelsisan World knows that Lieutenant General Callum Osouf used his super-secret security clearance to fuck his girlfriend behind the Labrum's waterfall."

The seamstress' back straightened, and the wrinkles around her mouth grew more prominent as she pursed her lips.

"Yeah, what was that between you and Callum's mother?"

She waved me off with a slender hand. "A discussion for a different time."

I rolled my eyes. "Oh, sure. We can talk about my sex life, but not the beef between you and Freyja."

"Exactly."

I sat on a velvet couch behind Aletheia, waiting for the seamstress to finish up her work on my friend so I could get my Gala dress fitted. I had asked Aletheia earlier that day why we couldn't get a dress from *Paradigm,* and she nearly bit my head off. Apparently, despite how precise *Paradigm*'s technology was, a true Excelsian woman will always go to a designer for a Gala dress. 'It ensures the originalism and quality of a gown,' she had told me. However, Aletheia designed our gowns and picked out the fabrics herself. She then gave the designs to our seamstress, whom Aletheia had been working with since she was a young girl. Though Aletheia and the seamstress had obviously known each other for years, they seemed no closer than two strangers off the *trames*—even within Excelsis, there were clear hierarchical boundaries, or Aletheia just really did not like making friends.

"In my defense, I did not choose to go to the Labrum; I was dragged there. *And* the Circus was too gruesome for me to bear." Though I was conversing with my friend, I kept my eyes on my COM-tab's three-dimensional holo feed, flipping through the online Chirps and various news headlines.

"Adellaide, there are some things you will just have to deal with here in Excelsis, so get used to it." There was a sharpness to my friend's voice, like a callus that had broken open.

"Why? If I don't like something, then I will just not participate. No one can force me to do otherwise."

Aletheia turned to me, and the seamstress backed off to give the Private some space. "If you do not participate in the status quo, you will be ostracized. You will be pegged as different and not given a voice. If you do not conform, they will take everything you love away from you." Her words were a harmony of Callum's.

They will erase you like you never existed if you step one foot out of line.

Who were *they*? Callum and Aletheia were a part of the Coalition Military. Callum's father was a part of the Government. Who could they possibly be afraid of? Who could they not protect me against?

I met her stern gaze, and I saw pain flicker in the Private's dark eyes. "If I can only say what they want me to say, then I already have no voice at all. I refuse to give in to the pressures of this world just to live the ghost of a life someone else wants for me."

Aletheia turned from me. "Then remember, you won't be the only one to pay the consequences, but everyone you love will have to pay them too."

If someone really loved me, then they wouldn't mind paying those consequences. The words rang in my mind, but I didn't feel like arguing with Aletheia. Maybe it was cowardice, maybe it was laziness. But the reality was, Aletheia had lived in the Coalition far longer than I had. She knew the rules, written or unwritten, and her words came from a place of survival in a world filled with difficulty, even within the Coalition's highest society. I bit my tongue as the seamstress continued to work on Aletheia's gown, and I scrolled through the feed on my COM-tab until something red and familiar flashed across the three-dimensional image. I scrolled back to find the video that caught my eye. It was a recording from the Circus. There were nearly a dozen humans, male and female, with crimson-red hair firing weapons at moving targets, though I couldn't quite tell from the video what they were shooting at. Each red-haired individual hit their respective targets dead center. Next to the video panned an article headlined: *Prometheans: The New Military Special Ops is Here and Ready for Duty.*

I played back the footage and pinched open the three-dimensional image to get a closer look at one of the females. She looked like—

"Aletheia… What is this?" I zoomed out and played the video for my friend. She peered through the mirror.

"Oh, that's what you missed yesterday when you were fucking Callum's brains out."

I glared at Aletheia, my teeth grinding together at her annoying comment.

She rolled her eyes before she released a relenting sigh. "That was the super special sixth set from yesterday's Circus. The Circus Masters called them Prometheans, I think, and apparently, they are super soldiers that were crafted in Freyja's lab. Freaks of nature, if you ask me, but the Military is all giddy to have new toys."

"But they are human?

"Kind of, I guess. I think, technically, they are another 'breed' of humans. They are stronger, faster, more accurate, and more precise in their aim because their brains can work through mathematical probability more quickly. Oh, and they can heal faster, almost immediately. It was pretty wicked."

I clicked on the article to find more videos, and sure enough, there was clip after clip of each test they were given. During the last test, each Promethean was given a knife, and they had to slit open their wrists. Within moments of cutting themselves, their skin stitched itself together instantly, leaving nothing more than a thin trickle of blood from their wounds.

"Crazy, huh?"

My brows furrowed. "Yeah…" I breathed, uncertain of what to focus on. "Why the red hair?"

"Fuck if I know. Looks badass? It's extinct within the Coalition's population, so now everyone will know a

Promethean when they see one. Not very stealthy if you ask me, but whatever, I'm not in charge of the mutants." Aletheia spoke of them with such disdain, like the very thought of them was nothing more than gum stuck to the bottom of her shoe.

I leaned forward, my elbows on my knees as I continued to watch the 'mutants' as Aletheia called them. I scanned back to the beginning of the holo feed and zoomed in. The Prometheans weren't just shooting random moving targets. They were shooting *people*. A chill crawled over my skin. The 'mutants' had perfect aim, their blasters striking true in the head or heart before their victims shuddered violently and fell lifeless on the ground.

"Aletheia, who are they shooting?" My voice shook.

Aletheia shrugged, then winced when a needle must have punctured skin with the movement. "Their 'targets' were Resistance sympathizers and operatives."

My heart plummeted into my stomach, and the air from my lungs seemed to vanish, but Aletheia continued, unaware of the panic growing within me.

Frantically, I paused and zoomed in, and each face was set in more terror than the last as I tried to discern each Resistance member. My anxiety grew with each passing face, waiting to see Niahm, Balor, or Ulysses—especially the latter, since I knew he was in the city—but I did not recognize anyone.

Were they all internal operatives I never met?

I scrolled all the way down the article, and sure enough, each 'Traitor to the Coalition' was listed with their mug shots.

Out of eight individuals, not a single person was from Base.

How is that possible? Is the Resistance in the city really that large?

Even though my fellow Resistance members were slaughtered, I couldn't help the flood of relief that washed over me after I confirmed no one was from Base. But relief was quickly replaced by guilt. Even though I did not know these people, they still had families, and they were still a part of our team in some small way.

I scrolled back up to the top, pushing the faces of the murdered Resistance operatives from my mind. We all knew the cost of our vision.

I chewed on my lip as my eye caught a glimpse of red hair once more. "Aletheia, why are they called Prometheans?"

The seamstress stood up and gave Aletheia a single nod. My friend stepped down from the raised platform with all the grace of a black swan as she carefully held the flank of her pinned gown. "Not sure. Though I think Freyja may have mentioned a Prometheus Project or something like that."

The Prometheus Project.

Human super soldiers—created to take down the Coalition Resistance Forces.

CHAPTER 31

I had spent a good part of my workday trying to get any information about the Prometheus Project I could get my hands on, but all the files I managed to find were still classified, locked with codes or chip-reading technology. Every time I tried to ask Hlín for more information, she chastised me for not focusing on the work at hand.

So, I trudged up to Callum's apartment after a hover ride home, downtrodden by the lack of Promethean information I was able to find, despite the blowup in the media about the new experimental creatures.

As I stepped through the door into Callum's apartment, something felt all wrong. The flat was dark—pitch black, actually—and the air hung tightly in an eerie stillness. Usually, the light of Excelsis would be shining through the balcony doors or the windows in the dining room, but all the curtains must have been drawn because not a ray of light lent its aid to my eyesight. I moved to shut the door, and as my back turned to the seemingly empty room, the small hairs on the back of my neck stiffened.

I was being watched.

I crept toward the kitchen and racked my brain, trying to remember if there was a night mode in the contacts Ulysses had given me, but if there was, I didn't know the cue. I felt around on the countertop to gain my bearings until my fingers touched the smooth wood of the knife block. I lifted my hand and grabbed a cool hilt of a steak knife. Just as I was about to unsheathe the knife from its home…

Crunch.

Before I could process the sound, I whipped the knife from the block, aimed toward the sound, and flung the knife into the darkness.

And then it hit me. *The sound. It was like a—*

A wet rip emanated from where my knife landed across the living room. With a click, a lamplight flickered to life to reveal Bellona with an apple in hand, poised right in front of her nose. The hilt of the knife I'd flung protruded from the red and green fruit, and liquid fell from the apple in small droplets, landing silently on the soldier's black leggings. Bellona drew the fruit away from her impassive face, and light glinted off the blade poking through the other side of the apple, juice dripping from the tip.

"Nice throw." Bellona wiped away droplets of apple juice from her face with the sleeve of her black shirt, then examined the apple.

My heart pounded in my chest. "Luck, I guess."

Bellona nodded once. The Major General removed the knife from the fruit, sending more juice spewing before she took another bite.

"Are you going to tell me why you are ominously sitting in a dark, empty flat that is not your own?"

She swallowed a bite of apple. "Now I know you weren't expecting anyone."

I crossed my arms. "Who could I possibly be expecting? Callum told me he had to work overnight, Aletheia is going out, and…well, that pretty much completes my social circle."

Bellona took another bite of the apple and flipped the knife in her right hand. The owl inked on the Major General's skull appeared to be staring at me and the steak knife simultaneously.

"Oh, right." I turned to the fridge, opened the appliance door, and pulled out a half-empty bottle of wine. "I could be expecting my 'Rebel friends.'" I popped the loose cork from the bottle and poured myself a glass of the blush-colored wine.

I lifted the bottle, silently offering Bellona a glass, though she declined with a shake of her head. I left the bottle out on the counter—*Skies knew I was going to need another glass after whatever discussion Bellona had planned*—and sauntered over to the living room. I sat in the armchair across from the Major General and crossed a leg. "I am assuming you already went through all my things, examined every inch of the guest room, noted my clothes still on Callum's floor, and maybe even sniffed his bedsheets." I took a sip of wine and cocked my head. "Oh, Skies. Please don't tell me you peed on his bedpost."

Bellona rolled her eyes. "You know it's not like that."

"Actually, I don't."

"Jealous already, *Rowyn?*"

My spine straightened at my name. I knew Callum told her. He told me as much this morning before I left for work, but it was distressing to hear my name spoken from her lips. "No, but I think you are."

Bellona weighed the knife in her hand, then balanced the tip of the blade on a fingertip. "Lieutenant General Osouf and I have a strictly professional relationship."

I grimaced. "Oh, like you two aren't the best of friends."

"I don't have friends," she said flatly. For a brief moment, I felt pity for the soldier.

"Maybe that's because you keep scaring them away by entering their homes and frightening off their significant others."

"I am here"—Bellona flipped the knife and turned her head slightly, revealing more of the grey-scale barn owl—"because I decided to do some digging, Rowyn Eloise Darrow. Would you like to know what I found?"

"No, but I don't think that's going to stop you." I settled back into my chair despite my pounding heart and took another sip of my wine.

Bellona set the knife on the coffee table, metal clinking against the glass as it was placed with precision, an equal distance between us. Was she daring me to make the first move?

Bellona leaned over on her knees, the apple core clutched between two fingers. "Not a whole lot. Not a birth certificate, no proof of vaccines, no medical records at all, actually. There are no school records—"

"I was privately tutored before my family left Militum," I answered.

"No academic placement records or tests. And the only pictures I could find of you were with your father, whom you look nothing like, might I add."

I was painfully aware.

Bellona's eyes flicked to my hair. "And your natural hair color is red? Peculiar, don't you think?"

I ground my teeth. "Genetic anomalies happen every day."

"Not in the Coalition." Bellona stood, finally turning her back to me as she wandered around Callum's living room. "As I was saying, even structural genetic analysis gathered from the few pictures found minute similarities that offered no more resemblance than two complete strangers picked off the streets. Regardless…" Bellona had slowly made her way to Callum's fireplace and picked up the small rock I had thrown at my friend all those years ago. She rolled it around in her hand. "I decided to research Janus Cornelei Darrow, and do you know what I found on him?"

I let her continue because I genuinely wanted to know. Skies knew I hadn't had the access nor the guts to investigate my father over the past several weeks.

"Not a lot." Bellona placed the rock back on the mantle. "More than you, but still minimal. I did find his birth certificate, medical records, and school records. Your father was a genius, accelerated in every field, but particularly his course of study, which was—"

"Genetics."

"Correct." The Major General continued circling around the room. "*Dr.* Janus Cornelei Darrow was a highly respected genetics researcher specializing in nuclear and mitochondrial DNA sequencing and coding, focusing on the interactions of the two, in addition to epigenetic effects of programming, processing, and final expression of genes." She took a breath. "Although his multitude of awards for various theories, research, and experiments have proved him to be essential to the cellular and molecular biology community, when I look up Janus Darrow's research in the Coalition Library Scientific Database, you know what I find?"

"What?" I sighed, feigning disinterest.

"Redaction after redaction after redaction. Papers, dissertations, research, theories—all redacted. Which is implausible, really, because the deeper I dug into genetics research, the more I found recent biological articles from around the world still using his theories to report or prove their findings —even for medical testing and treatments."

I was speechless. I didn't know what to say; I didn't know how to process, so I remained quiet as the Major General continued.

"With the help of some technologically inclined Military personnel, I was able to access the Coalition's Biological Database, and you know what I found?"

I rubbed my face, growing impatient. "Holy Skies, Bellona! I didn't pin you for such dramatics!"

She rolled her eyes, her arms crossed as she paced the room. "Your father worked with—"

"Dr. Freyja Osouf..."

Bellona nodded once. "According to witness reports, Dr. Osouf and Dr. Darrow had a large public dispute at the Militum Research Laboratory five days before your father took a new job offer here in Imperium. In addition, just one day before the disappearance of your family, there was an anonymous report filed detailing another argument between Dr. Osouf and Dr. Darrow at the Osouf Manor in Militum. Do you know about either of these encounters?"

I shook my head, which was only half a lie. I knew about the second argument—it was the last of the very few memories I had from my childhood in Militum. The memory floated through my mind like a leaf on an autumn breeze.

Callum was playing his viola for me when we heard shouts echoing from Freyja's study. I had never heard my father yell before—I had hardly seen him furrow a brow in anger—but he was menacing as he grabbed my small hand in an iron grip, screaming at Freyja that she would never keep the project.

"We have shared intellectual property, Janus! Or have you forgotten?" Freyja's retort was sharp, and she was on our heels as my father bounded down the stairs, dragging me behind him.

"I have guardianship!" my father cried over a shoulder, though whatever guardianship meant in relation to a research project, I did not know. My father walked out the door as Freyja scoffed, and mentioned something about a paper trail, then he turned on her, a single finger held out in a straight, tight line. "You will never see my family again." My father picked me up and tossed me over his shoulder. The last thing I saw of the Osouf Manor in Militum was Freyja's steely grey eyes. I didn't even get a chance to say goodbye to my only friend.

Bellona must have seen the memory flash in my eyes because her lips were pursed into a tight line, and her dark brows were creased. She obviously did not believe my lies. "Do you blame Freyja for your father's death? For your family's death?"

"What?"

"Do you think if your father and Freyja did not have these altercations, your father would have retained his career path in Militum, thus your family wouldn't have fled the Coalition and perished on a hunting trip?"

Everything.

Callum told Bellona everything.

Betrayal settled like bile in my throat, burning and throbbing. I shook my head. "No, of course not." My voice was a rasp. I hadn't even thought about how this could all be Freyja's fault. I thought maybe she was angry my father took the job, not necessarily that he took it because they had poor working relations at the time.

"You are telling me that you didn't intentionally weasel your way into a lab job to ruin Freyja's reputation? That you didn't seduce Callum to destroy Freyja's family like she destroyed yours?"

Bellona towered over me as I sat in the armchair, and my jaw went slack at the Major General's accusations. "First of all,"—I stood and held one finger in the air—"I did not *weasel* my way, nor did I *seduce* anyone to get anything. My job was *offered* to me! Callum's grandparents brought the position up at dinner. Secondly,"—I held up another finger—"Callum and I have something that dates back to childhood. It is by the grace of the Skies above that he and I found each other again. Forgive me for falling into this Skies-forsaken faerie tale and running with it. And so what? I saw an opportunity, and I took it. Do I want to find out more information about my father? Sure. Did I see this job as an opportunity to do so? Yes. What are you going to do? Arrest me? Try me for treason? I haven't even had the guts to look around the database because of you and every other Military official watching my ass every hour of every day!"

Bellona took a step closer to me, and the way she could look down at anyone, everyone, was astonishing. "It's awfully coincidental how you show up out of the blue for a *second* time."

"How was I supposed to know as a *child* that I had no birth records—no medical or testing records?" I was yelling, infuriated by all her 'evidence' clearly out of my control.

She tilted her head like she was listening to the owl inked above her ear. "Seems like something the Resistance could take care of—erasing any trace of their new recruits from the Coalition Database."

I stepped closer to her, forcing the Major General to back up a step. "And do you have any proof of that? Do you have any indications that the Resistance could be interfering with your database?"

She ground her teeth together, which told me all I needed to know. *She has nothing.*

I tossed my hands in the air. "You know what, Major General, if this is a formal interrogation, then at least have the decency to take me onto Base with a fucking warrant. Otherwise, get the fuck out." And as I pointed to the door, Callum stood there, still in his Military uniform, which was as perfect and polished as it was this morning when he first pressed the fabric.

"What's going on here?" he asked as he stepped over the threshold and pulled off his cap.

"Why don't you ask your Major General..." I nodded to Bellona as I crossed my arms and stepped back.

"Major General." Callum's eyes narrowed into dark shadows. "I asked you to stand down." It was more of a question, a 'why the fuck are you here right now?' kind of insinuation.

"Lieutenant General, sir—"

"I *ordered* you to stand down," Callum growled.

Bellona stepped toward her commanding officer. "Sir, I found more evidence that might—"

"Major! I have seen all the evidence. Skies-damn it all, I *am* evidence! I am a witness! I am *involved*—"

"And that is what I am worried about, sir—"

"Are you undermining my authority?"

Bellona straightened, shoulders tightening into stone. "No, sir. I—"

Callum held a hand up. "You know what, Major General? You are off this mission. Actually, this 'mission' is terminated. I will file it myself within the hour. You are free to leave."

Mission? Was I a mission?

Bellona's jaw twitched, and her throat bobbed, but she remained still and quiet, a soldier waiting for further instruction.

Callum turned to me. "Rowyn, do you have anything you'd like to say to the Major General?"

"Yeah." I stood with my arms crossed.

Bellona turned to me, her eyes dark with rage. For a moment, I saw something familiar in those dark brown eyes. Someone familiar.

But I pushed the thought aside and rolled my shoulders back. "Stay the fuck away from me."

She audibly ground her teeth as she made to storm out. But as she passed Callum, he grabbed her by the arm. "And that's an order," he growled into her ear.

Bellona shook her arm loose and slammed the door behind her.

CHAPTER 32

The moment. One I never knew I had dreamed of. Two huge white doors opened wide to reveal a grand ballroom alive with the lilting music of a chamber orchestra, glinting golden accents, and the mingling of glamorous guests. The moment of grand doors as they boomed shut, demanding all heads to turn toward the sound, when the gazes of the assembled finally fell on you, eyes wide and mouths still as they hung open in awe. The moment when a woman feels wholly and painstakingly beautiful.

But that's all it was—just a moment—because suddenly, my body started to fold in on itself, and my hands trembled as they stretched, longing for something, anything to hold onto. My breaths were short and shallow, my chest constricting under my tight gown, and sweat beaded at my brow and pooled under my breasts. I had never felt so exposed. I wanted to turn and run from the party as I scanned the room for Callum but found the ballroom void of him, of anyone I knew. *He said he was going to meet me here. He said he was going to enter with me.* But the doormen had ushered me along despite my protests, and now I was alone.

Maybe if I got closer…

I took a small step, struggling to straighten my shoulders and neck as I moved toward the grand staircase. Glancing down, I gently placed my hand on the intricately carved railing, ignoring my urge to grip it tight, and took another step. When I glanced back up, people were whispering to each other, their eyes still pinned on me. Some of their brows were furrowed in curiosity, others' high with judgment, and others' lowered in pity.

Then, a strong arm hooked through mine, smooth fabric brushing against my bare skin.

"Sorry I'm late, Wynnie." A low whisper brushed against my ear as the scent of earth and wood wafted through the air around me. Callum's lips gently pressed my cheek, sending warmth to spread over my body like warm butter. I leaned into him. "You look…" His breath hitched. "Ethereal."

My cheeks burned, and I glanced down at my golden shoes as he led us down the staircase. "I feel like an idiot."

Callum squeezed my hand. "But you're my idiot."

"You're not helping," I gritted out through a smile.

When we reached the ballroom floor, Callum turned me toward him and eyed every inch of me. His gaze was full of wonder and mischief as he flashed me his gorgeous half-smile. "I look like the idiot for showing up late. You look like a woman with enough courage to enter alone."

With unearthly grace, Callum wrapped his arm around me, pulled me in, then whipped me down into a low dip. His emerald eyes shone brightly in the golden light of the ballroom, and I was so mesmerized that the feeling of his soft lips on my own startled me, jolting me further into the embrace. Though, once I realized his lips were on mine, I lost myself in the silky warmth of his skin, and the need to touch him—to feel him— overcame me. I wrapped my arms around Callum's neck, urging him to kiss me deeper, to love me fully. He complied. His lips moved with mine as he held me tighter to him, then, with a small rumble in his chest and his soft smile on my lips, we parted. Our gazes met again, and his eyes were a shade brighter, mischievous blue and gold flecks dancing in an emerald sea.

Callum twirled me up to my feet, and I had nearly forgotten about the ballroom of people as they applauded and cheered for our display. I glanced at Callum sheepishly, but his returning smile exuded confidence as he led us through the crowd, my left arm hooked around his right. The assembly practically separated itself as we made our way toward the front of the great hall. Callum nodded to various officials and patrons, sneaking small, light kisses on my cheeks between his general greetings. Violins, cellos, and violas resonated in the huge hall, weaving masterpieces with every swipe of the bow and pluck of a string. Herbal notes of thyme, rosemary, and sage wafted through the air as hors d'oeuvres were passed on golden platters, and my mouth watered despite the turning of my stomach from our exuberant entrance.

Callum wrapped an arm around my waist, pulling me to his side. "You are absolutely stunning. I can hardly keep my eyes off you."

"You clean up nice, yourself," I replied with a laugh as his lips tickled my ear.

I felt Callum straighten beside me, and I followed his gaze across the room to find Erebus, Callum's father, talking to another man. Of course, Laurunda was dutifully only a few feet away, donning a lavish and sensuous gold and robin-egg blue gown. Freyja was standing at Erebus' side. She was clothed in a modest yet ornate white and gold gown as she looked upon her son. A smile was plastered across Freyja's lips, but in the widening of her eyes and the tensing of her neck laid pure indignation.

"Should we go talk to—"

"No," Callum muttered as he changed our course toward a towering marble column near the eastern gardens. "I need one more moment. Just the two of us." Cal's voice was a breathless rasp as he pinned me against the column. I expected him to lean in and kiss me, but instead, he took my hands and stepped back. His eyes trailed every inch of me, starting from the bottom of my slate-colored, see-through gown and traveling up. His eyes gleamed against the large glittering golden feathers sweeping over my legs, hips, abdomen, and breasts, then his lashes flickered almost like he was watching the black velvet ravens flittering around the golden plumage in worship. Callum's throat bobbed as his gaze settled on the glitter on my collarbones and neck, and it lingered there before slowly traveling up to my lips. His callused fingertips grazed my cheekbone as he tucked loose strands of hair behind my left ear, then gently cupped the gold, glittering bird studded in my lobe. A smile crawled across his face as his fingers brushed down my neck, around my shoulder, and slid down my arm. Chills ran up my spine, though if it was caused by Callum's tender touch or the cool marble against my back, I wasn't sure. Our fingers found each other and intertwined as Callum leaned into me. Our lips met. Gently at first, then urgency grew with every ebb and flow of Callum's lips.

"Achem." A sharp grumble emanated from behind Callum. The Lieutenant General's groan vibrated against my lips before we parted, and I opened my eyes to find Freyja standing behind Callum, her eyes like screws drilling into the back of his head. I tried to separate myself from him, but with one firm hand, he held tightly to my waist.

Callum set his other hand on the marble column behind me and hung his head. "Yes, Mother?"

"This is no time to be fooling around with *some girl*," she snapped.

My heart throbbed.

Callum whirled. "Well, thank the Skies that wasn't what I was doing. I was enjoying some *alone* time with my *beautiful date* this evening."

Freyja peered over her son's shoulder to look me up and down, her lips pursed in distaste. "Surely, you have had enough *alone time* with Ms. Stevens." The doctor's eyes then settled on the Lieutenant General. "You are supposed to be mingling. Come," she ordered with a crook of her finger and turned, "there are people you need to meet."

I removed Callum's hand from my waist and pushed him off. "Will you stop that?" I straightened his lapels in frustration.

"Stop what?" Callum ran a hand through his hair.

"Aggravating your mother." I moved onto adjusting his Military pins on his white and gold formal jacket.

"But she makes it so easy."

I rolled my eyes. "After the Circus, we should probably suck up a little bit. I need her to like me, and you are not making it any easier."

Callum took my cheek in the palm of his hand. "You don't *need* anyone to like you. Except me," he said with a wink.

I glanced around the enormous ballroom where several people from various social groupings were staring at us. "Well, it sure would be nice, Cal. They still look at me like I am a lowly Median."

"I could fix that if you would just—"

I shot him a warning glare.

"Not the time… Got it." Callum pulled me in, pressing his lips to mine again. They were firm yet smooth and gentle, moving against mine like rainwater. When we parted, my head was dizzy, and my lungs struggled to hold breath.

He cocked a brow and shot me a crooked grin. "Then let's go charm the fuck out of some people."

———

When Callum said, 'charm the fuck out of some people,' I thought we would follow Freyja, and she would introduce us to Mr. and Mrs. Pompous-Ass and Lady Snob or Sir Mansplainer. I had expected much ass-kissing and my best attempts of fake laughter. However, all of these scenarios were quickly shoved from my mind when, instead of following his mother, Callum weaved through the crowd, not making any eye contact with anyone, my hand firmly clutched in his own.

His hand was warm and slick like he was… *Skies, is Callum sweating?*

He proceeded to the platform near the chamber orchestra, and when he turned around to face me, he was flushed and, yes, that was indeed sweat beading on the Lieutenant General's brow.

I looked from him to the stage. "Is it customary for a Military official to prepare a speech?"

"No." Callum raked his fingers through his hair before straightening his jacket and cuffs. "Not really. How do I look?"

"Umm, great." I blinked in confusion. "But why—"

He grabbed my shoulders. "You should stand right…here." He moved me so I was standing center before the platform.

"Cal, what is—"

He kissed my forehead. "I love you, Rowyn," he whispered against my skin. "I love you so much."

My heart sank. Not at the words, but *how* he said them, like they were words before a goodbye—the kiss before the betrayal.

Before I could utter another sound, Callum turned and walked onto the stage. In moments, Sancus was beside his friend, donning a plumb and gold uniform, while he handed Callum a microphone, and I couldn't believe I hadn't noticed the Second Lieutenant until now. I glanced around the room, trying to find someone else I knew, someone I could stand next to so I wasn't alone, but Sancus remained on the other side of the stage. Aletheia was nowhere to be seen, and Skies knew Bellona wouldn't come within ten feet of me.

"Ladies and Gentlemen of Excelsis, Imperium, welcome to the Spring Gala. It is an honor to be with you all tonight."

I glanced back up to the platform, to Callum.

Everything is fine, Red. It is just a small announcement. Just a welcoming message. Yet, somehow, with Callum's last words to me, the thought did not ring true.

"As most of you know, either from word of mouth or various

holo gossip feeds, I have had the pleasure of hosting a participant in the Excelsis Integration Program, Ms. Adellaide Stevens." Callum held a hand out toward me, and the entire company applauded. Heat rose to my cheeks. I tried to smile as I waved to the crowd around me, but joy was the farthest emotion from me right now.

"Ms. Stevens—" Callum chuckled. "I mean Adellaide, though a previous citizen of Media, is not all as she might appear."

My throat went dry, and I couldn't even hear Callum's words when he continued speaking. The world was too far from me as a pit formed in my heart, and my stomach began to churn.

He knows. Callum knows I am a spy, and he is going to reveal it in front of everyone. The Coalition will make a spectacle of me, they will record how the soon-to-be General of the Coalition caught a spy in their capitol.

I had to get out. *I need to run...now.* I was sure all the exits were blocked or manned, but I had to try.

I gathered my dress in my hands, but as I started to turn, an invisible string pulled tightly on my spine, and Callum's voice returned like a whisper in my ear. It was a question, a very important question. And the four words were so close, yet so far from me.

Breathless. I was utterly breathless as I glanced around the ballroom, and every eye was fixed on me, on my reaction. I stifled the urge to gasp for air, my lungs burning as they longed for oxygen, but I couldn't breathe as I struggled to process Callum's question.

What did he ask? Did he ask if I was a spy? Did he ask if I was a murderer? If I was a Rebel?

I turned my body to face the Lieutenant General, and the sound of my heels against the white marble floor clacked loudly against my eardrums as everything blurred—the scene whirled around me, soggy and slow.

My eyes found his, and all I could do was mouth one word: *What?*

With preternatural grace, Callum jumped from the platform to land on one knee right in front of me. He reached into the inside pocket of his Military jacket. I flinched, ready for a knife, or a gun, pepper spray… I was ready for just about anything except the black velvet cube he held in one hand. He set the box in my cupped hands, then slowly lifted the lid.

"Will you marry me?" Callum's words finally clicked as a large ruby glinted in the golden light of the ballroom.

The silence in the vast space was deafening. Not a whisper, cough, or mummer escaped the lips of a single person in the crowd—almost like they held their breaths with me—but I didn't look around. I dared not to look from him—from Callum, from the only man I could ever love. If I dared to look away, I would fold in on myself, I would run, and never look back. His gaze—Callum's emerald eyes—gave me strength as the weight of everyone's stares settled on my shoulders…

And, in that moment, I suddenly hated him. I hated Callum for doing this so publicly, for embarrassing me by putting me on the spot. I hated him for making me feel weak in this way—in front of my enemies—and I loathed him for forcing me to rely on him for strength. I despised him for making my cheeks turn crimson and for my buckling knees. I wanted to say *no* to spite him. I wanted him to feel agony in that moment as well—to feel the excruciating embarrassment that covered my body in hives from head to toe.

Though, as my mind slowed and as I recalled his words from the Circus, I knew why he chose this event. I knew why he chose to propose so publicly. How it could prove beneficial to our true, private happiness.

Because of Freyja. Because he would do whatever it took to protect me.

In my periphery, I could see the stony expression on Dr. Freyja Osouf's face. Emotionless. Calculating. In this moment, *she* was powerless, not me. Freyja couldn't object or change her son's mind. She couldn't hide the engagement or have someone intervene. Suddenly, Freyja seemed so small, and I saw what Callum was doing—he was giving me the power.

It wasn't only his mother that was powerless...it was the 'they' everyone was so afraid of. Due to a public engagement, it would be harder to rid me from the Coalition—it would be harder to erase me. It wouldn't be just the minds of the few *they* would have to contend with, but the minds of the many—emboldened by us. By me.

My eyes were still fixed on the ruby, but Callum's gentle voice pulled my eyes to his. "Well?"

I swallowed. In his face—in the unspoken way we could communicate—I saw everything confirmed. He did not want to propose to me like this—he would have preferred an intimate engagement, but perhaps this was the only way he thought he could secure our happiness. Our future. He was protecting me.

And there was no way I could protect him.

The Lieutenant General was promising his life, his strength, and his allegiance to a Resistance spy. Eventually, this was bound to crumble. He would either discover I was with the Resistance, or I would have to leave him. Once again, Callum was giving me a rose, and eventually, I would have to throw another stone.

Eventually.

I forced a slow, hesitant smile, but when Callum beamed back, my guilt was overcome by pure joy.

After what felt like a millennium, I opened my mouth, and one simple word escaped. I didn't hear my own voice over the pounding of my heart thumping against my ear drums. I didn't fully process what I'd said until I saw Callum's eyes light up and a smile stretch across his face.

"Yes?" It was cute how full of unbelief Callum's breathless voice seemed.

My smile grew wider, and I nodded excitedly. "Yes."

Callum plucked the ring from its home, chucked the black box behind his back for Sancus to catch, and then pushed the gold and ruby ring onto my finger. When he stood up, Callum wrapped his arms around my waist and swung me around in a circle, pressing his lips to mine. The crowd around us clapped and cheered. Serving staff quickly scuttled around, popping bottles of champagne, filling glasses, and passing crystal flutes.

Callum set me down, and a throat cleared behind us. Startled, I jumped back from my fiancé—S*kies, Callum Osouf is my fiancé*—pursing my lips like I was trying to hide the evidence, but it was only Sancus who stood on the stage behind Callum with three glasses of sparkling wine balancing between his fingers.

Callum grabbed two glasses from his friend, passed one to me, then wrapped an arm around my waist like he was afraid to let me go.

"Sorry to interrupt you two love birds," Sancus proclaimed into the microphone, "but I wanted to be the first person to properly congratulate you." The Second Lieutenant lifted a glass. "Well, cheers to you, Adellaide, for proving to everyone that Callum is, in fact, interested in women." The crowd laughed. "And cheers to you, Callum, for actually loving something more than work and your mum." More laughter emanated from the crowd. Callum gave his friend a crude gesture. "Alright," Sancus said, holding up a hand in surrender, "all joking aside, congratulations to you both. Adellaide, you truly make Callum a better person, filling him with so much joy and love, he's actually bearable to be around now. And Cal," Sancus sighed, "you don't deserve her. Not one bit. Remember that."

My stomach knotted.

"*Salularia!*" Sancus proclaimed, raising a glass.

"*Salularia!*" Callum, myself, and the crowd echoed. The ring of clinking glasses filled the room before people partook of the toast. Notes of apple and pear flooded my palate. The champagne was as fresh and crisp as the spring evening air.

Sancus jumped down from the stage, landing right in front of Callum and me, his champagne sloshing to the ground. He clapped Callum on the back. "Congratulations, man. And you, darling Adellaide," he said before kissing me on the cheek. "If you have the power to change Cal, you have the power to change us all."

It was a whisper, and Callum looked as confused as I was. Before I could utter a word to Sancus, he tipped his glass to the crowd before us. "Well, good luck."

We turned in the direction of his gesture and found the whole gala turned toward us, pressing in on each other as everyone longed to congratulate the Lieutenant General and his new fiancée.

CHAPTER 33

After hours of mingling, various introductions, congratulatory niceties, standing, dancing, and smiling, I finally claimed fatigue and excused myself from the ballroom. I felt only slightly guilty for leaving my new fiancé alone with three of his father's bureau colleagues as I slipped out into the eastern gardens through two glass French doors.

My fiancé. I sighed at the thought as I strode along the cloister. A few Military personnel were positioned around the gardens, standing still in the shadows like ominous gargoyles on a medieval cathedral. I took a deep breath of fresh air as I settled against the railing of a balcony and rested my arms on the cool, white wood. Though it was never cold in Excelsis, the fresh garden air seemed a bit chilly, a stark contrast to the stuffiness of the ballroom. The aroma of the flowers was indescribable, mostly because I couldn't pick out just one floral scent—all the bouquets from all the flowers and leaves combined into one beautiful symphony. I glanced around the oasis. It was dark, but when I closed my eyes, I could imagine all the colors and textures of the plants. And, after a few moments, I finally mustered enough courage to open my eyes to behold the ring that now adorned my left ring finger. I moved my hand from side to side, examining how the light reflected off each precious stone. The ring itself was simple enough, a plain gold setting, but the dozen small diamonds shone brightly in the dim light filtering through the window from the ballroom, their facets dancing around the fingernail-sized ruby. Colors of gold, red, and orange flickered off the diamonds in tendrils of light, like a little flame on my finger.

"Do you like it?" As he approached, Callum rested his chin on my left shoulder as his strong arms wrapped around my waist. I leaned back into my fiancé, breathing him in.

"Very much so." I smiled, moving my hand back and forth to make the ring sparkle and shine. "But I am surprised it's a ruby since your family has such a propensity for emeralds."

Callum laughed. "Well, if I were to give you an Osouf family heirloom, then my mother would have found out before I actually asked you—"

"And Skies-forbid she try to interfere."

"Exactly." He held me tighter. "And this ring actually fell out of the book your father gave me when I was younger. I thought it was fitting that you have it back."

"Wait." I turned to meet Callum's gaze, though his arms remained wrapped around me. "This ring was in the '*Winnie the Pooh*' book? Where?"

Callum shrugged. "I don't know. I was reading it one night when I was little. I went to put the book away and heard something small clang against the wood. When I searched for the item, I found the ring."

I set the hand with my ring on Callum's chest. "Why would my father give it to you?"

He shrugged again. "Maybe a little something to remind me of you." He kissed my nose. "Did you read the inscription?"

"There's an inscription?" I fumbled with the ring as I hurried to take it off.

Callum unraveled himself from me. "Whoa, careful there. Let me help you." He slid the ring from my finger, turned it nimbly, and pointed to the script engraved on the inside of the small golden circle.

"*A spark to light the flame.*" Callum's eyes remained fixed on me as he relayed the phrase from memory. I took the ring from his fingers to inspect it for myself, and sure enough, those were the exact words engraved in the precious metal.

"This was from my father?"

Callum nodded.

"But why?"

He gave me a crooked smile. "Maybe your father was a hopeless romantic, like me, and wished that somehow we could find each other."

Or, what if the ring was hidden with the message in the back of the book—the message that was for me? But how could my father possibly know that I would ever see his words?

My head started to whirl.

Callum placed the heirloom back on my finger and lifted my chin to meet his eyes. "Better than an Osouf family emerald?"

I pressed my mouth to his. "Much better." I smiled against his lips. Callum wrapped his arms around me again, pulling me in tighter, and his lips met mine. They were urgent, every kiss filled with yearning and desperation. I was equally zealous. I held his face to mine, winding my fingers through his hair and grasping at the fabric of his jacket, wanting more than anything for nothing to be between us. Not clothes, not sheets, not air.

Callum pulled back, my chin grasped between his fingers, and I lazily opened my eyes to look at him. "Look, Rowyn, I want you to know that this isn't the way I wanted to ask you. And I know it was rather sudden, but—"

I placed my hand on his cheek and rubbed a thumb over his stubble. "I know. This is you protecting me."

Callum sighed in relief. "Yes. And we don't have to get married right away. We can wait two, five… Skies, we can wait ten years if you want to."

Years. My throat went dry. We didn't have years. We hardly had weeks. Callum thought keeping me close to him would be the best way to keep me safe, but the only way I could be truly out of harm's way was to leave the Coalition forever.

I tried my best to laugh off his words. "We will take it one day at a time. I was shocked, and I needed some time to process. I was furious at first—I could not believe you were making such a spectacle of us."

Callum took my hand in his and brought it to his lips. "I know, and I am so sorry. You can take all the time you need. In the meantime, I will propose to you a hundred different times, a hundred different ways to make it up to you."

I smiled mischievously. "And I expect a new ring every time."

Callum laughed. "You strike a hard bargain, future Mrs. Osouf."

The knot in my throat throbbed. "That will take some time to get used to."

"We have all time in the world."

If only that were true.

"Achem," a feminine throat cleared from behind us.

"You have got to be fucking kidding me. Can't you see we are—" He paused as he whirled to see who was interrupting us. "Major General Anderson." Callum nodded. "What do you need?"

Bellona stood straight, her head tilted high in a formal Military stance. She must have volunteered for duty tonight—I knew she was on the guest list, but instead of a gown or formal Military attire, she wore her on-duty uniform. "General Daniels would like to speak with you, sir," she replied.

Callum waved a hand. "Tell him we will be there in a minute."

"Actually, sir," Bellona interrupted before Callum could return his attention to me, "he would like to speak to only you. He made that quite clear. Something about a bottle of thirty-year MacTavish and Cubans in honor of the 'newly chained'."

Callum ran a hand through his hair. "Adellaide, darling, you look fatigued. Maybe we should call it a night."

I bristled at the use of my alias around Bellona; she knew, after all. "Nah, I am fine. Go have fun with your men."

Callum turned to Bellona. "Please tell General Daniels it is getting late, and we were just about to leave—"

"No, we aren't," I argued. "The night is still young."

Sancus popped his head out of a nearby window, a fat, unlit cigar hanging from his mouth. "You heard the girl, Lieutenant General. Get your ass in here!"

I couldn't help but laugh.

"Fine," Callum grumbled, straightening his jacket. "I will be right in."

Bellona nodded, and with a sharp turn of her heel, the Major General left us to wait inside the ballroom for her commanding officer.

Callum turned to me after waving Sancus off, who bellowed a long, loud whistle before pushing himself off the windowsill and into the presumed presence of General Daniels. Callum kissed me on the cheek. "I'm sorry. Do you want to come inside?"

I shook my head. "Actually, I would like to enjoy the night a little longer, if you don't mind."

"Not at all." Callum kissed my forehead. "Stay out here as long as you'd like. But if you have any mercy, please come save me at some point."

I could tell he wanted to linger with me in the moment. I wanted that too, but I didn't want the wrath of Bellona or the General to come down upon us, so I pushed him away, urging him to attend to his General.

"Fine," he yelled to me as he walked backward toward the gala. "But later…" Callum didn't finish his sentence. Instead, he flicked his eyebrows twice, a seductive gleam sparking to life in his eyes.

I bit my lip in anticipation. "Then we better leave soon,

Callum Osouf. Because I want you to make a thorough job of me."

And with a wink, he disappeared.

I returned to where Callum had found me, leaning on the balcony looking over the gardens, studying my ring—my father's ring—and suddenly it didn't seem so simple anymore. Everything about it was intricate. Complicated.

Just like my life.

The weight of the decision I'd made settled on my shoulders. I said yes to Callum, but I never took a second to determine what was best for my mission. I never once thought of how my decision could impact the Resistance. Hell, I didn't even think of Reign.

Did I really say yes?

No. I couldn't have because that would mean I said yes to a future here. In the Coalition. With Callum.

With Callum.

But I did say yes. I said yes to a life with Callum because that's what I wanted. Because I was crazy.

So fucking crazy.

Crazy in love with a Lieutenant General of the Coalition Military.

Okay, stop. Just think logically for two seconds, Red. I released a deep breath. I tried to remember why I was here in the Coalition in the first place. I was here for a mission. I was here to gather intelligence about the Coalition government, Military, and security, as well as information about my father and his research. I was here to aid the Resistance—to ensure a good life, not only for me, not only for Reign, or Niahm, Lyella, and Darragh, but for the whole country. *And even though I agreed to marry Callum, it doesn't mean I have to follow through. I am a fucking spy, for Skies' sake.*

Though, maybe it's not so bad here. I mean, I am happy...ish. The thought snuck through a dark crevice in my mind, like a weed that found a crack through a rock bed and then, exposed to sun and air, grew rapidly.

I could bring Reign here. I could find a way to bring her here, and we could build a life together in the Coalition. With Callum. Maybe…maybe Callum and I could change the country together, from the inside. The Lieutenant General had told me various things he wanted to change in the Coalition, and I agreed with most of his suggestions. It was a start. And maybe once more changes were set in place, I could see everyone else again.

Cal and I. We could make the Coalition better. We could make this place ours.

A bush about twenty yards from me rustled violently, and I glanced up from my ring to see a shadowed human figure dart from that bush to another. I looked around the garden to see if the guards saw the figure as well, but they were all gone. Every single one of them stationed around the garden's perimeter had left their previous posts. It must have been time for rotation, though I found it odd that all the guards would leave their posts at the same time to switch with the next shift guards.

My gut twisted at the peculiarity of it all, but my curiosity propelled me forward as I gathered the light skirting of my gown and crept down the marble staircase leading to the garden. I stopped dead when the figure, who was noticeably smaller than any full-grown man or woman, darted into another bush. I tiptoed down the stairs and kept my eyes on the bush, waiting for the figure to reveal himself, but they stayed put. When I reached the bottom of the stairs, I crept behind a large marble pillar, hiding deep in its shadow, when, suddenly, the trespasser shot behind the tree next to the staircase, no more than ten feet from the pillar I stood behind.

Before the intruder could turn, I grabbed for their wrist, pulling their arm far up and behind their back, and with my other arm, I wrapped my elbow around their throat.

"Don't move an inch, or I will make sure this breath is your last," I whispered tightly into the miscreant's ear.

"Red?" a familiar voice rasped out.

Quickly, quietly, I swung the trespasser around so their back smacked hard against the pillar. The air left their lungs in a heavy grunt, but I quickly placed my arm against their throat again, not daring to take any chances. Their pulse throbbed against my skin. I reached a hand to finger the trespasser's hood, and as I pulled it up and over, the light revealed the disheveled, mousy brown hair and mischievous eyes I didn't know I missed so much until that moment.

"Darragh," I breathed. I instantly released my arm that was crushing his windpipe, and he gasped as I pulled him in tight. "What the hell are you doing here? Are you okay?" I pushed him to arm's length and scanned every inch of him.

"Um, I think so. I don't know. Are you going to hurt me again?" Darragh's rubbed his throat.

"No, of course not. But Darragh, why are you here? Where is Balor? Does he even know you are here? Does Hoenir?" I touched his face, his shoulders, his hands, unable to fully believe Darragh, my adopted little brother, was standing before me.

"Ulysses sent me."

"Ulysses did what?" I stifled a yell.

He crossed his small arms. "Yeah. He said Hoenir and Dad make stupid rules, and if I wanted to join the squad, then I had to prove 'em wrong. So that's what I'm doin'," Darragh said with a firm nod before his eyes grew wide. "Wow, Red. You look really pretty."

"Darragh, does anyone else know about this?" I placed the back of my hand on his forehead, checking for a fever, then turned him around, checking for any scrapes or blood. Nothing stood out, but the garden was dark.

"Nope. It's gonna be a surprise! Dad is gonna be so proud! By the way, was that you kissin' some boy up on that balcony?" Darragh pointed to where Callum and I were standing not minutes ago. "Who was that? Do you love him? Wait until my brother finds out! He's gonna be so—"

Niahm? What would Niahm think?

I cupped Darragh's face between my hands. "Darragh, honey, focus. If Ulysses sent you, where is he? Why are you here?"

The little boy's eyes lit up as if he remembered something. "Oh, yeah! I am supposed to tell you to hurry up. Ulysses said Hoenir's getting really impatient, and you're probably gonna get demoted when you get back. But I don't think so because I know that whatever you're doin', it's gonna really help us, right, Agent Red?"

"Right, Darragh," I sighed. "Wait… He said I have to hurry up? I am waiting for an extraction!"

Darragh shrugged.

I ground my teeth. *Fucking Ulysses.*

"How is Reign?" I asked as I glanced around the garden and upper cloisters, checking for guards or lovers looking for some privacy. Nothing caught my eye.

"She is good. She really misses you. But Niahm has been teaching her lots of stuff in the tech lab. She loves helping out there. It seems like everyone has their place on Base except for me. But now that I am on my very own mission, I can join the agent team!"

"Oh, Darragh." I pulled him close again. "I am really happy to see you, but you shouldn't be here, bud. It's not safe, and you are not old enough. You better tell your dad to kick Ulysses' butt when you get back. Okay? You can tell him that Red told you."

Darragh shoved me off. "I am too old enough! And this isn't my first mission. It's my second." The small boy stood with his hands on his hips. "A few months ago, Ulysses had me hide a leather book in this old shack. He said I was giving valuable information to other Resistance agents, but it just looked like a bunch of mumbo-jumbo to me. But I completed my mission all by myself, too. I mean, Ulysses drew me a map and told me when to go, but I made it to the secret hideout and back all by myself. I had to be quick, and I couldn't let anyone know I was gone." Darragh touched his forehead, where a scar now marred his tawny skin. "But that's how I really split my head open. On the way back, I slipped on a tree stump and fell headfirst onto a big rock." The boy clapped a hand over his mouth. "Oh, shoot! I wasn't supposed to tell anyone. Please don't tell Ulysses I told you! Otherwise, he will kick me off the team!"

My jaw fell slack.

Darragh was the one who put the journal in the Shed? Ulysses knew about the Shed and my family—my father—this whole time?

How?

And how the hell did he even know I would be here tonight? How did he know I would come out to these gardens?

I pushed aside the questions growing in my mind like a hurricane. I needed to get Darragh out of here, now. I squatted low to get a good look at the boy's eyes. "Now, Darragh—"

"Agent Dare."

I groaned. "Agent Dare, was there anything else you needed to do?"

"Oh, yeah! The switch out!"

I rolled my eyes. "Okay, what about the switch out?"

Darragh pulled out a lens case from his pocket. "This set has a file depicting the plan of how to get you out of here. Ulysses said that Metis said he couldn't do it over a satellite signal because it could be hacked. Oh, and I need your lenses in exchange."

I rubbed the bridge of my nose. "Well, why didn't you mention that when I told you I was waiting for an extraction plan."

Darragh shrugged again.

I hated Ulysses, so I was kind of glad that he didn't come himself, but Darragh was just a boy and clearly unfit for this job. Something didn't feel right in my gut, and I hadn't felt right about this mission since Ulysses found me in Media, but I needed a safe plan out, and right now, I didn't have one. Hell, the only plan I had was to stay here forever.

"Why do you need my lenses?" I asked Darragh, scanning his eyes.

He gave me one firm nod. "For the intel you gathered, duh."

I pinched my lips tight, glanced around the garden one more time, and then sighed. "Fine. Give me the case."

One by one, I plucked my lenses out and placed them into Darragh's dirty little palm. Then I held my hand out for the new case. He dug deep into his right pocket and pulled out a silver lens case. I quickly placed the new lenses in my eyes and gave the case back to Darragh so he could stow the old ones in the silver case.

"Okay, good?"

"Good." Darragh held up a thumb.

"And they should work just like my other ones, right? They still record and everything?"

The little boy shrugged. "I don't know. No one told me about what other stuff they do."

I stifled a groan as I pressed my right temple for three seconds and tapped twice. A red dot bloomed in the corner of my vision. *Recording.* That was proof enough.

"Now, how far is Ulysses?"

"Just on the other side of the garden." Darragh pointed. Quickly, I shoved his arm down, hoping no one saw where he pointed, or that we were down here. But the gardens were empty.

"Okay, well, let me walk you back to him." I started to take his hand, but he wrenched it from my grasp.

"No!" he nearly shouted. "I can do it on my own! I am Agent Dare!"

"Okay, okay." I held my hands up, trying to hush the child. "But make sure those lenses go straight to Metis. And remember to tell your dad that he needs to beat up Ulysses."

"Yes, ma'am!" The little boy saluted.

I scanned the garden one last time, but there was no one in

sight. The garden was silent—too silent. Even the birds and bugs seemed still, and it made me uneasy. Darragh couldn't linger any longer.

"You better hurry back, you hoodlum." I replaced his hood and rubbed it into his head. Darragh batted me away and straightened his hood and cloak before he darted in the direction he had pointed to earlier.

After a few steps, Darragh whirled around. "Oh, wait! Red!" he called out in a hushed tone. "Ulysses said he has a surprise for you! Just wait a couple minutes after I leave, and he will give it to you."

I furrowed my brows. "What's the surprise, Darragh?"

The small boy shrugged. "He wouldn't tell me because he didn't want me to spoil it for you. So, I guess it's a surprise for both of us! Bye, Red!" Darragh waved a small hand before he dove into a bush.

I crept in the shadows to the other side of the garden, so if there were cameras, we wouldn't be seen leaving the same place. I continued left toward the staircase of the gardens, and, occasionally, I heard the rustling of leaves from Darragh sneaking into another bush. I ascended the western staircase as new guards started to take up positions around the garden. Panic shot through me like a bullet down my spine.

Darragh will make it. He is a smart boy. I can only hear him because I have great hearing. I can only see him now because I'm looking for him. He will be fine. I sighed as I reached the top step. *Darragh is always fine,* I thought to myself as I turned one last time, though I prayed I wouldn't see him. If I couldn't see him, neither could the guards.

From the north, a glimmer of light caught my eye, followed by a faint *click.* I turned toward the spark of light and the familiar sound of a safety switch. It was a soldier, and his rifle was aimed, light glinting off the barrel, and he was…*smiling? Is that a smile on the soldier's face?* My mind clicked in recognition—I knew that hawk nose and malicious smile. *But*

Darragh said he was supposed to be... The rifle moved, jerking against the soldier as a big *BOOM* resonated through the garden air. I whirled to see Darragh's head jolt back just before his body fell limp onto the grass.

I returned my horrified gaze to the soldier, hoping he could give me some clue that what I saw didn't happen—what I witnessed wasn't real. But the soldier turned to me, a dark smile still painted across his face, and with a wink, he ran, abandoning his post.

No. "No!" I ran toward Darragh as my eyes stung and my vision blurred. When I reached the small boy, guards began flooding the garden, and the faint music from the gala faded into silence. I gathered Darragh's corpse into my arms, and a sob escaped my chest as warm blood pooled onto my hand.

"No. No. Come on, honey, come on." I patted his face, hoping his eyes would flutter open. "Wake up! You have to wake up!" I yelled. The thud of boots marched closer, matching the loud thundering of my heart.

"Please. Please, just wake up." I dropped my forehead to Darragh's. "Please," I sobbed into his ear.

A firm hand grasped my shoulder. "Ma'am—"

"Don't touch me!" I growled at the soldier towering over me, but he gripped harder. "Don't touch me!" I snapped up at the commander. He backed away slowly, but apparently still had the gall to tell me the child dead in my arms was a trespasser.

"He is a boy! One of your men shot a child, Commander!"

My mind screamed, the truth pounded against my skull. *Ulysses killed Darragh! A Resistance agent snuck through the Coalition's Military Ranks and killed a child!* But I couldn't tell the commander, because if I did, then I would have to tell everyone that I was a Resistance agent, too.

Callum broke through the crowd of officers.

"What is going on?" he demanded, not quite seeing me, but then his eyes met mine, and his face softened. "Stand down,

Commander." Callum pushed the man hovering over me out of the way.

"But, sir-" The Commander grabbed Callum's shoulder.

With a jerk of an elbow, Callum shoved the man off, and a growl ripped through his chest. "I said *stand down*."

"They shot him," I whispered to Callum before he could even ask. "They shot him, Callum. They shot a boy." A sob broke through. "He is just a boy." I ran a hand through Darragh's warm, sodden hair.

How could this be? Darragh was just talking to me. Niahm's brother—Balor's youngest son—he was just here with me, and now he's—

Callum bent down to one knee, and with two fingers, he folded Darragh's eyelids shut.

"He was just a boy," I whispered again because it was the only thought running through my mind.

Callum cupped my face. "I know, darling. I am so sorry." We stayed there for a minute. Or eternity. I couldn't tell. But we just stared at the boy in my arms. Silent as guards hovered around us, still and silent as well.

At some point, Callum reached under Darragh's body and lifted him up.

"No," I whispered, my voice hoarse. "No."

Callum stood and approached an officer, then placed Darragh's body into the officer's arms. "Bring him to the infirmary."

"No. No!" I reached for Darragh, but I paused when I noticed red staining my fingers, coating the ring that now donned my left hand. Blood pooled on the grass around me. It stained my dress, the gold feathers now painted crimson, and the black velvet birds slick with the dark liquid. Iron stung my nose. "No." It was so much blood. *How could such a small boy have so much blood?*

My hands clutched the slick grass, my mind desperately trying to keep a hold on reality as my consciousness started to slip into the unknown, then something sliver caught my eye.

There, laying in the pool of blood, was the lens case Darragh had held. I slowly grabbed for it, clutching the metal case like it was my life—like it was Darragh's life.

"North entrance. Now. You. Get me a towel. Or a blanket. Anything." I vaguely heard Callum's orders in the back of my mind as the earth tried to pull me down toward it. The crimson-stained grass called to me, and the tangy tendrils of blood clutched my nostrils like a bull ring, and they dragged me down.

Then nothing. The smell was gone, all sounds vanished, and all feeling fled from me. I couldn't feel the metal case in my palm, the ground beneath my hips, or the grass under my legs. I couldn't even feel the blood coating my skin. I couldn't feel anything. Not pain, nor sorrow. I was numb.

"Adellaide. Darling?" A distant voice hovered over me. "Adellaide, let me help you."

Adellaide. Who was Adellaide?

"He was just a boy." Another distant voice whispered in my ear. Or did it echo in my mind? *Was that my voice?* "He was just a boy."

I think I cradled my legs to my chest, and I think Callum knelt down. I felt pressure under my chin before staring into emerald oceans. "Let me help you."

Callum stood up and moved to stand behind me. I felt something large but thin cover my shoulders. Instinctively, I clutched it tighter to me, and then, the vague presence of the lens case crept to the forefront of my mind. Slowly and discreetly, I slid the case beneath the bodice of my dress, right between my breasts.

A strong hand pressed tightly against my elbow, propelling me up, and the world shifted around me. My legs felt wobbly, knees threatening to buckle and ankles shifting uneasily.

"Come on, my darling." Another distant voice. Familiar. Soothing. But distant. "Let's get you home."

My head was weak, my vision fixed on my crimson hands clutching white fabric around my chest. Black water droplets fell onto the fabric in small, oily dots, and more droplets fell onto my hands, creating grey trails through a scarlet terrain. But I didn't feel them. I couldn't feel them—the tears. Nor the deep sorrow that should accompany them.

He was only a boy.
He was only a child.
He was only a boy.

CHAPTER 34

I didn't remember leaving the Gala. I didn't even remember arriving at Callum's flat. As I lay lifeless in Callum's bed, eyes wide against the night, I could only recall a pool of pink water, strong hands, and the smell of lavender soap before being carried to bed. But warmth didn't surround me as I lay wrapped in thick, gray blankets. Neither did the cold.

Darkness was my only companion, even as Callum stirred beside me. I lay there, numb to my senses and emotions. I could feel the dark abyss staring back at me like a mirror—it filled me. Engulfed me. Consumed me. And as I listened to Callum's steady breathing, I silently begged the darkness to take me—either in sleep or in death. I didn't care, but I was too afraid to close my eyes as I waited for either to come. Even when I blinked, I saw Darragh's lifeless eyes—the eyes that once sparked in mischief, grew wide in adventure, and dewy in love were now empty. The child who was so pure was now stained crimson in my mind. Because of me. Because of my recklessness, because of my own selfish ambitions and dreams, Darragh was dead. Because I couldn't keep to my mission.

No. NO. I screamed silently, shutting my eyes tight. But

instead of more darkness, a devil's smile sliced across my vision. *Ulysses*.

Ulysses said he has a surprise for you!

I guess it's a surprise for both of us!

Darragh's words morphed in my mind, stretching and deepening until it was Ulysses' voice, which echoed off the boundaries of my mind, taunting me. Torturing me. *I have a surprise for you, Red.*

Red.

Suddenly, my name felt like a curse—a prophecy.

Blood pooled in my vision, and I forced my eyes open, focusing on the darkness, daring it to take me—daring it to claim waste to my very soul. I was so ready for it. I was ready to dive deep into death myself.

Ulysses. It was fucking Ulysses who shot Darragh. I knew it in every fiber of my being. It was his nose, his cruel smile, his taunting wink. I should have known the moment I saw Darragh that Ulysses had planned something devious. I should have known that very second that Darragh's life was on the line. I should have guessed he would have sacrificed Darragh to prove a point. Though what his point was, I had no idea.

What could he have possibly gained from killing an innocent child?

What if Ulysses tells everyone back at Base that Darragh was dead because of me?

My heart pounded, and my mind raced. *I have to go.* My feet twitched in anticipation. *I have to get the fuck out of here. I need to go because the longer I stay here, the longer I hide, the more guilty I look, and the more Ulysses will force them to believe his lies.* My breaths escaped in rasps, my mind grew distant and fuzzy, and my stomach heaved. I pursed my lips tight, fighting against the sickness.

Callum stirred.

Focus, Red. I forced myself to take a deep breath, pushing my lungs hard against what felt like a cobra wrapped around my abdomen, but my body buckled in panic.

Dammit, Red, just calm down.

But I couldn't. My stomach lurched, and I gagged over the side of the bed though there was nothing left in me to wretch up. Dry heaves shook my very bones as my body felt like it was trying to purge my intestines from my body.

A firm hand rested between my shoulder blades, and another hand tucked back my hair. Cool air caressed my neck, a slight relief from the burning pressure inside of me. My eyes stung as tears threatened to fall again, and though I willed them back, a sob still escaped my lips. The mattress shifted as Callum crawled around to me. I was still looking down, and his toes curled on the cold wood floors as he crouched before me and cradled my head in his hands, our foreheads touching. His brow was bone dry against my warm, slick skin. Callum said nothing as tears flowed from my eyes, crawled onto his palms, and trailed down his wrists. He said nothing as chopped sobs escaped from my chest. He simply held me as we breathed the same air. When I finally calmed a bit, a headache bloomed from one temple to the other, and I leaned back to lie down. Callum followed me, nudging me to his side of the bed so he didn't have to let go of me, and he pulled me onto his chest. He pressed his lips to the crown of my head as a deep breath left his body.

"Let's push back the engagement party," he whispered softly.

Engagement party? A distant memory of last night—Aletheia messaging her mother's party planner to arrange a date that very minute. The party was in six days, and suddenly, the ring adorning my left hand felt heavy.

"No. It will be a good…distraction." The lie was choked.

"You need time to process. Trauma like this… You need time to make sense of it all. You need time to heal." He kissed me again.

"I am no stranger to death, Callum." My words were empty. Numb.

"But to the murder of a young boy?"

I flinched. *Not just any boy,* I thought to myself. Darragh was like a brother to me—I loved him like he was my own flesh and blood—but I couldn't tell Callum that. The Coalition was probably linking Darragh to the Resistance as we spoke. I was sure they would run DNA tests to find out who the boy was and to whom he belonged, and if they ever had Balor's DNA—which they probably did since he was in the Military—they would be able to find the relation between the two of them. They would know Darragh was from the Resistance.

"I'm sorry, Rowyn. I just want to give you the time and space you need."

"Thank you, but I need to keep moving forward. I need life to remain normal." *I need to get the fuck out of here.* But I didn't know how, not without the Coalition tracking me. I fingered the spot where my chip was implanted.

My whole body jerked, and I bolted upright.

How could I have forgotten?

"Are you okay?"

"Sorry. I—I think I need to be alone right now." I rushed out of bed and ran into Callum's living room.

The mattress creaked as Callum hopped out of bed to follow me. "Rowyn, I can help—"

"No!" I snapped, still trudging toward the guest bedroom. It had been weeks since I slept in this room, but I needed the… "No, I—I will just keep you up, and I just need some space to think." The guest room's door handle was cold as I pushed the door open.

"Rowyn, please. Let me help you."

Before Callum could reach me, I shut the door in his face and switched on the lock. The doorknob rattled beneath my hands as Callum tried to open the door.

The remaining tattered pieces of my heart ached as Callum pounded on the door. "Wynnie, let me in."

"Callum, please." My words were a quiet plea for solitude.

He must have heard the desperation in my voice because the pounding stopped. I heard his muffled sigh through the wooden door between us. "Please come back to bed when you are ready."

"I will." My words were choked, a sob threatening to break through, and I covered my hand over my mouth as I heard Callum's feet padding back to his bedroom.

Slowly, I walked to the bathroom.

As I stared at myself in the mirror, I once again saw a stranger. Brown hair. Brown eyes. But it was the stranger's eyes that held the proof I needed.

I had been too distracted when we got back to take my contacts out. Well, not distracted—I had been in shock when we got back—and Callum must not have found them important enough to remove either. When Darragh found me, we switched contacts, and then I tested them by starting a recording. I pressed my right temple for three seconds, and the contacts blinked to life. I held each temple for two seconds to bring up a selection screen before scrolling down to previous recordings. With a tap to my right temple, a message passed through my vision.

Play-Back Latest Recording?

Another right temple tap. The contacts recognized the movement, and the list of clips consisted only of one long recording. I selected it, and my vision went blank before I saw it all again. The contacts recorded Darragh's smile and laugh, the message he relayed from Ulysses, and they recorded the fatal shot that pierced through Darragh's head. As I witnessed the whole scene play out, I was certain the guard who shot Darragh was indeed Ulysses.

But how could Ulysses have possibly infiltrated the Coalition Military?

As I stood in the bathroom, my eyes saw Darragh's blood pooling around my dress and staining my hands. My cries reverberated through my mind, along with my last words to Darragh as I cradled his small head in my arms. My heart shattered into a million pieces all over again as the guards tried to pull him from me, grabbing the boy so viciously, though I knew they couldn't hurt him anymore.

And then there was Callum—he was gentle and strong, kind and commanding. He was perfect, until I saw that the Lieutenant General's hands were also tainted crimson with the blood of an innocent child.

And who knew how many others? The thought jarred me.

The contacts had recorded until the storage was full—sometime after Callum laid me in bed—and when the recording had stopped, my vision was returned to me, but another message scrolled across.

Would you like to…

1. Delete recording

2. Save recording

I swept above my brow twice and tapped.

Recording Saved.

I rummaged around in the bathroom drawers. It had been so long since I used this bathroom, but it was where I had stored the extra pairs of contacts Metis had given to me. I had completely forgotten about them because, according to Ulysses, they were useless.

But now, they were my saving grace.

I nearly sighed when my fingers brushed against the cool plastic container tucked in the back of the bottom drawer of the vanity. I replaced my current contacts with the originals Metis made for me, blinking them into place before powering them on. Notifications instantly panned through my vision. I had received twenty-four video messages from Metis and six different file drops, including an extraction plan.

And just as I suspected, Metis didn't know.

Either he didn't know his contacts were compromised, or Ulysses lied.

I didn't have enough time to watch all the recordings or scan through the files. Callum was waiting for me, but I gathered enough information from Metis to know he was not the one who demanded Ulysses give me new contacts. Based on Metis' confusion as to why I wasn't responding, I had a hunch Metis didn't even know about the new contacts.

Pressing my right temple for three seconds, the contacts blinked to life. I tapped my right temple twice, and once the red dot glowed, I breathed on the mirror. Condensation clung to the cold surface.

I'm sorry, I wrote with a finger, a chill running down my spine from the cold mirror. I leaned forward and pushed another breath from my lungs onto the mirror.

Darragh is dead.

I breathed onto the mirror again.

Ulysses is a spy.

Another breath.

I have evidence.

One final exhale.

Extraction. Three days.

I tapped my right temple twice. The recording stopped.

`Send. Send and Save. Save. Delete.` Using my forefinger, I rubbed down along my eyebrow to select send and tapped once.

`Message Sent to Dr. Metis Barnes.`

I washed the mirror with soap and water to dissolve any oils from my finger that would cling to the glass.

Before I returned to Callum's bed, I checked both sets of contacts to ensure the extraction plans were different. They were. I replaced Metis' contacts over my eyes and exited the guest room. Callum was sitting up waiting for me. I crawled into bed next to him and laid my head on his lap.

He ran his fingers through my hair. "Are you okay, Rowyn?"

I sighed, tapping and swiping above my brow in the dark, trying to look like I was fidgeting. "I will be," I whispered as a message scrolled across my vision.

`View plans for "The Red Run"?`

I tapped once.

———

The next morning, I snuck out before Callum woke up, and as I wandered around Excelsis, I felt like my eyes were open for the first time. I noticed the blank stares of the Excelsians as they passed by, their eyes glued to COM-tabs and completely unaware of the world around them. I saw people, but I didn't see life. Instead, I saw Darragh's eyes—his pure ocean eyes, iced over, cold, and empty. I saw his eyes in everyone, and in everyone, I saw death.

In my unconscious search for life, I found myself at the Labrum. Sunlight glinted off the waterfall, every droplet of water sparkling like a facet in a diamond. The trees were full of green, some starting to bud with flowers. And despite the cascading waterfall, the lake, which it poured into, was still and quiet. Orange and white fish swam beneath the calm surface, flowing in circles and whorls. They looked so peaceful. So free.

I glanced around the park to find it empty. Not a single person was strolling along the walkways or staring at their COM-tab on a bench. It was unnerving. Though it was nice to feel like, in that moment, the whole park was mine. Sometimes, when I was out in the woods, I would have a similar feeling— like nothing and no one could take the woods from me, that it belonged to me as much as I belonged to it.

Tentatively, I sat on the grass and pulled off my shoes. When I dipped my toes in the water, a chill ran over my skin. Relieved to feel something, I plunged my feet in the lake. The icy water was refreshing and invigorating.

My COM-tab dinged.

That's odd, I thought to myself. *I'm sure I turned my ringer off.*

I closed my eyes, ignoring the notification. I didn't want anything to take this moment away from me. Not even Callum.

Ding.

I peeked at my bag through one eye, perturbed by the disturbance.

Ding.

Who the fuck wants to get a hold of me this badly? I shut my eyes tightly and hummed to myself in a desperate attempt to regain focus.

Ding. Ding. Ding.

"Ugh!" I reached into my bag and pulled out my small COM-device. A message appeared on the screen as I lifted the device to my face.

`This is a reminder not to submerge your feet in the pond. It disturbs the delicate balance of the ecosystem and is distressing to the fish.`

I stared at the screen, and my mouth fell open. I whipped my head every which way to find out who was watching me, but I didn't see anyone, nor did I see any cameras or surveillance equipment hiding in the trees or on lampposts. I threw my COM-tab back in my black purse, ignoring the 'reminder' as I wiggled my toes and kicked my feet, sending ripples into the lake.

Ding. Ding. Ding.

"You have got to be fucking kidding me!" I roared, jerking my feet from the water. In a huff, I grabbed my shoes and slung my purse over a shoulder. I stomped toward the waterfall and mumbled incoherently to myself as another notification chimed from my COM-tab. When I reached the waterfall and was safely tucked behind its roaring waters, I turned on the contacts Metis had given me. Sure enough, there was an unopened message.

As soon as I opened it, Metis' gruff face appeared before me, and I nearly sighed in relief. But his brows were pinched tightly together, and dark circles rimmed both his human and his bionic eye. His usual annoyed demeanor was gone, instead replaced by worry.

"Red. Stay in the city. That's 'n order," Metis urged, glancing around him like he didn't want anyone listening. "I was relieved to see yer face, but I dunno what the fuck's goin' on. If yer right 'n Ulysses is a spy, then it ain't good." Metis rubbed a hand over the human side of his face. "Darragh went missin' days ago. I don't have the heart to tell Balor what ya told me, though the Owens family is furious 'n confused. Rightfully so. Ulysses hasn't returned to Base, 'n Hoenir's been denyin' meetings with me and Balor left and right. The safest place for ya is in the city. No one is in their right mind to do an extraction, 'n for all I know, Ulysses is waitin' to ambush ya. I dunno if Ulysses knows about 'The Red Run,' but it's safer to assume he does. So, stay put. Get any information ya can, wait out this storm, 'n most importantly, trust no one. I mean that, Red. Keep yer head on tight 'n trust no one."

Metis' face disappeared, and reality came back into focus. The waterfall rushed beside me, spritzing water against my skin and clothes.

"Holy fuck!" I screamed at the top of my lungs and pulled at my hair.

I just want to go home! I just wanted to mourn Darragh properly. I wanted to cry in Niahm's arms. I wanted to hold Reign as she cried herself to sleep. I wanted to hold Aine's hand as she tried to remain strong and train with Balor to distract him when the emotions were just too much to handle. I wanted to help. I *needed* to help. But I was stuck in the newly discovered hell that everyone had warned me about. I was too distracted and blinded, just like everyone else in this Skies-forsaken Circulum.

I dropped to my knees, and small rocks jabbed through my leggings, puncturing my skin. I held my head in my hands as tears fell from my eyes and sobs escaped, jerking my chest in awkward, uncomfortable motions.

"You knew him, didn't you?" A familiar voice sounded from behind me.

I did not dare to turn around. "Mourning for a child does not have to be personal."

Boots crunched behind me, and I cursed my loud sobbing

that prevented me from hearing it before. "I saw you speaking with him. We have surveillance."

"Is it now a crime in this city to speak to a child?"

"No. But colluding with Resistance spies is a crime punishable by death."

"He was a child!" I finally stood up to face Bellona. "Not a Resistance spy!"

The Major General stood straight, the hair on her head hanging in dark, natural waves down to her shoulder. "We have evidence proving otherwise."

"You have *evidence* that a *child* was a spy?"

Bellona lifted her head. "He is related to a suspected defector."

I stood to my feet. "I didn't realize it was so common for a *child* to be a *spy.*" I took a step closer. "I thought he was curious, or his friends dared him, or maybe he was just fucking bored. I don't know. I told him to run along before he got caught by someone who would tell his parents."

"You thought an Excelsian child would sneak into one of the most highly guarded events of the year, in clothes that were clearly not from this Circulum, talk to a complete stranger, and be on his merry way?" Bellona's face was stoic. Unreadable.

"Believe it or not, Major General, I don't really follow Excelsian children's fashion trends, and the 'most guarded event of the year' was missing Military personnel in the garden for a good eight minutes—there was no one in sight when I saw the kid arrive, that is why I decided to check it out."

Bellona's chestnut eyes widened in surprise.

"Yeah. Check your footage. I guarantee you will see all the patrol positions empty not two minutes before I found the kid. So, maybe you should be asking why your men decided to abandon post that evening."

I stepped to turn, but Bellona spoke. "You gave something to him," she accused.

I turned back to her. "What?"

"What did you give to him?"

"N—nothing," I stuttered, shaking my head in disbelief.

Bellona stepped toward me. Her eyes were searching mine, but I knew she wasn't searching for lies; she was looking for… "I know you gave the child your contacts, and he gave you a pair in return, but the only objects on his person were a small pocketknife and a small piece of cloth, neither of which had your prints on them. Did you take them back during the commotion? Why? What are you hiding, Ms. Darrow?"

I stared down the Major General, though I still felt small under her gaze. "We have been through this before, Bellona," I sneered. "A proper interrogation has to be done on Military property."

Her jaw worked. "The Military is the Coalition, and everything in this city belongs to the Coalition. Ergo, we are on Military property."

I crossed my arms. "I didn't pin you as the loop-hole type."

"I will do anything to keep my country safe."

"Then arrest me, Major General," I challenged, taking another step closer. "If the boy is actually a Rebel, and you have footage of me conversing with him, then arrest me. Put me on trial."

"Believe me, Ms. Darrow," the Major General's voice was hard, "I will." Bellona turned on a heel, leaving me behind the waterfall. Alone.

CHAPTER 35

After Bellona's threats, I felt the ticking clock of my time in the Coalition dwindling down with every heartbeat. I always knew my time here was limited, but the feeling of doom that settled in my stomach wasn't so much caused by the thought of Darragh's death—which still haunted my every waking moment—or leaving Callum, especially since my extraction was postponed. I simply couldn't help but wonder if the clock ticking down wasn't for my time here in the Coalition but my time here on this earth.

Then there was work. Returning to the Research Facility two days after the gala was like ripping off a bandage only to find that the wound festered underneath, and an oozing scab clung to the dressing. Everyone—doctors, researchers, janitors, and the like—congratulated me on my engagement, pleading to see the ring before asking personal questions. Many people practically invited themselves to the wedding.

The wedding.

That was the festering wound. I knew that it would eventually be called off. I knew if Callum didn't end this engagement, I would have to, so every time someone mentioned our wedding, my stomach would churn into a large knot, and my chest would constrict. But I smiled, showed them the ring, and pretended like I wasn't dying of guilt on the inside. I tried to convince myself that if I had said 'no' to Callum, things would be a lot worse.

Some people weren't as gracious. My skin crawled as women and men alike gawked at me from across the room. In all likelihood, they had read all the *Propas*, which, as of that morning, included Adellaide's 'real' identity as a Median brothel worker due to some 'anonymous source.' However, I couldn't help but wonder if they gawked because they heard my clock ticking down as well, or if they stared so as not to miss a show.

I hurried up to the usual Laboratory Hlín and I used on Mondays. The best part about Hlín was that she didn't care for gossip or social news. When Hlín and I were working, she practically reprimanded me any time I would try to engage in small talk. So, as I rode in the elevator, away from the mass of people in the Research Center's lobby, I almost felt excited to spend the day with Hlín.

When I walked into the Laboratory, a familiar astringent aroma hanging in the air, I greeted Hlín, who was carefully stowing away nano-pipets and test tubes. "Do we have a different project to work on today?"

Hlín jumped at the sound of my voice. "Oh, dear! Ms. Stevens, you can't just sneak up on people like that! It is not polite!"

"Sorry. I just assumed—"

"You are not supposed to be here." Hlín's eyes were wide.

"Why? It's Monday. This is the Lab we use every Monday."

"Yes, well." Hlín gently placed the strap of her bag on her shoulder. "Dr. Osouf informed me of your time off this week. She has scheduled other work for me during your absence."

I grimaced and took a step forward. "I'm sorry. I was not aware."

She turned her head sharply. "Yes, yes. Dr. Osouf does not want the party planning and new engagement to distract you in the Laboratory. She is afraid it will have horrible consequences on your work. Did you not check your COM-mail?"

I closed my eyes and took a deep breath, stifling my frustration. "No."

"Ms. Stevens," Hlín *tisked*. "You need to check your COM-mail. Dr. Osouf sent you a message this morning."

"Well, I am here now. There must be something I can help you with today."

"Oh, no, no." Hlín backed away from me like I was trying to brand her with a hot iron. "The project I am working on today is highly classified. Way above your clearance." She laughed gently. "I simply stopped by to grab a few things."

I glanced around the lab. "I am sure there is something I can work on here. Do you need me to count cells or run simulations?"

"No, no, no, Ms. Stevens. You must go home. If you are not scheduled to work, you do not work. Trust me, I have tried." Hlín started shooing me out the doorway. A small sound chimed from her COM-tab on the table. The translucent screen lit up. From the corner of my eye, I read the text glowing from the device.

It was a reminder. *0830. Prometheus Project. Level-3.*

"Oh, dear," Hlín cried. "Ms. Stevens, you must leave." Then Hlín started pushing me out of the ray-door. "I only have fifteen minutes! I cannot be late!"

I was dazed. My mind whirled.

The Prometheus Project.

I stumbled through the door, nearly toppling over Hlín as she shoved past me, and everything clicked into place, the tiniest pieces of a plan beginning to form.

"Now, go home, Ms. Stevens. You are off the entire week. I'll see you next Monday." She hurried toward the elevators, the small bun on top of her head stiff despite her haste.

When Hlín disappeared around the corner, I pulled my COM-tab out of my leather work bag. I quickly pressed the screen a few times, brought the device to my face, and pressed record.

"Hey, wanna play hooky? Meet me behind the waterfall at zero-ten-hundred."

———

We had a plan. A plan based on a lie, and there were a lot of variables that couldn't be fully worked through in such a short amount of time. So, we had half a plan based on half a truth.

I felt bad for lying to Alethia. She had been nothing but kind and welcoming toward me, despite her hard exterior, but I couldn't exactly tell her I needed clearance to sneak into a super-secret lab to find my dead father's old research. Instead, I told her I needed clearance to sneak into lower research levels to make sure all the Epimetheus Creatures were safe and well-fed.

She tried to refuse, but I pulled the whole 'I know what it's like to be used and abused for *'entertainment,'* and she was putty in my hand.

So, the lie was planted, and it was time for the research. Most of our planning time was spent digging up information on Lydia Martinez, the Skies-awful woman who worked the Research Facility's front desk, but as it turned out, she had a very handsome grandson in the Military whom she adored.

"I think I may have shagged him," Aletheia noted when his picture popped up on the CCD.

I gave my accomplice a begrudging look.

"Well, the wench probably doesn't know that," was Aletheia's only defense. "Plus"—she tossed her long, dark ponytail over a shoulder—"I'm a catch."

I rolled my eyes. "What else do we have on her?"

"Nothing." Aletheia sighed. "She is clean as a Medic Bay. That's pretty typical of receptionists. They don't like to jiggle the jam if you know what I mean."

I gawked at her. "No. I don't."

"Oh, you know." Aletheia made some odd movements, like she was indeed jiggling a jar of jam.

I couldn't help but roll my eyes. "You got that from your brother, didn't you?"

Aletheia shrugged. "Sometimes Sancus is funny."

"You literally have never said Sancus is funny. Theia…" I took a step closer to my co-conspirator to get a good look at her dark eyes. "Are you fucking high right now?"

The lithe girl shrugged again. "What? You said we were playing hooky? What good is playing hooky without a little…" Aletheia gestured as if smoking a joint.

I rubbed the bridge of my nose between two fingers. "Holy fuck, this better work."

———

Around twelve-hundred, Aletheia made a quick stop at the Military Base before we met outside of a *prandium* about a block down from the Research Facility. With her was a tall man around the age of twenty-five. His hair was dark and stretched down his face in a full but tidy beard.

"Adellaide, this is Brutus."

"Pleasure to meet you, Brutus." I stretched out a hand to shake his, but instead, he grasped it gently and pressed my knuckles to his lips.

"The pleasure is mine, Ms. Stevens." His voice was a low caress, and I had to stifle a blush as his crystal-blue eyes met mine. It wasn't a mystery why Aletheia had chosen to hook up with the beautiful man.

"Alright," Aletheia interrupted with a yawn. "Let's get this over with." I understood she was donning a mask for Brutus, but I saw the twinkling of excitement in her dark eyes—she was ready to cause a little trouble.

"Now remember," I urged, trying my hardest to focus my friend through her drug-induced haze, "the biggest variable is—"

Aletheia waved me off. "The security cameras, I know."

"So, you have to make sure—"

Alethea whipped her head toward me. "Oh, don't you worry, darling Adellaide. This will be my best performance yet. Ms. Martinez will be too frazzled to even think about checking the security cameras. She might even delete all the feeds just to rid the world of our display."

I was unsure. I took Ms. Martinez as a detail-oriented individual. If I were to move one thing out of place, she would definitely suspect tampering and then check the security footage for the culprit. But as long as Aletheia's distraction was long enough and I didn't have to rush, then everything should go as planned.

Aletheia and Brutus linked arms as we all walked down the street, appearing as though we had just finished up a luncheon together. We talked casually. I asked Brutus typical 'get-to-know-you' questions since the reality was, I knew nothing about him, but I also just wanted to hear the low, creaminess of his voice. Brutus was polite and engaged in the conversation easily, which was probably why Aletheia had not kept things going with the soldier.

Brutus congratulated me on the engagement. When I asked if he attended the Gala, he mentioned he was on duty that night but was manning the front gate, not the gardens. I managed to swallow the lump in my throat to keep on with normal conversation. Aletheia and Brutus played their part well as they walked me to the front steps of the Research Center and ran off together.

As I made my way into the building around the time I usually came back from lunch—on the off chance I would get a lunch— Ms. Martinez was in her usual spot, sitting behind the large front desk, typing away on her large COM-pad screen. The desk was a large half-circle made of intricately carved marble, and I knew that below the top of the desk, the COM-tab screen was another half-circle about half the length of the desk. She not only monitored every entrance in the building, but she could also do any additional filing, communication, or detailing she needed all on one screen. If anything were to happen on any other level, it would be taken care of by security first. But the first floor was Ms. Martinez's domain, and if she saw a problem, she would be on it like a mutant momma bear protecting her den.

I felt the old woman's eyes pierce through me as I strode toward her desk.

"Good afternoon, Ms. Martinez," I chimed, pretending to keep striding past her desk.

"Ms. Stevens," she said in a tone indicating for me to stop. I prayed she didn't know I was supposed to have the day off and that she hadn't paid much attention to me leaving before nine earlier this morning. But if worse came to worse, I could feign the need to do research off campus this morning. "Was that you with Aletheia and Brutus outside?"

"Um, yes," I answered, my shoulders slouching in relief. "Do you know them?"

"Well, yes. Brutus is my grandson. My *favorite* grandson."

I turned toward the older woman and leaned on the desk. "Is he really? He is so charming! I can see why Aletheia is so taken with him."

"Aletheia? Taken?" Ms. Martinez scoffed. "She is a troubled soul, dear. You should not be aquatinting yourself with such riffraff."

The shock written across my face was not forced. "Ms. Martinez, Aletheia is a good friend of mine. And of Lieutenant General Osouf."

The woman tapped her stylus impatiently on the desk. "I have heard things, Ms. Stevens. Uncouth things." She looked me up and down.

"And here I thought mindless gossip was beneath you, Ms. Martinez."

The woman leaned back in her chair with a huff, still tapping anxiously. Then, her eyes jerked to the left side of her screen.

She stood up in alarm, shoving her chair to the side as she bolted around her desk.

"This is exactly what I was talking about!" I heard her mumble in her tizzy.

Once she was out of view, making her way toward the south door, I glanced around the lobby, ensuring the coast was clear, and crept behind her desk. Her potent floral perfume still lingered in the air, mixed with a faint body odor I did not care for. I stifled a gag as I glanced at the giant COM-screen and immediately clapped a hand over my mouth to prevent the laugh threatening to burst from my belly. There they were, Aletheia and Brutus tangled up outside the southern entrance. My friend was hoisted up on a sleek rail, her skirt so far up her thighs you could have seen her underwear if Brutus hadn't been pressed so tightly against her.

I had to force myself to look away, though I desperately wanted to watch Ms. Martinez's rage scene unfold. It only took me seconds rummaging through the receptionist's desk and drawers before I found the chip wand.

"Okay, now how do you work?" I muttered to the wand as if it could tell me all of its secrets. I pressed a button, and lights flicked on, the screen on the wand shimmering blue.

For Amethyst clearance, the screen read *1011.* I pressed the arrow button on the wand.

For Lapis clearance, 1022.

I paged through several times.

For ALL clearance, 4024.

Slowly, I punched the numbers. Lights flickered in a rainbow sequence. I stole a quick glance at the monitoring screens, and I saw Ms. Martinez yelling at Aletheia and Brutus, her pointer finger wagging violently between the two of them.

I placed the two prongs of the wand on either side of where my chip was inserted deep into my forearm tissue and pressed the green button on the long device. After it lit up in a rainbow sequence again, a jolt ran through my arm, and the word *Success* blinked across the screen before the wand went dim.

I glanced at the security screen. Ms. Martinez was dragging her grandson by the ear through the southern door, leaving a shocked Aletheia outside. Hand shaking, I placed the wand in the same drawer from which it came, skirted around the front desk, and casually walked toward the front door. As I left, Ms. Martinez was dragging Brutus through the research facility, yelling in her native tongue. There were only a few people in the lobby, most of them waiting for the elevator and one straggler walking while talking to someone on his COM-tab, but they all turned toward the old woman, their eyes wide and mouths agape. Before Ms. Martinez was in view of her desk, I crept through the front door.

Aletheia and I met back at the *prandium* because we never actually had lunch. I found her sitting outside on the patio, feet propped on a chair in front of her and running scarlet red lipstick across her plump lips. Pulling out a chair for myself, I asked, "So, what exactly did you promise Brutus in exchange for a beating from his grandmother?"

Aletheia rubbed her lips together and gave me a devilish, feline smile. "Let's just say *that* was a little bit of foreplay."

I sat down and picked up the glass of iced tea she must have ordered for me. "Cheers to foreplay," I said, raising my glass.

Aletheia also lifted her glass of iced tea and winked at me. "Cheers indeed, little fox."

CHAPTER 36

My eyes met those of the stone Direwolf prowling over the gigantic front door of Osouf Manor, the same color of dress I now wore for my—our—engagement party, and the twins to Callum's eyes. After my family fled Militum, I had always dreamed of seeing his eyes again—always wondering how the years had fared for him, what our lives would be like if we had still known each other—but here he was, standing beside me, dressed in a formal obsidian tuxedo with a velvet jacket and satin bowtie, and I didn't have to wonder anymore. Sure, he didn't end up becoming an interstellar space astronomer like his younger self always dreamed of, and he never discovered an underground ancient civilization that died out millennia ago, but the years fared him well.

Callum was strong, intelligent, and kind. He had worked extremely hard to climb the Military Ranks in record time and managed to grow a conscience within the debilitating Coalition. I couldn't help but wonder if staring into those emerald-green eyes for the rest of my life would be the worst thing. Maybe, with time, I would mourn Darragh and move on from the Resistance. With the help of Metis, I could sneak Reign into the Coalition and finally reveal more of my life to my fiancé. Maybe the three of us could be one happy family. But as I found myself getting lost in the eyes of the Direwolf, I couldn't help but wonder if I was being sucked in—if I was being hypnotized, only to be devoured in one bite. As if Darragh's death six days ago was just a warning snap of teeth before the monster finally attacked.

My breath hitched as a cold shiver crawled down my exposed spine like an icy millipede.

"Breathe," Callum whispered in my ear. I gave him a small smile. Arms linked, Callum pulled me closer and pressed his warm lips to my temple. "Try to enjoy yourself, Rowyn."

Before I could utter a sarcastic retort, the muffled, booming voice of the Osouf's butler reverberated through the thick wooden doors, slowly growing louder and clearer as the entry doors opened wide.

"...the Lieutenant General and future Mrs. Osouf!" The foyer stretched before us, filled with people dressed to the nines, and I barely registered the applause as the name 'Mrs. Osouf' rang in my mind. It was everything I had ever hoped for, but it seemed surreal, like this life of mine belonged to someone else. Because it did.

As Callum led us through the doorway, some guests clapped their hands together while others gently patted their thighs with one hand because their other was clutched tightly around a crystal glass. A small group of young ladies stood atop the balcony of the stairs, all their eyes set in disdain as they looked down on me. I felt small beneath their glares. Each one of the girls was probably enraged that some random Median snagged the Coalition's number one bachelor.

Freyja and Erebus were the first people to greet us, each embracing their son and pecking his cheeks with a light kiss, and then they bestowed a similar greeting to me.

Callum's grandparents greeted us next. "We are so excited for you, darling," Rheamarie cooed as she clutched my hands in hers. Tears rimmed her joy-filled eyes. "Odin and I could not imagine anyone more perfect for our Callum."

I kissed Rheamarie on her rosy cheek. "Thank you, Amma. I am honored to be a part of your family." The older woman beamed at her beloved title, then she pulled me in close.

"And whatever happens, *do not* let Callum's mother get under your skin," Rheamarie whispered in my ear. "If you have any problems, you come straight to me."

"Amma…" I tried laughing off her comment, but she held tight.

"I am very serious, Adellaide. Straight to me." She released me only to hold my shoulders tight until I nodded. "Good girl," Rheamarie said with a pat on my cheek.

As Callum's grandmother parted from me, I overheard Odin's warning to Callum. "Do not screw this up, boy. She's a good one," the older gentleman whispered in Callum's ear as he jabbed a crooked finger into his grandson's chest.

Callum laughed. "Oh, I would not dare, Affi."

A long line of close friends and family followed the older couple. Aletheia and Sancus were two of the first, the former dressed in a chic, black satin gown accented in gold, while Sancus wore a colorfully beaded jacket with twin tails.

"I know we have congratulated the two of you already," Aletheia started, voice tainted with apathy as she embraced me with one arm, a glass of champagne sloshing in a golden glass over my shoulder. "But I have to keep up with appearances." As soon as my friend let go, she gave me a sly wink and strode away, her slender hips shifting softly from side to side.

Sancus greeted Callum first, clasping hands and pulling his friend in to clap him on the shoulder. "Congrats, man." Sancus pulled back, taking both of us in with a sigh. "Wow." His eyes traveled up and down. "You two really look like a Coalition Power Couple." Sancus shook his head in awe and then embraced me. "I'm just glad he is finally settling down so I can have a turn at the ladies."

I rolled my eyes and playfully shoved Sancus off. "Oh, you pig."

"You know I am kidding, darling Adellaide." Sancus batted his big, dark brown eyes at me. "Enjoy your party. If you need me, I will be by the food."

I glanced at Callum, who had already moved on to greet the next in line, a couple I didn't recognize, but they kind of looked like—

"Adellaide," Callum started as he turned toward me, "I would like to introduce you to Dr. and Senator Gillian."

"Oh." I smiled politely. "Are you Sancus and Theia's parents?"

"Yes," Senator Gillian replied. She was dark and slender like her daughter, though quite a bit shorter.

Dr. Gillian laughed. "Though we do not like to admit it in public," he said jokingly. Dr. Gillian was tall and fair-skinned, with freckles bridging his nose like his son.

Cinnamon and vanilla mingled with the air around me as my friends' mother embraced me, her arms strong, warm, and comforting. "It is a true pleasure to meet you. We have heard so much about you." The senator's voice was soft and melodic. I couldn't imagine her reprimanding a dog, let alone speaking on the council's floor or arguing policies with her fellow lawmakers.

Dr. Gillian patted his wife's back. "Okay, dear. We will have to talk with them later. Maybe invite them over for dinner. But for now…" He nodded toward the line behind them.

"Oh, yes. Of course." Senator Gillian nodded. "Congratulations, you two. Marriage is a beautiful and sacred union not to be taken for granted."

"They get the point, dear. Now, come on." Dr. Gillian gently pulled his wife away.

I instantly loved her. Neither Sancus nor Aletheia seemed to have gained any of their mother's personality traits. Senator Gillian was so…mellow. So calm and tame. Aletheia, especially, was none of those things.

More guests tugged at our attention, each desiring the

consideration of the Coalition's new 'Power Couple,' and I had no choice but to let them distract me. They were our guests, after all, and each of them probably brought gifts for which I would be truly grateful, though we lacked for nothing. At least not in a physical sense. No, the things I desired could not be wrapped or bought. They had to be won and fought.

———

Time droned on as the never-ending line of guests slowly dwindled, and mouthwatering hors d'oeuvres were passed before us, remaining just out of reach. My stomach ached and grumbled as the delicious aromas of roast duck and smoked chicken wafted through the air, and my throat grew dry and ragged after thanking so many guests. Luckily, as soon as the line was through, Callum and I were able to breathe.

Like a bountiful goddess, Aletheia breezed over to Callum and me, two glasses of champagne in tow.

"Oh, my Skies," I sighed. "Where were these twenty minutes ago?"

"It is rude to drink while you are greeting guests, Adellaide," Aletheia chastised, though a playfulness clung to her words.

"Well, you could have at least brought me a shot," I muttered, taking a sip from my crystal-and-gold champagne flute.

"Don't be so dramatic."

Callum wrapped an arm around my waist and pressed his lips to my temple. "You did great."

"Of course she did. Darling Adellaide is captivating as fuck!"

"Theia," Callum breathed. "How about you go enjoy the party."

"You call this a party? Honestly, Callum, you are such a bore. Look around." She waved a hand through the air, long, sharp nails cutting through the scene in glittering gold. "Nothing but a bunch of over-dressed stiffs here."

Callum gave her an incredulous glare.

"Fine," Aletheia sighed. "I will go scrounge up some food for the princess. Go mingle. I will find you in a few."

The slender woman turned, but Callum caught her arm before she could walk away. "Aletheia, where is Bellona?"

She shrugged. "Hell if I know. Probably sulking around somewhere."

Callum nodded.

"Careful," Aletheia warned. "She's been in a mood."

"As usual," I muttered.

Aletheia winked at me with a playful smile on her full lips. "Don't drink too fast, Adellaide. That champagne will go straight to your head." And with a swish of her hips, Aletheia turned toward the long tables of food set up in the drawing room.

"Please bring me the duck!" I yelled after her. She gave me a thumbs-up as she continued walking.

"We will be in the gardens!" Callum called after her as well. She held up another thumb.

"The gardens?"

"You look a little warm," Callum answered, pressing the back of his hand to my cheek. "And there is a string quartet. I was hoping we could dance."

I gave him a small smile and nodded.

Callum led us through the crowds of people gathered in every room. We would stop about every twelve steps to greet someone or to thank a guest for celebrating with us. We passed the large table in the sitting room overflowing with gifts of all shapes and sizes. I swear I saw one of the bags moving.

When we finally reached the southern gardens of the Osouf Estate, we were greeted by the romantic ambiance of a thousand small, twinkling lights floating through the air like blinking light bugs. Music ebbed and flowed through the garden in gentle movements that soothed and entranced my senses.

"Are the lights—"

"Yeah." Callum smiled, reading my mind. "They are in sync with the rhythm of the music."

"Fascinating."

Callum pulled me toward the small, cobbled space in front of the band, and with a strong arm, he twirled me around, then pulled me in close. The garden air smelled of crocus and snapdragons, and although the temperature was comfortable, I yearned for the nip of a spring breeze. I wished for goosebumps and a chill running down my spine so I could appreciate the warm embrace of my exquisite partner even more.

"Enjoying yourself?" Callum whispered after a quiet moment.

I huffed a laugh. "It has only been an hour, and all we have done is hug and greet strangers."

Callum's returning smile was tainted with disappointment. "This *is* our party. From now on, you can do whatever you want."

I gave him a mischievous smile. "Anything I want?"

"Anything." His voice was a low, seductive rumble.

"So, I can chug champagne from one of your mother's antique vases and slide down the banister of the grand staircase?"

Callum barked a laugh. "Okay, you can do *almost* anything you want." He twirled me in time to the music.

"It was nice to meet Sancus and Theia's parents," I said once Callum pulled me back into his embrace.

"Yes. I can't believe I had never introduced you to them before."

I blinked. I supposed the Gillians were important enough that they should have been at the Gala, but Callum was probably so preoccupied with the engagement and then with Darragh...

"Do they have other children? Or just Sancus and Aletheia?"

Callum bit his lip, like he didn't want to tell me. "One. Mira. She lives in Humilis."

I raised a brow, silently asking for more.

Callum swallowed. "It's a story for a different time."

I could tell from the weight in his words that it wasn't a happy story, and right now wasn't the best time to pry. "What exactly does Dr. Gillian do?"

"In a way, he works for my mother—she oversees all of the Biology Research here in Imperium, and Dr. Gillian is a Virologist."

A crowd began to form around us as we danced, slowly filling the cobbled courtyard.

"Will there be this many people at our wedding?" I asked quietly.

"There will be about five times as many people at our wedding."

My jaw dropped. "You have got to be kidding me."

He shook his head.

"Can we just elope?"

Callum shrugged. "Only if you want to be disowned by my family."

I grimaced. "That might be a risk I am willing to take."

Callum laughed. "We will have plenty of time to discuss everything. I'm sure we could cut the guest list down to only four times this many people."

I couldn't help but roll my eyes. "I'm sure six hundred people do not need to see us get married."

"No," Callum acknowledged. "But at least a thousand will want to."

"Gross," I muttered.

Callum kissed my forehead. "I know."

"Can I take it back?"

"Take what back?" Callum brows knit together.

"The engagement. I don't know if it's worth it." I winked at him, though the words echoed in my heart.

"Oh," Callum growled. "I will make it worth it." He pulled me in tight to his chest, and his lips met mine with urgency.

"Is that a threat?" I asked when our lips parted.

"No." *Skies his voice alone is going to make me—* "That is a promise, my darling."

"Well, I am going to hold you to it," I purred, brushing my lips against his.

"Please do."

Before our lips could meet again, Callum twirled me one last time as the song ended and pulled me into a dip. The growing crowd around us clapped and cheered as Callum bent over me, pulled me close, and pressed his lips against mine. I wrapped my arms tightly around his neck as our lips ebbed and flowed together. The taste of him consumed me, depleting me of all my other senses. And just as I brushed my tongue against his lower lip, he pulled me up, forcing our bodies to break apart. Nodding to the crowd, Callum escorted me off the dance floor as the beat to the next song picked up. A gap formed in the crowd for us as we made our way to a carved metal bench surrounded by blooming cabbage roses.

My fiancé sat me down on his lap so that I was just above his eye level. He looked up at me, brushing my curled tresses away from my neck, and smiled as he leaned into me. Our lips met again, softly at first. Then Callum's hands were on my hips, drawing me into him, and I couldn't fight my restraint anymore. My will crumbled under the monumental tension that had been building all night. We were a tangle of lips, teeth, and tongues, wanting more of each other with every shallow breath.

Callum parted sharply, his forehead resting on mine as we caught our breaths. "I want to take you home right now," he whispered.

"It is *our* party; we can leave when we want to."

"You really want to piss off my mother, don't you?"

I laughed. "No, I just like your—"

"Achem," a throat cleared behind us.

Callum rose his head and peered over my shoulder. His jaw clenched, and I turned to see the person responsible for his mood change.

"I apologize for the interruption," the Major General intoned.

"Really? Because it seems to be your preferred method of beginning a conversation."

Bellona, donned in her work uniform and her hands were clasped behind her back, ignored my jab and my presence altogether, her eyes remaining fixed on Callum. "I wanted to formally congratulate you two on your engagement."

I felt Callum straighten his shoulders while his strong hands tightened on my hips. "Thank you, Major General. I didn't realize you were working tonight. I made sure you were on the guest list."

"I picked up the shift," Bellona explained.

"For party security?" Callum asked suspiciously.

"That's an unusual job for someone as skilled as you, isn't it?" I asked before Bellona could answer.

"No. I was doing a round, and I was in the area, so I thought I would stop by."

"But you were invited, right?"

Bellona nodded to her commander.

"Who called off their shift?"

The Major General shrugged. "I don't know. Ask one of the hundreds of soldiers that are here getting drunk off their asses."

Callum gave his subordinate a tight smile. "I'm sure it has been quiet tonight. I will call you off. Just enjoy the rest of the party."

"If it is all the same to you, sir, I would like to continue my shift. I also need to return to Base and finish some work up at the office."

She probably has more dirt to dig up on me.

Though I couldn't see Callum's eyes, I could feel his stare, hard and heavy against my cheek. "I will call and see if someone can finish your round. Surely your other work can wait until tomorrow."

Bellona crossed her arms. "That would be an abuse of resources, sir. I would rather continue my work for the evening."

Silence stretched between them, forcing the air around us to chill and stiffen.

"You know what?" Callum said with a wave of his hand. "Forget about it. Please, go back to your duties." Something in Callum's voice broke, and whatever it was reflected itself in Bellona's dark eyes.

With a sharp turn of her heel, the Major General left.

I twisted to look at Callum. "What the fuck is her problem?"

Callum ran a hand through his hair. "She will come around." He sighed, more to himself than to me.

"And if she doesn't? Will that affect our relationship?"

"No, of course not. But—"

"Oh, here we go." I stood up. "The but…"

Callum pulled me back down. "Rowyn," he whispered my name. "Bellona and I have been working together for a long time. We were partnered together for most of our training and have been in the same unit for years. We trust each other, and we know each other very well, including all our strengths and all our weaknesses, and to some extent, she was right about you." He raised his brows. "She is just being cautious because that is her job. Does Bellona get carried away? Sometimes, yes. But—"

"But what, Cal? She already knows everything! You told her about me and my family."

"I think she is suspicious because you don't want anyone else to know. She thinks you are still hiding something. If we could—"

"No." I held up a finger. "I know where you are going with this."

"Wyn, if we would just tell everyone who you are, you wouldn't have to keep secrets, and you wouldn't act so suspicious all the time."

"Callum, I can't—"

"You can do anything you want."

"I can only do anything I want because of you," I said,

jabbing a finger in his chest. "Besides, I don't even know if Rowyn exists anymore."

Maybe I didn't want her to. Not if it meant giving up Callum for the Resistance. Not if everyone Rowyn loved died. I thought of my father and Aura. Darragh's lifeless eyes shadowed my own. A shudder coursed through my body.

Callum took my hands in his. "Rowyn," he whispered. "I am sorry. I didn't mean to pressure—"

"Well, you are." I ripped my hands from his. "And you have been. And I just… I need time to think." I stood from his lap.

"Think about what?"

I turned from him. "I don't know." My eyes burned as tears pooled. "I'm sorry. I'm just overwhelmed."

Callum stood behind me, and gently he pressed a hand to the small of my back. His other hand cupped my cheek while he slowly turned me so our eyes met. "Whatever you have to think about, I will give you all the time you need."

"Thank you," I breathed.

Callum's smile was gentle and loving—kind. "How about you go find a washroom? Take a few minutes to yourself. I will satisfy the masses."

I nodded, kissed him on his cheek, then wandered off.

CHAPTER 37

I crept through a small service entrance that led to a narrow hallway. Once I reached the end, there was no handle or knob. No door.

A warm draft floated through a thin crevice in the wall. Curious, I braced both hands against the smooth surface and pressed. The wall gave and a panel pushed out and then pulled back into the right wall, opening like a pocket door. It revealed a back staircase that led up to the third floor, through another paneled door, and out into a broader hallway. The carpet was Coalition Plum with gold accents. The light gold walls were lined with intricately carved doors and portraits of distinguished-looking people.

Though Callum had suggested a washroom, any room would do. I just needed some time to collect my thoughts—to remember why I was in the Coalition. To remember who I was. So, I opened the first mahogany door. Blindly, I reached around the corner and switched on the lights. A giant chandelier revealed a private study.

My eyes were drawn to the southern wall where neatly lined mahogany bookshelves stretched from floor to ceiling, the highest shelves only accessible by a rolling ladder.

Consuming the eastern wall was a window made of stained glass depicting the Osouf family crest. The Direwolf's emerald eyes and white teeth glistened as the twinkling lights from the garden floated beyond the panes. The masterpiece of glass and lead was the backdrop for a large mahogany desk intricately carved with vines, leaves, trees, and flowers, like it was telling the story of the forest it could have been carved from.

A few small, gilded picture frames were perched upon the desk's surface. I walked around the desk and studied each one. My eyes met those of a little girl with grey eyes and a toothy smile.

There was another picture of the same girl, though older, dressed in a black robe and cap holding a rolled scroll of parchment. Something in her smile was different. Dark. Void of the joy the little girl had in the previous picture.

Freyja.

It's strange how time changes people.

I didn't know what that younger, fragile Freyja had gone through, but something in her expression echoed in my soul. I was a Resistance spy who had fallen in love with a Coalition soldier. A man who aids the very government that might as well have killed my family. And the Resistance… I didn't even know what they stood for, not really. What was their purpose?

What is my *purpose?*

I forced my eyes down the line of frames to a photograph of Callum's official Military photo.

I chewed on my lip. That was someone with a sense of purpose. Everything about him—his eyes, the set of his jaw, the straightness of his neck—was poised to move with tenacity and dignity.

The next photo was of Freyja and Callum when Cal was just a boy. He was cast upon his mother's hip. He was grinning ear to ear while Freyja looked at him like he was the only beautiful thing in the world. Her silver eyes were alight with pride and something else…something I couldn't quite place.

The last two pictures were different. The frames were simple and engraved with names—Aureliea Lilith and Benjamin Augustus respectively. The pictures were just swirls of black and white.

My breath hitched.

They were sonograms.

I stood and glanced around the room. Something didn't make sense. The whole study felt as though it was plucked from the past. There was no COM-tab or computer on the desk—nothing electrical or technological for that matter—and every drawer was empty. No pens or utensils, no pads of paper; no files, no sign of any work actually being done in this office.

Whose study is this?

Erebus'? Maybe the pictures were doting reminders of his wife and son.

Freyja's? With memories of her life's biggest accomplishments and biggest heartbreaks?

There was no dust on the desk, and from my quick glance at the bookshelf, there was no dust there either.

I continued my walk around the room. On the north wall, there was a large fireplace, big enough for two people to comfortably enjoy tea inside the hearth. It wasn't electric like in most homes in Excelsis. No, it was a natural, wood-burning fireplace created from ornately carved white marble. The stone leaves and vines crawling up each side shone starkly against the mahogany framing the stone. No wood or ash lay on the bottom; no soot marks against the back of the space or signs of smoke. There was an iron log holder in the center, but it looked untouched.

The banister of the fireplace was decorated with a few golden statues of various animals and small busts of probably important people. I had only recognized one. It was Gregor Mendel. He was originally coined the founder of modern genetics—if you call the limited knowledge of the nineteenth-century *modern*. I tried to pick up the bust of the famous geneticist, but it didn't budge. I reached for the golden statue next to him, but it didn't budge either. None of them did. They were all adhered to the banister.

Odd.

I examined Mendel again. His hair was cut short and parted to the left, and he wore a small pair of round spectacles. A cross necklace was placed around his neck, and in the pocket of his jacket was a small golden plant. I recognized the organism as a pea plant because Mendel's pea plant experiments really defined the first laws of genetics which were later coined as Mendelian Inheritance. Tentatively, I touched the small plant with the pad of my finger.

It wiggled.

Curious, I plucked it from the bust and placed it in the palm of my hand. I heard a faint *click* and before I could look up from the golden pea plant, the back wall of the fireplace had vanished. It was replaced by a dark hallway gently lit with blue LED lights that hung from the ceiling.

I glanced down at the pea plant that I held in my hand, then back up at the peculiar hallway. My pulse thumped against my eardrums, making it difficult to hear if anyone was in the hallway.

I could put the plant back, I thought, taking a deep breath. *I could put the plant back and hope that it will close the door. Then I could come back on a different day to explore. A different time that isn't during my* engagement party.

I fingered the small plant and lifted the tiny golden branch.

You don't know if you will get another chance, Red.

The Osoufs were occupied with almost two hundred people in their home.

Surely, no one would sneak off to their study during such an event.

Then again, that was how I ended up in the study.

But what could the Osoufs possibly have to hide?

Freyja and Erebus were two of the most influential people in the Coalition. Each of them was probably the most influential person in their field, and they had a secret corridor in one of their studies.

If there wasn't a secret to the Coalition I could access through this corridor, there was no way I would be able to access any secrets whatsoever.

And if this was Freyja's study...

The Prometheus Project.

I took one glance behind me, tucked the pea plant into the tight waistline of my dress, and took a deep breath.

—————

A light *thud* startled me into a jump as the door shut behind me. My stomach dropped. I thought about turning back, trying the door by pushing, or rummaging around in the dim light for a handle or switch—Skies, it was tempting—but the secrets at the end of this tunnel seemed to call to me, propelling me forward one soft clap of a heel at a time.

The corridor smelled of mildew and wet rocks, and humidity hung heavy in the air. The dampness made my hair and dress stick uncomfortably to my skin. The tunnel was constructed of cold, hard concrete that was rough yet slick to the touch. Along the corridor was an iron railing on each side and I clung tightly to the right, afraid that if I let go of the cold metal rod, I would be consumed by the dark abyss surrounding me. The blue lights were few and far between, casting ominous shadows along the walls and floor. The corridor continued down in a gentle slope, twisting around and around until finally it bottomed out. A ray door stood at the Base, glowing white.

A white door? I've never seen a white ray-door!

I glanced down at my forearm where my chip was implanted. I knew I had access to all colors, but white wasn't a color. It was white. The absence of color. Just as black was the culmination of all colors. I glanced back to the white ray-door.

I slammed a fist against the railing and the reverberation echoed around me and all the way up through the metal rod. *I got myself stuck down here for nothing?*

I could try to go through, and if I set off an alarm, I could just lie. I could say I was looking for a place to rejuvenate, I stumbled into the study, fiddled with the busts, and the door opened. Who wouldn't have ventured down a strange tunnel that was hidden behind a fireplace? I was curious. No harm no foul. And who knows—getting caught might be the only way I can get out of this damned cavern.

I closed my eyes. I breathed deeply, filling my chest, willing the oxygen to fuel my brain—to give me another option. I thought about the chip wand. I activated my chip for all the doors. For the rainbow. *And when all the colors of light come together...*

I opened my eyes to stare directly into the blinding white light. Releasing a deep breath and relaxing my shoulders, I stepped through the ray-door.

Nothing.

No debilitating shock, no alarm or spikes shooting from each side of the corridor. No ring of fire engulfing my body in flames.

I glanced behind me.

No pack of mutant wolves stampeding down the hallway to devour me. I breathed deeply again, and I felt my racing heart slow. When I turned back around, I faced the room the white ray-door was protecting. It was dark, only the faint glow of small emergency lights peeking through the void, but as I took a few more steps into the room, one by one the lights flickered on. It took only a moment for my eyes to readjust to the ancient fluorescent lighting, the same lights the Resistance Base had, though I had never seen fluorescents in Excelsis. When I looked around, I found just what I was hoping for.

A laboratory.

Honestly, I was hoping Freyja wouldn't be so cliché, but there are some things that people are just drawn to, and I guess scientists are drawn to secret labs like mice are drawn to cheese. But this wasn't an ordinary biology lab. There were no beakers or centrifuges; I did not see a bio-hood, nanoscale, or any steel incubators. But there was a lone stainless-steal desk polished to a shine, and perched above the desk was one big, long holo-screen.

With two taps to my right temple, I glided over to the desk to get a closer look, the bottom of my dress feeling damp and heavy. The holo-screen was curved and divided into six different sections with six different feeds. I watched strangers moving about, carrying on with their lives like they were in fact not being monitored.

"Who are you watching, Freyja?" I whispered into the darkness.

Before I could get a good look at the faces on the screen, something flat and utterly plain caught my eye. On the desk, next to a COM-tab, were paper files. Dozens of almond-colored file folders were scattered throughout the desktop. My fingers edged toward the smooth paper products, but I stopped short, not wanting to disturb the unkemptness, nor leave my fingerprints.

This could be your only chance, Red, a small voice in my head whispered.

Carefully, I picked through the papers. I glanced at the file tabs, searching for anything familiar, and there it was, all the way to the far right of the desk, and tucked under a paper notebook was a file labeled: "Prometheus Project." I shimmied it out from under the notebook, careful not to disturb anything, and opened the file.

Empty.

"Of fucking course." I slammed the file shut before sliding it back into its original spot. I glanced around the room. *I can't possibly rummage through all of this crap!* Not only did I not have the time, but there was no possible way I could return everything back to its exact placement in the room. *Though, it's not like everything is meticulously organized. Would Freyja really be able to tell if things were slightly moved?*

Then I thought of Metis. He would have called this lab 'organized chaos.' *It may look like three tornados ran through here,* I heard his grumbling voice in my head. *But I know exactly where everything is.*

And he did. He always did. However, I didn't pin Dr. Freyja Osouf as the 'organized chaos' type. It seemed oddly uncharacteristic of her personal profile.

I turned back to the COM-tab on the desk. *Maybe all the paper files have already been transferred...* With a tap of my finger, the device opened up to its home screen right away. *Dr. Freyja Osouf must be pretty freaking confident in her secret passage and white ray-door.* Most COM-tabs I had come in contact with only opened up to the owners' fingerprints or facial recognition.

I flicked three fingers up on the screen to project a holo image in the air. I searched the COM-tab for any files containing the words 'Prometheus Project.' Only one file popped up, but it was a folder holding nearly five hundred terabytes of information. I double-tapped the file.

`Folder locked. Please enter passcode.`

"And I thought this was going to be easy," I sighed.

I worked my fingers across the holo feed. `Freyja is the best`

The feed shook. '`Password incorrect`' flashed in red letters.

`Freyja is a genius`

Nope.

`Laurunda is a whore`

No.

I slammed my fist on the desk. *I could be here forever trying to figure this out!*

Another message scrolled across the screen. '`Hint is available. Would you like to use the Hint?`'

"Yes!" I practically screamed as I pressed the hint button.

The hint appeared in blue letters on the holo feed. *'Tucked deeply in the woods…'*

WHAT. THE. FUCK. I wanted to grab the COM-tab and chuck it against the wall. *Freyja's house looks like a whole Skies-damned magical forest! This hint could literally mean anything!* I leaned my hands on the table, dropping my gaze to stare at the outdated COM-tab.

Outdated COM-tab. It was bulkier than the most recent ones, and the screen was opaque, not the clear fiberglass like all the others I had seen. It was clearly decades old.

What if this isn't Freyja's COM-tab?

I racked my brain. "Okay, Dad…" I sat in the desk chair. "What is tucked deeply in the woods?"

The Shed? No. He wouldn't have had the Shed when he started this project. But he could have changed the password when he started preparing for us to leave.

I typed in the word *'Shed'*

'Incorrect Password'

I worked my fingers against the holo image, when my ring caught my eye, the gems glittering in the light. I cocked my head, remembering something.

Ring. I typed.

'Incorrect Password'

The Ring, I tried again.

'Incorrect Password'

I roared, my agony echoing around the room as the rumble bounced off the solid stone walls. I studied the ring again, something deep in my gut, screaming that I was so close. I took it off. The engraving on the inside caught my eye.

A spark to light the flame

With a deep breath, I typed the words onto the holo feed.

And the folder opened.

CHAPTER 38

The folder held hundreds of documents, videos, holos, graphs, charts, and other files. Just by scrolling over the image, I could see how large the document was, who created it, and when it was created.

"Dad?" I whispered after opening one of the many files created by Dr. Janus Darrow, and in the first time since I was a child, I saw his face again. He was a lot younger in the video, eyes bright with curiosity and blonde hair neatly combed.

"Prometheus Project. The date is September twelfth, twenty-two ninety-four." His voice was softer than I remembered. It was almost pure. Innocent.

Twenty-two ninety-four. He couldn't have been more than thirty-five years old.

"Dr. Osouf and I ran the sims last night, and when we arrived this morning, they looked very promising. Data file is attached."

A file popped up in the right corner of the holo feed. I almost tapped it, curious about what it contained, but I couldn't say goodbye to my father just yet.

"We are running the gene printer right now. It's our eleventh time using the machine, and it is still so fascinating to watch. The gene printer works similarly to the technological age's three-dimensional printer but at a much more precise level. It literally takes the building blocks of life—nucleotides—and builds an entire genome from them. Of course, we can't see the DNA being built with the naked eye, so we use the nano-cams attached to the device to track the progress. The process is long. It will take the next two days, but after that, we will insert the genome into a human egg that was donated. My companion here—" My father gestured to Freyja in the background. She, too, was much younger and full of hope, though I could still see something in her eyes that didn't settle right in my stomach, almost like a shadow. "—assured me the egg was harvested from a superior specimen. Of course, we will be extracting the DNA within the ovum. Then, we will insert two new strands of DNA or a full chromosomal set of a human genome. And that is the tricky part.

"For an unknown reason, sometimes the genome and eggs are not compatible. Currently, Dr. Osouf is researching the key to egg and genome compatibility. We think it has something to do with nuclear protein alignment and attachment, but we are not sure. Hopefully, we will find something within the next week or two if this experiment fails again."

They are creating humans. From scratch. My father was building human genomes and creating human beings from those genomes.

The holos of the Prometheans ran through my mind. Their speed. Their strength. Their red hair.

A chill crept down my spine.

The video feed ended, and I felt empty again. My heart throbbed, desiring more of my father.

I clicked on another video file. Then another. And another. Most of them were the same—a small brief of the research my father and Freyja were working on and problems that needed to be addressed.

I was beginning to think my father's project was a failure when I clicked on a video the year I was born.

"Prometheus Project. February eighth, twenty-three thousand

and three." My father looked fifteen years older, though only nine years had passed. His eyes were dim, with dark circles ringing them, and his hair was a mess, like he was continually scratching at a problem in his Cerebral Cortex in an attempt to coax the solutions from the lobe. "This is the one thousand and twenty-fifth time we have run our gene printer. We are noticing that the more we use it, the more mutations occur in the genome we create, essentially ruining our designed DNA.

"Some appear to be small superficial attributes, but other instances included coding for extra limbs, infertility, diabetes, and other physical deformities or genetic impurities. We have not had a human embryo breach the first trimester as of yet, despite promising simulations."

My father ran a hand through his untidy hair, reminding me of Callum. "This project has really been testing my patience, and it has been worrying my colleagues." His voice was a low rasp. "Dr. Metis Barnes is worried that I am creating Frankenstein's monster, but I don't think he was referring to the project." My father sighed. "Maybe he is right." He ran another hand through his graying hair, though it did nothing to tidy the matted mess. "After this trial, it might be best to retire the project. Either all together or attack it from a different angle, I don't know. I did try a few new algorithms to perfect binding the DNA to the egg and to limit the rejection of the DNA from the zygote to a developing blastocyst, but we are struggling to get the blastocyst to implant within the artificial womb. Somehow, the hormonal signals are not matching up, but we do not yet know if it is a problem with the artificial womb or with the blastocyst." My father rubbed his face with a hand and laughed to himself. "Who knew creating a human could be this complicated? Maybe we should just stick to the old-fashioned way." The video clicked off.

I opened another holo video from a few months later.

My father looked drastically different. He was nearly glowing, and the dark, purple circles that had previously shadowed his face were faded—there was a sparkle in his blue eyes. "Prometheus Project. May eleventh, twenty-three thousand and three. One-zero-two-five has made it past the first trimester and is thriving. She is growing at an above-average rate compared to 'normal' human babies." My father hooked his fingers in the air to show quotation marks. "But nothing that is alarming. And boy,"—he ran a hand through his hair and smiled —"she is beautiful. I have never seen anything more beautiful in my entire life." Dad moved the holo-cam over to zoom in on an odd aquarium-looking thing. It must have been their womb simulator because floating in the spherical glass was a small fetus. It was attached to the simulator wall with a placenta. Like normal babies, its toes and fingers were flexing like it was actually alive.

Because it was, I reminded myself.

"There are sensors all around the artificial womb," my father continued, "and they give us hourly readings on one-zero-two-five to check her HCG levels, cellular division, nutritional absorption rates, heart rate, and movement capabilities. Basically, the only thing the womb simulator can't do is read electrical impulses from the brain. However, we can gather rudimentary brain information from the movement capabilities and her responses to certain stimuli." My father moved the camera back to his face. In the last video I saw, he had grown a grungy-looking beard. Now, he still had the beard, but it was neatly groomed, resembling more of the father I grew up with.

"Data gathered so far is attached." A file popped up in the bottom right corner of the holo feed for a brief moment before the video stopped, and the holo image returned to the Prometheus Project File screen.

I opened up a video titled: `Birth of One-Zero-Two-Five`

"Today's the day!" My father's face popped up in the three-dimensional holo video in front of me, a wide grin peeking out from under his beard.

"Janus!" Freyja scolded him in the background.

"Oh, right. Sorry." He ran a hand over his beard. "Prometheus Project. November second, twenty-three thousand and three. One-Zero-Two-Five is at thirty-nine weeks, but all of our sensors and data indicate she is ready for delivery." My father panned the camera over to the artificial womb. "We have Dr. Osouf, Dr. Barnes, and Dr. Oliver, an actual physician, here today to assist in delivery." Dad took a few steps closer to all the doctors.

"Dr. Osouf will be taking written notes on her COM-tab, Dr. Barnes will be recording, and I will be assisting Dr. Oliver in the delivery. Of course, this will be very different from a normal human delivery..."

"But hopefully just as easy," Dr. Oliver, a bald young man, chimed in.

My father handed the holo-cam over to Metis. "Theoretically, but this is uncharted territory, Dr. Oliver." Dad started to pull on medic scrubs over his clothes. "We do have to take sanitary precautions because the baby's immune system is still elementary. However, unlike natural births, we do not have to worry about the health of a mother in this situation."

As soon as my father and Dr. Oliver were gloved and masked, they approached the synthetic womb. They turned the sphere so the opening was toward the tiled floor, and with a quick jab, Dr. Oliver popped the synthetic amniotic sac, fluids flowing onto the laboratory floor, and the baby slid down with it, landing in the arms of my father. He wrapped the screaming baby girl in a soft towel and gently started to pat her dry. My father's eyes grew wide and wet with tears as he dried the baby's hair, and when he pulled the towel away from her head, I finally noticed the color of the child's hair.

It was red.

———

I panned the holo back, beginning the video over again.

"Prometheus Project," my father's voice started again. "November second, twenty-three thousand and three. One-zero-two-five is at thirty-nine weeks, but all of our sensors are showing she is ready for delivery."

November second, twenty-three thousand and three. "That's my birthday," I breathed out into the universe, though I had a feeling it already knew. I swiped my finger on the holo display to scroll to the end of the video. I watched again as my father dried the baby's head and revealed her crimson hair.

My father smiled to Freyja, the newborn still cradled in his arms. "We did it. We did it! And look at her beautiful red hair! The MC1R gene hasn't been expressed in humanity for a century! We did it!"

Freyja reached for the baby. "May I?"

My father nodded and carefully placed the child into Freyja's arms. She was a natural.

"Do you think Callum will like her?" Freyja asked, gently rubbing the baby's cheeks and nose.

Janus smiled. "I think he will be infatuated with her."

My stomach churned.

The screen shifted, and a light *thud* sounded, but the view was still upright, capturing most of the laboratory the team occupied. Then Metis stepped in front of the camera, limped over to my father, and clapped him on the shoulder. I finally got a good look at my Resistance mentor. He didn't have a bionic eye. Instead, it was bandaged over, like the wound was fresh, and he, indeed, was hobbling on a crutch. It was in that moment I realized Metis never told me exactly what had happened to him. Maybe I never asked.

"Good job, mate," Metis said to his comrade, my father. "What are you gonna name her?"

"Well, I was think—"

"No," Freyja cut him off, handing the child to Dr. Oliver.

Something snapped in her—something either broke in place or out of place, and the change was reflected in her steely eyes. Dr. Oliver carried the silent child over to a table to be measured and weighed. "It is a child of the American Coalition. It will have no name."

"That's a lil' harsh, don't ya' think? Every child needs a name. We could even name her Coalitia." Metis laughed.

Freyja shook her head, standing firm in her decision. "It is best not to get attached. One-zero-two-five is our first successful trial of our Project. Rigorous testing will need to be performed on it throughout its whole life."

"You can at least call the baby a 'she,' Freyja."

Freyja ignored Metis. "We need data to understand the progression of the new species. We will need to know if it expresses the genes we intended, and if not, we may have to edit the gene expression of one-zero-two-five. It might need improvements. One-zero-two-five might yet fail."

"Fail?" my father asked.

Freyja stepped closer to my father. "Do not get attached, Dr. Darrow. Experiments fail every day. Babies die every day. There is no guarantee one-zero-two-five will survive. Even if this portion of the experiment proved successful, we still have years of opportunity for failure ahead of us." She turned from the doctors and left the room.

"Killjoy," Metis muttered as soon as the steel door closed behind Freyja.

"No," my father breathed. "She is right." He started to clean up the lab, organizing papers and packing up tools and tubes. "We have already brought to life and killed thousands of fetuses. The chances of the same happening to babies and children will be high." My father turned toward the door.

"Are ya mad?" Metis yelled after my father. "Ya can't just leave her here!"

"Yes, I can." My father's voice was cold. "We already have designated rotations with our assistants."

Metis hobbled a few steps toward my father. "Even serial killers start out as innocent babies."

"Well, good thing the government is paying us to create assassins."

Assassins.

My throat went dry, but I couldn't pause to think about what my father meant. I couldn't pry my eyes away from the scene unfolding.

Metis hobbled again, shoving himself between my father and the door. "Ya gotta think of the psychology, Janus. If ya isolate the child, it'll grow rebellious 'n unstable. If yer creatin' soldiers, or assassins, or whatever ya wanna call 'em, yer gonna need humans who'll listen to orders." Metis jabbed my father in the chest with a strong finger. "I don't care what that she-witch says. Yer job doesn't end with the data. It mightn't even start there. Ys see that?" Metis pointed to the baby. "That there is a real human. I don't care if it was made artificially. She's still real 'n alive."

"Just like your creatures. And look what happened to you!" My father nodded to Metis' leg. "You lost your leg, your eye, and your whole left side was nearly torn to ribbons!"

"'n maybe if I would've stopped lookin' through my lab spectacles for five minutes, 'n actually learned to communicate with the Obsidian Pheasox, it wouldn't've charged me when I tried interactin' with it."

My father adjusted his glasses. "Look, I don't tell you how to do your research, so don't tell me how to do mine." He shoved past his friend, leaving Metis speechless, staring at the door as my father slammed it in his face.

"She still needs to eat," Dr. Oliver muttered after a long moment of silence.

Metis grumbled, hobbling over to a small incubator on the opposite side of the room, and grabbed a bottle of milk. He sat down on a lab stool next to a simple wooden crib, then gestured for the doctor to hand the child over to him.

"But you only have one good arm."

"They're both good enough to feed a damn baby if she needs food."

Hesitantly, Dr. Oliver set the baby in Metis' good arm and tucked the blanket covering the child into Metis' chest.

My heart stumbled beneath my ribs. I had seen that blanket before—that pattern before. I zoomed in on the fabric, and my mind raced back to the day I found my father's journal and the piece of cloth placed as a bookmark in the middle. But it wasn't just a random piece of cloth—it was my baby blanket.

Had my father kept it in his journal as a keepsake? Did he purposefully give the journal with the patch of blanket to Metis?

I zoomed back out as Metis used his slung arm to reach over and feed the child. She took it easily, soothed by the warm milk and light bobbing as Metis moved the leg she was resting upon up and down.

"There ya go," Metis cooed. It was unfamiliar to my ears. "Don't ya worry, wee lil' one, he'll come around." My mentor lifted an eye to the doctor, still hovering over the baby. "You can go now. I'll manage."

Dr. Oliver nodded, leaving the room in slow, quiet movements, careful not to disturb the peaceful baby.

Metis didn't watch as the doctor left. He continued to stare at the child in his arms. "There ya go, Red. There ya go."

Red. It wasn't my official name, but it was the first name given to me. By Metis of all people. I hadn't realized just how close he was to my father—to me.

I watched the rest of the holo, transfixed by the gentle side of Metis I had never experienced before. Well, obviously I had, but I didn't remember. Once she was done eating, Metis rocked the child to sleep, then tucked her in the crib, careful not to jostle her head. He winced at the movement, but his arms remained steady. He smiled at the child, caressed her cheek with a finger, and right before he whispered good night, Metis ripped off a corner of the baby blanket and tucked it in his pocket.

Tears pooled in my eyes as I watched Metis as he, too, left softly and, like everyone else, forgot to click the holo-cam off.

I checked the time on the video. It ran for another ten minutes. Either the battery died, or someone came back, noticed the holo-cam was still on, and turned it off. I scrolled through, stopping when I finally saw someone enter the frame. It was my father, and in his arm was a baby carriage. He pulled the child from the wooden crib, tucked her into the carriage, and glanced around the room, gathering a deep breath in his lungs. He released it in a loud sigh before noticing the holo-cam. He pulled a blanket over the carriage, walked over to the camera, and the screen went blank.

A single tear ran down my right cheek. Quiet consumed the laboratory around me, but my mind raced loudly.

That child was me. I was a lab experiment. I was created to be an assassin. Some sort of weapon. My world began crashing down around me, the weight of everything I learned crushing against my shoulders, my chest, my stomach.

Pushing the agony from my mind, I grabbed my clutch and pulled my COM-tab from the accessory to check the time. It had been over an hour. Callum was probably worried. People were probably asking for me or looking for me before they retired for the evening.

I glanced back to the old COM-tab. *But there are still so many files I needed to look through.*

Tapping the holo-feed, I pulled up the settings and scrolled through the options. *There! Data Drop.* I pressed the option, and my father's COM-tab scanned for devices. When 'Adellaide's Com-Tab' popped up, I clicked on the words. I certainly did not have three hundred terabytes of space on my small COM-tab—I had to go through and manually pick the files I wanted to drop. I selected files and feed related to Prometheus Project One-Zero-Two-Five. Some of them were growth charts and hormonal activity, others indicated fitness and stress testing, and a select few were of normal baby accomplishments, like when I first began to walk and talk.

Scrolling through the files, I noticed there were files and holo-feeds created after my family had fled the Coalition. Curious, I clicked on a file called 'The A Twins,' wondering if other experiments after me were successful. On the first page of the file, there was a picture of two children, one boy and one girl, both around the age of eight or nine. They shared the same falcon nose, almond eyes, and golden skin. Upon further inspection, I couldn't help but feel like I knew these children.

I scrolled the screen down to find more pictures of the two children, but they were gruesome and horrifying. Each child had been taken apart and put back together again. The girl's right side of her head was stripped away, grey matter revealed and probed while she sat still in a chair, arms and legs strapped and eyes focused, lined with tears.

My stomach churned, and I clasped my hand over my mouth to keep myself from hurling as I recognized the child.

Bellona. With the child's right side of her skull shaved and bare, it was blatantly obvious.

But who was her twin? I couldn't recall a time when Bellona mentioned having siblings, though I didn't know if I'd cared enough to ask. Again, my selfishness stung like bile in my throat. I scrolled down through the documents of the file and clicked on a picture of the boy. He had a gun in hand, aiming at a target twenty yards away. It wasn't his stature or eyes that revealed his person to me, but the smirk on his face.

Ulysses.

My chest constricted to the point of pain as anger boiled my lungs. I forcefully scrolled down to the bottom of the folder until I hit the last photos. The two teenagers stood at attention in Military uniforms. Below the picture read: 'Sergeant B. Anderson and Sergeant O. Anderson'

O?

Using my father's COM-tab, I searched the CCD for an 'O. Anderson.'

A match was found in Militum's Excelsis. I clicked on the name Odysseus Anderson. A picture of the Coalition Citizen loaded, and Odysseus was undoubtedly Ulysses. They shared the same dark eyes, prominent nose, and— *Skies-damn it all, was he fucking smirking in his Military picture?*

Bile rose to my throat.

With his picture, the Citizen information on Odysseus Anderson included his background, academics, training, previous accomplishments, and Military placements. Though the most recent placement was from two years ago, and it was listed as 'Classified.'

"Helpful," I muttered. But then I paused. *Ulysses had joined the Resistance no more than two years ago.*

I clicked on his Military experience link. Odysseus' Classification Level was an O-6 Colonel, and the word 'White' was in italics next to the rank. I clicked back to find the Operative groups he had belonged to. Most recently, he was affiliated with the 'Kelpies.' According to the CCD, he was working with the Kelpies to gather intel on SEICRF.

SEICRF?

I had seen those letters when I first walked into the lab. *But where were they?* I scanned the room, rummaging through files and opening drawers, then I turned around to glance at the large screen I saw when I first entered the lab. Live footage fed into the screen, different panels recording different rooms, and in the bottom right corner of each panel, there was a number followed by 'SEICRF.' I walked closer to the large screen. Focusing my attention on the far top right panel, '8SEICRF,' I saw her.

Reign.

She was braiding Lyella's hair in the greenhouse. I shifted my gaze down one, to panel '16SEICRF.' Metis was in his lab. He hobbled around his desk holding a camera to his face, like he was recording himself. My eyes found Balor in another panel, training in the gym and tears streamed down the former soldier's face as he beat fists into the familiar, faded leather punching bag.

No. No, no... "No!" I screamed.

I glanced from panel to panel, my brain struggling to keep up with the quickness of my shifting eyes. I reached for the screen to touch Niahm's face.

But a message popped up.

Switch feed to...

The prompt listed 3 different options. There was a 'NWICRF,' 'NEICRF,' and 'SWICRF.'

Confused, I pressed the pad of my forefinger to 'NWICRF.'

All the feeds changed, and different people appeared on every screen—people I did not recognize, but they were similar to the people I knew from the Resistance. Similar clothes, and the same hopeful look in their eyes. I tapped the screen again, this time selecting 'SWICRF.' Different people. Similar living style and state. They certainly were not Coalition Citizens.

They were Rebels. Each location was a different Coalition Resistance Force.

ICRF. Imperium Coalition Resistance Forces.

I scanned through the feeds again. Southeast. Northwest. Southwest, and Northeast.

And each one is being watched.

I clicked back to my family's Base: SEICRF.

Has Freyja known what and who I am this whole time? What the actual fuck is going on here?

Frantically, I circled back to my father's COM-tab and finished dropping files into my personal COM-tab. I included various Prometheus Project Files, the Anderson Twin Files, and some random shit to be thorough.

I can go through all of this later. Sort through it. Study it. Record it and send it to Metis. But I needed to get the fuck out of here now.

After I finished dropping files, I disengaged the drop network and killed the holo display. I glanced around one more time, checking myself for my purse, my COM-tab, my earrings, and my engagement ring.

But before I could turn around and make my exit, a soft, venomous voice cut through the air, "Welcome to my lab, Ms. Darrow."

CHAPTER 39

Dr. Freyja Osouf's silver eyes pierced into mine, and a playful yet dangerous smile danced across her lips.

"I have to admit," she purred, "I was getting a little impatient with you, Rowyn."

I turned my head innocently. "What are you talking about? What is this place?"

Freyja laughed. "Do not play coy with me. I have been watching you down here for the past hour and a half. I have seen everything you have seen." The white-haired woman took slow, deliberate steps toward the desk. "I have heard everything you have heard. I watched your wheels turn as you pieced everything together. It was fascinating, really. Better yet, I know everything you have yet to find out—I know the final pieces of the puzzle you have yet to place." Freyja sat atop the sturdy metal desk, crossing one leg over the other. The doctor sat straight, neck long and elegant as she cocked it delicately to one side. "So, tell me Ms. Darrow, do you have any questions?"

I gawked at her. I was at a loss for words. I had no idea if I was a player in her game or if I was a mere pawn on the board. Regardless, I was certain I was in check.

"What is the Prometheus Project?" My voice was low and

quiet. Slowly, I slipped my clutch, which held my COM-tab, under my arm.

A crooked smile twitched across her face. "I think you already know the answer."

"Humor me."

"*You* are the Prometheus Project, Ms. Darrow. Or should say, one-zero-two-five. It has always been you. Of course, it is not just you anymore—a reveal your cloying conscious ruined—but you were the very first successful experiment. And you continue to play such an important role in our research."

Without moving my head, I scanned the room, searching for something, anything to use as a weapon. Skies knew I was useless in this dress.

"Do not bother," Freyja waved an elegant hand, the light white sleeves of her square, modest gown rippling with the movement. "Even if you are to get me down and out, Bellona and Callum will be here in minutes. I left some clues for them as well as deactivated the ray-door." Freyja must have noticed the shocked expression painting my features. She flattened her lips. "Now I distracted you. I apologize. Please, ask me more questions." Another flick of her wrist.

"Wha—" My voice croaked. "What do you mean 'the first successful experiment?' Do you mean Bellona and Uly—Odysseus?"

Freyja released a dramatic sigh. Maybe she was disappointed in my question. Or disappointed in them. "No. They were just a fun little side project. After your father left, all his research was either erased or secured so tightly that none of my best technical workers could access his files. I had his COM-tab for years"—she pointed to my father's device—"before I was finally able to access the data. No, Bellona and Odysseus were different. They were fraternal twins from Media. Their parents had hidden them from the Coalition Government—you know we only allow citizens in Media to have so many children. They were confiscated around the same time I had theorized a project based on your father's research.

"You see, Ms. Darrow, without your father's algorithms, research, data, and notes, I had no idea how to continue the work. Your father was truly amazing at creating DNA, while I preferred to edit the genome and DNA expression. Bellona and Odysseus were my own personal little projects. I hoped to make them the perfect soldiers and assassins by editing their DNA. But as soon as I published my findings, the experimentation was seen as 'unethical.'" Her tone was edged in disgust, as if she truly thought ripping children away from their families and experimenting on them wasn't immoral on every level.

"It wasn't any more than four years after I started their experimentation that I was finally able to access your father's research. Of course, I couldn't let a project go unfinished. So, although my research with the Anderson twins was prohibited, I saw to it that their training was completed. Then, I decided to restart your father's work. Next question, Ms. Darrow," Freyja ordered rather impatiently. "You might not get another chance like this."

"What?"

Instead of answering, she waved one hand, insisting on another question, while using the other to flatten out the wrinkles across her lap.

"Okay," I breathed. "Why did my father leave?"

Freyja shifted to tap the pad of her finger on my father's COM-tab. She pulled up the holo-screen to the day of my birth and forwarded to the first time he held me. With a tap in the air, she paused the footage, then turned to me and placed her hands neatly in her lap. The doctor had the gall to purse her lips like she really cared. "I did warn your father not to get attached. But did he listen?" Freyja shook her head, her straight, white hair swinging with the movement.

"I will admit, Ms. Darrow, it was a challenge for me as well. You were quite captivating. Intriguing even. However, testing was very difficult. Janus described your testing in the very same way the Board of Genetics Research described the Anderson Project. 'Unethical,'" she spat. "But can something be unethical if it is for the greater good? If it benefits our society? I suppose it is a question fit for a philosophical debate —tormenting one life to save countless others—but Janus was so in love with you that he couldn't proceed with further experimentation. Even after we implemented precautions like memory blockers and processing inhibitors during your testings. During physical and stress experimentations, we couldn't eliminate your pain, but we made sure you would never remember."

Her words rang in my mind. I knew there were gaps in my childhood memories, but I thought that was normal. Surely one couldn't remember their whole childhood.

"Janus attempted to terminate the project several times, he even went to the Board of Research Control, but I assured him if he presented our *Classified Research* to the board, his career would be ruined, and his reputation would be tarnished. I would have made sure of it. So, he left." Callum's mother shrugged. "Created some story about accepting a new position here in Imperium, only to fake the death of himself and his family. As you know, Janus had prepared to live off the grid for the rest of his life, but we found him a few years later."

My heart stopped. "What?"

Freyja nodded and pursed her lips. "Yes. I found your little Shed deep in 'The Wastes'." She used her fingers as quotation marks. "I had a feeling he wasn't dead. He was too smart to die an unfortunate and unforeseen death. He had made too big of a ripple in the universe only to perish in a hovercraft accident. Please. After the news reports came out, I hired some very deadly people to track him down and bring him to me. It took a few years, your father was one sneaky bastard, but we found him. Aura too. It was quite the reunion."

"My—my father is alive?"

"Oh, no." Freyja pouted. "Unfortunately, I needed information, and I used whatever means necessary to extract it."

My father's COM-tab.

My eyes grew wide at the cruelty of her statement. "I don't understand. Why didn't you take me as well? I was what you really wanted. Why did you kill my father when all you needed was my DNA to replicate the process?"

"Very good question!" Freyja's voice was enthusiastic as she stood from her seat on her desk and began to walk around. The doctor's white cape and gown were stark against the dark laboratory as it ran along the dirty concrete floor, yet the image was fitting. "You see, after some very deep thinking, I realized your father had a valid point. We were testing you in excruciating ways. I do wish I could have given you more time down here so you could watch your testings, but that is beside the point. I realized your testing was so hard on you when I noticed your serotonin and dopamine levels drop significantly.

"You became depressed, isolating yourself not only emotionally but physically as well. It became clear that testing you directly was not effective and skewed our data drastically. After all, lab stressors are not the same as natural stressors, and natural stressors are not effective unless natural caretakers are present as well. Ms. Darrow, you needed an environment that would challenge you, yet you needed adult guidance and discipline. So, although I could have observed you and your sister in the Shed, making you a rather preferable control group, I wanted to see how you responded to adult supervision and guidance in a Military-like system.

"I decided the best way to do this, while I kept your father under lock and key, would be to push you toward the Resistance and have you raised there for the remainder of your childhood. All it took was a teensy little virus exposed to your sister to push you two out of the Shed and into the Coalition Resistance Forces. And there you were, the perfect little experiment in the perfect little petri dish."

I struggled to wrap my head around Freyja's words.

"Then, with your acquired DNA and the few missing pieces I gained from your father's last confessions, I reinstated the Prometheus Project and started from scratch. I created more genetically enhanced humans and used you as a control."

More genetically enhanced humans. "The Prometheans."

Has anyone ever told you that you are unusually strong? Callum's words echoed in my mind.

"Yes. I was utterly disappointed when you did not see my little display live at the Circus. I was quite excited to show them to you in person and see the look on your face when you saw their wounds heal right before your eyes." Freyja smoothed out the invisible wrinkles on her lap. "Alas, there is a time and a place for everything."

I glanced behind Freyja, the live video footage from my Resistance Base glowing. I saw Reign. Lyella was gone now, and she was sitting alone next to the small apple tree, her knees tucked into one of my sweatshirts she now wore, which completely drowned her small frame. "Why—" Before I could finish my question, footsteps echoed in the corridor, and seconds later, Callum appeared with Bellona trailing behind.

Callum's eyes found mine right away. "I have been looking everywhere for you." He took my hand in his. "Where have you been? What is this place?"

"Do not lie. I know you are so fond of lying, but I have the footage," Freyja warned, her eyes still fixed on me.

Callum glanced at his mother, then to me. "I—I have been stuck down here."

"You have been snooping down here," Freyja corrected.

"And what is *here*?"

"It's your mother's lab," I answered.

"And why are you down here?"

"I was just curious," I breathed. My mind whirled. *How did I end up here? What was Freyja's plan? How did I set off this trap?*

"Okay." Callum grimaced. "No harm, no foul. Let's get back to the party." He started to pull me back toward the entrance when Freyja stopped us.

"Wait, Callum. Do you not want to know a little more about your *Rowyn*?"

Callum stopped dead in his tracks, and he turned slowly, like a cornered animal. His emerald eyes met mine. "Did you tell her?"

I shook my head. Bellona stared at me, her eyes threatening and cold.

"I have been watching her for quite some time, Callum." Freyja gestured to the security footage of my Resistance Base. "Did you know that Ms. Darrow was sent from the Resistance as a spy to gather Intel?"

Callum gripped my hand tight, and I watched the ever-quickening rise and fall of his chest.

"It's true. Tell him, Rowyn."

Callum's eyes never left mine, silently begging me to tell him Freyja was lying.

"Cal, please—"

The Lieutenant General must have seen the truth in my eyes because his hand fell from mine, leaving me cold and hollow. Bellona pounced, grasping my wrists tightly and pinning them behind my back. I tried to break free, but her grip was firm, and her arms were strong. We were equals—one in the same —superhuman.

"Callum," I shouted. "I was just trying to find information about my father. I just wanted to know about his Prometheus Project. That's all!"

Callum's eyes were flooded with hurt and betrayal, but he straightened himself, standing tall amidst the chaos. "Mother," the voice of the Lieutenant General boomed, "what is all this?" He gestured to the screens, unable to look at me any longer.

"I have been performing invaluable research as well as keeping track of the Resistance."

"Why? How did I not know about this?"

Freyja sat in her desk chair. "It is my job, Lieutenant General."

"Elaborate," Callum growled through his teeth.

"I apologize, Callum. I cannot."

He took a solid step toward his mother. "I am a Lieutenant General of the American Coalition. I outrank all of you here. Now brief me, or I will take you in for obstruction of justice."

Freyja crossed a leg and turned toward the giant security screen.

"Not quite." Freyja's teeth flashed. "Lieutenant General, what if I were to tell you the Coalition controls the Resistance Forces?"

"I would tell you you're crazy."

Freyja's brows rose. "It's true."

Bellona's grip loosened around my wrists, but as soon as I tried to take advantage of it, she snapped back down with such force I thought she would sever the blood circulation to my hands.

"I proposed a solution to the 'rebellion' problem we had many years ago. After properly squashing the uprising, I suggested we let the anti-Coalitionists have their 'Resistance.' Most thought I was mad, but my theory explained how the people who resisted were genetically impure. The people who made up the rebellion were people who did not respond to government-mandated hormonal treatments, like the treatments provided through the chips and pheromone diffusers, nor did they respond correctly to herd mentality.

"I explained that no matter what food we fed them or what drugs we gave them, these genetically impure citizens would maintain Rebel tendencies, and we could not allow these people to live or reproduce in the Coalition. These impure citizens would continue to spread chaos and possibly influence those who are genetically pure. I proposed a Resistance for the impure citizens—Bases on the outskirts of each Coalition City that would be controlled by the Coalition Government. I created a special operation called the Kelpies to run the anti-Resistance program."

"So Uly—"

Freyja held a finger up to me. "It's rude to interrupt. I am getting there." Freyja cleared her throat. "Lower-ranking Kelpies monitor the lower Circulums and spread rumors about Resistance Bases. People of a rebellious nature will be intrigued by the prospect of a Coalition Resistance and either ask for more information or seek out the Resistance themselves.

"Furthermore, higher ranking Kelpies run each Resistance Base, controlling the Rebels from the inside. They monitor any individuals who pose a large threat to our society and squash them, using mental and emotional manipulation tactics. These 'Resistance Leaders' ensure very limited damage is done to the Coalition, but just enough to make these people think they are making strides toward their cause. The goal of the Resistance Leaders is to keep their Base and their citizens in a 'comfortable sweet spot' where the Rebels feel like they are making a difference, but not willing to do anything drastic to uproot their new and perceived happier lives."

Freyja turned to me. "Yes, Ms. Darrow," she answered before I spoke, "all those meetings you had, begging for the Resistance to actually resist the Coalition, were all in vain. Odysseus and Hoenir were both in the Coalition pocket the whole time."

"Odysseus?" Bellona asked.

Freyja simply nodded to the Major General. She must not have known about her brother's work.

"Why was I not aware of this operation?" Callum asked, crossing his arms.

Freyja's foot bobbed. "Only the Coalition Generals, a few high Bureaus from every City, and the even fewer chosen Kelpies know about the facade. General Daniels was to brief you next month after your induction."

"Why exactly are *you* monitoring the Resistance Bases?"

"For science!" Freyja nearly jumped from her seat. "These *Rebels* are genetic anomalies within our carefully structured society. Against all hormonal treatment and psychological manipulation, they still have the inclination to resist. I observe them in their preferred habitat and perform regular tests to see how they respond. It is quite intriguing."

Callum ran a hand through his hair. "I'm supposed to believe, Mother, that you created a Resistance program that is not actually a Resistance?"

"Oh, no," Freyja started to clarify. "It is a Resistance, the Coalition just controls the productivity of the Coalition Resistance Forces. Anyone who joins the Resistance, except for the director and one, maybe two other Kelpie spies, are, in fact, traitors of the state."

"And what about Bellona?" I asked, nodding my head roughly toward my oppressor. "Does she know everything you did to her and her bother?"

Freyja rubbed her temples. "I must admit, Ms. Darrow, I did not anticipate you looking into *those* files. I thought you would be too preoccupied digging through your father's research to be deterred by later experimentation."

I felt Bellona shift, but she remained quiet.

"So, she doesn't know that you treated her and her brother like lab rats? Bellona doesn't know she was stolen from her family in Media? A family who loved her and her brother so much they risked their lives to save them, only for them to be tormented so furiously that the Board of Genetic Research dismantled the project because it was deemed 'unethical'? Then you disregarded their directors and continued on with the project in secret?"

Bellona straightened, though her grip held firm.

"Every decision has consequences, Ms. Darrow. You, of all people, should know those consequences can be dire. And look at her now." Freyja gestured to the Major General. "She is living in Excelsis! She is a Major General and moving up rapidly.

Without her parent's poor decision and me making her who she is today, Major General Anderson wouldn't be here." Freyja looked to the woman standing behind me. "I did you a kindness."

"The life she lives should be her own choice, not what you 'designed' it to be."

"And it is! I merely improved her options."

"She could have a family!" I growled, feeling the absence of my own family tugging at my heart—the family Freyja had stolen from me as well. I pulled at Bellona's hold on me. The Major General let me slip, just briefly, our palms touching before she jerked back and held me tight again.

Freyja gestured between Bellona and Callum. "And she does! The Major General and my son are practically sister and brother."

"That is not the same, and you know it," I spat.

"Over the many years of my life, Ms. Darrow, I have come to realize that we gain the family we choose."

"It's not a choice when you eliminate all of her options!"

Bellona stood in silence. Maybe she was processing, maybe she couldn't find the words. Maybe the Major General was pissed that we spoke of her like she wasn't in the room. I would have given anything to see her face, to see her reactions. It was one of the many advantages Freyja had over me in this moment. Though part of me knew Bellona wore her typical stone-cold mask of a Coalition Soldier.

Freyja rolled her eyes, an expression I had never seen her use. "Shall we stop speaking of Bellona like she is a child and start discussing where we go from here? Now we have everything out in the open, so let us have a frank, civil discussion." The Dr. turned to Bellona. "Major General Anderson, do you have any questions?"

"Where is my brother?" Her voice was distant, indifferent.

"Southeast Resistance Head Quarters. Well, right now,

Odysseus is in the city awaiting further instructions from me. We ran into a little *snag*."

My blood boiled under my skin. *Is she referring to Ulysses killing Darragh? Was Darragh's murder nothing more than an inconvenience in her grand scheme?*

"What will happen to me now that I know information above my security clearance?" Bellona asked.

Freyja smiled sweetly at Bellona, another unusual expression for the doctor. "Nothing," she reassured her. "As long as you can keep this secret between the three of us, you can remain on track for your promotion."

I audibly gawked. This was what Bellona was worried about right now? Her *promotion*?

I felt Bellona nod behind me.

Freyja turned to her son. "Questions?"

Callum considered me. "How long before you were to leave me?"

I stared right back at him. "I don't know," I whispered, tears brimming in my eyes. "My extraction was…deferred."

Callum's head twitched like I landed a physical blow to his ear. "And what were you going to do with the information you gathered?"

"I was going to relay the intel to Hoenir and Balor, my captain. From there, I wanted to devise a plan to draw more people to our cause so we could be big enough to actually do something."

"And what about all these people?" Callum gestured to the other Resistance camps on the large screen, his voice hovering just below a yell.

I flinched at his tone. "I didn't know about all those other camps. I—I thought we were the only one."

"Yes, that's true," Freyja cut in with a firm nod. "The population of genetically unfavorable peoples was growing rapidly. Keeping the different Bases small and secluded limits their options. If groups were too big, they would be more difficult to control and might try to overthrow their directors once they proved ineffective."

Callum ignored his mother, eyes still set on me. "Was it ever real?" His low, hushed words sent a fissure through my heart.

A tear finally fell down my right cheek. "It was more than real." My voice cracked. "You were never the target. You were never part of the plan. Ulys—Odysseus fucked me over. He ruined everything." I turned to Freyja. "But I suppose that was all a part of your plan?"

Her smile was feline. "We will get to that."

"What really brought you to Imperium?" Callum asked.

I took a deep breath. "A few days before you found me, I was at Base, and we noticed the Coalition had hacked our server. We decided to sneak into Humilis, extract the data from a security outpost in Ward Ten, and plant a virus to keep your servers down for a week or two so we could move our Base. We knew you had discovered our location, and we weren't safe anymore." I turned to Freyja. "Though, I suppose the data extraction you performed on our server was a routine check-up on our Base, and Uly— Odysseus was always on duty during the extractions."

Freyja nodded. "Yes. It was a routine data transfer. Though, it was quite an inconvenience that your little friend, Niahm, had to find out about the transfer. Alas, I am adaptable. I saw the little slip-up as an opportunity to set a bigger plan into motion, and here we are." She opened up her arms, motioning to the whole laboratory.

"Are you going to enlighten us?" I snapped.

"Patience, Ms. Darrow. I do not think Callum has finished asking questions." Freyja nodded to her son.

"You said you wanted to learn about your father's research. Why? How were you going to do that if my family and I were not the targets?"

Sweat beaded at my brow and neck. "Th—the virus we planted had a back door. It would allow us access to the Imperium Data System so that once we returned to Base, I could scan through the Data System and copy files about my father's work.

"My father died when I was young, Cal! I just wanted to know more about him. I hoped his research would tell me more about why he gave up his whole life to go live out in the wilderness." Air shuddered from my lungs. "I just wanted to feel close to my father again. I–I never wanted to join the Resistance, but my sister got sick, and I had no choice. I was never trained as a spy; I was only a soldier who got caught in a bad situation, and I had to improvise. We decided, as a team, that remaining in the city to gather Intel would be beneficial to our cause."

"Why didn't you leave the Resistance once your sister got better?" Callum's eyes were no longer alive like an emerald ocean, instead, they were cold and unyielding like the gems they resembled.

"Even if Hoenir would have let us leave, which he didn't, I wanted a normal life for my sister. I wanted her to have a family that cared for her and friends to grow with. Though it wasn't ideal, the Resistance provided more than I could ever give my sister alone." Reign's flowing chestnut hair, freckled nose, and quick smile warmed my soul, but only for a second.

Callum took a deep breath and turned away from me. With every moment of his silence, my heart thumped harder and harder in my chest, and I felt like a million horses had trampled it by the time he finally ran and hand through his hair and approached me. He was mere inches away, and I wanted to relax in our intermingling breaths, but everything about him was cold and unyielding. "Was it ever real? Were *we* ever real?"

"It's complicated." My voice was weak, and I hated it.

Callum slammed a hand onto the steal desk. I jumped back into Bellona, but she was unrelenting, forcing me further into the Lieutenant General. "Uncomplicate it," he commanded.

"Of—" I swallowed the terror in my voice. "Of course, it was real."

"But?"

I chewed on my lip, not wanting to release the truth he demanded. "What do you expect me to do? Abandon my sister? Desert my friends?"

"I expect you to choose me!"

Tears stung my eyes. "I—I can't."

Callum grew silent, the air chilling around the four of us.

"Any other questions?" Freyja prompted, but Callum shook his head, his eyes finally drawing away from mine.

"Now it is your turn, Ms. Darrow. Any more questions?"

"Only one."

Freyja tilted her head expectantly.

"Why did you bring me here?"

Because obviously, she did—I was part of a greater plan for the geneticist.

A feline smile grew across her face. "I have been growing tired of the leadership here in Imperium. They are slow and old, pumping themselves full of rejuvenation chemicals and whoring around." Freyja looked to me. "I would say *no offense*, but you were never a whore, now were you? In any case, I know you, too, have seen the corruption in the system, Callum. You have grown tired of women getting passed over for positions they were clearly more qualified for, of Humilian families struggling to survive because of our 'culling' policies."

"Yes, your culling policies," I surmised.

Freyja gave me a stern look, her nostrils flaring before she continued speaking to her son. "There is no doubt the Coalition needs change. And you have been working diligently on small projects during your time in the Military. But deep down, you know you cannot fix everything. You know there are bigger problems that even as General of the Coalition Base might be too difficult to address and change within our current system."

Callum was unreadable. "And what do you suggest?"

"I suggest—"

"A coup," I breathed, finishing Freyja's sentence.

Freyja swung around. The back of her hand slammed against

my right cheek, jerking my head to the left, and a stinging pain bloomed from my cheekbone. "Manners!" she growled. Callum started to take a step toward me but caught himself. Freyja straightened the jacket of her pure white gown and turned to face her son again. "Yes. A coup d'état. You are almost General. And at that time, you can gather your forces, and with the help of our Resistance camps, we can overthrow our withering government."

"Why the Resistance?" I growled, my face still tingling from the impact.

"Because," Freyja purred, "then it will look like we are for the people instead of warring political powers. Actually, Ms. Darrow,"—she waved a finger as if remembering something— "that is where you come in. I want you to lead the Resistance."

I balked at the woman.

"You were once the darling of the Coalition—the Coalition's beloved daughter, a feat of science, the talk of every dinner table. You, Rowyn darling, were created *for* the Coalition."

"But the project was classified…"

Freyja tucked her snow-white hair behind her ear. "The project was classified, but the results were flaunted. We needed more funding, and what better way to gain funding than by promoting the ingenuity of Coalition Scientists? So, when your father faked the death of your family, the whole Coalition mourned for *you.* If they see you now, leading the Resistance, they will believe your cause is worth fighting for."

Freyja sat in the black leather desk chair and folded her hands neatly in her lap. "Now, my question for you, Ms. Darrow: Will you join my cause and help us lead a coup d'état so that you may later sit in a seat of power and decide how this country will be run? Or will you choose to be executed for acts of treason against the Coalition?" Before I could spit in her face, Freyja held up a hand. "Keep in mind, if the whole Coalition watches their darling become a martyr to the government, they will rebel. They will no longer trust the government they serve. I will still use your death to further my gain."

Bellona held tight to my wrists behind my back. I glanced from Freyja to Callum. Back and forth until my eyes finally settled on Callum's emerald eyes.

"You first. Do you believe in the Coalition your mother stands for?"

Callum looked away from me, not able to meet my gaze for more than a few seconds, and I knew, even if I were to join Freyja, Callum would never look at me the same way again. He would never trust me. Either way, I was dead to Callum. Again.

I stood straighter, looking Freyja in the eyes as I spat at her feet.

She stood up. "Well, that was unnecessary. A simple 'no' would have sufficed." Freyja started to walk past Bellona and me, but she stopped shoulder to shoulder with the Major General. "Rowyn's COM-tab data chip, Major General?" Bellona maneuvered to hold both my wrists with one of her hands, then passed Freyja the data chip I had slid into Bellona's hand when our palms touched.

Fuck.

"Thank you, Major General Anderson. Now, incarcerate Ms. Darrow, please." Freyja continued toward the exit. "But take her out the back door. We don't need a scene. I will handle our guests."

"What happens when everyone finds out a Resistance spy duped the great Lieutenant General Osouf?" I turned to yell at Freyja. "Won't that ruin your son's reputation and chance for promotion?"

Freyja laughed like I was a child trying to trick her into reading another story before bed. "We will tell everyone how we suspected you to be a Resistance spy the entire time. It was merely a ploy to gather intel from you, and when we no longer found you useful, we decided to try and execute you—the leader of the Resistance. To the government, Callum will be a war hero, and to the Resistance, we will say he was in on the ploy, and you sacrificed your life for the cause."

I turned to Callum. "Please," I begged. "Please don't do this. You know she is using you. You are giving up your dream of what the Coalition should look like. Do not throw away everything you believe in, Callum. Please."

He turned from me, his shoulders slumped and heavy. "*You were everything I believed in.*"

Callum walked toward the dark corridor, and with each footstep, everything we could have been shattered into pieces.

CHAPTER 40

Callum was there. Not as a Lieutenant General of the Coalition Military, but as a child. Callum Orion Osouf was a serious child. He always carried himself elegantly, dressed neatly, and had an air of professionalism, so when I could get him out of his comfort zone, I was always very proud of myself.

I was five, Callum was seven, and I was waiting for him to arrive home from school. I climbed to the very top of one of his mother's prized Cherry Blossom trees, which lined the front drive of Osouf Manor in Militum, but, of course, I picked one of the front two so I could watch for Callum in the distance. I nestled myself between the branches and pulled out a book from the bag strapped across my back.

He was late.

When Callum finally strode down the cobbled road, forty minutes later than usual, his blonde hair was strewn in every direction, white shirt untucked from the front of his khaki pants, and eyes as bright as two twinkling green stars. I had seen Callum arriving since he turned the corner. I pretended like I didn't know he was there, though I was perplexed by the disarray of his school uniform.

"What are you doing up there, Rowyn?" Callum called up to me.

I tried not to look at his crooked smile, that, even as a child, took my breath away. "Reading."

"Well, aren't you going to come down?"

"I don't know." I shrugged, nose firmly planted in the book. "I am pretty comfortable. Plus, you're late. I waited for you. Now you have to wait for me."

"Oh, come on, Rowyn! It's not my fault!"

I shut the book with a hard clap. "Then who's fault is it? Why are you late, Callum Osouf?"

"Detention," the small boy muttered sheepishly, but his eyes still shone brightly.

I bolted upright, nearly flinging myself from the branches. "What?" I shouted. "Did perfect Callum Orion Osouf finally get a detention? What did you do?"

"I got in a fight, but Percy started it!" Callum yelled up to me. "He said you must be super dumb if you can't even go to school. But I told him that you are too smart for school, so you have to have special teachers. But then he said he didn't believe that, and I was even more dumb for having such an ugly girlfriend. So, I punched him."

I gawked down at him. "Well, Percy is the most dumb if he thinks I am your girlfriend!" I laughed.

"But aren't you?" Even from the top of the tree, I could see Callum's cheeks flush.

"If I am your girlfriend, that means you have to kiss me. And you, Callum Osouf, have never kissed me."

"Well, fine." He crossed his arms. "Come down here, and I'll do it right now."

"Oh, I don't think so! If you want to kiss me, you have to come up here!" I hadn't expected Callum to climb the tree. He never liked to dirty his school uniform, so I opened up my book and began reading again. Then I heard the hard *thump* of his book bag hitting the driveway and the scraping of his shoes against the cherry tree.

"What are you doing?"

"I. Am. Coming. To kiss you," he grunted between breaths, feet slipping against the bark.

"You are never going to make it!" I taunted before closing my book and stowing it in my bag. Then I twisted myself to sit on the branch, legs dangling over the edge so I could watch when Callum finally fell. But he never did. Instead, he climbed all the way up to me, straddling the same tree branch I sat on as he faced me. He was smiling through his gasping breaths—a toothy smile, his eyes full of pride.

"Okay," he huffed. "I made it. Time to make you my girlfriend." Callum puckered his lips.

"You don't make me anything!" I raised my brows and crossed my arms.

Callum opened his eyes. "Well, I climbed all the way up here! I think I at least earned a kiss!"

"Oh, you think so, huh?"

"Yeah," Callum pouted.

"Okay…" I smiled playfully. "Then close your eyes." He did. Callum leaned in and puckered his lips. Slowly, I leaned over…

Thump.

The force from my feet hitting the ground reverberated through my bones, but I kept my balance and bounded down the long driveway."

"Rowyn!" Callum called after me.

I laughed. "You gotta do a lot more than climb a tree to get a kiss from me, Callum Osouf!"

———

The memory was vivid in my sleep. That memory, and so many more, haunted me every time I closed my eyes.

It had been three days, according to my meal rotations. There were no windows in the dark, dank prison cellar that smelled of mildew and grime. No one came to visit me. Not Sancus. Not Aletheia. And certainly not Callum. I was beginning to wonder if I would ever see any of them again.

For me, the hardest part about being alone was allowing myself to be. Naturally, as humans, we are drawn to each other— our lives become centered around family, friends, significant others, and even acquaintances. And, I believed, between every human being, there was an invisible string, linking people together. Sometimes, the string was thousands of miles long; other times, it was just two feet. And when a person was alone, some strings started to tug, pulling the person in a direction. That was the hardest part of life, discerning when to give in to the pulls or when to cut the string. I should have cut the string when I first walked into this city.

I bet Callum wished the same. All the chances I had to run, all the times Callum should have let me. That was all I thought about in the Skies-forsaken prison cell. The past two days, I had nothing to do but dwell. I remembered all the times I had a chance to get out, all the times I should have asked for an extraction… Though that wouldn't have done me any good since Metis wouldn't have received the messages, but I could have tried, yet I never did. Whether it was because of pride, insecurities, or just blatantly lying to myself that I could have the best of both worlds—that I could build a life with Callum yet hate the Coalition—I didn't know.

While the first two days my mind was tainted with the shadows of depression, the third day was crippled by the churning waters of anxiety. All I could think about was Reign. How I would never see her again. I would never be able to hold her in my arms or braid her hair again. No longer would I have the chance to tell her stories about our father or teach her how to shoot a rifle. I thought about Metis and his research he would now have to continue alone. I thought of Niahm and the inevitable life we would have had together in the Resistance, even if I would have been settling. I thought of Aine and Balor, how they risked their lives to flee from the Coalition, but they just ran deeper into the corrupted oligarchy. I thought of Darragh. My little Darragh. A beautiful life senselessly lost.

I dwelled on how I would die. I wondered if they would torture me, though that seemed unlikely since Freyja knew everything about the Resistance. I contemplated death by a shooting squad, hanging, or euthanasia. The latter seemed the most humane, so probably not.

Maybe they would put me in the Circus with a pack of raptors.

It was painful to think about but not as excruciating as thinking about Callum. In fact, I might have thought of a million ways to die just to avoid thinking about the Lieutenant General —about the pain in his eyes and the knife I cleaved through his spine. However, each way I envisioned death, I couldn't help but wonder how Callum would react. My thoughts always spiraled back to him. I longed for him. I yearned to see him again, to hold him again, to breath him in and taste him again. To talk to him again. My heart ached, desiring to speak to him once more—I needed to make him understand how Freyja, his *mother*, truly orchestrated this whole thing. I ended up at the Resistance not because of me or my sister's immune system, but because of Freyja. And that, while I was in Imperium. Every time I thought of returning to Base, it hurt. My heart swelled and constricted at the thought of leaving Callum to go back to something that wasn't even real. I wanted him to know that, if it wasn't for Reign, I would have abandoned my mission months ago. Because with him, with Callum, everything was better.

I tried to remind myself that Callum had abandoned me. That Callum chose his mother—his controlling, abusive, and psychotic mother—over me. I tried to remind myself that I broke Callum and everything we had beyond mending. It didn't matter if I could see him one last time because nothing would change. The damage was done—the stone was thrown.

I sat on my cot with my arms wound tightly around my legs when keys jingled outside of my cell door, and the metal slab swung open in a slow and even *creak*. I lifted my head to find the Major General standing in the doorway.

"It's time."

ACKNOWLEDGMENTS

First and foremost, thank you to my Savior and Lord—the Creator of the Universe, whose soul dwells in me and has blessed me with the gift of creation. I pray for Your continued wisdom and guidance. I pray You continue to display Your creativity through me.

Thank you to my husband, Drew. I am so grateful for your continuous support for my wild and crazy ideas. I am so thankful for you as you hold my hand through late night breakdowns and the occasional broken spirit. Thank you for giving me space to live my dream and sacrificing much of your time to build a home, family, and life with me. You are a better husband than I deserve and a better partner than I could ever imagine.

Thank you to my sister, Alyssa, and my best friend, Sam. You read the earliest drafts of this novel and still believed in me— you still believed in my story. Because of you, I continued. Because of you, I did not give up. And for that, I am forever grateful.

Thank you to my parents, Jay and Marianne, who inspired me to dream. Even though I often lived in my own little world as a child, you encouraged my goofiness, my creativity, and my passions. Thank you for not shying away from my big ideas and supporting my dreams.

I'd also like to thank Danne for starting Fabled Spirits with me and joining me on a fun and creative journey.

A special thank you to all you mangy Howlers out there in The Den. Shit, I haven't even met you all in person, but you amazed me by the immediate support and love when I joined. Thank you for sharing my journey and joining my fan base before my book even hit the shelf.

And thank you Phantom House Press for granting me the opportunity to share my story with the world. I had nearly given up hope for Rowyn and her journey, but you saw her potential.

Thank you to my editor, Jane, who breathed new life into my story. I am in awe of your magic every round of edits and I am so grateful for the experience and lessons you have given me. I can't wait to continue this project with you all.

Lastly, thank you. Yes, you. Thank you for picking up this book. Whether you bought it or borrowed it, finished it or just started, liked it or hated it, you gave me a chance, and for that I am truly grateful. I can't wait to continue writing books for you.

TARYN L. DAVIDSON

Writer by day, bartender by night, Taryn L. Davidson loves to create unforgettable experiences for her readers and bar guests alike. She lives in Wisconsin with her husband, two mischievous cats, and one spunky dog. Taryn's background is in Cellular and Molecular Biology, but she traded in research journals and microscopes for fantasy worlds and barspoons. Taryn is co-founder of Fabled Spirits, a platform that combines her love for books and booze by creating cocktails inspired by her favorite fictional characters.

Be sure to follow Taryn on social media.
@tarynldavidson